J M BRISCOE

THE
VOICE
THAT
TWISTS
THE
KNIFE

Reader reactions to
The Girl with the Green Eyes,
the first book in the Take Her Back trilogy:

5.0 out of 5 stars **Cleverly constructed story** draws you in to the start of a series. Beautiful example of show not tell.

5.0 out of 5 stars **Delicious Book** This book is like a perfect chocolate torte – rich, dark and bittersweet. As soon as you've devoured it, you'll be clamouring for seconds!

5.0 out of 5 stars **Gripping from the first pages** I am not a sci-fi fan but this book may well have changed that for me. Bella and her story caught my attention from the first pages. It was hard to put down because I wanted to know more about her journey both as a young child and older adult. A great read with dark and twisty turns.

And for The Child Left in the Dark:

5.0 out of 5 stars **Amazing!** OMG! If you thought the first book was good you need to read book 2. I have run the gamut of emotions reading it and am totally wired and DESPERATE to read book 3. I am not commenting on the plot/story line, don't want to give anything away but I'll just say READ it ,it's great!

5 out of 5 stars **Brilliant** book. Brilliantly written, so many threads running through the storyline. The author is a master of keeping everything moving along until it all comes together perfectly. Can't wait to read the final book in the trilogy.

The Voice that Twists the Knife

by

J M Briscoe

Cover photo by Dmytro Tolokonov-unsplash

Cover design by Jason Anscomb

Interior design by BAD PRESS iNK

ISBN: 978-1-8384577-9-2

published by www.badpress.ink

To my children, for the sci-fi

Thank you

Thank you firstly to my publisher BAD PRESS iNK. A few years ago they took a chance on me and my story and because of them I managed to achieve a life-long dream by the age of 34, something for which I will always be grateful.

Thank you to my band of loyal proofreaders: Gary, who is best at spotting my over-use of certain phraseology; Celine, who was the speediest by far and didn't judge me too harshly for the decidedly darker 'before' version of chapter 49. Mandy, the language expert who helped tremendously with my tautologous tendencies (also for teaching me the word tautologous). And Mum, for her expertise both botanical and medical and for explaining why I could not shorten 'Mollitiam' to 'Molly' without changing the entire dynamic of several chapters.

Thank you (again) to Gary, my wonderful husband, for providing all the love, encouragement and support at every single junction of this trilogy's journey. The one who told me that the only way it wouldn't happen was if I stopped trying.

Thank you to my children – because of you I have been able to take a fascination with fictional parent/child strife and twist out a story so far removed from my own experiences it can only really be described as science fiction.

And last, but definitely not least, thank you to you, my readers (particularly those who've made it this far!). Your messages, encouragement and positive reviews mean more to me than my own words ever will.

January, 2020

She can feel him. When she shuts her eyes, he is there – a malevolent smudge bruising into the horizon. And when she opens them, he remains. Waiting, beckoning. Wanting her, always. She shouldn't go to him. They made her promise she wouldn't. He is dangerous, they say. He wants you. If he catches you, he will kill you before he lets you go again. *Let him try*, she snarls inside her head. She remembers the feel of spilling words as easy as breath from a normal mouth and tongue. Everything is sharp and short now. Her words slough like her feathers under the burn of the sun. It doesn't matter. They know what she means. Well, Ralph does. And Bella, most of the time. Except when it suits her not to.

Nova stands at the small, child-sized hole in the stones beneath the Manor's eaves. She shouldn't go to him. But he's *right there*. She can see the ARC easily from here, her sharp eyes picking out the people hurrying to and from the vehicles in the driveway like darting rats. They'd arrived yesterday in their large boxy trucks. She'd known they were here long before she first heard the flurry of raised voices and questions flowing up from the floors beneath her. She'd felt him come. She'd felt it in the darkness blooming across the inside of her eyelids, the slide of his voice around the edges of her soul. She can't hold

1

conversations in her mind like Bella, but Nova knows when the man who made her into a monster is nearby.

'We don't know what Daniel's doing,' Bella had told her, when she and the others had all finally stopped arguing over one other and she'd come to find Nova up in the attic nest. Nova had fixed Bella with one of her looks; one of the set expressions she has come to rely upon when speech is too much effort.

'OK, we have our suspicions... It makes sense for them to have brought the hybrid project here. I suggested it myself.' She'd looked away then, the way she always did when she was remembering the walled, pointed prison of the Beaumont facility back in London. Then, just as Nova was trying to work out whether the thoughts swarming Bella's face were sad, angry or something else altogether, her friend had given herself a little shake and all traces of reflection abruptly disappeared.

'Anyway, I know you want to go and see for yourself. I know how you feel about Daniel, Nov.'

She'd come closer, reaching out to touch Nova's feathers. But Nova hadn't wanted to be touched, even by Bella. She'd turned herself away, towards the hole in the wall. Towards him. Bella had sighed.

'Just... wait, OK? It's not safe for you. Wait until we know more. Dom and Tess are going to go and have a look later, once it's dark. I'll come and find you then and let you know what we know. Promise, OK?'

Nova had given her a dismissive noise. She hadn't bothered turning to watch Bella pick her way delicately across the filthy floorboards. Bella was wrong; she couldn't know how Nova felt about Daniel, the boy she'd once sat in a classroom with, the man who'd made her what she was now. This half-thing, this un-being, this *other*. If she had, she would never have asked such a thing of her.

Clicking her hard lips together, Nova glances behind her once, just quickly. It's early. Not yet seven. There are no sounds coming from the rooms beneath her bare feet. The twigs, leaves and heather strewn across the room behind her shiver with the sweet whispers of the early air beyond the hole. Nova lets the beckoning fingers of sky ruffle along her back as she turns to the opening, slips through and plummets like a raindrop. She falls for several heartbeats before unfurling her great shimmering wings and beating them once, the exhilaration soaring to the tips of her soul; twice, and everything is lightness and wonder as she kisses through the sky, saturated in joyful darkness.

As she beats her way through the air, Nova recalls the feeling of being a neat, featherless body, the graceful whip of her limbs, the poised movements. She remembers, too, the tight band of pressure reminding her to point her toes, locate the audience, turn just so, remember the positioning of her arms. The sharp thrill of getting it right; a bitter ache when she messed up... She remembers the screams and the darkness. The rough stones pushing around her. The first time she stepped into air and dropped. The empty, hollow longing like a gnaw at her very core... She pushes those thoughts away now. Her wings still feel clumsy when she remembers the streamlined dart of her former body, but there's a safety in their slow propulsion, their sinuous strength and the frissons of air dancing to the fringe of every feather. They won't let her down. They won't leave her alone in the cold, dark places of the world.

The ARC looms, a glimmering tower of blackness. She feels the sky lightening as she swoops high, just a large blur of a bird to anyone below who might be looking up. The

3

people are mostly the heavy-set Guard – the 'old-school' models, Ralph and Dominic would call them – designed for heavy labour and not much else. They have worked through the night and are showing no signs of stopping in their relentless unloading; crates, computers, desks, various pieces of lumpen machinery. Nova cannot see any other hybrids. The crates are empty. She wheels around the ARC as low as she dares, waiting, knowing none of the Guard will look up without reason, their programming does not allow for curiosity. The sky brightens with every circuit. He is coming. She feels him emerge. She knows he will look up. She knows he feels her too.

Daniel is a small shabby figure in the entrance of the ARC. His face is a smear of grey, his eyes two distant blots as he tracks her. She feels his gaze in her stomach, in the parts of her which hate and burn and yearn in equal, confusing measure. She thinks about swooping down suddenly, raising her talons like a hunting eagle, making him cower, making him scream. She feels how delicious that would be. Or she could simply shit on him. She is still considering her options when he gestures to a Guard person next to him. Her human senses are fully engaged in the sweetness of contemplation, of her winged superiority, of how much Ralph and Dom will laugh when she tells them... The gunshot shatters the image first. Then her left wing explodes and the world is wrenched into hideous, unimaginable agony.

Summer, 2019

'Again.'

'But I'm tired.'

'I don't care. Try again.'

Ariana sighed and stared at the pencil on the large, black table in front of her. She stared until the shapes of the plastic chairs, the white screen at the head of the room and the gleaming blue sky behind the large windows all blurred into nothing. She tried to grab onto the seething frustration of the blank power within her, tried to manipulate the well of feeling into invisible strands of outward energy. The pencil did not move. She groaned loudly and sank her head into her hands.

'Don't get cross,' Lychen muttered, his own irritation easy to hear beneath the cold veneer of calm.

'It doesn't work unless I get cross, I *told* you,' Ariana snapped, glaring up at him. He stood with his hands behind his back, leaning against the wall opposite the window. She could tell that his mind wasn't fully with her in this room he'd had converted into a temporary classroom over the last week. She didn't need to pry into his closed bastion of a brain to know his thoughts were several storeys above them, on the rooftop where they had last seen her mother hurtling backwards over the edge of the balcony.

'You should not have to rely on clumsy emotion to

5

execute the powers within you,' Lychen said, more measuredly this time. She blinked at him. He blinked back, his black eyes as empty as glass.

'Maybe it's all just... gone,' she murmured, turning back to the pencil so he wouldn't see how much she feared the words might be true. *It's not,* the blank voice whispered. *It's still here. I'm still here.* So why couldn't she reach it? It had been two weeks since the man standing next to her had thrown her mother off the balcony upstairs. Fourteen days since Ariana had leapt, heart pounding in every strand of her hair, every shred of skin from her scalp to her toes, to the edge of the railing, staring below, listening for the shattering thump which had never come, eyes unable to make sense of the flurrying mess of golden feathers... A fortnight since her strange, cold new father had imprisoned her in her mother's old room and Ariana had used her strange, cold new power to force her way out. Two weeks since he'd regarded her like she was the most important thing in the world, called her extraordinary, a *source of untapped potential equal to none*... And she hadn't so much as made a pencil twitch since then.

'Is it because of Marc?' Lychen muttered quietly, his voice barely lifting with the question.

'No,' Ariana mumbled. Though for all she knew, it might have been. Lychen had given her responsibility for the old man who used to push her on the swings and buy her sweets in a paper bag. The practical stranger who had come to rescue her and been rewarded with imprisonment for his troubles. Ariana had got as far as basic board and lodging. She hadn't made up her mind any further, yet.

'Because if he is a distraction, he can be disposed of,' Lychen added, the warning ringing clear this time.

'It's not that. I don't... It's not like I *know* him, I don't care that he's my granddad.'

'So why—'

'Because he can be useful! Because he knows things about me and my mother. Things that might be helpful for your scientists to know if they're serious about finding out more about me and why I can do what I do. Or could, anyway. And... and maybe he could be useful to you too, if you want to get to her. If you still want to, I mean.'

She looked up when she dared and saw that she'd surprised him. He wore it coldly, as he wore everything, but nonetheless there was a respect which simmered, briefly, on the surface of his blank projection. Then his eyes flamed with anger, pain, and something she couldn't define. She looked away, knowing that his thoughts had turned back to her mother, the balcony, the impossible tussle of longing and loathing.

'Noted,' he replied, slowly.

'What are you going to do about her?' Ariana stared at the pencil again so she wouldn't have to look back at him.

'I haven't decided yet,' he muttered, pushing away from the wall and striding towards the door.

'Keep practising on your own. Remember, do not grab at it. It is yours to channel, not the other way around.'

'I thought you said you were going to bring in an expert to help me,' she whined.

'I am. I've a team working on it. The individual in question is proving somewhat challenging to locate. I have had to invest heavily in his procurement, much like I have invested in the adaptation of this room, your education, the guest suite in which you sleep, watch your enormous television and play on the state-of-the-art games console you had to possess...'

She looked up at him, biting her lip, suddenly not feeling in the least bit powerful or extraordinary.

'I do this, Ariana, not because you are my daughter, or hers. You could be anyone's for all I care. Ralph's, Daniel's, some drug addict off the streets outside this building... No, Ariana, I do this because two weeks ago you showed yourself worthy of it. Do not make me regret deciding that.'

He shut the door firmly behind him, leaving a trail of cold fury which swelled into her nose like the smell of singed flesh. She shivered. *He's lying,* whispered a voice at the corner of her mind. Ariana turned it away, coldly. As she had done every time she had felt its gentle but insistent nudge to be heard. She stared at the pencil. It did not move. She shut her eyes and reached for the blank swell beneath, before remembering she wasn't supposed to reach for it at all. It didn't matter, the blankness didn't so much as ripple. She pushed her breath out slowly and dropped her head forward again until it rested heavily on her folded arms.

What, Mother. What is he lying about? The whole thing about not caring about me being his daughter?

He might be, I'm not sure about that. It is Lychen, after all. He doesn't think the same way about family as everyone else does. But that's not what I was talking about.

What, then?

He's lying about me. He knows what he's going to do. He wants to kill me. He tried and failed. It's a job half-done, a loose strand, a chaotic thread beyond his control. He hates that.

Ariana frowned, anger tumbling into sadness and creating a murky haze of confusion.

Is this real, Mum? Are you really talking to me, from

wherever you are?

Yes.

Are you... What ha— Are you OK?

No. Not really. But I will be.

OK.

Never let your guard down around him, Ri. Trust your own instincts. He's a liar.

Takes one to know one, Bella. Get out of my head now, I've had enough.

And she did, to Ariana's surprise. Ariana blinked and turned back to the pencil. She thought about her mother's voice, about the sight of her father lifting her by the throat and throwing her off the balcony like a ragdoll, about how she was not OK, *not really*. But would be. How the words had sounded less like a reassurance and more of a threat. To whom? Maybe the person who'd used a thought-weapon to slash her across her perfectly designed face, thrown her back against the balcony, into his reach...

The pencil gave the briefest echo of a shudder. As if it had met the touch of her mind and found it chilly.

Summer, 2019

I was given fourteen days to wallow. On the fifteenth, the door shushed briskly across the rug and Ethan's footsteps creaked across the floor of my childhood bedroom. Brightness pressed insistently against my closed lids as he pulled the cream blinds upwards. Smells drifted into my nose, reminding me that I hadn't eaten properly for weeks.

'What we have here,' he announced, determinedly, 'are three types of pastry and a fresh pot of coffee. You have to open your eyes for them, though.'

I stayed motionless, trying to ignore him. I'd been drifting in Ariana's dreams, the place I felt calmest these days, despite their tumbling confusion.

You have to wake up, Bella. They're talking about interventions. Felix is all for shipping you off to the hospital. Ralph hasn't slept properly for weeks. And then there's Nova... We need you, my love.

My eyes snapped open. The bandage had been removed from the left side of my face, but I'd barely bothered contemplating the room since I'd arrived. There was a sharp edge to the pain in my left leg, no muzzy painkiller to nestle my brain back into its comfortable stupor. I twitched my toes and felt the edges of a plaster cast. I wondered, dully, who'd put it there.

You can't call me that, Ethan.

10

His gentle face folded into a smile as I flickered my gaze onto his. The last vestiges of the bland Guard had all but disappeared, at least when he was looking at me. Even his bristly haircut had begun to lengthen into dark, tight curls. He reached for me and I knew I shouldn't let him, but the feel of his hands easing around my shoulders, bringing my body upright, nestling me back against the pillows was so normal, so un-awkward. It was like he was a large, male, extension of myself. I thought about the Guard, about the way their brains had been manipulated by electricity, chemicals, probes; erased into a cold slate, ready for the insertion of a master's wishes and wants. I shuddered. Ethan's brow creased in response.

'It's not like that with us,' he murmured, pouring a cup of coffee and handing it to me. Black, unsweetened, just the correct amount of finely ground Italian bean. The bitter liquid warmed against the soreness of my throat, still bruised where it had borne my weight against the crush of Lychen's fingers.

'Of course it is,' I whispered hoarsely. 'Why else would you be here, doing this? How else would you know the exact way I like my coffee? Why else would Felix be so determined to do all she can to get you as far away from me as possible?'

He didn't look away. His large brown eyes clouded briefly at the mention of his wife, but they hid nothing. There was no point.

'There's no tether anymore. There's no obligation. I'm here because I choose to be,' he said, a hint of the metallic Guard curling ironically around his words. He smiled as I drank, feeling all of the everything within me and smiling all the same. When I had finished the cup, he held the plate of pastries out.

11

'I've got cinnamon, almond, and an apple turnover. All freshly made and I went out especially, so you'd be plain rude to refuse...'

I rolled my eyes and took the cinnamon.

We can't carry on like this, Ethan. It's not fair on Felix. I'm safe now. I've got Ralph and Nova. The Youth Guard are ready to be called upon if I need them.

Lychen will come for you. He has an army of Guard at his disposal. Even if you summoned the Youth, they would be no match for his numbers.

I shut my eyes for a moment, concentrating on the crisp snap of hardened sugar, the tang of the cinnamon. Trying to pull together the threads of the plan which had seemed so much clearer before my daughter had strode across the balcony of the Beaumont with murder in her gaze.

If that happens, you won't be able to save me either. But I don't think he will do it like that. He does not know about the Youth. He does not think I have any weapons or resources to warrant traipsing an army across the country. The only reason he hasn't come yet is because—

It's because you found a way to threaten him. I felt it. The mind-link. You told him you were coming for him. It terrified him.

I frowned. I should have felt annoyed at the intrusion, of course. But that would have been like getting annoyed at part of my own head for listening to the other.

It's not safe, Ethan. Even in my head. If he sensed you...

He wouldn't be looking for me. He probably thinks I'm dead or that you're all keeping me unconscious or something – that's the logical conclusion if he's tried to reach me by mind-link himself and failed. It wouldn't occur to him that I am no longer Guard.

Exactly. So if he sensed you and realised you were alive and back to normal—

The door opened and we both turned sharply towards the sound.

'Beast! You're up!' Ralph's face erupted in relief, even as his eyes drooped a little at the sight of Ethan and me.

'I was beginning to worry,' he admitted, his voice almost as croaky as mine as he strode across the room. He stopped short of the bed, glancing from Ethan to me and back again. For the first time since I opened my eyes, I felt self-conscious. Though most of me was still beneath the large purple eiderdown of the old sleigh bed, my top half was clad in an unfamiliar white T-shirt, my hair was loose and felt strange, almost like it was coated in something. I brought a hand up to my face and winced as the barely scabbed cut stung underneath my fingertips. *Has it gone?* The last words I'd said to Ralph jolted back into my head.

'How're you feeling?' Ralph's eyes lingered on my hand, the cut on my face. His pinched eyes were all the mirror I needed. It was gone. My beauty. My relief was immediately swamped by fear. Who was I? *What* was I, now?

'Better,' I rasped, swallowing and wincing. I glanced at Ethan. Why was it none of this pain and self-consciousness had occurred to me when he'd come in?

'You look better,' Ralph said, his hands flapping a little.

'I'm sorry I worried you,' I muttered. 'I could really do with a wash... My hair...'

Ralph gave a short quiet version of his bark-laugh.

'Your hair looks fine, Beast. And I'm not sure a shower would be the best idea... In case you hadn't noticed.' He gestured at the lump which was my left leg.

'I was hoping we'd get away with a boot, but the break

13

needed total immobilisation,' Ethan said. I stared at him, remembering Felix questioning him about his X-ray vision during that long pain-filled night when we'd arrived back here.

'We managed to fix one of the old scanning machines,' Ralph added. I looked at him, catching the ghost of a frown. Ethan grinned.

I told them they didn't need it but he had to see for himself.

'I can ask Fee if she'll help you wash—'

'No,' I snapped. They both stared. I stared back as blandly as possible. It was surprisingly difficult, not knowing what I looked like, not having the usual confidence of my face just there, a given to call upon whenever I needed.

'How's your dad doing?' I asked quickly.

'Still unresponsive,' Ralph sighed, 'though they say there's been a little more eye movement in the last few days.'

'They're still saying it's a stroke?'

'That's what they're treating it as. Bleeding on the brain. Of course, none of us know what really happened between him and Ariana.' He glanced down bitterly, folding his arms.

'I doubt she would know even if she were willing to share,' I rasped, my throat beginning to narrow around the effort of so many words. Ethan felt it too.

'We should let you rest,' he said, firmly.

'I've done nothing *but* rest,' I muttered.

'He's right,' Ralph remarked, taking my plate away. 'Your voice sounds like an eighty-year-old chain-smoker. We can talk more later.'

'OK,' I mumbled. 'I'll rest if you do. You look worse

than the poor sod who was thrown off a balcony two weeks ago.'

He gave his bark-laugh a little more convincingly. 'Yeah, right,' he muttered, moving out of the room. He glanced back at Ethan when he reached the door, but Ethan was bending over the coffee tray, solicitously balancing mugs and the remaining pastries. As soon as Ralph had gone, he stopped.

I'll help you wash.

Make sure Fee's not here. I don't want to give her more incentive to smother me with my own pillow.

I'll talk to her. I know she's not coping with all this, but she shouldn't take it out on you. It's not your fault I'm like this.

I sighed, suddenly exhausted in every shred of my soul.

Just... make sure she's not about.

He smiled tightly and took up the tray. I watched him leave, feeling the closeness of our mind connection stretch only minutely as he trod heavily along the corridor and down the stairs into the kitchen. It couldn't last. I felt safer with him near me than I could ever remember feeling my entire life. Certainly safer than I had felt all the other years I had lain here in this bed, contemplating what I was and all the people who reached for me, grasped me too tight, pushed me too hard... But it couldn't last because he wasn't mine to keep.

It's just you now, Bella.

Ana's voice was loud in the space left by Ethan.

I know.

You can't rely on anyone else anymore. Not Ralph. Not Nova. Not the Youth Guard. Not even Ethan. He might love you but you still ended up going over that balcony, didn't you? You must get stronger. Ethan's right, Lychen will come for you. And you're alone.

Except you, Mamma. I smiled. Now I was here, now I could hear her voice again I could almost see her sitting on the edge of my bed, her hair caught up in the bright yellow scarf she'd liked to wear with her favourite cotton summer dress. Her absent eyebrows puckered and she leant forward, her arms whittled with wiry strength as they reached for my hands over the top of the duvet. I squinted as she shimmered into the tight smile she'd wear when she didn't trust her face not to split into the passion of emotion frittering beneath. Then I blinked and she was gone, and I was every bit as alone as she had pointed out.

January, 2020

Dominic is a computer geek. He'd been told at the earliest age that computers were his allies, that he could talk to them like no one else and that his natural place was in front of one. He knows now that much of this was Project C bullshit, but he also knows that there was a reason he was able to do what he could for so long… and still, sometimes, almost, can. And that those reasons lie within the crave of the smooth plastic keys beneath his fingers, the glowing beam of screens, the rashy discomfort of spending too much time beneath a natural light source. He has lived in Cumbria his whole life and has only ever participated in treks, hikes and other outdoor-based misery under duress. So why he has been tasked with checking on the Manor's herb garden on a miserably freezing January morning is, quite frankly, beyond him.

OK, so technically no one asked him to come out here so early. He was supposed to have done this last night, when he and Tess had shuffled as quickly as they could down the path towards the ARC, ascertained that there were a bunch of lorries and Guard people but no hybrids to be seen before scurrying back again to the warmth of the Manor and the game they'd paused. He'd been thinking about Minecraft, about the mob cave he'd been in the middle of exploring, as Tess had entered the code Dom had never bothered to learn in the back door alarm system. It had only been later, when he'd come across a farming village in the game, that he'd remembered Ralph asking him to check on the damn herbs in their cloches.

He could have lied. Even if sod's law meant that tonight of all nights the garden was raided by herb-ravaging wildlife who could scale seven-foot walls, he could have just lied and said that yes, of *course* they'd all been fine when he'd checked on them earlier. If it had just been for Ralph, he probably would have. But the garden had been Bella's idea – all to do with the potions and medicines she and Ralph were calculating and cooking up in their brand new lab. And though he can at least now bring himself to meet that acerbic green gaze most of the time, Dominic can't even contemplate the possibility of lying to it, let alone construct a story about how the cloches had looked and whether there was frost on the ground or pawprints around the patch... Besides, Tess had been with him – she idolised Bella, thought she was some sort of pioneering saviour for spending so much time developing cures for hybrids, Guard, and the rest of the world to boot... She'd waste no time dobbing him in. Which brings him here now, at the ungodly hour of twenty past seven on a Tuesday morning, stamping over iron-hard soil in his ill-equipped Converse, muttering about how he is a computer geek, he was *literally made* to be a computer geek, he has no business at all checking on unidentifiable vegetation and he isn't entirely sure what a cloche is anyway—

The crack of the gunshot abruptly splinters the frigid, icy air. Dom's body whips towards the ARC before his mind can catch up. He can barely see the tall black building from the Manor's back garden thanks to the new towering stone wall lining the property's perimeter. An ugly precaution none of them had pretended they were not relieved to see constructed back in the summer. Birds skewer into the sky, shrieking. Dominic glances from them back to the Manor and, as the shrieks morph into a long, hauntingly human-sounding wail, back in horror to the grey clouds ahead. A shape is lolloping awkwardly across the sky and he doesn't need to squint to know it's Nova. He's seen her fly enough times to recognise the colossal sweep of her golden wings, the eerily impossible shape of the feathery not-fully-human between them... He knows it's Nova and he knows she's been horribly injured because the flight is uneven, her left wing crumpling more and more with every attempt to beat it. She's not so much flying as tumbling unevenly through the air.

'*Fuck*,' Dominic groans, instantly feeling guilty because his anguish is definitely not as great for Nova as it is for himself, being the person she's flying towards, the person who is going to have to do something important and decisive. He turns back to the Manor. Should he fetch someone? Should he wait to see if she lands?

'Come on,' he mutters, turning from the dark back door of the house to the shape tumbling towards the wall, crying and falling lower every moment. 'Come on, you can do it... a little further...'

She falters and he catches a blur of her face, tight with pain and concentration, as she collides with the top of the stone wall and somersaults, like a feathery boulder, into the garden.

'Dom? What's happened?' He hears Ralph and registers the swoop of relief even as he begins to run towards the fallen mass of bird-girl in the grass ahead. Ralph vaults into step next to him.

'I think she's been shot,' Dom puffs. Ralph quickly

overtakes him, throwing himself onto his knees next to Nova.

'We've got to get her inside... Help me lift her,' Ralph mutters urgently. Nova's eyes flutter as he folds her uninjured wing into her body. Dominic glances nervously from her face to the mess of bloody feathers on her injured wing, still outstretched. Despite Bella's insistence that they all treat Nova as one of them, he's not actually been this close to her since the day she arrived here six months ago. Ralph, he sees, is doing a far better job of concealing any uneasiness as he gently rocks his hands under the feathery body, bringing her close to his chest and lifting. Nova screams as her injured wing slackens on the ground. Dominic attempts to lift it but she snarls and lurches at him with a talon, narrowly missing his chest. She rolls away from Ralph and crouches around her injured wing, blood dripping steadily onto the white-tipped grass.

'Ralph? What's going on?' Bella's voice snaps Dominic's attention. She strides across the lawn towards them, wrapped in a fur-lined coat. Her cheeks flush with the icy air and her eyes grow into saucers of jade as she contemplates the mess in front of her.

'Grab some towels and blankets,' she says, barely sparing Dominic a glance. He is halfway towards the house before he knows he's begun to move, his will as hollow as a Guard's.

It takes too long to get Nova inside. First, I have to send Dominic back again for the necessary drugs when it becomes clear that even my gentle firm commands are not going to be enough to persuade Nova that she needs to let Ralph carry her. She snaps her mouth at us, furling herself defensively, and her eyes when she glances up are wild, full of fear, mistrust, and pain. It's like the shock of the injury has transformed her back to the beast in the cage I met last year. And of course, there's no mind-link for me to use, no tentative nestling into her thoughts to reassure her – there never has been with us. It makes me wonder, as I watch Ralph take the syringes from Dominic with his back turned so Nova doesn't see, whether I've become too reliant on my new way of communication these past few months.

There is no time for these musings now, though. I talk to Nova, distracting her with quick promises about going for a hike over the fells in the next valley, seeing whether the waterfalls have frozen over, how she will be able to skim the ice of the lake with her toes once she has healed… I cannot reach her mind and I cannot command her when she is more bird than woman, so I turn my voice into a sweeping paintbrush until I see the beat of her wings echo into the esoteric blue of her eyes as Ralph creeps behind her with the needle. I murmur for her to be still as I hold her with my eyes and she is, having finally let enough of me in to seize her. When the needle pierces the soft skin beneath the feathers of her back there is no flare of realisation or accusation. She just blinks once and when she slumps Ralph catches her, Dominic ready with the blanket.

'She's cold,' Ralph murmurs as I make sure she's unconscious before folding her injured wing into her body and using a towel to bind it there.

'The thermometer in the utility room said minus six when I came out,' I reply, tucking the last of the feathers into the surprisingly small bundle in his arms. He stomps easily up to the house with her. I glance at Dom who is staring, rather sickly, at the feathers and blood on the

21

ground.

'You alright?' I ask. He looks up and gulps. I know I still make him shivery. I feel it billow from him as obviously as smoke from a candle. It has its uses – transforming the attic room from his lodgings into a nest for Nova was extremely easy, for one – but I try not to take advantage too often, for Tess's sake as much as his. I know she watches and thinks of Ethan and Felix, the mess of our living situation last summer. I wish I could show her that it's nothing like the same.

'I'm fine.' He glances at the stone wall and beyond, to the loom of the dark tower just visible. We head back to the house in silence. Tess meets us at the bottom of the stairs, wearing long-johns under her fluffy dressing gown, her hair a scattered puff of yellow straw, mismatched bed socks on her feet.

'Wha—?'

'Nova was shot in the wing,' I say, shrugging my coat off and placing it quickly in the coat cupboard under the stairs. Either Ralph or Dom must have lit the boiler when they got up this morning because even the often-draughty hallway feels like a sauna compared to outside. Dom still stands in his inadequate coat, his hands shoved into his armpits. His teeth chatter so hard I can almost feel the flagstones vibrate beneath his feet.

'Beast, where are you?' Ralph calls from the lab. I tread quickly across the floor, pausing only to replace my hiking boots with plastic sock coverings just outside the door. Dominic mutters about going to warm up as I step quickly into what was once Ana's dance studio. The sprung floor still meets the balls of my feet with whispers of turns and jetés, but apart from Mamma's old portrait hanging next to the large bay windows, the rest of the room is unrecognisable. The ballet barre has been replaced by sinks and I cross to them first, tapping a pedal with my toe so I can wash my hands without contamination. I glance over my shoulder as I scrub. The back of the room holds three rows of work benches and stools; Ralph has placed Nova on the closest bench, the books and microscope it formerly held piled haphazardly on the floor. I dry my hands hurriedly and pull on a pair of gloves.

'We could use better light,' I mutter, as I take Nova's wing in my hands, propping the uninjured tip onto the adjacent bench. Ralph nods, not needing to point out that with the space under the large windows at the front of the lab now filled with a mixture of old equipment from the ARC alongside several new procurements I've made over the last six months, there's simply no other option for an injured bird-woman hybrid.

'How long have we got until she begins to wake up?'

'I had to guess her weight... I'd say maybe a couple of hours at least, but I've got another dose ready...'

'Were you thinking we could—'

'Use Mollitiam? No Beast, it's too risky...'

'Well clearly you *were* thinking of using it. It's worked on all the test subjects—'

'This is *Nova,* even with the work we've done using her DNA, we can't begin to understand what effect it might have—'

'So what, then? Just treat her like a bird with a shot wing? Come on, Ralphie. You know as well as I that she'll never fly properly again. I don't even know how she made it back from the ARC to the garden...'

'Can I do anything?' Tess mumbles from the doorway. I unlock my gaze from Ralph's clear-eyed frown and she balks a little as we both turn to her.

'Have you got your phone on you?' Ralph barks.

'Er... yeah?' She frowns, reaching into the pocket of her dressing gown. I stare from her to Ralph, knowing what he wants to ask her, longing to cut through all the clumsy words bumbling through the air and talk to him in his head. He glances briefly my way, a glare in his eyes which tells me he knows exactly what I want. I drop my eyes in frustration, reaching for a clean piece of gauze and dab away some of the dirt encrusted in the blood of Nova's feathers.

'Look up how to treat a bird shot in the wing,' Ralph says, a little less brusquely. I sigh again, reaching for a disinfectant which I spray directly onto the peppering of wounds left by the shotgun pellets. I have to pluck a few feathers out of the way first. I glance at the pale face to make sure she's not waking up. I can almost feel the tearing agony this would cause if she were conscious; the sting of my old wounds whisper with the memory of Felix's rough fingers. I swallow the feeling. Nova doesn't flinch. She's fine.

'OK, so there's a bit about immobilising the wing, er, but you've kind of done that...' Tess glances up, turns a delicate shade of green as she spots the bloodied cloth in my hand and hurriedly looks down again. 'Says here that gunshot wounds aren't so bad if they don't involve bone, but um... would you say the wing's been *shattered*?'

'Do I look like a bloody vet?' I snap, knowing my eyes are spitting every ounce of the clamouring frustration I'm feeling. 'Ralph, she's losing blood. We're dealing with several wounds here and the wing was all bent wrong, I think she must have fallen on it. It's probably broken. Neither of us know what the hell we're doing. We've got to use Mollitiam or she's going to die.'

'She won't *die*, Beast—'

'If she can't fly, she will kill herself. She will throw herself off the roof. She won't wait around to see if we ever finish the Naturalisation Application to turn her back to a human. I'm not being dramatic. I know her. So do you.'

Please Ralph. I won't make you.

He watches me, exasperation battling with the excitement I know I've reached within him with my scoop of words. He wants to try it as much as I do.

'Bugger it. OK.'

'Yes,' I breathe, smiling and feeling the now-familiar tightness of my scar. Ralph crosses over to the machinery at the front of the room.

'Mollitiam? The isolated resilience material?' Tess looks less ill but she carefully does not look my way as I fold Nova's wing in and prepare to bandage. 'I didn't realise you'd managed to formulate it into drug doses...'

'We only finished it last week,' Ralph says, shortly, opening the fridge and reaching for the green vials we placed in there only last Thursday. 'Testing has been sparse, to say the least. Ideally the samples should be brought up to room temperature...'

'The application works better closer to the time of injury,' I warn him.

'Yeah. Yeah, OK.' He crosses over to me and, glancing once at Nova's face and then up to mine, hands me one of the vials with shaking fingers. Everything blurs around us. Tess, the tens of thousands of pounds worth of equipment, the taps and the sprung floorboards, Mamma's portrait. All that exists is his hand holding the stoppered tube of silvery emerald, his eyes shining with exhilaration barely kept in check by the damper of fear. I don't bother hiding mine. I take it from him, grab an empty syringe from the dish on the bench behind me, draw up ten millilitres and plunge it

25

directly into my former protégée's chest.

Summer, 2019

The windows were dirty and the leaded diamonds of this particular one made it hard to see through. Still, her eyes had been sharpened by bird DNA and Nova could glimpse enough to know that Bella remained a still unmoving shape in the wide purple bed. She shut her eyes until she saw backwards, past the rambling old house and over the hill to the shining black tower beyond... The classrooms full of bright colours and laughter. The days of fingers, thumbs, clear speech and whatever version of normal it was she had once known. Rudy's hands lifting her like a log high above his head, warning her to stop giggling because it was making him unsteady, Verity creeping behind him with a feather from the craft box... A shriek with nothing beneath it but fun and joy. All of them landing in a heap of limbs, laughing so hard one of them said they were going to pee. Bella watching them, pretending to disapprove but all of them knowing she didn't really. Bella's hand in hers, her voice a twirl of silken ribbon around her heart. Bella showing the ballet class a movement on her toes, her entire body a sinuous line of control and fast whiplike movement. Bella's hand tightening until it was on the edge of being painful. Bella moving across a stage, dancing out of reach of the predators who grasped for her like deathly magnets. Bella should not be lying still. Bella needed to be able to move. How else will she escape, when the predators come for her?

Nova sat in the oak tree, nestled in a knot of branches because it was more comfortable than perching. The thrill of flight still tingled along her wings, and yet... She didn't stray far. She wanted to. She burned to. She knew the sweetness of the soft summer air would caress along each feather, she could taste the joy of plunging through it, however clumsy it still felt. But Bella was lying in that bed and it was her fault. The words battered around her head with more clarity than the urge to fly, tussling against the pull of the sky, wrenching her back from sleep, yawning over the increasing hunger and aching thirst that the few droplets of rain from the leaves around her could not quite quench. She had to keep watch. It was her fault. It was her fault and yet it also wasn't...

She didn't know how many days it had been when Ralph came to sit beneath the large tree. She barely recognised him from the impossibly tall, glasses-wearing genius the children had whispered about back at the ARC. He was going to cure the whole world, they'd said. She looked down at him now, at the rounded shoulders and the wasted sadness of his gaze and she wondered if he even understood what a cure was. It was another two days before she swooped down to meet him, and that was only because she was ravenous and he held a tray of food.

'Hello, Nova,' he said, placing the tray carefully down. 'I thought you'd be hungry, but I didn't know what you might like to eat. So I've brought a mixture. There're nuts and seeds, berries, pasta, bread, a bit of beef from yesterday's roast...'

He left the tray and stepped back. Nova inched towards it, her bird voice warning to keep an eye on him, her human stomach moaning at the sight of the feast. Ralph watched in silence as she ate using her talons to scoop, her feet to steady the bowls. There was a large water bottle at the edge of the tray, a straw at the top. She tried to say thank you, but the words came out as a grunt, a sort of stutter. Instead she gestured and nodded and Ralph smiled, and though it was a sad smile, she knew he had understood.

'Bella?' She could manage that word. It had been with her the longest.

'She's OK. Healing. Slowly. You saved her life, you know.'

'I... hu... hurt...her.'

'She would be an awful lot more hurt if you hadn't caught her.'

Nova watched him, clicking her mouth. She bent forward and took another long drink through the straw.

'Are you alright out here? In the tree, I mean? There's plenty of room inside if you wanted...'

'No... Out. Outside.'

'OK. Just... Don't fly too far. I mean, I'm not trying to tell you what to do or anything. I wouldn't. You're a grown... well. You're not a child, is what I mean. It's just...' he reached into his pocket and drew out a piece of crumpled-looking paper. Nova felt her head cocking to one side as she tried to place in her scattered memory what it was he was showing her. Words. Print. News... *Newspaper*.

'People saw you, the other week. There's been some coverage in the Press about it. People speculating about what's really happening at the Beaumont. They claim to be all about transparency, of course, with their Guard projects and the whole song and dance about the Prime Minister visiting earlier this year... But they kept quiet about the

29

hybrids. People are pretty angry. Animal rights groups have been protesting. They don't know anything for certain – the pictures of you that came out of it are pretty hazy at best, but you can definitely see a wing. The BFI have had to put out a statement saying that everything they're doing is under government approval, within the bounds of licensed scientific exploration or however they spun it. They're even organising tours for the Press so that they'll be able to see for themselves what they're doing. I imagine they'll try and use it as a positive spin for the Guard Home Assistance launch, but... well, it's still going to be a PR nightmare for them, trying to cover up all Daniel's operations. Especially without Bella as their spokesperson.'

Nova bristled and spat on the ground at the mention of Daniel. She could feel her entire body shrinking in on itself, becoming more bird-like as she shuddered. Daniel, watching her and Rudy, not smiling, not wanting to join in even when kind-hearted Verity had held out her hand to him. Daniel, his face a twisted sneer: *Rudy's dead, you know. Do you want to know why? Do you?* Daniel older, standing in a dark doorway with a syringe in his hand, explaining that it would help, that it would stop the nightmares... His voice soft, kind, but his eyes still watching the way they always had, whispering of nothing but a cold thirst for pain.

'Anyway, I just wanted to see if you're OK and let you know... Well, it's probably best to keep a low profile if possible. You should be safe enough around here – you don't get many more remote places than this. That was the whole point, after all. But if you do see people, try and stay clear. Loathe as I am to actually do anything to *help* BFI, the last thing we need are a bunch of activists and Press showing up here...'

She gave a squawk of acknowledgement and when he got to his feet, she didn't allow herself to flinch backwards.

'I'll leave the tray. And I'll bring you more tomorrow. Don't worry about Bella, she'll be OK. You don't need to keep watch anymore.'

Nova waited, and watched him as he trudged back to the large ramshackle house. She cocked her head again and gave a small mournful sounding call without really knowing why. Just that he had been kind to her and that he was sad. Shaking her head a little, she turned back to the matter at hand. Once she had eaten as much as she could, Nova shook herself clean, unfurled her wings and stepped out of the shadow of the oak branches. She broke into a run, opened her wings and began to beat them until she was soaring, at last, into the wide and glorious sky.

Summer, 2019

I felt her eyes on me from the moment I stepped outside. The sun shone upon the overgrown grass, dappling shade from the apple trees onto the old half-rotten climbing frame and swing set, but it wasn't particularly warm. Her gaze, however, blazed like dragon's breath on the back of my head. She must have followed me from one of the rooms downstairs. I didn't turn around straight away. I hobbled, the unfamiliar crutches yanking painfully against the scars on my arms, until I reached the old wooden furniture set on the small weed-strewn terrace.

Finally, once I had propped my bad leg up a little, placed my crutches where I could reach them and lowered my sunglasses over my eyes, I looked around at her. She was closer than I'd realised, standing only a few paces behind my chair.

'Was there something you wanted, Felix?'

She scowled, shifted her weight between the scuffed combat boots on her feet and squinted at the sun as if it had been rude to her. Up close I could see the deepening grooves of her forehead and eyes, the tinge of shadows underneath.

'I see you're doing better,' she grunted.

'No thanks to you,' I replied, sharply, turning back to face the end of the garden. I could just see the path through the overgrown grasses of the meadow beyond the gate. The large ash trees, sweeping oaks and tall proud pines. The ARC stood beyond all of them, a looming tower of solid midnight. I stared at it and remembered what Ariana had said about going there, breaking in, finding Blake, finding answers, seeing the horror of her own conception. I waited for the echoes of feeling to come, but to my surprise there was nothing. I felt wrung out, like I had used up the remainder of my lifetime's emotions in the last few weeks alone. It was an oddly cleansing sensation.

Felix rounded her shoulders, folding her arms and glancing at the chair next to mine but not making a move to sit in it. She bobbed a little on her toes, glaring from the ARC back to me.

'You probably shouldn't wear sunglasses. Let the air get to your face. It might help with the scarring.'

'Forgive me if I don't rush to take your medical advice,' I replied. Nicely enough, I thought.

'Yeah.' She scuffed a weed out of a crack in the paving with the toe of her boot. 'The thing with the morphine and stitches and that. I was angry. I might've let it get the better of me. Sorry.'

I watched her, not removing my sunglasses. A familiar bird call caught both of us off guard and we turned at the same time to see Nova flying, the beat of her wings still a little clumsy, over the roof of the manor and to the west, over the moorland where red deer spotted the hills and valleys.

'What's your plan, Bella?' Felix turned to me, eyes bulging with sudden urgency, biting her lip as if holding back a hundred more words. 'Ralph mentioned you told him you had something up your sleeve… You know, when you spoke to him in London.'

'Didn't include getting thrown off a rooftop, shockingly.'

'OK, but short term. Now you're on the mend. Are you staying? Planning a raid on London to try to take Ariana back by force? Or have you given up?'

I watched Nova swoop and tumble in the air, legs tucked neatly into her body. From here she really did just look like a giant bird. I hoped it would appear the same to anyone else who might find themselves beneath her flight path, remote as the Manor's location was. Ralph had told me he'd warned her not to be seen, but none of us could know what she would actually choose to do... Our training sessions had not even come close to this level of trust at the Beaumont. There had been so much more to do. And not just with her.

'I've told Ethan that he doesn't need to look after me anymore,' I muttered, quietly. Felix sat down in the chair so suddenly it gave a wrenching creak. Wrapping her arms around herself, she looked up at me, her face a mask of confusion, anguish and mistrust.

'I've found us a place near the sea close to where I grew up,' Felix said. 'Near enough to the city, plenty of wealthy homeowners with houses to paint and decorate if he ever stopped for a minute to think about his business. If he ever stopped for a minute to think about *anything*, except you. He won't leave unless you make him. You know that. So I'll ask you again, what is your plan?'

'I take it your research into my nefarious plot to expose my and my daughter's whereabouts to her psychopathic father is not going terribly well, if you feel the need to ask?'

'Are you worried about that?'

I turned from the swishing undulation of Nova in

flight, now no bigger than a dandelion seed drifting in the distance, to regard Felix.

'My plan…' I turned my chin to meet the sun as its fingers slanted through a heavy cloud. 'There aren't any children living here and that decrepit old swing set over there is serving no purpose I can see. If we had it taken out there'd be room for a herb garden, which could come in handy. And over in the east corner we could remove all those old rose bushes, Ana never liked them anyway. That would make enough space for a decent perimeter. Stone, to match the house as closely as possible. Seven feet high, maybe more. A locked gate at the front and the back here.'

She snorted. 'Sounds like a Beaumont 2.0.'

'No,' I replied, keeping my voice soft even as it longed to leap and sharpen at her throat, burn all the things that had happened to me there into *her* memory, her body. 'No angles, no octagons. Just a wall.'

'It's not going to make Ethan want to leave you anymore.'

'It might make him worry a little less. He knows I have other protectors.'

'What, Ralph and Dom?' She snorted again. I almost smiled with her.

'Hardly. There are others.'

'Other Guard? Cos I can't see how anything else would even count as a contender against the resources Lychen has…'

'Yes. Other Guard. Different Guard. No one so devoted as Ethan. I don't know exactly what happened there…'

'The link – the *bond* – was made too deeply so he could keep tabs on your Project A curse,' Felix recited. 'So if he just gets away from you, severs the link properly, maybe he can come back to himself properly. Maybe our marriage might actually stand a chance.'

'I agree.'

'Well then, we're on the same page, from the sound of things.'

'I've already spoken to Ralph about the wall. Construction begins tomorrow. I will tell Ethan he must go.'

'I'll stop digging, if you do.'

'Dig all you like. There's nothing there to find. I could have told you that the other week, if I'd the breath spare.'

She had the grace to look ashamed. Only for a second, though.

'A wall, eh? So that's your game... Wall up and hope it keeps Lychen out long enough for you to muster whatever other flesh robots you've enslaved?'

'Yes and no,' I murmured, making her wait for it. 'A wall because it's logical, particularly once BFI start using the ARC again as I suspect they might.'

'You think they'll use the ARC again?'

'Oh yes. They can't keep the hybrids in London, not after what happened with Nova. And the cost of a new facility is too high. I suggested myself that they move the project here.'

'You wanted to have an excuse to be closer to Ariana?'

I shrugged, 'It doesn't really matter now, does it? Now our positions are reversed. In any case, a wall won't stop Lychen. He'll get here long before it's even partially constructed. By the end of next week, I'd wager.'

'What? You... How could you possibly know that?'

'I'm Subject A, remember?'

'So you read minds like Ariana, is that it?'

'No.' I crossed my arms as the sun was swallowed by another cloud. 'What Ariana does isn't mind-reading, to start with. She perceives desires. A bit like Reuben from Project C, before he lost the ability. And it's more about resilience than a core ability. It's the resilience gene from me, working with the modifications Lychen made to his own DNA during his experimentation phase. That's what I've gathered, from the last few days, anyway.'

'While you've been comatose?'

'While I've been consolidating what I know, what I feel... And reading Dr Blake's Project A research papers.'

'Ah. And where did you get— actually, never mind. He certainly wouldn't have left anything lying around that he didn't want people to read.'

'Quite. But getting back to the point in hand, I believe Ariana's abilities stem from her desire – her *need* – to keep herself safe, physically and mentally, and that is how this resilience manifests itself, sometimes violently.'

'And you?'

'I can't be sure. I need to... I need a lab, is what I need. Proper instruments that aren't decades old and patched back together. I need actual resources.'

'Yeah, well. I'd like a million-pound mansion by the sea.'

'There are always ways, Felix. I'm only working on theories at the moment, but I think I can prove them. My own abilities have always been tied to my resilience gene, but that's not the only enhancement... I think that when I was scarred, when my beauty was damaged, the resilience compensated. You see it all the time in human physiology when one area is compromised. Perhaps that part of me realised that I could no longer rely on my face to get what I wanted, so I would need a greater power. In any case, I've been able to link to more minds, using the same methods I used to use to communicate with my bonded Guard. Not many people, and only those with whom I have had an intimate relationship – people whose minds are familiar to me, in other words. I wouldn't be able to just leap into the Prime Minister's head and read his thoughts or anything… But I can tell that Ariana is safe and that she sleeps somewhere warm and comfortable every night. And I know that Lychen is consumed with emotions even he can't decipher and that it's slowly driving him mad…'

'Wait. Are you saying you can read Lychen's mind?'

'Not easily and not every time I've tried. But when he is least guarded, when he's asleep or almost… I've broken through twice now. Scared the shit out of him.'

Felix laughed shortly, snappishly. Then her face clouded over again.

'It sounds like you're needing less protection by the minute.'

'Perhaps. But I don't know how long this power is mine to wield. I don't know how else it can be applied. If it's genetic, how much did Ariana inherit? Will it run out, like the other Project A characteristics? Will it turn on me? Will it turn on her?'

Felix blew her cheeks out and exhaled in a long, mournful sound.

'Wow. Some parents, eh?'

I glanced at her sharply.

'I meant yours… But, well, can't say I fancy Ari's chances much either.'

I couldn't quite bring myself to agree with her out loud and so we lapsed into silence. The sun slid free of the cloud but its beams had slouched too far across the long wild grasses to reach us now. There was no sign of Nova to the west. Up ahead, the ARC lost its gleam and became tarnished, blocky. Like an incongruously large piece of Lego dropped by a giant careless child.

'End of next week, you say?'

'Mmm. Probably sooner.'

'Well,' she stood, her body springing more lightly on her feet than it had before she'd sat down. 'I'd better go and talk to Ethan about mustering up some explosives. Just in case.'

I didn't turn to watch her go. I did remove my sunglasses though, once she had gone. I let the air nip into the ripped, torn skin on my face. Just in case.

January, 20209

Once we've done all we can for her wing, we move Nova
into what was once Dr Blake's office. By pushing the sofa
back and using one of the spare mattresses from upstairs,
we're able to make a comfortable enough bed, though as
soon as some consciousness trickles back to her, she curls
herself into her good wing, her human feet and legs tucking
in, transforming her back into more bird than woman once
again. I place towels around her injured, strapped wing but
we don't cover her with any blankets, opting instead to
keep the fire burning behind the large heavy grate.

Ralph, Dominic, and Tess bumble in and out for a
while, but once the rush of excitement is over and they see
that she's not going to do much but sleep for the next few
hours, and that no one is coming charging over the hill with
a shotgun to finish her off, they drift away. They all have
jobs to do, their keep to earn. The Manor is not how it was
when I arrived in the summer. And it is certainly nothing
like the sprawling estate replete with schoolroom and
hired help I knew as a child. There are only a handful of us
here now, but we all have our roles. Tess and Dom work
remotely for a big, well-paying tech company based in
Manchester. They are also in charge of general surveillance
of BFI's digital activities. Felix sometimes helps them on an
advisory basis, though from what I'm given to believe she

hasn't been consulted on much at all recently. Her presence has all but disappeared since she and Ethan left us last summer, even their old bedroom has been transformed into a joint office for Tess and Dom; the bed removed and replaced with an abundance of screens, desks, office chairs and machines which hum and whirr through the old, wooden door frames and out into the landing beyond. Despite the far-reaching views from the ornate bay windows, heavy blackout curtains ensure the room exists in almost perpetual darkness. A large gaming chair points at a vast screen in the darkest corner. My bedroom is next door; I have grown used to falling asleep to the sounds of Dominic building worlds and battling enemies late into the small hours.

'Any change?' Ralph cuts into my reverie. I've settled on Blake's old desk chair at his writing desk in front of the window. The fire ensures a soft press of warmth as I write up my notes on Nova's injury and treatment, the echo of memories sifting gently around me.

'No, she's stirred a few times but I think you got the sedative dose about right.'

'How will she react, do you think? When she finds out we used her as a guinea pig?'

I accept the cup of coffee he offers me and peer over its rim at the feathery shape on the mattress.

'If it works, she won't care.'

'And if it doesn't?'

I shrug. 'Us trying Mollitiam on her will be the least of her worries. Besides, she's expressed an interest in trying the Naturalisation Application more than once.'

He snorts. 'I still don't know why you told her about NatApp. It's even further off being ready than Mollitiam.'

'Nonsense. You've seen the results with the rodents.'

41

'That was melded animal DNA, not human. And two out of five still died.'

'Still, it shows the application works in theory, once you've corrected the formula I don't see why—'

'I told you; I want to finish the work on Serum X first.' His voice tightens with frustration as the fire glazes golden flames across his glasses.

'You've got it down to one dose now, you said.'

'It's still untested though. If you hadn't killed—'

'I know, I know,' I sigh. 'Let's not start that up again.'

The day has gloomed over outside and the only light comes from the desk lamp, pointing carefully away from the sleeping figure and the soft glow of the fire. The shadows age Ralph, particularly coupled with the white flecks along his hairline. He holds his own coffee cup in one hand, the other resting nonchalantly on the back of my chair. I can feel the warmth of him angling towards me.

'If it's Guard you're after, there are ways and means of acquiring them,' I remark. 'It's easier than ever now they've rolled out the Home Assistance programme. I could order half a dozen today...'

The warmth of him drops away as his gaze clouds over and he snatches his hand from my chair.

'No, Beast. It's one thing using Serum X against one of them in defence, but ordering a batch of former people here to experiment upon is another thing entirely.'

'Even if it could help save the hybrids? You know what Tess and Dom saw yesterday. You know who did this to Nova. Daniel's project is very much alive... And growing, by the looks of things. I hope I'm wrong, but I expect he's found a way to apply the familiarisation methods I used with Nova and—'

'I know, I know.'

'We don't stand a chance of getting anywhere near the hybrids without a proper weapon against the Guard…'

He frowns. 'I'm not sure if it's quite so cut and dry as that, but I see what you're getting at. I'll keep working on NatApp. And I'll think about Serum X. It may be that there's a safer way to test it. Let's just concentrate on Nova for now, see how she takes to Mollitiam first of all. Hopefully it will heal the wing. Maybe it will bring her back to her human self a little more as well. Who knows, maybe it will prove useful for NatApp and X. They're born of the same purpose after all – to revert, regenerate, boost humanity.'

'And Mollitiam's is to boost natural resilience.'

'Perhaps it will do more. It comes from you, after all. And you're always surprising me.'

I grin. 'Twelve-year-old Ralph would never have admitted such a thing.'

'Well. Maybe I'm maturing at long last.'

We sip our coffee silently for a few minutes. I don't pry into the unspoken words between us but I can feel them hanging in the still air of the room like breath on a winter's day.

'Any more news of Ariana?'

'No.' I sigh, swallowing coffee so I don't have to swallow the stone of worry that bundles into my throat every time I think about my daughter. My daughter whose voice I haven't heard for over six weeks now.

'What about… Tom, is it? The Youth fellow still at Beaumont?'

'He can only find out so much without raising suspicion. Lychen's become obsessively paranoid about security, it seems. All I know is that she is alive, unconscious and safe. As safe as she can be there, anyway. I still don't really know what happened – Tom wasn't anywhere near

43

the building in question... And it's all been hushed up, of course. All we know is someone died. Still don't know who, how it happened, whether she was the one who did it...'
My words are swallowed by a shudder which echoes across Ralph's body in turn.

'What about Lychen?'

'He's unravelling a bit, but he's still so angry. He's found a way of blocking me most of the time, a sort of wall. I can still hammer my way in at night occasionally, but it takes a lot of energy. From what I can gather, his view of Ariana is one of enormous frustration and no small amount of fear. I think whatever she did, she disappointed him, but she also scared him. Enough so for him to have effectively put her on ice for the last month or so.'

'You get all that from... what, his dreams?'

'His subconscious, his anger, the flavour of it. The great well of emotion he puts his energy into dismissing and diminishing when he's awake. I'm working my way through it.'

'Does he... Can he *feel* you doing that?'

'Sometimes. When I want him to.'

'OK... you know what you're doing, right?'

I look at him. He looks away, gulping bulkily.

'I'm sorry, it's just...'

'It's just you can't understand why I haven't driven down to London and battered down the walls around Beaumont until I find my daughter?'

'Well...'

'Ariana is OK. I know enough to know that. Besides, if there's one thing the last couple of years have taught me, it's that she is more than capable of self-preservation.'

'Why do I feel like there's a whole lot more you're not telling me?'

I stare at him impassively.

'You said you wanted a normal relationship, Ralph.'

'I know, I know.'

'You can't shut me out of your head and then expect an unreasonable amount of access into mine...'

'Al*right*, jeez!' He turns away, taking my empty cup along with his so that I know he's not really cross. He glances at my notes before he steps away from the desk. The fact he does not point out any mistakes or omissions tells me what I've written is correct.

'Are you walking later?' He pauses at the hearth rug as Marble the cat slinks into the room, takes a long look at Nova, twitches his tail imperiously and settles himself in front of the fire, his eyes remaining on the still, feathery figure. Ralph bends down to scratch him behind the ears.

'Maybe. Depends on how she does,' I say, going back to my notes.

'OK... Well, let me know,' he tries to keep his voice casual. I know my evening walks worry him, though I rarely go far at this time of year. 'I'm cooking tonight. Something with sausages. Dishing up at seven.'

'OK,' I reply, keeping my head down until he's out of the room. I glance back up once he's gone, letting the relief come as a sigh as I look from Nova to Marble.

'Normal relationship,' I mutter, rolling my eyes. 'Like either one of us knows what *that* looks like.'

Marble does not spare me a glance. I am far less interesting than the enormous bird person to whom he has never been able to get this close before. He doesn't even twitch when Dr Blake slopes into the room from the open doorway, his figure stooped and his movements fumbling but eyes as sharp as ever.

'He's trying, Bella.'

'I know he is. I wish he wouldn't, sometimes,' I murmur.

'You'll have to tell him the truth one day,' he nags, softly. He glances at Nova and Marble, his eyes sparkling with humour at the bizarreness which has befallen his office. 'He needs to know that you don't love him back.'

'This is really none of your business, you know,' I glance up, letting a little of the sharpness I'd shown Ralph knife back into my voice.

'You make it my business. He is my son. You are hurting him by letting him believe that one day you might feel about him the way he does about you...'

'Well, who's to say I never will? Who knows what may happen if we're successful in what we're trying to do here? I can't just put everything on pause and fall into his arms. I'm not a stupid teenager anymore.'

'Bella. You were never a stupid teenager.'

I stare at him and he glances away, his mouth caught between amusement and the unmistakable twitch of fear.

'Let's not travel that path today, old man.'

'Fine. I'm just saying I know how Ralph thinks, how he feels. I know him better than anyone. He may act like he's fine but there will come a point when his patience breaks. Don't let it come at the moment when you need him the most. Because you *do* need him, Bella, and not just for the calculations of Mollitiam and the Naturalisation Application project...'

'Point taken.' I look down and begin writing again until I can feel that he's gone, sloping off in his uneven, shuffling way to impart more wisdom at someone else who won't listen, no doubt. The next time I look up, the only eyes I meet are Marble's yellow, unblinking circles of indiscriminate scorn.

'Don't you start,' I mutter.

Summer, 2019

The man was taller than Lychen by at least six inches and had smooth, richly brown skin and hair cropped closely to his head. His huge dark eyes were framed with a set of lustrously thick eyelashes above high cheekbones, which set his jaw into angular relief. He was dressed in a casual, open-necked shirt and neat jeans which made Lychen look stiff and overdressed in his suit and press-lined trousers. Realising she was staring, Ariana shut her mouth and stuffed her hands into her pockets, horribly aware of the small orange juice stain on her T-shirt, the wild tangle of her hair spurting unbrushed around her ears; the red, tight areas of skin brewing spots on her chin... everything. All of her blemishes and imperfections seemed to scream from every angle as she dropped her gaze from the stranger's and looked at the school desk in front of her instead.

'Ariana, this is Mr Teaque. Mr or Dr?' Lychen turned to the man questioningly.

'Mr,' he said, smoothly, as if this were just a normal introduction between tutor and student. As if he hadn't been kidnapped or blackmailed or whatever else Lychen must have done to get him here.

'He teaches mathematics. He is also extensively experienced in the field of empathic perception. I shall let him explain further.' He turned to the man, Mr Teaque, with a twitchy sort of impatience that Ariana had come to associate with his wanting very much to be elsewhere. She'd only known Lychen a couple of weeks but she'd already grown used to his apparent distaste for spending too long in her company, particularly since her powers had stopped working properly. She suspected her resemblance to Bella was to blame.

'Lessons will be conducted between nine am and twelve noon. The afternoon will be spent planning the following day's tuition while Ariana dedicates her time to her schoolwork under the supervision of her Guard tutor.'

'Guard tutor?' Ariana frowned.

'I have instructed Sigma to memorise your curriculum. She will be ready for your lessons tomorrow. That should suffice for the remainder of this school term, at least.'

'May I have full use of the facility?' Mr Teaque addressed Lychen politely, though there was a steely resentment Ariana could feel wafting deliciously from the low rumble of his vowels. She smiled a little as she saw it pull Lychen's eyebrow upwards.

'To what purpose?'

'To deliver the instruction and tutelage in order to produce the results you have demanded, I need space.'

Lychen paused for a few moments. 'You may move freely about the North building and its gardens. Access to the rest of the facility will depend on her improvement. Ariana knows she's not supposed to leave the North building until her abilities are under control. I will check on progress regularly. You will be assigned a Guard person. He will not interfere with lessons but will take steps to ensure you do not venture out of bounds, where necessary. See that you work hard,' he added, staring at both of them before turning abruptly and heading out of the classroom door. Ariana heard him speak a few words to a Guard person just outside before his footfalls faded away down the stairs.

Ariana stared at a spot of carpet near Mr Teaque's shiny brogues. She felt horribly awkward, heat trickling all over her. When he didn't say anything, she made herself look up and meet his steady brown gaze.

'So. Did he force you to come here, then?'

Mr Teaque smiled tightly, though it didn't reach his eyes. Ariana tried to concentrate on the feelings locked behind them, but other than the glimpse of resentment she'd felt directed at Lychen earlier, there was nothing to read. What was it he'd called him? An expert in empathetic... empathic... something.

'I was sought out, offered a position and strongly *encouraged* to take it, let's say,' the man replied, smoothly.

'He said you know about empath-something or other... The reading feelings thing I can do? Although I don't know why he's concentrating on that, that part still works fine. It's the other things I'm having trouble with,' she sighed, frustratedly.

Mr Teaque sighed as well and looked out of the window, his hands in his pockets.

'Tell me about your abilities,' he said, eventually. 'Tell me about how they started and what you can do and the trouble you are having with them. Then I will tell you about me. And we had better hope, for both our sakes, that I can help.'

Ariana leaned back against the school desk. She tried not to think too much about what he had meant by both their sakes.

'Well. I don't know. I suppose it all started with being able to tell things about people. I didn't know that's what I was doing of course. For so long, I just thought it was normal, to sense what other people didn't say. Then it got stronger about a year ago... Something to do with me growing up, apparently. Other people started to notice it, I was able to see things that they couldn't, not just about people but patterns and stuff. I solved a computer code thing without knowing how to read it... Then... I don't know, a bunch of stuff happened. I found out that people I'd trusted had been lying to me. I got angry. I was angry all the time. And that's when I started being able to do other stuff. Make people hurt, make them tell me things... I could still read their feelings but I didn't really care about that anymore. I attacked people. I hurt them, without ever touching them... But then it all sort of stopped. And now I'm left with nothing but the useless feelings thing again. And even that doesn't work on everyone, especially round here where most of the people I see are *them*,' she gestured at the Guard man still waiting impassively outside the classroom door.

As her voice trailed off, Mr Teaque got to his feet.

'Come on, let's walk.'

She followed him from the room. As they passed the Guard man, he fell into step a few paces behind them. Ariana followed her new tutor halfway along the corridor before he spoke again.

'The power. How do you envision it within you?'

'The reading feelings power?'

'All of it.'

'Well... I don't know. The feelings thing I could always do, so I never really envisioned it as anything in particular because it was always just *there,* you know? But the other stuff... It's like this dark, blank well inside me. It would talk to me. And when I was angry before, it kind of swelled and took over and made me dark and blank as well. Then it would kind of just… shoot out of me…'

'I see. And how did you come to think of it that way?'

Ariana frowned. 'I don't understand.'

They were at the end of the corridor now, but Mr Teaque simply turned on his heel and walked back the other way. Ariana had to take two steps for every one of his long strides just to keep up. She glanced at him, but his eyes were fixed down and ahead. Everything about him was wired with concentration. She could easily imagine him as a teacher in the classroom, pacing up and down as he explained some impossible quadratic formula without looking anyone in the eye.

'Did you perhaps come across a description of a similar power that invoked images of this dark, blank well within you?'

Ariana felt her frown deepen. 'I… Well, yeah. I overheard… people. I thought they were my family. I thought they cared about me. They were talking about me and saying that there was this blankness, a darkness… That it was getting bigger, making me disappear. That's sort of when I started thinking about it like that, I guess? But what does it matter, how I look at it? I can't reach it anymore, anyway.'

'Because,' he addressed the looming wall ahead keenly, 'because the first thing you must do is stop separating your abilities. They are all as one. They are all yours; they are all you. There is no empathic perception without the dark well of emotion-driven telekinesis. You are the only thing stopping yourself from accessing both.'

'Lychen said I have to stop grabbing for it. That it should come to me.'

'Dr Lychen does not know what it is to harness this

power. But he is correct in some sense. If I'm right in what I have ascertained so far, you will eventually be able to scoop whatever power you seek to control at will.'

'Right,' Ariana said, sarcastically. They had reached the stairwell on their second lap of the corridor. Mr Teaque eyed her briefly, before turning abruptly and setting off down the stairs. The movement was so swift it took Ariana by surprise and the Guard person who had been tailing them also made an odd, hitching movement at the sudden change of direction.

'You seem sceptical,' Mr Teaque remarked, mildly, as Ariana jogged a little down the stairs onto the floor below. He barely hesitated for her to catch up with him before he began to stride once again. It was as if he were measuring the building's width in step counts.

'Well yeah... You've known me for like twenty minutes and you're making all these big assumptions about what I can do...'

'I've known *you* for twenty minutes. I've known your power a lot longer than that.'

'OK... Is this the point where you're going to tell me all about you now? Are you some empathic wizard who has seen into my mind and now understands all the stuff I can do perfectly?' She tried to sound nonchalant but she knew that he had heard the desperate strain of hope in her words. He didn't react, merely put his hands behind his back as they continued to pace, the Guard's eyes never leaving them from his post where the stairs met in the middle.

'Hardly. I haven't been able to read a person's desires for a great many more years than I ever could. But there was a time when I was able to do it to a degree that, in some cases, I could manipulate those desires to my own end.'

'Mind control? Like the old guy from the X-Men... Professor X?'

'Not quite that slick, but that was the direction I was heading in for a while. I was one of the most promising Subjects of Project C. You are, of course, familiar with Project C?'

'The ARC children with special powers? Yeah. I lived with Dominic last year. He wasn't so impressive.'

'He was when he was your age. We all were. That's when we peaked. The beginning of adolescence, tripping along the line between childhood and self-awareness... That's when your abilities began to grow, yes?'

'Yes, but I'm not like the Project C kids, I wasn't given genetic properties to match my abilities or special tutoring to make me believe I could do them... I wasn't even planned.'

She shuts her eyes and shakes her head so that the images don't crowd in. The warm summer air spilling lazily across the office floor. The sharp, purposeful stride of the young man across the room. The unaware gaze of the younger woman, the crack of his hand against her head. The vision hadn't troubled her when she first saw it. The blankness had been in control then. It had told her that she didn't care and she hadn't. So why did it churn her stomach with nausea now? She looked at the man next to her, realising, as she did so, that he had come to a standstill. They were outside a door. She knew without looking that it was one of the ones which still bore her mother's name.

'I know who you are, Ariana. I know where you came from. I knew your father back when he was the lead of our Project. He never had much time for me, especially as I had begun already to lose my grip on my abilities as his own esteem grew. He would have disposed of me back in the children's home I was plucked from as an infant, if the choice had been his. Dr Blake was the one who offered me a position as a junior apprentice. He always displayed more sympathy for his failures because, of course, the fault was ultimately his.' There was no bitterness to his voice, nor any warmth. It just rumbled smoothly like water over a stone. He turned to look at the name again.

'Let me guess,' Ariana scowled, staring from the name to him. 'She was the most magnificent, beautiful, powerful person in the whole world and no one will ever have a hope of matching up, least of all me...'

'Beautiful? Yes. Of course, she was designed that way. Powerful in her own way I suppose. But magnificent? No. I saw her, you see. I saw all of what she was. What she wanted. She knew it as well and avoided me. She favoured the small, the young, the impressionable. All those who could give her the approval and love she sought so desperately as a child. Her power was in her resilience which manifested as command over others because that is what her innermost perception of power was. She chose to be able to have the ability to acquire what she needed. Your resilience is borne of the same ilk. It manifests as a power you harness in any which way you determine will protect you.'

'So... the reason why I can't do it at the moment is because I don't need protecting?'

'No, it's because that's what you believe. I told you, you are the only block between yourself and your ability.'

He began to move in that quick, unexpected way again. She sprang to catch up.

'You haven't actually told me anything about how to stop that, though?'

'What makes you think I know? I merely explained what I thought, based on what I *do* know...'

'But Lychen said—'

'Dr Lychen is undoubtedly hoping that my memories of how I once read and manipulated desire will lend some insight into how your similar powers can be harnessed. But we are two very different individuals, and our abilities were never created equally. I will try and help you, because I have a family whom I would very much like to see again.'

'What did he do to them?'

'Nothing. He has gifted them a Guard Assistant, however. Under the guise of testing the Home Assistants in the field. It will remain with them – watching, monitoring – until I return. I very much hope that will be sooner rather than later.'

'Right. Um. Sorry, I guess...'

'It's not your fault.'

'Well. I'm kind of the reason.'

'You are not. You are just a child caught in the middle of an impossible mesh of genetic hubris, experimentations and fools who play God. As was I. For now, I would suggest you take some time to yourself. No distractions, no expectations, no other voices in your head but your own. Listen to what it says.'

He glanced at her once as they came to a stop. She realised, with the same wrong-footed jolt she'd felt when they'd landed outside her mother's office, that the room they now faced was her own suite. Shrugging, she put her hand on the handle.

'OK then. Guess I'll see you tomorrow, Mr Teaque.'

'Please. Call me Reuben.'

Summer, 2019

Nova lived for the sky. For the limber flow of air beneath her feathers, for the rhythmic beat, the bob and list which flowed more naturally every day. She slept in the same alcove of the oak tree she had discovered in her first few days. On cooler nights she drew her wings tightly around her bare legs and knew, with a logic that loomed as certainly as her new-found flight, that when the colder seasons came she would need to find a better shelter. Still, for now the temperature did not bother her, not when there were dew drops to shake free and a looming, white-scored sky to spear through.

Ralph still brought food and talked to her. Sometimes she would talk back, but mostly she listened. Sometimes she felt the gaze of the others upon her as she soared high above them. The wonderment of Dom and Tess who gazed the longest but had not yet found the words to speak to her. That was fine. Nova did not require company. She didn't care that the birds avoided her, skittering in fright whenever she rustled herself free of the drag of sleep in the mornings. She couldn't remember a time before the loneliness. Even as a child of the ARC, tight friendships had not been encouraged. There had been laughter and jokes and gentle teasing, but she hadn't felt close to anyone. Only her.

Nova watched as Bella grew in strength, tapping her slow way on her crutches outside to sit in the weak rays of sunshine. She watched the narrow gleam of Felix's glare upon the slighter figure and knew she meant her harm. She felt the strong devotion of Ethan, the helpless adoration of Ralph. And as she did, it occurred to Nova for the first time that perhaps she *did* care, just a tiny bit, that she was alone.

'Nova? Nov? Are you awake?'

She awoke to the sound of the silken ribbon voice and moved, startled. They hadn't spoken properly since they'd come here. Not more than a wave and a nod, anyway. And now Bella stood under her tree, leaning heavily on the crutches, her eyes twin shards of piercing green visible even through the thick emerald of the oak leaves. Nova shuffled to a space in the branches, jumped and opened her wings, sailing in a large circle to land clear of the lower limbs, a few paces from her former mentor, who smiled in admiration.

'I always said the leash impeded you,' Bella remarked, her voice still a little hoarse but already almost back to its normal, musical self. Nova blinked at her bandaged arms and broken leg in its cast.

'I know,' Bella said, a flash of self-consciousness making her almost unrecognisable. She brought a hand to her cheek and it was then that Nova saw the long, livid scar there. She hadn't noticed it until then. 'I'm a mess. But it looks worse than it is. And it hardly hurts anymore. I wanted to thank you. If it weren't for you... Well.'

Nova tilted her head.

'You know about the Press coverage?'

Nova nodded.

'It's not safe for either of us at the moment. Not really. They'll want you. They'll want me. I'm having a wall built around us here…'

Nova laughed inside and it came out as a strange squawk which made Bella jump a little. Bella frowned again. 'I know, it doesn't sound like much. And it won't be ready before Lychen comes for me. But if things turn out the way I think they will, it should help in the future. Anyway. I wanted to warn you that there'll be people here, building the wall. It shouldn't take too long, but if you could stay out of sight while they're around…'

Nova nodded, her mind already skittering upwards, away. She'd caught sight of a narrow, glimmering spit of a lake on her flight yesterday evening. She could dip low enough, try and catch a fish with her toes… That would keep her busy while the people built their wall.

'Thank you,' Bella shifted her weight from her good leg to her crutches. She was in pain. It laced through her movements like lead. Nova gave another sound, a piteous little coo that she herself didn't quite understand. She watched it nestle through Bella though, soften some of the sharper lines the pain had left on her face.

'I wanted to ask… How was it you came to my rescue? How did you know I was falling? You were in the Yard; I was the other side of the building entirely…'

Nova concentrated, mustering the words, knowing they wouldn't all come.

'Sh… shout… ing.'

'You heard the shouting? From all the way in the Yard?'

'D… d. Da— day…'

'Day?'

'D… Danger.' She shut her eyes and turned her face upwards before looking back at Bella, who was frowning in confusion.

'Danger? You mean... you knew there would be danger? From the shouting?'

Nova gave a small sigh. She longed to fly, to sweep away from all this mess of confusion and feeling and broken, boring, humanity. But she tried one last time, because she wasn't in a cage anymore. She knew what it was like not to be in a cage, and Bella was why.

'I... ffff. Fff. Feel... danger. You.'

'You felt I was in danger?'

Nova nodded, relief flooding through her even as a part of her, a small, calculating human part said that yes, it was all very well and good Bella having got her out of her cage, but would she have been in a cage in the first place if Bella hadn't left her behind all those years ago? Shuffling from foot to foot, she gave another small wild call and looked away, to the sky. Bella sighed.

'Well. Thank you.'

Nova cocked her head, turned to the grass and ran, hopped, and sprang up and away. Really, though she was lonely and often too cold and didn't know how it felt to be loved like Bella, being a bird was so much easier than being a human.

Summer, 2019

Felix watched her husband working, her body rigid with irritation. He looked so normal, bent over the table in her office, the remaining monitors carefully moved to one side, sorting through some of the old explosive-making supplies she'd saved.

'Do you have what you need?' She asked, mostly to let him know she was there. He turned; his mouth too small without its usual easy grin. His hair was too long and his eyes were too soft.

'I think so. I may need to raid some of Ralph's supplies... Does he still keep a chemical store in the upstairs office?'

'Yes. There's talk of turning the old dance studio into a bespoke lab. Dom's already moved some of the old surgical equipment from the ARC out of there.'

'I know,' he turned back to the box. Of course he knew.

'I need to give an answer on that property by the end of the week.'

'Yep.'

'Eth?'

'I'm not going anywhere if Lychen's coming here. We'll all be needed. You too.'

Felix sighed and turned away. She'd known he would

61

say as much. She tried to tell herself that she agreed with him, that she wouldn't feel comfortable leaving Ralph and Dom behind knowing Lychen and however many Guard people were coming. But the truth was, every passing day she spent in this house felt like it was leaching a little more of her energy, her soul. The parts of her which gave a shit about anything or anyone.

'Do you think he'll bring Ariana?' She asked, looking up and squinting. Ethan stood up, his back suddenly rule-stick-straight. It was a Guard movement and it made her shudder.

'Why would he?'

'As a weapon?'

He turned to her, fear and shame battling across his face. His hand shook a little as he placed an aerosol back in the box carefully.

'Strategically, it would give him a greater advantage in terms of physical and mental damage impact. But her abilities are still unpredictable and her emotional state is bound to be even more unstable, particularly here... I don't think he will, no.'

'You aren't still connected to him at all?'

'No. I am no longer a Guard. My assumptions are based on what I knew of his intentions when I was.' He retained the mechanical tone, too, when he spoke about it. But his eyes softened once again as he glanced at her.

'Don't worry about me, I'll be fine.'

'What will he do when he sees you're no longer his? He'll realise there's a way back, he'll realise we've developed Serum X. Perhaps it would be better if you weren't—'

Ethan turned around and took her hands in his. From the neck down, it was almost the old Ethan. His grip was the same, the ripple of muscle formed the familiar undulations beneath the tattoos he'd acquired in his twenties. One of them a black and white cat in a stupid, drunken homage to her. His face, though. His mouth and his eyes and the curly hair she'd asked and asked him to try growing out... None of it was hers anymore.

'If he gives any thought at all to my anomalous status after seeing Bella, I think he will deduce that it was born of our unique connection. He will conclude that its design has proven ultimately detrimental to my status as a Guard. Any further blame will be placed on Bella. I don't think he gives the Blakes enough credit to have come up with a means to counteract the Guard process.'

'But he wouldn't hesitate to have one of them kill you on the spot—'

'The same can be said of any of us, apart from Bella, whom he will want to kill himself.'

'You won't leave her.'

'Not until I know she is safe without me. In the same way you are still concerned for Ariana... You don't want her brought here for *her* sake, not ours.'

'It is *not* the same, Ethan,' she threw his hands back at him. He frowned.

'You love her—'

'Like a child, Eth. Like *our* child, who would have been about three months younger. Oscar. Remember him?'

'Of course...' but his frown deepened, as if he couldn't quite work out what she meant by the word *remember*.

'That's what I think about, when I see her. She isn't the same. Of course she isn't. But she still deserves to be loved and protected as we would have loved and protected him. If we'd had the chance. That is *not* the same as this weird, residual compulsion you have to protect Bella D'accourt.'

Ethan looked down. He didn't say that the need went deeper than that. That he felt Bella in the depths of everything he was. That he could barely breathe without reaching for the gentle flutter of her thoughts in the darkest depths of his mind. That it couldn't just be a Guard thing, because he wasn't a Guard anymore. That he didn't want to be free, if being free meant not seeing her face or hearing her voice again... He didn't say it, but Felix heard it all the same. She walked away without another word, trudged up the stairs and slammed her bedroom door.

She didn't cry anymore. That day last month, when Ethan had come back to her in part but had chosen to stay in London... That day had been the last time. The tears had wrenched themselves out of her long after she had cried herself into a deep, throat-burning dehydration. Then she had slept for a few hours and, when she had woken in the early hours of the morning, she had gone downstairs and collected up the most useful of her computers and brought them back up here to her room. Now they stood on a desk in front of the window. She crossed over to them and brought the three screens to life. Ignoring two of them, she concentrated on the one nearest to her as she slid her office chair closer to the table and settled into a reverie, her eyes skating over lines of code like the blades of an ice dancer.

She hadn't been able to find much yet. But searching through Bella's old emails, perusing forums from years ago, examining more and more obscure usernames, metadata tags, Instagram images... It had become relaxing in a strange sort of way. Felix didn't even really know if she truly believed she would find an answer to that old dull nag. She wondered if perhaps she was remembering the instinct wrong in the first place. It had only been momentary, after all. The briefest of conversations with Ralph, who would look at her in horror now if he knew how many hours she had spent trying to prove it.

'...number two is that Bella knows exactly what's happening and that this is all playing into some bigger plan. Which means...'

'We're playing into her hands and doing exactly what she wants us to do...'

'Yep...'

Felix dragged a window showing a parenting chat forum onto the second screen as it ran a search for various keyword combinations she'd auto-loaded. She refocused on the encryption code for a Twitter account belonging to a French name with a scientific reference in the bio. *Dig all you like,* Bella's voice taunted her. She glanced out of the window, watching as Bella herself hobbled towards the gardener she'd hired to remove the dead rose bushes. She was becoming stronger on her crutches by the day, the pain still evident but less obvious in her movements now. She paused briefly at the edge of the path and pivoted as gracefully as it was possible for a broken-legged ballerina to do as a call came from the house. Felix narrowed her eyes. From this angle she couldn't see the scar which ran jaggedly from the left side of Bella's forehead to her chin. From this angle, the petite woman looked as perfect as ever as she smiled at the figure approaching. Ralph joined her on the path, his face as open and easy as Felix had ever seen it. Everything about his body, angled towards Bella, hands quick to offer a hand onto the grass, everything about the shine of his face as he spoke to her, everything was so bloody *obvious.*

Felix shook her head and turned back to her screens.

Maybe she was mad. Driven into the heady realms of obsession by the woman who had taken her husband. All she knew was that it was easier to keep doing what she was doing, lose herself in the infinite searches and stretches of digital possibility, than to simply do nothing. Feast on the image of finding something, anything, to prove herself right. To swipe the hateful, pitying looks from all their faces. Felix smiled a little to herself as she settled her mind back into its happy place, blocking out the distant notes of Bella's laughter mixed with Ralph's short, bark-chuckle. There most likely wasn't anything to find. In all probability she was treading a dangerous line between vengeful preoccupation and heart-clenching grief. But she'd keep doing this for now, if it stopped her from crying herself raw or snatching one of Bella's crutches and beating her senseless with it. She'd keep doing this for now, even if she was mad. Because maybe, just maybe, she wasn't.

January, 2020

When Nova has not shown any signs of wakefulness by five and the heady oppression of the Manor and all its inhabitants threatens to implode inside my head, I decide to take a walk after all. Darkness nestles around the Manor like a predator as I pull my heavy coat around my shoulders, tug the fur-trimmed hood over my head and wrap a thick alpaca wool scarf around my neck. Still, when I open the back door and step outside, the cold air shocks against my exposed skin like a breaking wave. I take a moment to inhale slowly, letting the fresh scent of mountains, lakes, wildness, flood into my lungs and warm up as it flows back out. Sometimes this is the only time of day when I feel like I can truly breathe. When no one is watching me, waiting for my next decisive moment.

I step out into the garden, the frigid ground lit by the warm glow spooling from the Manor's windows. Pulling on a pair of suede gloves, I step lightly onto the path and down towards the large, uneven shadow of the wall.

Ralph doesn't understand my walks. He doesn't try to persuade me not to go anymore, he's even stopped muttering under his breath about what the point was of constructing a bloody great wall when I was just going to swan off out of it every night. But I know he still doesn't get it. I don't pry into his mind but I can as good as feel his anxiety pressing out of the very walls of the Manor, feathering against my back like the clutching fingertips of an anxious parent. It's enough to make anyone crave the open, empty air.

I type the six-digit number into the key pad on the large heavy wooden gate set into the stones at the bottom of the garden and swing it open. Passing through, I make sure the lock clicks loudly back into place behind me. It's the only sound I make as I turn away and set off over the frost-flattened ground of the meadow, gleaming in the moonlight.

It wasn't so bad in the warmer months. Ralph used to come with me then, sometimes. We'd wander slowly over the newly-mown grass, him ready with a steady strong hand to catch or help if my bad leg gave way. It's hard to know when things began to change. Lychen's visit. The wall. Ethan. Dr Blake. At some point, Ralph started looking at me differently. As if I might disappear entirely if I stray too long out of his sight. Which is stupid, because it's only now that I'm finally beginning to feel as if my disappearing days are behind me.

Sighing, I put Ralph out of my mind. I've reached the trees now and I wait a moment. Not because I need to rest, my leg is stronger than ever and, thanks to my new habit of daily walking, my body is as fit and poised as it was in the days when I'd train with Ana in the studio until my toes bled. I wait in the shadow of a tall pine tree, watching the ARC and gathering myself. Clearing my head, I concentrate on the tall column up ahead, sending my mind out on an invisible thread. I shut my eyes as my inner vision reaches past the trees, up the hill and over the gate Ralph used to jump in one swift movement when he felt like showing off. Past the old expanse of lawn where the amphitheatre had been, over the walled boundary, round the corner, past boarded windows and across to the front. The gravelled driveway still holds two lorries and the floodlights are up.

I rarely venture towards the ARC in mind or body these days. Most nights I simply stick to the moorland on the outskirts of the Manor, finding a quiet spot to wait while my mind reaches the rest of the distance. There was never any point my venturing to the ARC. I'm not like Ariana. There are no secrets in that building for me. Neither do I ascribe it feelings of resentment; stolen innocence; a life wrenched off track. It is just a building. There is no monstrosity in a building. That is what I try to remember as my mind hesitates at the threshold, at the large double doors I pushed open without a care every day for almost ten years, heels clipping neatly across the shining black ocean of floor, tossing the lights of the chandeliers into a thousand dazzling crystals in my hair... It is just a building. And I need to see inside. Go, Bella.

Nothing.

I open my eyes, my gloved hand outstretched before me. Shaking my head, I try again, trying not to give in to frustration as my mind drifts once again through the frigid twigs, up the frosting path and over the gate. Back round the corner, past the boards and tarnished broken glass winking echoes of artificial light. Back to the door and this time I don't hesitate to dwell in useless memory, this time I just push.

Nothing.

I scowl, balling my fist in frustration.

Well, at least you know for sure now. It's not to do with you, when you can't get into Lychen's mind. Whatever defence he's using is here too.

Yes. Somehow he and Daniel have used it to cloak the

building. How on earth did they do that?

Don't panic. It doesn't mean—

No. You must go, Mamma. I have to check them all. You have to go.

She sweeps clear of my mind like a leaf lifting in the breeze. I sort hurriedly through the connections. All twenty of the Youth Guard remain tethered, loosely. They're the most likely candidates for hijack, of course. I quickly glimpse each of their present circumstance but everyone is where they should be. Tom is at the Beaumont, running on the exercise track in the Guard quarters, tailed by seven of the new generation of Youth Guard Lychen has tasked him with mentoring. None of them have even come close to replicating the success of my original twenty, I've been happy to learn. Karl, Hugh, Liz... All good. Bette is fine, too.

When the next generation of Youth Guard failed to live up to my success, the first twenty became even more valuable, which led to Lychen redistributing Bette from Daniel's service. As much as I enjoyed the sour look on Daniel's face as I watched the transaction from Bette's eyes, it was a blow to lose my best means of keeping tabs on him. Now Bette, like many of the others, is linked to a government official. Eve, of course, remains my most prized asset. I barely need to touch on her link to know she is exactly where she is supposed to be, in the most important position of all. No, my Youth are fine. I should have known it would take more than the likes of Lychen's limited knowledge of mind-links to break them. So how has he masked the ARC building against me?

I touch my link to Lychen next. It's the thinnest I hold because he has learned new ways to block me out over the last few months. Nowadays I often reach no closer than the slippery outer walls of his mind, shouting my taunts over the top with the hope he hears at least a shadow of them. The walls are only slightly more scalable when he is asleep, and even then I sometimes find myself ricocheted abruptly back to my body. Tonight the walls are in place as usual. I tiptoe close without touching and hear an echo of his cold, clear voice telling someone – a Guard person presumably – to bring him a double measure of the single malt. I smile as I come back to the trees, though I still don't have my answer. The drinking is a good sign. It's not him doing *this*, though. It has to be Daniel then. I don't link to Daniel. I have never tried. I am not so arrogant that I have forgotten the dogged calculation of his gaze, the unknowable darkness beneath it. The hints of an entirely different kind of monster to the one I shared a bed with last year.

Ariana is a remote black well of unconsciousness when I try to reach her. I flutter around, touching every space I can reach, but she's gone. Fear spirals deep inside as I return to myself.

What's wrong? I don't even have to reach for the last link because, as always, he is waiting for me.

Daniel is back at the ARC. I can't penetrate it psychically. They've erected some sort of blockade against me.

Is it the same defence Lychen uses?

I think so. But I don't know how they have managed to place it on an entire building. Lychen's is not strong, he only wields it sporadically. Yet somehow it has been manifested into a cloak big enough to cover the entire ARC.

Calm down. Let's look at this logically.

I feel him sit down in his favourite large easy chair so he can fully immerse himself in the conversation, like my presence is a VR headset he can place over his eyes, blackening everything else out.

I can't calm down, Ethan! If they can block me from seeing into a building they can block me from people! How am I going to connect with Ariana?

Is she—?

Fine for now. I tried her. But what if they put this cloaking mechanism on her too?

Don't jump to conclusions – look for the logic. Did you test your connection with Lychen?

Yes. Couldn't get all the way in but I got far enough to hear him ordering a drink.

So if they have found a way to mask an entire building, wouldn't they have started with him? So you wouldn't even—

—have caught a glimpse. You're right.

It must be Daniel.

But how?

You've never linked to him?

No. I wouldn't. Not until I have more control, anyway.

A sound filters through the link. A click and hiss which sounds particularly out of place under the moonlit trees. I shut my eyes and taste the cool sour tang. I've grown used to the flavour of beer over the last few months without a drop ever passing my lips. He feels me and grins, the warmth of it curving around the place where I am in his head like a caress. We both feel the guilt of it at the back of our throats and, as one, swallow it together.

If Lychen's decided it's beer o'clock...

Lychen's drinking single malt whisky. Not a half price lager from Tesco.

It's a pale ale actually. But it was half price, you're right. Divorce is an expensive business. How are things in the ramshackle laboratory of hopes and dreams, anyway?

Nova was shot.

No way! Is she OK?

I think so. We used Mollitiam on her.

Ralph agreed to that?

He didn't have much choice. And no, I didn't make him. But she might have lost use of her wing if we didn't try. And so far it seems to be healing well, from what I can see. I should be getting back, actually.

Yes, you should.

You're only agreeing because you don't like me being this close to the ARC.

I don't like you being that close to Daniel. The ARC is just a building.

I know. I'm going back.

But I linger and so does he. It's comfortable and warm in his small living room, the taste of beer on my tongue, the softness of his touch in my head. The longer I stay, the more I feel – the wisps of woodsmoke coming from the fireplace, the slight musky scent of sweat and paint, the cotton brush of his shirt against the skin of my cheek. I sigh and withdraw. He strokes the whisper of me as I do.

Turning back to the Manor, I begin the slow ascent up the hill. My limbs feel stiff with cold, the warmth of Ethan seeping out into the air around me. I frown, hating to leave the puzzle unsolved. Ethan is right, Lychen can't know about the cloaking thing otherwise he'd do it to himself. Has he told Daniel about my mind-visits? He wouldn't want the younger man to think he was losing his grip on his control, his sanity... But his terror has always been so desperate, his anger untethered... Has it driven him to seek help at the cost of a small portion of dignity? Has Daniel taken that knowledge and, knowing he'll be near me, used it to construct some sort of mind-repulsion protection on a scale the size of the ARC? I can't understand how such a thing would be possible, but then I wouldn't have thought it possible to replicate one's desires and place them into a mind-altered human being before I met one of the Guard.

My mind continues to circle around itself as I unlock the gate and pass through to the garden. Feathers still splay on the ground where Nova lay twelve or so hours ago. I frown again. Had Daniel been the one to shoot her? And, if so, how had he known she was going to be flying over the ARC? Had he felt her desire to seek him out as I had sensed it too, when I went to see her yesterday? Why else would he just so happen to be carrying a gun on his person? Unless he'd seen her and told one of the Guard to fetch it, but why would she have given him that opportunity – surely she would have identified the danger as keenly as she'd detected his presence in the first place? None of it makes sense, and none of it is good.

I turn towards the Manor, its higgledy-piggledy windows either glaring light at me or staring blankly. I take a moment to feel for the presences within. Nova, still wrapped in muddled, drug-induced stupor, but fluttering closer to the surface every minute. She will need an extra sedative to get her through the night without pain. Ralph in the kitchen, stirring lentils and chopped tomatoes, his mind flicking agitatedly between a mathematical problem in the NatApp formula and all the horrible things that could be happening to me out here in the dark. Dom, plugged into a game on the X-box, only vaguely aware of Tess who sits on the chair beside him, scrolling jealously through the social media of an old university classmate, her mind spiralling slowly around the question of what the hell she is doing with her life. Marble curls closer to the fire and thinks about the strange smells he can smell and whether one of them might be sausage. Dr Blake lingers in the laboratory, hands behind his back as he frowns at the genetic machinery. Behind him, Ana smiles fondly at the back of his head as she points her toes and launches a slow, perfectly controlled turn in the small, isolated remains of her dancefloor. Beasts, friends, lovers and the ghosts of love... all waiting for the strands of me to bind them together.

Summer, 2019

Ariana lay on the white sea of sheets, staring at the neatly carved patterns of the four wooden posts. They stretched up from the bed in a strange, half-done kind of way. She blinked and tried to concentrate on what Mr Teaque – Reuben – had said. It seemed to have been one of those explanations which made a lot more sense at the time, when it was being delivered by a grown-up in a voice full of authority and self-assuredness. Breathing slowly, Ariana tried to clear her head as she shut her eyes. The well of blankness lurked sulkily in its usual spot. *Not blankness. Not darkness.* Dr Blake had been the one to call it that, the look she got sometimes. *It's sort of black. Blank... There's something growing in her that's going beyond us. Some sort of darkness, a confidence... the more it emerges, the more she seems to just... disappear.* The power stirred a little and she realised that it was in reaction, almost like a shudder, to the pinpricks of guilt spraying into her stomach at the thought of her fake grandfather, the memory of his rumbling voice.

Follow it. See where it goes. It was her own voice. Her *mother wasn't in here. Ariana touched upon the area where Bella's voice usually came from just to be sure, but there wasn't anything there. Find the block. I'm the thing that's stopping me. Find the block.*

Why, though? This was another Ariana again. The first one had been older, but this questioning seemed to come from a smaller, gentler part of herself. The part which wondered whether this time might be better spent playing Roblox after all.

Because... I need to stay here. It took so much to get here. And if I don't show Lychen that I'm worth it, he might throw me out and then where will I go?

Back to Cumbria. So? It's not like I actually like him.

What about Marc? The image of her grandfather bound and helpless in the centre of the squash court flooded into her head.

Lychen wouldn't need him anymore, maybe he'd let him go.

She thought about where Marc stayed now, in the bare prison-like room a few floors beneath her, sitting on his bed as he always was when she visited. His face, thinner already than it had been in the squash court, his eyes older, though always ready with a smile, guarded though it was with the memory of the pain she'd inflicted on him.

What do I care? It's not like he's ever been a proper granddad to me. I'm not supposed to be visiting him for cosy chats, he's here to practice on. I could do that. I did it before, when he annoyed me. I could hurt him, if I could make it work again...

Could I? He—

I don't want to think about that anymore. That's not the block. It didn't stop when I saw him in the squash court. I still used it against him.

It stopped the next day. When everything was new and different and I stopped fighting everything...

It stopped when I thought about how I hurt Mum and Dr Blake... I don't even know what happened to him.

I could ask. I could ask Fee or Ralph.

Lychen blocked and erased their numbers on my phone. I'm not supposed to contact them.

I'm not supposed to be going to talk to Marc twice a week either. Lychen doesn't know everything. He doesn't know about inside voices.

I don't want to talk to Mum. I don't want her in my head.

But the other thing, the not-blank power, it shivered as the thought came to her. She went deeper.

I miss them.

Another shiver and another. The sea of darkness began to tremble. She couldn't work out if it was reacting in scornful opposition to what she was feeling or had been titillated by it.

I miss Ralph and Fee. I miss Dr Blake, his stupid sticky-uppy hair and the way he said my name, even when he got it wrong. And I miss my mum. Her smile. Running across the sand and thinking she was the most wonderful thing in the whole world. I miss me. I miss who I was.

The power shifted and slurped and suddenly, there it was, right there in her head. It spoke to her:

They were weak. We hurt them. We were right to do that. They deserved it. They hurt us too. They hurt us when we were that person. That person was weak.

True.

And just for a moment, the voice swarmed and flowed into her and they were the same, in agreement, both aching for the people they'd hurt while loathing them at the same time. Ariana opened her eyes and her mouth fell ajar at the same time. She was no longer lying in her four-poster bed. She was no longer lying on anything at all. Trying hard not to move her head in case she broke the spell, whatever it was, she glanced sideways. Her eyeline was level with the top of the posts. She was lying in mid-air... She was *levitating... How the hell am I—* and she dropped, abruptly. Coughing, sitting up, Ariana shook her head. She could fell the power retreating again, draining like water flowing into an open plughole.

Where are you going? Come back!

Nothing happened. Ariana sighed, settled back into the bed, and tried to go back to what it was she had been thinking about when it had reacted. Mum. Dr Blake. The block. The child she had been, when she'd cared about things... Something shivered and it wasn't her. She concentrated very hard on not grabbing or reaching. Whatever it was faltered and slipped away. She sighed and let her mind wander into the corner, sensing rather than smelling the faint aromas of sandalwood and cedar candles, bergamot and jasmine shampoo.

Mum? Are you there?

No answer, but there was an echoing shudder somewhere far away. Not the power voice... This presence was as different as ribbon to rope, and slowly, because she was waiting for her, listening for her, Ariana felt her mother's presence drifting delicately, gracefully as always, into hers.

Ariana? Are you OK?

Yes.

Ariana opened her eyes and felt her mother see through them, felt her react with unfamiliarity as she surveyed the four posts, the large white bed, the cream carpet and minimalist, expensive furniture.

You're in one of the guest suites in North?

Yes. I've got my own 60-inch TV in the other room.

Bloody hell, Ri! What do you need a screen that size

for?

Playing PlayStation, mostly. Tell Dom I've got the new PS5, he'll be sick—

Are you doing any schoolwork at all?

I've got a few books and a new computer. And I'm getting a Guard tutor, apparently. She's memorised the year eight curriculum and is going to be overseeing my studying in the afternoons.

Well. That's something I suppose. What will you be doing in the morning?

Working with my other tutor. On my other skills.

She didn't say any more and very carefully shut away all thoughts of Reuben. She wasn't sure if it was instinct telling her to stay quiet or a stubborn want to keep the information to herself, knowing the name would mean so much more to Bella than it did to her. Luckily, if she noticed Ariana was holding back, Bella did not say anything.

Did you call me for a reason?

Ariana focused on the voice, trying to get an idea of what her mother might be doing. She caught a sudden scent of cut grass, the feel of sun on tight painful skin, a gnawing ache in her left leg. For some reason, it all irritated her. She bit back a sarcastic retort about her mother having somewhere better to be. After all, she was the reason why she didn't. A memory of Bella pacing the floor back in the Flintworth flat, tapping her hands against her slim elbows impatiently when her laptop stopped working on a Saturday afternoon swam into her mind. The power shifted again and Ariana had to frown in concentration to keep the mind-link intact.

I want to know about Dr Blake. I need to know what I did to him.

Why? Did Lychen—

No. But it's something to do with why my powers aren't working as they were. It's a block.

I see. Well, he's in a coma but there have been some small signs of improvement. The doctors think he had a stroke. That may have been what you did to him, or it may have been a side effect of whatever it was... I'm hoping to go and see him this week.

OK. That's good. I think.

You think? Of course it's good, Ariana. What's happened to you? A few weeks ago you were begging me to save Nova and the other hybrids even though they terrified you. Now you're not sure if it's a good thing you didn't kill your granddad—

Ariana broke the link with a satisfying little tug away. Her mother's words still stung around her head like angry wasps caught in a jar, but she turned away from them. She wasn't a murderer. She hadn't been in full control of herself, that's why what had happened had happened. She needed to embrace all the parts of her, including the dark, blank part, that's how she'd be able to do as Reuben said, scoop whatever resources she needed at will.

Ariana spent the rest of the afternoon lying on her bed, imagining herself flying, turning invisible, shooting flames and ice from her limbs. She imagined her mother and father trapped into small, meaningless worlds, pacing, tapping their elbows, circling one another, waiting. Her body raised itself a few inches once or twice, hovered and then dropped. She did not notice.

January, 2020

'Out! Ouuuuuuuut!'

'A little more water first, please,' I say quietly, holding her gaze. Nova scowls but lets me hold the bottle to her small mouth. Though her nose bears more than a passing resemblance to a beak, I've never seen her use it to drink and, for the most part, she takes in nourishment like a human who has limited use of their arms, which is why her nest upstairs has a large water dispenser with a straw mechanism fitted into it. It's strange to see her sitting up like a person, her feet tucked beneath her, her good wing folded on one side and her bad wing strapped to her other. The soft glow of the fire glints golden fingers along her glossy feathers and, as she watches me from her quick, aquamarine eyes, I consider her beauty. It's wild, other, unexpected… Admittedly grotesque in some ways – her taloned hands, strange nose and clawed toenails… But it's also undeniable.

'Outside,' she murmurs. Her speech is far easier to understand these days, but she is sparing with her words. Ironic really that her mind is one of the few I have failed to penetrate, yet wordless communication would probably benefit her the most.

'OK then,' I smile, lowering the bottle. 'Can you walk?'

She makes a dismissive sound which reminds me,

piercingly, of Ariana. I watch as she stands up without a fuss. At full height she only reaches my shoulder, but the width of her wings, even folded, means that the doors all have to be opened to their fullest, and even then she shuffles sideways, lurching slightly. Ralph has cleared a path to the back door but it still takes nearly ten minutes, with several stops. The door from the schoolroom to the hallway proves the most challenging and in the end I have to meet her round the other side and half carry her good wing through so she can manoeuvre herself around without tugging unnecessarily on the bad side. Even so she gives several squawks of pain.

When at last Nova has reached the back garden, she wastes no time in unfurling her good wing, lifting her face to the grey iron-clouded sky. I watch from the doorway as I pull on my coat and snood. Ralph joins us from where he has been waiting near the herb garden.

'Looking good, Nov,' he grins. 'How's the wing feel?' Nova shrugs her good wing and cocks her head. She holds the bandaged bad wing out as best she can, her intentions clear.

'Are you sure?' I ask, quietly. 'The medicine we gave you might need longer to take…'

'Off,' she says, blinking earnestly. I glance at Ralph, who shrugs, before reaching to unwrap the bandages as swiftly as I can before my fingers seize in the cold.

'Wait,' I whisper, as the last of the wrappings come loose. She shuffles impatiently, but allows me to keep hold of her wing. Ralph comes to help remove the last of the white gauze. There is a small smudge of blood on the layer closest to her feathers, but the wounds themselves…

'They've *gone*,' Ralph gasps, looking up at me with shining eyes. 'Completely healed… That's incredible.'

83

The area of wing where the shotgun pellets pierced is still missing the feathers we removed, but the skin is fresh and new-looking, the scars barely perceptible. I stare from them to Ralph and it's as if my entire soul has grown its own pair of wings. They unfurl and stretch and slowly, deliberately, begin to beat until I'm soaring higher than I've ever gone before.

'We did it. It *works*, Ralph!' I beam at him, knowing that the spiralling wonder is shining from my eyes because his are reflecting it back at me, though there's a guarded sense of fear in his gaze as well. *I* did this. We both know that.

'Let. Go. Wing!' Nova shakes her wing and, blinking, I gently detach my fingers, lowering the limb. She winces and opens her mouth as she takes the weight of it. I stand back next to Ralph. He places a hand on my shoulder as we watch her slowly flexing the tight sore muscles to extend the wing. She cries out a few times in obvious pain, the sound more birdlike than human as her forehead creases with a concentration I recognise from her ballet practice as a child.

'Mollitiam is still not ready for application, Beast,' Ralph murmurs softly, knowing that my mind has flittered past the newly-healed bird-woman before us and onto the possibilities she has created.

'Look at her. That injury should have grounded her for life... She's almost got full extension already and it's only been four days!'

'Yes, but Beast—'

'She'll be flying as well as before by next week!' I say it loud enough for Nova to hear and she turns to me with pure sunshine in her face. I beam back at her for a moment, ignoring Ralph's agitation until he puts his other hand on my other shoulder and coarsely turns me round to face him. I blink at him and though I am careful to keep my features calm, the abrupt roughness of his handling sends an icy shudder of fear right to my core.

'Bella, you have no *right* to make that claim!' He hisses right in my face. 'Mollitiam is made using *your* resilience gene, a Project A trait! You don't know how long the application to Nova will last – it could all rip apart in the next hour for all we know.' He's still gripping me too hard, too close. I can feel my panic beginning to echo outwards and I know he'll be able to see it on my face any second now. I can't have that, so I churn it into rage instead.

'Let go of me,' I spit. He removes his hands at once, shameful realisation swarming into his gaze.

'Beast, I'm sorry, I—'

I turn away, realising furiously that I haven't stopped the trembling after all. I watch Nova, who is still a picture of concentration as she continues to flex and retract.

'None of the other test subjects have shown signs of it waning,' I say, making my voice low and steady so that it doesn't tick and shudder with the memories swimming so close to the surface still. I let Ana in to try and calm it down. *It's Ralph. It's only Ralph. He would never hurt you like Lychen did. He just got carried away. He suspects what you are planning for Mollitiam. It terrifies him.* The trembles finally subside enough for me to trust myself to look up at him, take in his earnest, worried tone.

'...other test subjects are rodents. Nova is a completely different kettle of... well, bird. Just keep testing it. This is a positive outcome, but it's not a conclusive success yet.'

We watch Nova in silence for a while. I realise that my arms are wrapped tightly around myself and loosen them, bouncing on the balls of my feet a little to warm up. The atmosphere between Ralph and me has collapsed into blocky, cold awkwardness. I can feel his need to verbalise and sigh as it comes.

'Beast, you know I would never—'

'I know.'

'I shouldn't have grabbed you, I'm sorry. I know you're still dealing with a lot of shit—'

'I'm *fine*. It's fine.'

'I just don't want you rushing into anything. Particularly when it's all still so raw. Remember, what we're doing here isn't for revenge, it's about righting the wrongs.'

I glance up. His face has lost all the joy of moments ago and is now scoured with worry. He looks so much like Dr Blake I almost squint, just to make sure it's actually him.

'Look, I'm not about to go rushing up to London with a pocketful of syringes filled with Mollitiam. I know it wasn't designed to fix Ariana... And in any case, I don't know if it would do her much good anyway. She's got more than enough *resilience* to last her a lifetime.'

'And we have no idea what it is they're doing to keep her asleep...'

'No, you're right... It's just... if we can use the Mollitiam regeneration property alongside the memory enhancement of Serum X and NatApp...'

'I know. I thought about the hybrids and the Guard as well. But there's no way of testing it, not without subjects. Which means that when it comes to using it, we have to be surer than sure that it's safe...'

I sigh and toss my hair back, noticing his eyes linger on the line of my scar. My gaze snags on the ARC sticking up like a black chimney atop the stone wall. Five more times

I've tried to penetrate it and five more times I've come against the same barrier.

'I'm going inside,' I mutter. 'I've got more rodents to mutilate and dose up. Nov, you want to stay out a bit longer?' Nova looks up and nods briefly.

'Come in when you get cold,' I say, wanting to tell her not to try to fly but knowing I have no right to place limitations on her. She is not a child. She is not my child. 'We have more painkillers if you need them.'

I turn back to the house and go inside, shedding my coat only as I reach the front of the building because the chill from the open back door seems to saturate the very stones of the entire house. Slipping on a lab coat and covering my feet, I enter the laboratory, where the lights are brazen and the temperature is perfectly controlled.

'What are you doing?' Dr Blake's voice chimes an older, more worried version of Ralph's as he lurches behind my back. I don't jump, but I twitch in irritation.

'I'm just checking the isolations in the sample we administered to Nova.'

'You know what Ralph said, it's a success but it cannot be applied to—'

I need to check on the test rodents. You know they need quiet. If you must harp on, kindly have the courtesy to do so using an inside voice. I know you know how.

Sorry. I am not so practiced in these things. Bella, I know what you're planning. I think Ralph suspects as well. I was listening. I heard what you told him.

I threw him off with the pocketful-of-syringes comment.

Yes, your sleight of hand may have sent his fears spiralling in a different direction but he is not stupid.

I cross the floor to the back of the room and open a

door set into the newly-constructed partition wall in the back of the room. Inside the narrow cupboard-like space of floor-to-ceiling cages the air is cool, controlled on a different setting to the rest of the lab, and punctured with squeaks and rustlings. I do a quick head-count and turn to the computer on the small fold-up desk next to the cages, pressing a few keys until the latest results appear. All thriving; all fine.

It is not fine! And it's certainly not safe. You don't know what you're doing.

I know what I'm doing a darn site more than Ana did thirty-four years ago.

But self-administration is never—

It's my genetic material. I'm just... topping it up. You yourself told me that my resilience was finite. You told Ariana as well. I know now. I'm not waiting around for Project A to kill me like it killed my brother and sister. I have to be able to fight for her as well as myself. I can't do it as I am. I can't even see into the ARC, I can barely reach Lychen anymore. Since my body healed... Well, you know what happened, you're the one who explained it to me back in the hospital last summer.

A theory, Bella! Just a theory!

Well, I trust it. It makes sense. This will help defeat him. All of them. Or it might show me another way.

Or it might kill you.

I tip my head sideways as if easing a neck cramp. I've come out of the rodent cupboard now and am at the front of the lab once again. The windows overlooking the driveway are set above a panel of locked cabinets. Reaching for the door of one positioned on the far right, I tap in the code without looking. Blake flaps about anxiously in the corner of my line of vision, and as I look more closely

I can see Ana too. Her hair tumbles around her shoulders and her eyes watch me, burning with that same look – the one caught between love and hatred, the one which powered her hands to hold, stroke, pinch, twist... She never could decide. She tells me now, though, that she would do it too, if she were me.

I turn away from the pair of them as I draw up five millilitres, my brain already ticking ahead to consider how I might condense it into pill form. The medical supply bag is still where I left it after Nova's gunshot; before I can think myself out of it, I roll up my sleeve and grab a tourniquet.

Summer, 2019

They spent the first hour of the lesson walking the three sides of the triangular garden in the middle of the North building. Large panes of glass set into the walls surrounding the garden were positioned at equally-spaced intervals so that the manicured beds of flowers received the correct amount of sunlight. It also meant that although the morning had begun with a tinge of cold in the air, Ariana was soon sweating enough to remove her large black hoodie as she jogged to keep up with Reuben's brisk pace. Pulling her hair off the back of her neck, she scooped it into a messy ponytail, the breeze whistling coolly into the damp patches under her arms.

'So, tell me again what it was you were thinking about when you levitated?' Reuben turned, and realising Ariana had stopped, halted his quick pace. Chucking her hoodie onto a nearby bench, Ariana frowned as she stalked towards him, trying to remember.

'I think I mostly thought: What the hell am I doing up here?'

'No,' he stared at the nearest patch of poppies sternly, 'I mean, what was it you were thinking about during the moments before you realised you were levitating?'

'Um...' she stared at a bed of pink roses. She recognised the thorny twists of the bush more than the blooms upon it. There were hundreds of them in the Manor gardens, all scattered about the place in seemingly random patches, though Ralph had told her once it was so they could be seen from the windows. It had been some sort of project of his dad's when his mother had been too ill to go outside.

'Dr Blake,' she said, quietly. 'I was thinking about what I did to him and my mum...'

'And?' He was looking at her properly now, not her eyes, but her shoulder. So intently she glanced at it too to see if there was a bug there or something.

'And then I was floating. Oh wait... No, it spoke back to me. It said something like I was right to hurt them because they hurt me too. And I sort of knew that it was wrong, about being right to hurt them, but I also knew that it was right because, well... they *did* hurt me. So I don't know if it was about me agreeing with it or...'

'Or you understanding it, perhaps?'

'Yeah.' She looked up and he met her gaze with swift inscrutability. Then he turned in the opposite direction and began walking again. Feeling as wrong-footed as she had the first time he'd done it, Ariana jogged to catch up.

'I couldn't get the voice to talk again, the rest of the day. I did try.'

'You made progress by admitting your feelings to yourself. You say you contacted your mother?'

'Yeah, to ask about Dr Blake. I wanted to... I dunno, I needed to know what I'd done to him. Whether he was dead.'

'What difference would that have made to you?'

'I don't want to have killed him. He was nice to me. I think he liked me, when he wasn't worried I might be a psychopath...'

'And the voice? The other presence?'

'I… It… It didn't care either way. It just wanted him to stop being a block.'

It shivered in agreement and she looked up to find Reuben watching her again, for slightly longer now. He stopped moving and so did she. Something was about to happen… She could feel the blankness rippling in anticipation. But Reuben stood motionlessly. Waiting. And she realised that *she* was the one who was going to make the something happen. What? She looked around… Next to her was a spray of pink roses. She stared at them and thought: *I don't like roses.* Nothing happened. *That was stupid. I don't dislike roses. I don't care about roses either way.*

Neither do I.

And the pretty, vibrant petals curled and browned and shrivelled until they were nothing but lumpen, rotten clumps at the end of twisting, thorny vines. She looked back at Reuben. He nodded.

'I want you to show me how you did that.'

'*Show* you? How?'

'In here,' he tapped the side of his head.

'I thought you couldn't see into people's heads anymore.'

'I can't. But you can. You're going to come into my head and show me what you did just now, every thought process, every conversation.'

She frowned. 'God. I don't know if I can.'

'I need to understand where the ability blooms from in order to grasp how you'll be able to control it. Otherwise there is no point to me being here…'

She saw the shadow flicker over his face and knew he was afraid of what it would mean for him to be found surplus to requirements.

'OK... I'll try...'

It was harder than she thought, even though it had only just happened, trying to go back over the exact thought process... She had understood the voice, and it had... what, rewarded her with a dose of power? She lost the thread of logic even as she remembered she was supposed to be projecting the whole thing to Reuben. Concentrating, she reached her mind out to the tall motionless man waiting calmly in front of her. His thoughts were organised like a neat boxed desk drawer. There were no surface wants or needs, but she could sense them hidden away in the boxed areas. Ariana thought very hard. It took almost a full ten minutes of concentration to try and convey why and how she had killed the roses. By the end she was hot, exhausted and could feel a rashy prickle of sunburn on the back of her neck. Reuben remained as impassively cool as ever. She was almost ready for the abrupt lurch of his walk when he began to stride but still staggered a little as she followed.

'Did you see? Did I show you?' she asked, her voice sounding over-loud after all the internal work.

'Yes. It is as I thought. You must connect with the inner power, embrace it as part of yourself. I believe you're beginning to, which is why you are having these odd surges of power. It comes from you understanding it. But you must let it in if you want to harness it innately, without concentration.'

'OK... How do I do that?'

'Well, first you have to decide if you want to. I think that's what has separated you from the ability since you arrived here. Part of you doesn't think you should use it. Part of you thinks it is wrong – that is why you continue to think of it as a separate voice.'

'OK...' She swallowed, her brain muzzy in the heat. She wondered whether it was nearly twelve yet. Whether she might be able to find a quiet, soft place to lie down for a bit.

'You do have a choice, Ariana...' He was speaking more quietly now, his hands behind his back. They were in the corner of the garden now, a small neat shed shielding them from the sun and, Ariana realised with a small shock, from the gaze of the Guard person who stood in the garden's entranceway, always focused, always braced.

'What choice? You heard Lychen... You basically admitted he blackmailed you into coming here...'

'We aren't talking about *my* choices, here. What do *you* want, Ariana D'accourt? Ariana Lychen?'

'I... I don't want *that*. Those names. To be like them. My parents. I don't want to be a Lychen. I don't want to be cold and creepy and just... *dead* inside. I don't want the blankness to turn me into something like him. I want to be a person. But I don't want to be like *her* either. She's a liar. I just want to be something that neither of them are, I suppose. I want to take this power and make it mean something important, not just use it to get what I want and hurt people and skive off school and the stupid stuff I've been doing. But I'm scared of what it means if I do use it. I don't want to become a murderer... I don't want to just *not care*. But I also don't want to go back to being a stupid, powerless child everyone lied to.'

'So what if we could find a middle way, a way to unite your power with your humanity?'

'Yeah, let's do that.'

'OK.' He looked at her for a bit and sighed in a strange way, as if she had solved a puzzle for him but it had turned out to be far less complicated and interesting than he'd thought. Then he did another neat, quick little turn and was off, striding among the flowers once again.

15

January, 2020

Nothing incredible happens straight away. My dose is only a fraction of what we gave Nova. I'm in no need of immediate healing, after all. I spend the next few hours working on the formula and adding the necessary ingredients to the machine which dispenses drugs in tablet form. It's a long and complicated process and I could really use Ralph's help to check with some of the calculations, but I know asking him would lead to awkward questions about why I'm doing it all now and what the need is for tablet form when the injections reach the bloodstream instantly, etc, etc. Tess arrives and wordlessly helps restock the granulation fluid.

'What's the dosage?' She asks, as we watch the machine – old, large, and, like so many salvaged from the ARC, modified beyond recognition of its original state – rumble as it mixes and compresses.

'There will be a variety, so we can pick and choose depending on the recipient,' I glance at her sideways. She is wearing a large pair of goggles, her pale hair scraped into the standard net. She reaches for the samples of Mollitiam and, making sure they're all sealed tight, places them back in their insulated container. She then checks the progress of the genetic material separator – designed by Dr Blake himself – which is busy isolating samples of my blood. One of the best things about Tess becoming my unofficial lab assistant over the last few months has been the fact that she doesn't ask annoying questions. I don't know if it's a residual guilt from her part in the whole abducting-my-daughter plot or if that's simply the way she is. In any case, it's a welcome relief from the Blakes.

'You're pretty good at this stuff, you know, Tess. Easily good enough to get a job in a lab or start a PhD if that's what you wanted to do...'

'Thanks,' she grins. 'That's what you did, right?'

'Yes. But I'm sure it would take you far less time, without a small child in tow and an identity to protect.'

'Yeah... Maybe. I don't know... I kind of like it here. Especially *here,*' she gestures around the room, the hodgepodge mixture of machinery, makeshift work benches stacked with books, basic surgical supplies and instruments. The sprung floor has deep grooves where heavy things have fallen, scraped and gouged. The mirrored walls have been partially draped where they can't be used to reflect light.

'Really?' I raise an eyebrow. 'After working at the Beaumont?'

'Yeah. It has heart, you know? A soul. The Beaumont's all state-of-the-art and, you know, *shiny*... but the stuff you and Ralph are doing here is actually *good,* you know. You're trying to help people. Reverse the Guard process, heal people with this resilience stuff, maybe save the hybrids...'

'Well. That's the idea,' I murmur. 'But they do plenty of *good* work at the BFI as well, of course. It's not all Guard-making and animal torture...'

Something is beginning to happen. There's a tiny seed of energy firing along my veins, tingling its way to my right arm. I turn away from Tess, pretending to check a graph on the computer. She is busy adjusting something on the isolation machine, her thoughts lost in the swirls of her own career possibilities. I roll up the right sleeve of my lab coat and turn my palm upwards. The ugly, raised scar left by Nova's talons back in the summer is shrinking, the skin prickling as it smooths out the blemish. A few blinks later it has gone entirely. The energy dissipates like an effervescent tablet in water. I let my sleeve drop back over my wrist.

Not what you were expecting?

It's a start. But no, I didn't dose myself out of vanity.

I glimpse over to make sure Tess hasn't seen, but she's still absorbed in the machinery, her lips absently rolling the lipstick veneer between them. I catch sight of my reflection in the mirrored wall beyond Tess. I can't even see my facial scar from here but I know it's still there. I feel it like a tight rubber band even though all the physical pain of it has long healed.

Liar.

OK. I hoped it would be a perk. But I wanted an enhancement of my other skills first and foremost. How else will I be able to break into the ARC? How else can I continue to nettle Lychen? And find out what is really happening with Ariana...

The machine nearest me gives a satisfied little shudder and small white tablets begin to spurt from a narrow funnel into a tray underneath. Tess looks up and comes over, reaching to gather a few empty bottles on her way. I slip two of the smallest tablets into my pocket without her seeing.

'Would you sort them by milligram, please?'

'Sure,' she replies, placing the bottles down. I turn and head swiftly out of the room, taking off my goggles, lab coat and shoe covers at the door. It's still cold in the corridor and as I glance down the long dark flagstone passageway I see the back door still propped open. Shaking my hair free of its net, I slip quietly up the staircase. There's a window in the stairwell which looks into the garden and from there I glance out to see Nova in almost the exact same spot I left her hours ago. As I continue up the stairs towards my bedroom I cast my mind quickly through the Manor until, like an infrared sensor, I find Dom and Ralph in the dining room, eating soup as they discuss gaming strategy.

I close the door of my bedroom firmly behind me. I haven't made many changes to the room since I moved back in, except updating the wardrobe. Most of my former clothes have gone to the charity shop, but I kept a few timeless classics. Little black dresses. Killer heels. Designer jeans. And the hanger I reach for now, right at the back, the heavy contents ensconced in a protective covering.

I lay it on the bed and undo the zip. The emerald crystals sparkle as iridescently as I remember as I peel the dress out of its covering. Memories clamber in my chest as I quickly unbutton my blouse. The yearning heatwave of August 2005; Ralph's eyes scorching over my skin as I casually shrugged off my lab coat to reveal the glimmering jade underneath.

The scar at my midriff is long and, though less ragged thanks to Felix's not-so-gentle suturing, still raised and pink against the pallor of my winter-white skin. Before I can think too much more about any of it, I gather the dress towards me and step lightly into it. Tug, twist, zip, adjust and turn. It needs heels. In bare feet I am several inches too short. Otherwise, though the seep of the January greyness through the window sends only ripples of gleam from the emeralds rather than the luminescent shimmer of ten separate spotlights, the dress is as breathtaking as it was the day I wore it on stage. The day Ralph's gaze burned and Lychen's stare iced trails along every figure-clinging millimetre.

I smooth the front and turn, letting my hair tumble into the dip at the back, enjoying the soft sensation of curls against my cool bare skin. I select a pair of matching heels and step into them. My left arm still bears its scar and though my hair spills over half the line of the narrow blemish across my face, my eyes still seek it. I let my eyes seek it. The pills I've placed on the desk counter next to me whisper that they can make it go away. They can make me every iota as exquisite as I looked at nineteen-years-old on the stage with hundreds of eyes feasting upon nothing but me. Wanting nothing but me. But I don't need them or their wanting. I am my body. I am my scars and my beauty. I am my own best weapon.

Something catches my eye on the bed behind me and I turn, reaching curiously back into the covering. I'm confused for a moment as I pull a stretch of fabric out. It's a shawl in matching, sparkling green. I turn and meet my own eyes in the mirror and suddenly my breath collapses from my body like paper crumpled in a fist. A hand yanking my hair, the hiss of a warning in my ear. The dancing thrill of a tightrope high above them all, Ralph on one side, Lychen on the other. My office door opening. A blow like a bolt of iron meeting my skull. My own hair splayed beneath me, my desk an icy mortuary slab, cold air against my skin and I shut my eyes, bringing the wrap closer to my chest as the old pain wrenches its way inside me once again.

I don't know how long I sit there, how long it takes for the echoing trembles to stop wracking my body. They do, though. I am perfectly steady when I stand and cross the room to the desk, dropping the shawl on the floor as I do so. I take a pill and swallow it dry, meeting my own gaze in the wardrobe mirror once again and narrowing my eyes. *I am my body.* This time I try to control the drug as it slides down my throat and begins to break down. I tell it where to go. *I am my scars and my beauty.* I remind it of the memories, of the feelings, of the pain. *I am the weapon.* That first time and every other afterwards. I remind it who. *I am the voice in your head, coming to twist the knife in the darkness.* I remind it why. *You took everything from me.* And lastly, I bring it to the moment just a few months ago when he stood across from me in the room downstairs and reminded us all of exactly what he is. *I will take it back.*

Then I cross the room to the bed and carefully lie back upon it, smoothing the dress so it doesn't wrinkle, keeping my feet neatly tucked in the shoes. I shut my eyes and let the energy swarm into the parts I need, lighting a thousand tiny fires in its wake. I gather it all up and draw my mind like an archer pulling back a loaded bowstring. And, like I warned Lychen I would all those months ago, I come for him.

Summer, 2019

Ralph had to concentrate to stop himself helping too much. He watched Bella as she swung forward on her crutches, her face carefully clear of any winces though he knew the arm rests bothered her when they pressed against the long cuts there, still wrapped in bandages. She wore a white, fluttering summer dress under a denim jacket, her uninjured foot clad in a simple leather sandal. Her hair tumbled loose around her shoulders and down her back in thick gleaming spirals as it caught the afternoon sunshine. He knew she was aware every moment of the scar on her face, its unfamiliar curve of red livid against her pale skin. He wished he could tell her that she had never looked more beautiful, but even thinking the words made him cringe inside. She looked up as she reached the gravel of the driveway and he blushed, glancing behind him at the three mismatched vehicles on the drive.

'We'll have to take Dom's Polo,' he said, trying to banish the apology from his voice.

'Not the Fiesta?' Her eyes glittered playfully on the dusty little red car tucked behind Felix's van.

'Nah, it needs a new gearbox. That trip to Flintworth and then Cornwall and back last year really knackered it… Didn't you ever wonder why Ethan and I turned up so much later than you? We couldn't get it past fourth gear once we hit the M6.'

He offered her his arm as her crutches slipped on the loose shingle and felt slightly less stupid about it when she took it without hesitation. They cut a slow, faltering path towards the car. Ralph looked up as a soft coo came from the upper branches of the oak trees overhanging the driveway.

'Is that Nova?'

'Yeah... She's saying bye, I think.' Bella smiled and, though it wasn't really for him, Ralph felt it like a firework in his belly. He told himself to stop. He tried to think about his dad, tried to pull his thoughts in a more appropriate direction as he held the car door open and took her crutches as she manoeuvred herself into the seat with the sort of fluid movement only Bella could perform, even with one leg in plaster. *Dad*, he thought. Lying in hospital. *Dad*, he thought, sitting across from him at the table a few weeks ago... Talking to him about lost loves and soul mates. *Stop*, he told himself, as he crunched around the back of the car and opened the driver door, resisting the temptation to look up at the Manor and see if Ethan was watching. Probably. *Just stop. This is not the time. You don't know the half of what she's been through; of what that bastard did to her. Remember what Dad said: We don't know what toll it's taken. She's not ready for anything.* Let alone him and his ridiculous flapping heart.

'Right,' he slid the keys into the ignition and started the car. He turned his head as he reversed, spotted one of Ariana's school books on the back seat and swept it quickly onto the floor.

'What happened to your car, anyway? That swish BMW we chased all the way across the country?'

Bella sniffed and looked out of the window. 'It was

taken care of. Along with the flat in Flintworth, my old job at the university... Lychen has people to tie up loose ends. He has people everywhere.'

'Not here,' Ralph muttered, as they pulled out of the driveway and onto the main road.

'No,' Bella murmured, glancing into the wing mirror.

The journey wasn't a long one and, at first, Ralph filled the silences with whatever he could think of to prepare Bella for seeing Dr Blake. For her part, she mostly stared out of the window. At first he thought she was avoiding looking at him and spent a panicky few minutes wondering what on earth he'd said to offend her, but then he caught a glimpse of her expression in the reflection of the dirty window. It reminded him of the way she used to watch the Project C children as they performed their extraordinary abilities – too complicated an expression to define as one thing, but there were definite hints of wonder, jealousy, longing.

'What're you looking at so intently?' He asked, when he could no longer keep quiet, glancing to the right and left as he swung the car out onto an A-road. Bella blinked and cleared her face as she brought her gaze back to the car. He was sorry he'd spoken before she even answered.

'I'd forgotten what it was like up here. All the mountains, the lakes... so much space and emptiness...' Her voice was careful, still slightly hoarse although the bruises to her throat had faded into barely visible smudges.

Ralph avoided looking at them lest he punch a hole in the nearest hard surface, but the slight strain to Bella's voice also made his teeth clench. He shook the feeling away: 'That was the main idea, when they were looking for a place to build the ARC. My parents, I mean. Dad wanted somewhere hidden, Mamma said she wanted it to be picturesque. She grew up near Lake Como, you know. I guess the Lake District is the nearest thing in the UK, if you ignore the weather.'

'I wouldn't know,' Bella replied, softly. 'She always said she'd take me one day, but it never happened. She wasn't well enough. She showed me photos though. It looked wonderful…'

'It was. I went a couple of times as a kid, before she became ill. I'll take you,' he said, grinning as she smiled at him. 'One day, when all this madness has blown over.'

'How about today?'

He laughed shortly, but when she didn't he glanced at her. They were on the main road to the hospital now and large, H symbols were beginning to appear on the sign posts.

'We could just go… Head south to Manchester Airport, hop on a plane to Milan.'

'Materialise a couple of passports out of thin air…'

'Do you think I can't talk my way through passport control?'

He laughed again, because he was a bit nervous now. Glancing sideways, he could see she was more serious than he'd thought, her eyes wistful, her hands clenching and unclenching in her lap.

'We could be sitting lakeside by sunset. Local pizzeria, bottle of Chianti, no sound but cicadas…'

'Big bowl of *gelato* for dessert,' he took a left turn and pulled into the hospital car park. They did not speak again until he'd pulled into a space, the handbrake crunching a little as he pulled it sharply. When he looked up, Bella's face was closed off once again, and she'd dipped it forward until a lock of hair covered most of the scar.

'Shall we go, then?' He said, one hand on the car door,

his thoughts already tumbling ahead, into the large, grey building before them.

'Yes,' she replied, simply. It was only afterwards, when he replayed the strange turn the conversation had taken, that he realised she'd managed to put both hope and resignation into the one, small word.

One thing Ralph had forgotten to mention in preparation for Bella's visit was the Guard. Gunnersmore Hospital had taken stock of several following the acclaimed Press coverage of the Care Assistance Programme. Ralph had been taken aback to see the blank-faced individuals clad in scrubs wheeling patients up and down the corridors when he'd arrived shortly after Blake's ambulance. They all wore lanyards with a large G on them and though on that first occasion they'd drawn a fair number of whispers and pointing from members of the public, this had lessened every time Ralph had visited since. Even he had become used to them he realised, as he felt Bella freeze when they rounded a corner and saw a blank-faced woman providing a helping arm to an old, staggering man grasping a drip stand.

'I should have warned you about them, sorry,' Ralph muttered even as he felt her shake off the surprise and strike forward on her crutches once again.

'It's fine,' Bella murmured, though she avoided looking at the G-stamped woman as they passed her. Questions tangled themselves in knots in Ralph's head. He knew it probably wasn't the time or place, but something had occurred to him that he'd been wanting to ask for months.

'*Are* they all connected to him? Lychen, I mean?' He

kept his voice low lest the Guard woman spring into action at the mention of the name. 'I mean, I know Ethan isn't anymore, but he's hardly a normal example...'

'No, he isn't,' Bella paused and glanced behind her at the Guard woman. 'I should have expected to see them here. I launched the programme, after all... Helped, anyway. I didn't know all the locations, but it's been long enough that they'd be in most of the participating hospitals across the country by now. That was the directive for the summer...' She glanced at him before she began moving once again.

'The Guard mind-link is a complicated thing. With the earlier generations they all had a live connection with Lychen so he knew where each one was, he'd be able to give commands when required. But as their number grew, that method became unsustainable. Imagine five strands to five individual servants in your head. Then imagine five hundred. It's simply too much for one person to cope with... So they developed a way to copy a person's intentions into a small device placed behind their ear. They transfer that onto a Guard and they become attuned to that person's needs. The longer it's worn the deeper the connection...'

'Yeah, I remember that TV interview you gave explaining it all. So they *aren't* all connected to Lychen?'

'Not in the way you're thinking. When a Guard is created, they are given a core code of intention. It might be as simple as being told they are to be a Care Assistant and perform any task given by their Primary User. Then again, there are others whose core codes will be far more complicated. There could, for example, be a Guard person who has been coded to be a Care Assistant but also keep an eye out for certain individuals should they ever cross their path. Lychen told me he had quite a few looking for me across the country over the last ten years. There was a constant Guard presence at the end of the road where my parents live for many years, even my father noticed them. I remember him telling me about them – *goons in suits,* he called them. I always hoped he was just being paranoid. In any case, I'm sure those models have probably not been modified. In fact, I would put money on it. Lychen would have seen it as an insurance policy.'

'Ah...'

'But it doesn't matter. It's not like he doesn't know where I am. It's not like he couldn't find out where Blake is. I'm not running from him anymore. If he wants me, he can come.'

There was a steeliness in her voice now and a hardness to her eyes that, like so many things, reminded him of the old Bella. The child who would spit fire from her sweet, delicate mouth if he dared suggest she might not be as clever as him. The breathtaking young woman who had scorned and kissed him with equal, unrelenting fury. It was oddly comforting, especially when the things she spoke about made his stomach shudder with fear. Guard people with hidden agendas only triggered by certain things? What did that mean for the next few months, when BFI began putting them in households up and down the country?

'We can't let them launch GHAP.' He scowled as they reached the end of the corridor and turned down the one which would lead them to Dr Blake's room. 'We've got to get that serum finished. Who knows what he's put into some of them going into families' homes? They could be recording things, listening for certain words... Someone's elderly aunt could say, *Who's for more potatoes?* and the

108

whole street might go kaboom.'

She looked at him curiously. 'Lychen's not a mass-murdering maniac. He wants… control. Order. Improvement.'

Ralph frowned at her as they reached Blake's door.

'What?' She glared back at him.

'Nothing… Just the way you talk about him. After all he's done. I don't know how you're not more… I dunno.' *Angry. Emotional. Sad. Furious.* The unspoken words hung between them awkwardly.

She didn't bother replying, just gave him one of her looks. A sharp, narrow-eyed Bella-look to let him know that he really didn't understand her at all, before she turned, opened the door in front of them and hobbled through without hesitation.

January, 2020

It takes me a while to get it right. I find my way to his mind easily enough, I can feel the extra boost of resilience crushing his weak little walls and barriers like dirt beneath my feet. Projecting my body is another matter. Lychen is in the middle of a board meeting in the East building. They're using the largest conference room and there are at least fifty people seated around a large U-shaped table. Most of them are members of the Guard Home Assistance department, others I don't recognise, though I suspect they're investors of some kind. Dr John Bingham, head of GHAP development, is giving a presentation, complete with projected graph on the smart board behind him. It looks at first glance like some sort of progress report and projection for future sales.

Lychen sits on his right, at the very tip of the U. His thoughts are linear and I sift through them easily – surface frustration that Bingham is taking too long to get to the point tussles with boredom, there is nothing in Bingham's presentation or the graph that is new information to Lychen. Underneath lurk the physical wants: a slight thirst, a small but insistent itch on his left foot, a heavy, mind-sapping lull of weariness. I'm just reaching the interesting parts – buried deep because of course this is Lychen, but still easily discernible – heady swoops of anger tailed closely by shuddering fear, when he senses me with a hammer-blow of shock.

Good afternoon, Josiah.

I bat away his swipe at me as I feel him frown. He glances at the others, relief quick when he sees no one is looking his way, then his eyes snag on a green shimmer straight across from where he sits. A shimmer that becomes clearer by the moment, scintillating jade clinging to a body he knows as well as his own, hair tumbling smoothly, eyes glittering, face clear and set. She moves towards him and he flinches backwards. Bingham does notice this time and pauses, looking at him inquiringly. Lychen jerks his head to him, trying to ignore the woman as she laughs and steps neatly behind Bingham towards his chair.

Do you like my new trick?

Get. Out. He really tries. He keeps his eyes on the chart, though I can see through his eyes that I'm still very much a dominance of his peripheral vision. The dress is freaking him out as much as I'd hoped – it shoots his insides through with uncomfortable memories, tremulous lust tussling with fury and a wild drench of terror.

Yes, I thought you'd remember this dress. My expression turns serious. I'm standing directly across the table from Lychen now, and though he keeps his head turned, Bingham's words are buffeting nonsensically against his ears and he keeps stealing glances at me. My face. My body. His hands twitch and I can feel the wolfish hunger from the inside now, a strength I've only ever felt from his body and his hands on mine. Even now, even through this colossal ocean of anger and fear inside him, he still wants me. Perhaps more than ever.

How are you doing this? I put up a wall.

111

And I crushed it. Just like you crushed me. Over and over again. I am leaning across the table now, forcing his eyes onto mine. The man next to him — Dr Higgson from the same department as Bingham — is throwing him curious looks and he's not the only one. Lychen stares at me, sweat forming on his brow and top lip, hands tightening to fists on the table.

'Dr Lychen, are you alright?' Higgson murmurs, offering him a glass of water from the jug on the table. Lychen takes it and gulps desperately.

'Fine,' he snaps, making a concentrated effort to stare at Bingham once again.

You could always tell them you're suffering with constipation. You certainly look the part.

Are you here to throw petty insults until I've lost my mind entirely? He glares back at me.

Tell me what happened to Ariana.

Nothing happened to her. She's fine.

Really.

Without warning, I open my mouth wide and shriek right into his face. It's a long, penetrating scream which completely obliterates the sound of Bingham's drone, the shuffling breathing around him, the scratches of pens and pencils. Lychen's entire body judders backwards, away from the table, his irises black pools of alarm bulging from the whites. I pause to draw breath and he blinks as he realises the entire room is staring at him.

'Dr Lychen? Are you—'

'Excuse me,' he gets to his feet, his movements jagged as I lean towards him and shriek again. He moves stiffly past the baffled Bingham and the others at the front of the room, knocking over a briefcase but not pausing as he strides towards the door. I follow him, laughing as he grasps his head with his hands as soon as he reaches the corridor, letting the boardroom door bang shut behind him. He rounds on me in the corridor and I duck as he takes a swipe.

Oh no, that won't work this time, my love. No more blows to the face. No more bruises I have to hide with make-up and sleeves and wraps. You'll never lay a finger on me again.

My voice is vicious and I savour the moment I feel it cut into him. He begins to walk away from me but I keep myself in front of him, walking backwards nimbly on my heels, my dress swishing and glinting under the fluorescent lights of the Beaumont corridor. It's becoming harder to keep myself focused and I'm not sure if it's because projection is more difficult on the move or if the effects of the Mollitiam are ebbing.

Where is she, Lychen? What did you do to her? I push myself into his brain and find the answers before he can form a response.

Ariana. I see her cloudily at first, surrounded by dust… rubble? She's coughing and saying something but it mumbles into static and I can't make it out entirely… her voice is angrily triumphant and her eyes are… They're so *old*. The blankness I saw in the summer swirls with the child I raised and I realise she's managed to find a way to unite the two, invite the darkness in while refusing to let it dominate. She shouts something else and it comes slightly clearer this time, something about him not knowing the first thing about being a parent, how he can't tell her what to do, something about choking...

The image wavers and suddenly I'm looking up at her from the ground, there's a shuddering blast in the wall to my left which reminds me of Ethan's explosives back in

113

Futura. Shouts tumble from a sudden, jagged hole in the wall, dust swirls in angry tufts and then comes a wail of such unfiltered agony that I feel my own eyes watering even behind the lens of Lychen's memory. Face twisted almost beyond my recognition, Ariana turns into the dust, not seeing the Guard man approach her from behind. I throw a hand out, the warning on my lips even as he plunges a syringe into her arm and catches her as she crumples.

Ariana, alone in a blazingly white surgical room now, her body connected to machines. A Guard person stands over her, adjusting what looks like a feeding tube going into her nose. *Five weeks,* Lychen thinks as the question forms. *No, six.* Then, without any warning, I feel him gripping me in his head, like fingertips pinching a tiny errant hair on the surface of a thumb. He's standing still in the corridor, eyes firmly shut in concentration, one hand on the wall to steady himself. I feel the astral projection of myself waver and fade as I writhe in his hold. His grip loosens a little, but he still has me fast. He can't hold on for long, I'm stronger than him, but I stop moving as I realise he wants to show me something else. Curiosity overcomes the instinct to bolt. It's a room, familiar this time. The North building penthouse bedroom I once called my own. At first glance it looks unchanged from how I remember it, but gradually the changes begin to glare. The chandelier replaced with basic LEDs set into the ceiling. A huge, heavy bolt on the door to the adjoining dance studio. Ornate mirrors replaced with dull, reflective plastic nailed to the wall. All furniture removed except the bed, its posters stark without the diaphanous white drapes I remember. I shudder, noticing that the doors are not the only occurrences of chains and padlocks.

This is where I'm going to put you. You can play all the magic tricks you like but you're still just a person, Bella. This is where you belong. This is where you will die. When I decide I am done with you.

I wrench myself out of his grip and he opens his eyes to see me standing in front of him once again. He smiles as only Lychen can smile, a mutated, wretched imitation of the expression. I cuff past the echoing nightmare of images he is pushing back at me and fix him with a stony, cold glare.

I'd like to see you try. You know where I am. You want me, come and get me. Only it didn't work out so well for you the last time you tried, did it?

Careful, Bella. You know the tools I have at my disposal.

Yes. And now you know some of those at mine.

I summon all the last, ebbing fragments of the tablet, the injection and every scrap of hatred inside me that screams to punish him, to wrench him apart cell by cell. Then I swoop through his body and up to his head, skewering a raging headache in my wake.

I blink a few times at the plain Artex ceiling of my childhood bedroom, exhaustion pressing in at all angles. I sit up slowly, glancing at the clock. I've been 'gone' less than twenty minutes. I try to sense the others, but the images only come as a dull echo of uncertain probability. Sliding off the bed, I quickly make my way to the wardrobe and slip the dress off, changing back into my clothes quickly. Once the dress is safely stowed back in its sheath, the wrap folded neatly behind it and the hanger placed at the back of the wardrobe, I pass a hand in front of my face. I should probably eat. I should almost certainly go downstairs and make sure Tess has stowed the tablets away somewhere where Ralph is unlikely to spot them and ask awkward questions. Instead, I climb back onto the bed and am unconscious before my head reaches the pillow.

18

Summer, 2019

Of course it was a shock. Ralph had been wittering on for most of the drive and my slow laborious hobble through the hospital, about how Dr Blake would probably not open his eyes because he'd only been doing it intermittently, and about all the machines he was hooked up to, the breathing and heart rate monitors. He'd told me that he looked 'quite bad'. He hadn't told me to expect a sunken, corpse-like echo of my former mentor and father figure.

Dr Blake lay propped on pillows, a nasal canular plugged into his face. There was a drip hooked up to one hand and various tubes and drains leading under the bed. His face wasn't droopy on one side like some stroke patients, but his entire skull seemed to have melted into the pillow beneath, his hair a dirty white against the stark bedsheets. Without his glasses he just looked... ancient. Broken. Dying. The monitors next to him suggested otherwise, however, and as I lowered myself into the chair between his bed and the window, I took his hand in mine.

'Hi, Dr Blake,' I said, quietly, giving the paper-soft skin a little squeeze. Ralph hovered on the other side of the bed, his hands stuck in his armpits. The door to the private room was propped open a little and a nurse popped her head round, smiled, and left us. I wondered what she saw as I glanced back at the old man in the bed. A doting son and daughter? A vigilant relative and his wife? Certainly nothing near the truth, that was for sure.

'I've often wondered why I don't have a better name for you,' I said, quietly. 'Dr Blake seems so formal, but nothing else seemed to quite fit. Mamma was just Mamma. But I already had a dad. Still do, somewhere.'

'Remember when you went through that phase of calling him Dr B?' Ralph grinned. I returned it tightly, knowing it didn't reach my eyes.

'Yeah... Ramona told me off for being disrespectful. Must have really riled her, considering she didn't usually like to acknowledge my existence. I don't think he minded, but it never really stuck, did it?' I looked back at him. Dr Blake's eyelids flickered, but, glancing at Ralph, I could see that it wasn't anything he hadn't done before.

'The eye movements are random,' he explained. 'Sometimes he'll have them open for an entire visit, but he doesn't respond. They say that his brain activity is minimal, but may improve. Something to do with not knowing what damage was caused...'

'I'm sorry,' I whispered, looking back at Dr Blake. 'I'm sorry this happened to you. It was my fault. I should have been honest with Ariana. I should have realised that she had this potential in her. I knew it was a possibility. I knew it from the moment my father told me the truth about what he and Ana had done, giving me the resilience gene, making me the way I am. He knew it as well, of course. And Ri always had ways of knowing things she shouldn't, of influencing people in a way dictated by her own wants and needs... But I didn't want to see it. Just like Dad didn't want to see the darkness in me when I was younger, until I hurt someone. And now she's done the same thing, only worse. We've all come full circle and somehow ended up in an

118

even bigger mess.'

I shut my eyes, tried to connect to his mind, sensing my way ahead as I did with Ariana, Ethan, Lychen, and the Youth Guard. Nothing. Darkness. Emptiness. I went further, hearing Ralph from a distance explaining to someone that no, I was not his sister but that I had been brought up as one. And there... A tiny echoing flicker, underneath the heavy weight of sleep, a touch of the consciousness who would smile with crinkling eyes, slide his fist across the school desk and slowly extend his thumb upwards as he returned a piece of homework. The calming voice to counteract Ana's shrillness on difficult mornings. He didn't speak so much as reach to me and smile, as much as a spark of consciousness could. Smiled: *I love you both so much.*

'No,' I muttered, opening my eyes and giving his hand a little shake. 'Don't you start with how much you love us and the goodbyes. You need to come back from this, old man.' I glanced at Ralph, who was still talking quietly to a nurse in the corner of the room. 'You can't do this to Ralph. You can't do this to Ariana – she wanted to know how you were. She asked me. She came to me, after all the shit that's happened over the last few weeks... She cares about you. After everything. She was different, not so blank and unfeeling as she was before. But if you die, you'll make her a murderer and I won't have that, you hear me? I know you do. Wake up. Wake up properly.'

I squeezed his hand again and shut my eyes, going back in. It was easier to find the shadow of him this time. It was bigger, slightly; more corporeal. And it spoke: *It was never your fault, Bella. I went too far. We all did. You are right to hate me.*

I don't hate you, silly old man.

119

You were so angry last time we met. He was becoming stronger, as if the conversation itself was materialising him along with the focus. I knew if I opened my eyes his would be open too. I didn't need to hear Ralph's sharp intake of breath to know that it was a different kind of open this time.

Yes, I was angry. I blamed you for what Lychen did because it was easier than blaming him. And blaming myself.

You did nothing—

I did. I nudged him, needled him, pushed him – I might not have known what he'd do, but I knew he was dangerous. I knew I was playing with fire. But I know how to use that tension against him now. It's how he breaks. It's how I break him.

How?

Like this. Like that.

Bella, you must be careful. Your resilience allows you to do this but it's not a guarantee—

Hmm?

This isn't a game. One day the resources will be depleted, just like the other Project A traits...

What was that? I'm not sure if I heard you properly...

Bella! You can't use a mind connection as a torment – he will work out how to use it against you! Bella!

'Tell me, then. Tell me properly. Come back and tell me out loud.'

'Beast? What's going on?'

I blinked and looked up. Ralph was leaning over Dr Blake, holding a finger in front of his face. He turned and called to the nurse.

'He did it again! He's following my finger, come and see!'

I let the nurse bustle up and perform her checks, allowing their surprise and delight to waft around me. I was tired. His mind had been the hardest one to reach, even slipperier than Lychen's, despite his proximity, his willingness to hear me. I pondered what he'd said about the resilience being finite. I had suspected as much when I'd read through the notes and research I'd asked Ethan to bring to me, back when I was still bed-bound. I'd already begun working on the theory of genetic material isolation, synthesis... The notes were no match for the great well of encyclopaedic knowledge and experience which lay before me, though. The creator who had had a hand in enhancing the very genetic trait in question... The nurse went to fetch a doctor and Ralph crossed the room to me as I sat back, my mind flying through the possibilities. If we could figure out a way to replicate my resilience, apply it as a drug like Serum X...

'Beast? What the hell did you do?'

I glanced back at Dr Blake. He was following the doctor's finger now, I could see the flicker of his eye movement, a glimmer of blue, from where I sat. They tried moving the finger further away and the movement faltered a little.

'He needs his glasses,' I said, quietly, before I turned back to Ralph. 'Come on, we'd better get out of their way. They're going to want to run a bunch of tests and he'll be exhausted. He's not going to wake up any more than this today. Could you help me up, please?'

Wordlessly, with more than a hint of accusation mingled with the bemusement in his gaze, he helped me to my feet and handed me the crutches. Slowly, we made our way out of the room and down the corridor. Sticks, step, swing, sticks, step, swing. It was slow and my entire body began to throb before we reached the end of the corridor. I could sense Ralph's impatience like a wound-up toy beside me.

'I told you about the mind-link thing, didn't I?' I muttered, keeping my voice low.

'Your weird telepathy with Ariana and Ethan? You said it started with her and then your Guard bond with Ethan strengthened it or something?'

'Yes. I've been able to sense Ariana for a while now, not that she was really aware of it until a few weeks ago. Ethan's connection is what strengthened my ability to try it with others...' I paused as we reached the lift. I wouldn't ask for a wheelchair. I would do this.

'What's that got to do— oh. *Oh!*' He turned to me. Luckily none of the people around us noticed, still he followed my gaze as it slipped off him to our surroundings and he held in his questions until we had stepped into the lift, travelled down to the ground floor and I'd limped my way into the open foyer.

'So did you... You talked to Dad?'

'I woke him up,' I said, a little smugly. Perhaps more than a little smugly. He stared at me, wonder battling with worry and, to my surprise, not a small amount of anger.

'What did he say?'

'It was difficult to reach him at first... I'm not very efficient at it yet. It's really hard to focus on someone else's consciousness without all their surface thoughts and desires getting in the way. With him, it was mostly all buried under a mass of unconsciousness. And even then it was only a sort of echo. He knew we were there and said he loved us.'

'He did?' The anger was unmistakable now, swarming bigger beneath the cloudy surface of his confusion, wiring through his quick strides. I wasn't sure if he was holding it back for the sake of finding out as much as possible or if he just hadn't fully decided what he was cross about yet. In any case, I wasn't going to lie to him.

'I told him it wasn't good enough. I told him he had to come back, he needed to wake up properly.'

'So you forced him?'

I looked up sharply. We were outside by now, the summer breeze turning brittle and whipping our hair in front of our eyes. I removed one hand from the handle of my crutch to pull a wayward lock from my face and tuck it behind my ear. I could feel the force of my gaze pierce him, tired as I was.

'I told him that he was needed. That we cared about him and wanted him back. Was that not the truth?'

'Bella.'

'I apologised for what Ariana did. I told him it was my fault. He blamed himself, of course... And I told him it wasn't his fault what happened to me all those years ago.'

'And?'

'How d'you know there was any more?'

'Because all that sounds like you were making peace. None of it sounds persuasive enough to bring him back. The only reason he'd have come back to himself was if he thought he could do something meaningful to help one of us...'

'I told him that if he died Ariana would be a murderer... and when that didn't work, I let him think I wasn't taking the mind-link with Lychen seriously, that I was wasting the resilience resources I had left... I don't know, Ralph. Mind conversations don't happen the same way normal ones do, it's not like you have time to think and then speak... Wait, I can't keep up. *Wait*, will you?'

But he wasn't looking at me and I couldn't force him, my voice was too weak and I was too spent by my conversation with Blake to put anything powerful into the command. He strode ahead, pacing the narrow walkway next to the hospital and plunging into the depths of the car park. I thrust my hand back onto the crutch handle and followed him, cursing my leg, cursing Nova's talons and Lychen's anger for crippling me in the first place.

'Ralph?' He was gone, but I could still feel his rage. It flowed behind him like a contrail, billowing through me as I lurched through the car park, trying to see where he had gone, trying to spot the unfamiliar car whose location I had utterly forgotten. I couldn't even remember if the Polo was green or blue. A gust of wind shoved more hair across my eyes as a dark smudge of a vehicle swooped round a corner too fast. I felt the rush of air as I fell and for a moment I was back on that balcony, my body flying backwards, the open air reaching for me as I watched the horror dawning far too slowly in my daughter's eyes… Hands, furious but firm, gripped me, pulled me upright, out of the car's path and abruptly let me go. Ralph. Of course.

'What the hell are you playing at?' he snarled as the car screeched away, horn blaring.

'Well *obviously* I didn't see the car, Ralph. I didn't just decide that getting run over might add a quirky new dimension to my current injuries,' I hissed. He glared at me for a few moments before stomping away. The Polo was straight ahead. I followed him.

'Did you want me to just let him die? Because he was slipping away, Ralph. I could feel that the moment I tried to reach him. Another day or two and he might have been lost.'

He turned around, leaning against the car as he placed

a hand in front of his eyes.

'How can I possibly know if that's true, Bella? I know you. You'll say anything to get what you want in the end.'

'Oh, and what do I want, Ralph? Go on, tell me!'

He stared at me for a moment. Then he reached, with a quick preciseness which made me flinch, for the passenger side car door and wrenched it open. I lowered into the seat, too exhausted to care that the movement was laborious, slow, graceless. He handed me my crutches and slammed the door. I waited until he'd rounded the back end of the car and climbed into the driver's seat.

'So you're angry with me for saving his life, is that it?'

'I'm just... I just wanted him to go peacefully. If this was his time. No meddling. No *forcing...* I'd have thought you of all people would understand that.' He placed his hands on the steering wheel and sighed.

'But it's not his time, Ralph. It's *not*. He has more to do,' I made my voice soft, gentle because that was what he needed. It was an old trick but it had never failed, not with him.

'How can you know that?'

'Because he told me, in so many words.'

He waited for a minute, longing with every particle of himself for me to be telling the truth. I put every fragment of earnest persuasion into my eyes without demanding anything of him out loud. *Trust me.* He blinked as he heard my voice in his head.

'Don't do that. Don't talk to me like that,' he snapped.

'Why? It's more honest, I thought that's what you wanted—'

'What I want? What *I* want, Beast? When has this ever been about what I want?'

He glared out at the grey building, the rows of dull cars

125

filtered by shivering raindrops on the smeared windscreen as I waited. Finally he turned to me, anger seeping away at last.

'It's how you talk to them. Ethan. Lychen. I don't want that. I want whatever *we* have... whatever it is now between us and whatever it becomes... I want it to be normal, OK? Or as close to normal as we can get. I feel like that's the only chance we have.'

'OK.'

'OK,' he replied, not looking at me. He started the car. There was no talk of running away to Lake Como or anywhere else as we made the short, winding journey back to the Manor in a silence that felt an extremely long way from anything resembling normality.

Summer, 2019

Ariana breathed very slowly, keeping her eyes closed. She could see the outlines of the five glasses on the table in front of her as if they were seared through her closed lids. She could feel the stares on the back of her neck as well, though she tried hard not to waste energy on interpreting them. *Channel*, she thought. *It is mine. How they think and feel is not relevant.* She opened her eyes and stared hard at the first glass. *Lift*, she thought. Nothing happened.

Come on. They're watching. Lift.

Why, though? For what purpose?

To show Lychen. We have to progress.

He doesn't matter. He's nothing to us. He has nothing for us.

He has money. He has power. We can have it all, too.

We already have power. We—

Just lift the damn glass!

All five glasses shivered and then, as one, shattered. Ariana stepped backwards and collided heavily with the school desk behind her.

'Well,' Lychen's voice came smoothly from behind her right ear. She turned and glanced at him, trying to keep her expression clear.

'That was certainly an improvement. Sigma, the mess,' he gestured dismissively at the Guard person and she immediately moved towards the shards littering the desk and carpet beneath it. Ariana stole a glance at Reuben, but he was staring at the surface where the glasses had been, his face as calm as she was trying to make hers. Lychen checked his wristwatch and Ariana wondered, for a moment, if she might just have got away with it. Then he looked up at her, his dark eyes narrow.

'Did you mean to smash all five of them?'

'Um... Not exactly. But I did mean to move one... And technically, it *did* move.'

'True. It is progress. I had hoped for better by now though,' he sniffed. 'Your core abilities appear to draw from human interaction, from what we have been able to gather from the tests we've run so far on your genetics. I can't help but wonder if we would make greater progress using our test subject.'

'Marc? I'm... I don't know if I'm ready—'

'He is not here to be your grandparent, Ariana. Do you think I don't know that you go and visit him? I allow it so that you will have a greater understanding that you must sever the ties that limit you.'

'Like you have?' The words escaped her before she could stop them. She wondered if they'd come from the bundle of unpredictable energy she'd spent so long trying to embrace as part of herself, now soured with the bite of his disappointment. Lychen's eyes clouded with contempt as she caught Reuben flinch out of the corner of her eye. Too late, she thought.

'Do not push your luck, child,' Lychen said frostily, eyes narrowed to glimmers.

Perhaps it was his calling her *child*. Perhaps it was the lingering resentment of the empty voice within her, wondering why she still pandered to this cold, strange little man when his power was no match for hers.

'I'm just saying,' she sneered, chin held high, 'you're not the only one who *knows things.* Except I don't need my little robot slaves to spy for me. I don't need anyone or anything except what's right here, inside me. And yes, maybe I've not completely and entirely worked out how to control it yet, but I'm getting better. I'm learning. What are you doing? Swanning about trying to pretend that you're not missing her so much it hurts—'

He moved more swiftly than she thought possible. One minute she was standing there, fists clenched by her sides, instincts raging at her to shut up, shut up *now* as his face grew white and his eyes swarmed with molten rage, the next he was in front of her, one icy hand around her throat the same way she'd seen him hold her mother, right before he'd thrown her over the balcony. The other hand hovered above her face and she cringed, ready for the blow. It didn't come. Instead he threw her back down like she was something filthy he couldn't bear to hold any longer. Ariana staggered, hitting her elbow on the desk and catching her knee against the chair. Lychen shook out his shirt sleeves and neatened the cuffs unconcernedly. When he next looked at her, all traces of anger had gone. All traces of anything had gone.

'You will give your next demonstration in two weeks' time. It will be using Marc D'accourt as a test subject. If I am not suitably impressed, you will be held down while my employees sedate you and then use the considerable technology I have available at my disposal to do all they can to extract every remarkable piece of genetic material contained in your body. Then you will be woken up and thrown out of these premises, but not before Marc D'accourt is turned into a Guard person without anaesthesia, while you watch. In the meantime, I suggest you learn to control your mouth as well as your abilities if you'd like to keep using both.'

Ariana leapt to her feet as he turned and began walking away, his shoes crunching as they found some of the shards from the shattered glass Sigma had not yet finished cleaning up.

'You— you can't just *pull it out* of me!'

Lychen turned slowly, deliberately. He gave one of those weird face-twitches that she knew was supposed to be a smile.

'I have a multi-billion-pound facility with state-of-the-art equipment and some of the finest scientific minds of several generations. I have been pioneering the technology needed to remove a person's humanity and replace it with a will to do nothing but obey for longer than you've been alive. Do you really think I *don't* also have the resources to isolate and extract certain genetic properties which have, after all, been unnaturally modified in the first place?'

'But... Why didn't you do that to *her*?' She knew the answer, of course. It was a stupid question. He didn't bother replying, he just threw her a scathing, contemptuous look before muttering, 'Two weeks,' and sweeping, silently, from the room.

'Well. That was... interesting,' Reuben said, as the door closed with a click. At the front of the room, Sigma finished collecting the larger shards into a plastic bag and turned to leave.

'I lost my temper,' Ariana rubbed her neck ruefully. It ached a little where he'd grabbed her, but not enough to leave a bruise. 'The voice... That part of me, it didn't see the point of trying to move the glasses. It was like, *Why bother, we don't need his approval...* I kind of agreed with it.'

'That's because it was you thinking it.' He hopped off the desk where he had been perched. Sigma came back into the room with a vacuum cleaner and, his eyes trained on the Guard woman, Reuben gestured to Ariana. Silently, they slipped out of the room as the sound of the vacuum whined into life behind them. Ariana followed without a word as Reuben padded quickly down the stairs. She was used to his quick, decisive movements now, her body had picked up a muscle memory to follow without question. When they reached the ground floor, she drew up to a halt behind him. He was staring at the front entranceway. She could feel him weighing up the options in his head. Then he shrugged and turned to the small, triangular garden instead.

'Perhaps we've rebelled enough today,' he said, as he led her outside. The day felt muggy, as if Lychen's harsh words had followed her out here, bundling around her like a hot, wet press of discomfort.

'Your anger, your outburst – that wasn't what I meant when I said that interaction upstairs was interesting,' Reuben said, eventually, after one tri-circuit.

'OK...'

'It was your reaction. What did you do, when he angered you? What was your response?'

'I dunno. I said the stuff about mum. I got under his skin.'

'Precisely. You lashed out with your words. You didn't use your power to hurt him.'

'No...'

'Do you know why?'

'No.' The truth was, she hadn't even thought about it. She looked up at Reuben and realised he was giving her one of his knowing looks.

'Try again.'

'I really don't know. I probably should have thrown him across the room. I guess... I just said what occurred to me. He *is* a hypocrite for telling me to limit my ties with people or whatever. He still loves my mum, I can feel it pouring out of him like a... like a smell. Like everyone has their own smell which makes them them, but his is just wanting her. It's... It's the only thing that makes him almost like an actual human.'

'Which to Lychen...'

'Makes him weak! Which he *hates* more than anything.'

'Exactly!' Reuben looked at her triumphantly. She grinned back at him. 'You knew that all along. And you – every part of you – knew that *that* was the way to truly hurt him in that moment. Using words, not energy. It means you're uniting within yourself, Ariana.'

'Even though I didn't move the glass like I meant to?'

'Precisely.'

'OK. Except I made him so angry he threatened to have me wiped blank and sent on my way.'

'Well, yes. But I don't believe he would actually do that.'

'You don't?'

'No. There's only one of you. He does not want to waste the mass of potential within you. Not while he still has a chance of being able to control it, wield it for his own gain. Lychen is not the sort of person to rationally destroy a thing that can still be of use to him.'

'Right. Which is why he never took my mother's resilience from her.'

'Quite possibly,' Reuben's gaze turned dark, darker

than it had so far. Ariana opened her mouth to ask what, but at that moment Sigma appeared in the doorway of the garden. Ariana glanced at her watch. It was ten to twelve. Despite everything that had happened that morning, she felt a twist of hunger and turned towards the Guard person.

'Ariana,' Reuben held out a hand and caught her by the shoulder. It was the first time he had touched her and he didn't hold on for longer than a few seconds, but it was enough to gain her focus. 'Don't needle him about your mother again. I can't see much into a person's intentions anymore, but I can feel the darkness there. You must do as well... I don't know what he's going to do. I don't think *he* knows, but there's certainly nothing good to be gained by poking at it.'

'Yeah,' Ariana shrugged. 'OK.'

January, 2020

There's a long pause when I've finished speaking. I watch them all, gauging their reactions. Nova sits on the floor in front of the open double doors, her wings folded neatly around her, her eyes narrow to slits of glitter as they follow the flicker of Marble's tail. He's lying in his usual spot in front of the fire, though the twitch of his tail tells us all that he's more than aware of the bird-girl behind him. Behind Nova, Dominic perches on the armchair. He's been throwing her uncomfortable glances ever since he sat there as if wanting to offer her the seat but unsure if it would even be possible for her to get into it. Now his gaze flickers between Tess and Ralph, who sit on the sofa. I face them, sitting cross-legged atop Dr Blake's old writing desk. It has been three days since my Lychen intervention and today is the first time I've felt normal again.

Despite sleeping for more than fourteen hours after my dose of Mollitiam wore off, I'd still spent much of the next day feeling as if I were dragging a weighted blanket around my shoulders. I didn't know if it was the after effect of pulling off such a psychic feat or the comedown after such a massive boost. In any case, I didn't need Blake's warnings to tell me more work needed to be done before I could even think of taking them again.

Blake himself sits in his old desk chair, pulled up and

around the edge of the desk so he's part of the group. I feel the sternness of his gaze boring into my side and then lift away as he turns to watch how the others react.

Tess's quick glance tells me she suspects more than I've let on about the Mollitiam. Ralph is staring fixedly ahead, a small bulge throbbing in his jaw as he grinds his teeth together slowly.

'So… er. Ariana's being kept asleep?' Dom breaks the silence when he realises that no one else is going to.

'Yes. At the Beaumont. Looked like one of the surgical rooms in South East. That's where they perform most of the Guard transition processes. It would make sense to keep her there.'

'D'you think that's what he's going to do to her?' Tess looks up sharply. She holds my gaze far easier than Dominic, far longer than she ever used to.

'I don't think so…' I reply, slowly, looking from her to Ralph. 'I don't really think *he* even knows what he's going to do… I saw enough to learn that he's considered the option of turning her into a Guard, but then he'll be stuck with her. There's no way he can market a thirteen-year-old model. He had enough trouble with some of the younger looking Youth Guard. And as much as he wants to use her power, he can't stand to be around her anymore. She's… too messy, too highly-strung, emotional, hormonal, disrespectful. Too thirteen-year-old girl. And she has my eyes, so there's that too. No, I don't think he'll turn her into a Guard. He's considering the possibility of removing her special abilities. It's something he's been thinking about for a few months now. And at the moment, that seems to be the option he's leaning towards.'

'He can do that?' Dom stares.

'There are certain tools at his disposal designed for

such application. Removal of abnormal genetic materials. It's only been tested on Guard people as far as I'm aware, as one means of partially reversing the process. Of course, the only genetic interventions with them were fairly basic – propensity for strength, a boosted immune system, fast reflexes. The machines were able to take all that out, but the major alterations to brain chemistry which make the Guard... well, the Guard... That's irreversible. As far as BFI are aware, anyway.'

Nova shuffles a little on the carpet. I can tell she is beginning to feel antsy, there are too many people in the room. It's starting to feel like a cage. An image of the chains and the padlocks of my former bedroom flash painfully through my mind. *This is where I'm going to put you.* It might show on my face, because Ralph is looking up now and his jaw has stopped twitching.

'So what's the plan, Beast? I hope you're not thinking of trundling up to London to launch some half-cocked rescue mission...' He says it measuredly and I can tell instantly that he's trying really hard not to nag.

'No,' I reply. 'Not yet, anyway. It's not safe. Not now I've pissed him off to such a degree. It's not *him* that's the main threat, really,' I add, quickly, as Ralph frowns. 'It's the number of Guard at his disposal. You've seen the adverts. You've seen them in town. Since they launched GHAP there are tens of thousands of them now. And like I've explained before, he doesn't have an active link to them all, but they are first and foremost created by BFI. There's nothing to stop Lychen recalling an army under some guise of testing or updating, no matter what promises he made back in the summer. We need to act now. We need to take control, take the power back. Take the Guard.'

'How on earth—'

'I've got a plan involving the Youth Guard. It's risky – it's more than likely going to result in exposing their loyalty to me – but if it works, we can rescue Ariana and take control of Lychen's entire operation right from under his nose.'

'How?' Dom shakes his head, but I can already see it dawning on the others. Dr Blake clears his throat. 'Tom,' he remarks, quietly. The others blink.

'Tom? The Youth Guard left at Beaumont?' Ralph's glasses catch the light of the fire so I can't see his eyes.

'Yes. Tom, Bette, Karl, and Eve are going to be the main players, but all of the Youth Guard will have a part of it.'

'Eve... the one in the PM's household?' Ralph frowns.

'Yes. She's close enough to Shona Metcalfe now. I've seen it for myself. The woman treats her almost like a daughter...'

'Poor cow,' Tess mutters at her knees.

'Hey,' I say sharply, 'No place for sentimentality, Tess. Eve knows that. You should too.'

'Eve's a bloody robot,' Ralph bites, 'We're talking about a woman suffering from clinical depression, probably PTSD – who knows what else.'

'You knew where we going with this when Lychen appointed Eve to the PM's household.'

'When Lychen appointed her there *at your suggestion,* Beast.'

They are all staring at me now. I narrow my eyes, gathering all their agitation, accusation, weakness and spitting contemptuous venom back at them. Tess flinches. Ralph and Dom look down, ashamed. Dr Blake shuffles uncomfortably in his chair. Nova holds my gaze steadily, head cocked, small mouth smiling a little.

'I can do this on my own,' I say. 'It will be far more difficult and dangerous... But I can, if none of you want to help me actually stop him. Shona's situation is unfortunate, but it's a golden opportunity to discredit Lychen's entire BFI Guard operation. We won't get another chance. And we definitely won't get another chance to rescue Ariana. All Tom needs to do is get close enough and wake her up. I can talk to her then, tell her how she can get out. She might not need me to. Goodness knows she has enough resources on her side. She just needs to be given the chance to use them before he takes them from her.'

'Beast,' Ralph's voice is more measured now, 'if he *did* take them from her... Would it be such a bad thing? Didn't you want Ariana to have a normal life? Isn't that why you never told her the truth about Lychen, about how she was different, all those years?'

I look at him in exasperation. Does no one in this building use their brain except me? 'It's what he'll do to her afterwards that I'm worried about, Ralph. Not her being normal. Her being useless in his eyes. Expendable. Devoid of all the traits and abilities he prized in the first place.'

'But she's his daughter,' Dr Blake adds, quietly. I can tell from Ralph's face that he's thinking the same thing.

'Lychen... he doesn't care that she's his daughter. Not the same way you would, Ralph. He's too damaged by the way his parents treated him as a child. He doesn't think or feel for people in a normal way... it's why it never occurred to him that Ariana might be his in the first place, it's why it came as such a shock. His mind is linear and logical, he's determinedly made it that way. He prizes Ariana for her abilities just as he prized me for mine. The fact that she's his... it's a convenience, in some ways. And maybe there is a very small part of him that *wants* to feel a certain way about her, recreate the relationship he saw between you and your parents so long ago... See himself passing on his wisdom and his empire to her one day... but he's too fucked up to actually really *care* about her, of that I'm sure.'

'OK. Right.'

'So. I've got an idea of timescale. We're going to have to move fast. Plan A is that Tom wakes Ariana first. Then if all goes well with that, if he can remain undetected and Lychen never comes to suspect him – and that's a big *if* – we may be able to hold off on Shona until we've managed to finish the rest of the work on Serum X. Mollitiam I'm happy with. NatApp still has a way to go as well. Unfortunately, all this business with Ariana has sped things up a little bit too much. Nova, I know you're uncomfortable. Did you want us to go into a different room so you can relax in here, or do you want to go back outside?'

'Out. Outside.' She gets to her feet and shuffles out of the room. Her wing hasn't quite recovered enough to fly – though I've seen her beat herself a few metres off the ground over the last twelve hours – but she is able to fold it far more easily now to get through doorways. Handles can still be an encumbrance, however, and Dom springs to his feet to help her, eager to make up for his failure to at least offer her the armchair earlier. I look away in amusement to meet Ralph's gaze. Something has clicked into place, I can tell at once. Perhaps it was the mention of Mollitiam. I glance at Dr Blake out of the corner of my eye and, taking the hint, he pads out of the room behind Dom. Not before he raises his eyebrows in an irritatingly self-justified expression, though.

'You've never been able to hold a mind-link with

Lychen that long before, have you?'

'I guess I was luck—'

'Bollocks. You dosed yourself up on Mollitiam, didn't you? I told you, I *said*—'

'It's *my* bloody genetic material, Ralph—'

'And it's *my* research in part! You had no right—'

'He's got my daughter, of course I—'

A scream, shrill and unmistakably bird-like splinters through the room like a fire alarm. I watch Ralph's eyes bulge in echo of my own as he leaps to his feet, Tess already halfway out of the room as Dominic's yell – almost as high-pitched as Nova's – reaches us next. I spring from the table and follow them closely.

Nova is huddling close to the house, her wings wrapped around herself. Dominic is on the path next to the frozen herb garden, bent double. I think at first he's been struck but then he retches, falls to his knees and I look away just in time as he vomits messily into the grass. Tess reaches him and puts a hand on his shoulder. Ralph is there too, staring back at Nova in confusion. I turn to her.

'What happened? What's going on?' I glance around the garden, expecting to see Daniel or at the very least one of his Guard people lurking, shotgun in hand. There's no one, though. The wall is intact, the heavy gate remains reassuringly solid in its frame. Nova looks up, raises her good wing and points out a dark patch of grass near the cloches. Ralph and I follow the direction of her talon as one. What I've taken as late afternoon shadow is, in fact, a dark, messy smear of blood. And next to it, dirty and matted with blood, grass and clumps of hair—

'Oh *God…* is that a—' Ralph's voice heaves and he turns away. I glance up. Dominic's still leaning into the grass and Tess is keeping her eyes firmly averted from the bloody mess.

'Pig's head,' I whisper. I bend a little closer, my own gag reflex raising a warning in my throat as the smell hits – a mixture of blood, decay and something else. Something that instantly transports me back to the Beaumont. A large room with not nearly enough windows. Cages, straw and... I blink. There's no mistaking the misshapen snout, the too-long hair, the strange, angular ears...

'It's the pig hybrid,' I mutter, straightening up. Ralph stares at me, his face yellowing with horror.

'It's a warning,' he chokes. 'From Daniel... For Nova?'

'Why now, though? Unless—'

'Unless it's actually for you,' he finishes. We both turn and stare towards the wall, the gate, the looming hillside of the landscape beyond and the ARC, rising from the fist-like mound like a shiny, dark middle finger.

Summer, 2019

The second week of July crept fingers of weak sunlight around the corners of the cheap blind in my bedroom. I blinked a few times, twitching my face around the now familiar tightness of the scar running its length. Also newly familiar were the sounds that reached me as I sat up and stretched: Felix's stress-wired voice, Ethan's low rumble shot through with frustration. They'd been arguing almost constantly for the last week. I'd been keeping my distance as much as I could, but couldn't help overhearing. None of us could. Ralph had gone so far as to threaten to chuck them both out of the Manor without their keys if they didn't pack it in. Felix had replied in a low voice which I hadn't quite been able to catch from the landing, but I knew the gist was about Lychen and when he would supposedly pay us a visit. We were all waiting. I didn't have to delve into any minds to feel the spiky jolts of anticipation, the sideways looks of doubt.

Crossing the room, I opened my wardrobe and selected an A-line summer dress in electric blue. The skirt swirled around the cast on my leg and I counted, internally, the weeks until I would be free of it. I was getting better at balancing while dressing, at least, and the skin on my arms had healed to the point where the rub against the crutch handles barely bothered me anymore. I could feel the muscles in my good leg growing too, as it compensated. Pulling open the blind, I watched the gentle sway of the trees on the drive and smiled as Nova gave a soft call from one of them, opening her wings as if in greeting. I would walk, I decided, looking past the trees to the jagged horizon. When my leg had healed, I would go for long walks out there in the real, chaotic world. I'd strengthen my body and my mind together, explore the beckoning wilderness I'd taken for granted for too long.

The landing creaked in a worried-sounding way under Felix's feet as she slammed her way back into the bedroom she shared with Ethan. Outside the window, Nova continued to hover on her branch, head cocked as if watching me. She gave another call, slightly louder this time and I raised my hand in acknowledgement. The tree bounced as she launched herself from her bough, giving one last shriek as she swooped up and over the Manor's roof. I smiled a little as I turned away from the window, thinking about how much her bird cries had startled me not so very long ago. I still wasn't always sure what she was saying or trying to say unless she put real effort into her speaking, but the cries seemed to be less wild, more like just emanations of feeling or flight.

Ethan hovered on the landing as I made my way, silent except the slight creak of my left crutch where a screw had come loose, out of my bedroom. He rolled his eyes towards the room next to mine and I twitched a smile in response. Without speaking, he offered his hand. I handed him the left crutch and he took my arm with his free hand. We made our way downstairs like that.

It's happening today then?

Yes. You feel it, too?

Only through what you feel.

143

Nova senses it as well. She told me the other week that she can feel danger, it's how she got to me in time when I went over the balcony. She's loud this morning, I think she feels something is about to happen.

'Morning,' Ralph grunted at us as we entered the dining room. He and I hadn't discussed Dr Blake since our visit a few days earlier. He had gone back the next day and had grudgingly reported improvement when he'd returned, saying the doctors were 'cautiously optimistic' for a full recovery now.

'One of your orders arrived this morning,' Ralph muttered as I reached for the coffee Ethan had poured for me (old habits).

'Oh yes? Which one, the tablet machine or that new microscope?'

'Microscope. Beast, I've got to ask, how are you paying for all this? Not to mention the gardener and the guys putting up the wall… I know you're persuasive but we're talking thousands, possibly tens of thousands with all the equipment you're getting and what it'll cost to refit the front room into a lab. You can't still be on the payroll at Beaumont.'

I snorted. 'No, of course not. Lychen had my pay frozen before Felix hit the M25. He's got monitors on my bank accounts as well. The ones he knows about, anyway.'

'Ah.'

'Yeah. I had one under my old alias Elodie Guerre with my wages from the university where I worked, but when I was in hiding I also set up a secret one under a third name. It's where the bulk of my family trust fund money went, and when my brother and sister died I inherited theirs as well. There's a tidy sum now. I was initially saving for Ariana, but… Well, needs must. And we *need* this stuff,

Ralph, trust me. Serum X is just the beginning. Once we get that genetic isolation machine of your dad's up and running—'

Several things happened at once. There was an abrupt clattering sound outside the side window and a sudden, furious shrieking. Ralph turned, stunned, to see Nova beating her wings in a frenzied way against the glass. Ethan, however, was watching me as I stared, unseeingly, back at him. The flash of insight left my head as soon as it had come, but it had been unmistakable. I put my cup down so fast a splash of coffee leapt onto the dark, shiny surface of the wood. I gave myself one more second as Ralph got up to open the narrow stiff window. Ethan's soft dark eyes reflected my surprise and calmed it quickly, sending me his strength.

'Nova! What the hell?' Ralph muttered as Nova gave another squawk, her small eyes tearing around the room for mine. I turned so she could see me.

'It's OK, Nov. I know. I feel it, too.'

She calmed instantly, though Ralph was a picture of mystification as he turned to me.

'Feel what? What's going on?'

'He's early,' Ethan muttered, looking at me rather than Ralph. 'He knew you might sense him, so he—'

'He blocked me somehow. Until he got too close.'

'Eh?' Ralph stared at the two of us, his bemusement unable to completely screen his scowl of resentment.

'Lychen's coming. Now. He's nearly here.'

'What? Really? *Now*?'

'It's OK, he's only got Delta and two other Guard with him. It could be a lot worse. We've got to warn the others though.'

'I'll go,' Ralph got to his feet.

'No, Ethan, you go. Quick.' He obeyed without a glance.

'Nova,' I turned towards the window. Nova was throwing anxious glances towards the direction of the driveway, muttering squawks under her breath. I grabbed my crutches and moved as close to the window as I could.

'Coming,' she murmured.

'Thank you for warning us,' I said, trying to keep my voice as level and calm as possible, even as the tension rippled beneath it like snakes beneath a bedsheet. 'We'll take it from here. You have to stay out of sight.'

She stared at me for a moment, conflicted. Then she nodded, simply, and turned away. I heard her quick footsteps churning over the gravel and the beat of her wings as I turned quickly back to the others. Ralph was watching me with a wild sort of fear in his face.

'Ralph, you need to get as many vials of Serum X as you can.'

'OK... But it didn't fully work—'

'It doesn't matter, it will help. Remember what we discussed. You've got to leave me alone with him. No matter what you hear...'

'Bella, I'm not going to stand by—'

'I'll be fine. Ethan'll be nearby, he'll be ready if I need help. But the main threat is the Guard, they're the ones I need you to concentrate on. If I can distract Lychen—'

The sound of a car on the driveway froze us both into silence. I began to move as quickly as I could towards the door.

'Jesus Christ,' Ralph muttered as I passed him, pulling his hands through his hair. I had a sudden urge to grab them and kiss them. To send him to his room and lock the door.

'I didn't actually think he was going to come, you know. I know you said he was but... Wait, Beast. Let one of the others answer the door. You go wait in dad's office. I'll get the serum.'

I didn't argue. Hoping that Nova had managed to make it as far as tree cover at least, I made my way to Blake's office. The flagstones were chilly and I realised I'd left my right foot bare. Goosebumps shivered along my limbs as a knock shook through the house. Sunlight spilled through the leaded window, patterning the writing desk with diamonds. I made my way towards it, hoping that a little of the warmth would smooth the chill from my skin. Voices rumbled from overhead and footsteps approached the front door. Not Felix, I hoped. She'd show him right in. I held my arm out to the sun and watched the tiny bumps slowly fade. The sound of Lychen's smooth, clipped voice snaked into the room and I kept myself very still.

I am me. I am mine. Not his. I will never be his again. Ever. My body shivered as it remembered. Every bruise, every bloom of pain, every blemish. I let it all in, let it all hurt and then I shook it out and away. I kept my gaze steady as the door in front of me slowly opened.

Delta strode in first, holding the door for Lychen. He stepped inside and turned towards me. He wore a fresh, white shirt over his usual suit trousers and polished shoes. His hair slicked back, his face carefully impassive, though it faltered as his flinty eyes found my face, my scar.

'Good morning, Josiah,' I said, smoothly.

Movement caught my eye in the schoolroom beyond the open double doors. Lychen looked over as well.

'Bella,' he said, turning back to me. 'I've come to talk. Might we do so in private?'

'Of course,' I said, my voice as level as his. 'Dominic, if

you wouldn't mind shutting the door?'

Dominic's worried face appeared in the double doorway, staring wildly between me and Lychen as he pulled them shut. Lychen gave no sign of recognition, in fact he didn't so much as glance Dom's way as he crossed the room to the armchair facing the desk. I inclined my head towards Delta and, following my gaze, Lychen dismissed him with a wave of his hand.

Over to you, Eth, I thought, as Delta strode out of the door and shut it behind him. Lychen sat down smartly, back straight, feet firmly planted on the stone floor. I crossed the room slowly, swallowing my inner urge to swing away as fast as my crutches could carry me in the opposite direction. Instead I perched on the edge of the sofa furthest from him. I blinked and saw myself at nine years old, large-eyed and shuddery as I sat in the very same spot and listened to my mother talk loudly about all the things that were wrong with me. *Bella is defective. You need to take her back.* I leant my crutches on the arm of the sofa, blinked again as the vision changed, as I grew a little into a girl of fourteen in a clean, white dress, face alight with my own cleverness. I looked at Lychen and, because he was close by and his mind was swirling with conflict, nudged a little way into his head to see the same image.

'I would offer you coffee,' I said, cutting icily into the twirl of the child in his memory. 'But as you can see, I'm a little impeded. Besides, the last time I saw you, you threw me off a roof, so...'

'Yes,' he said, his eyes still riveted on the scar on my face. 'I apologise for that. I acted rashly, from impulse, anger.'

'Emotion?'

'I am not proud of it. But you cannot deny that you

provoked me...'

'How is Ariana?'

'She's fine.' A frown crossed his features. I could feel his frustration at my switch of focus, the power play of the conversation. 'I have appointed a tutor for her. She is showing signs of improvement with her abilities, though her temper needs a bit more control.'

'She got angry with you?' I smiled. Behind us, in the corridor, raised voices could be heard. I was tempted to see what was happening, glance through Ethan's eyes, but I knew I couldn't afford to drop a fragment of my attention from the conversation in this room. Lychen was leaning forward, I could see the tussle of impatience in his features and movements. It pulsed across the space between us.

'I handled it. She's fine. You can see just how fine she is for yourself if you come back with me today.'

I stared at him as another rumble of voices and footsteps reached us. He kept his eyes on mine. The same flinty black I knew, but not so expressionless perhaps. The longer I looked, the more I saw. Anger, of course. Always so close, always so quick. And underneath... weariness, frustration, conflict... pain?

'You really want me to come back?' I asked, measuredly.

'I can't pretend I'm not still furious about your deceit. But I am willing to overlook it if you would return to work. Your contribution to BFI is... valuable.'

I frowned at him.

'This isn't what you expected?' He remarked levelly, though his eyes flashed dangerously. 'Oh, I know you knew I would be coming... Don't think your little night time messages have gone unnoticed. And, as you've undoubtedly realised, I've already developed something of a defence against them. Not too difficult once I made the link with the Guard communication process. But I can't pretend your first, ah, *warning* didn't take me by surprise. Clearly I underestimated you. As I have done all year, perhaps, given your... revelations... last time we were together. It's certainly an interesting development. Think of the application, if we could harness it, if we could isolate your ability to infiltrate minds...'

I realised, a fraction before he stood up, what he was going to do and swung to my feet first, reaching for the crutches. I stepped away, turning my face so that he wouldn't see any interest sparked there. I moved back towards the sunlight pooling on the desk behind me. When I turned back, he stood in front of his chair mildly, his hands behind his back and a slightly bemused expression on his face. A crash nearby sounded loud enough to crease his forehead, flicker his eyes towards the door.

'Why would you think I would willingly come back with you?' I asked, mostly to gain his focus back onto me. I leant back onto the desk but didn't take my weight off my good foot, just in case.

'I have your child.'

'Who wants nothing to do with me.'

Eth, what's going on out there?

'She is young, impulsive, irrational. I have no doubt you are more than a match to win her round, should you want to. And then there's the Youth Guard project...'

Ethan?

'What about them?'

'I've been monitoring them. They are... spectacular. More so than I ever thought any Guard could be. I've initialised a launch – in the last week alone I've had enquiries from several high-end government representatives, including the Prime Minister... I know I can bring in a new mentor, a new instructor for the next generation but I cannot guarantee they will be as successful. I *know* this interests you, Bella. Despite all your other lies, your pretences about our relationship. I know your passion for that project was real, that it still is – I see the flames of it in your eyes. You aren't *that* good at lying.'

It's fine. All good. One down, two to go. All OK in there?

I hesitated.

'You're right. I did engage with that programme more so than any other. If it were just for them, I would come back. I'd make sure the programme was launched properly, I'd advise you that each one is worth at least ten times the conventional Home models, that with a bit of political tutelage, they could easily meld into any upper government staff. I'd put Eve forward for the PM job. I'd suggest keeping one – Tom, perhaps – back at the Beaumont to assist in training the next generation. Oh, I had ideas, I had plans... But if enacting any of them means I'd be working, living, *breathing air* within one kilometre of you again after all you've done to me...'

'Oh Bella.' He moved closer and, despite my pep-talk, I felt my body begin to seize as his eyes feasted on it. Ethan felt it too, I could tell. *I'm fine. I'm fine.* I closed the connection. I needed every morsel of concentration. This was everything, right here, right now.

'My Bella,' he spoke softly, as if to a child. 'When are you going to stop being so... so *victimised*? That's not the woman – the *goddess* I knew and loved over the last year. You can tell yourself it was all a lie, all for the sake of some deeper lie. But I saw you. I *know* you. Am I truly to believe in this new, weakened version you are presenting? That might be the face you want to show Blake out there, but it's not the one I see. I know *you*, Bella. It takes a monster to love their counterpart, after all...'

He was in front of me now. I stood, half propped by the desk behind me, my eyes locked on his. I needed him to be close, I told myself. I knew the mind-link was strongest the closer we were. This close, I could feel that the barrier he'd used to mask his approach was flimsy, chemical, transient. Still, my heart rattled so hard I could feel the thin fabric of my dress flutter with it. He was close enough to reach me. One hand, rising slowly, my throat clenched in anticipation...

'We could be a family,' he said, softly. His eyes changed into something I'd never seen before. I don't know if it was that or his closeness, but for a moment I blinked and saw a twelve-year-old boy, skinny and nervous-eyed under a heavy mop of too-long ashy blond hair. He stood in this room and wept. Lychen's hand shook as the image of the boy trembled through his head as well and instead of my throat, he traced a long, cold finger along my broken cheek.

'I can take it back. I can fix you,' he murmured. 'I can fix all the wrong things. I can give you a life you deserve. All the pain, all the scars... They can all be wiped clean...'

I shut my eyes for a moment and, without thinking about it, leant my mind into his. Into the odd dungeon of locked away desires. I saw myself, my body passing through one of his machines to erase the scars and emerge unblemished. I saw the three of us sitting around a table, served by Guard, smiling at one another. I saw him cup my cheek tenderly in his hand before it became cold and hard, lowering to my throat, pressing too tight as he lurched over my body, the gleeful sweetness of retribution... I opened my eyes, but this time he moved more quickly than I and swept my crutches to the floor. I knocked his hand away as he reached for my face again, my other hand holding firmly onto the desk. Anger swarmed into his features.

'I don't need to be fixed,' I breathed, pushing my face closer to his even as everything within me screamed in protest. He blinked. I registered the fear, I took it in and let it feed my hatred as I shut my eyes and pushed back. Back into his head, swirling the images of me enslaved, Ariana reverent and obedient, the army of Guard bringing the country under control… I pushed them aside and reached once again for the little boy, holding out my hand for his, bringing him here to this room where he'd stood in weakness and humiliation as his father had called him things that made Julia D'accourt look like Mother of the Year in comparison.

'Stop. *Stop it!*' I felt his hands reach for me, saw his intention to wrench me by the throat, throw me backwards onto the desk, force me into humiliating submission the way he had that first time, the way I deserved… *No,* I told the impulse. He froze, hands reaching in mid-air. I twirled the memory of me, an enchanting child in that clean white dress, twisted her face into mockery as she spun and laughed around the boy Josiah. No, *not* Josiah… He changed his name didn't he… What had it been? The answer reaches me in his tremulous, girlish voice: *Simon.* The girls had called him Simple Simey at school because he'd clammed up when called upon, spoke with a stammer under duress. They'd pushed him into the girls' toilets, pulled his pants down in front of the teacher, who'd just looked at him, pityingly, and walked away… *Simple Simey, Simple Simey, his breath smells bad, his hands are slimy…*

'Stop it! Enough! Get out of my head *now* and I'll

leave… I'll leave you alone!'

I opened my eyes. Lychen was on the other side of the room, hands braced on the arm of the chair he'd been sitting in earlier. His face shone with horror and his hair stuck out where he'd pulled at it. I smiled and slid myself easily onto the desk behind me. There was no more fear in its smooth, cold surface. No more surge of memories or panic-stricken warnings. I enjoyed it for a few seconds more.

Ethan? Status report?

Only Delta left. The other two are confused. We gave one three doses. The other got four. Delta took off upstairs, Ralph and Dom have gone after him.

Help them. I'm fine here.

'You'll leave me alone? You won't come after me or any of us here, ever again?'

'Yes,' Lychen straightened up, panting a little. When he looked at me, I could see that the fear was already diminishing, rage clouding in even as wonder shook through his mind.

'And Ariana?'

'What about her?'

'If the time comes that she chooses to leave you, you'll let her go, no questions asked?'

He frowned.

'Simey. I can do this all day.'

'Yes,' he sighed eventually, almost fully recovered now as he squared his shoulders, neatened the cuffs of his shirt sleeves and smoothed his hair. He threw me a contemptuous look. 'I've changed my mind. Keep that scar. It suits you. I'm glad I had a part in taking your beauty from you. That I was the last man who will ever want you.'

I smiled at him as the ceiling shook under the impact

of a large heavy-set body upstairs.

'You're lying,' I said, confidently. 'You want me now as much as you ever did. My face has nothing to do with it. If anything, you want me *more* now I've shown you a fraction of what I'm capable of. Now you know I'll fight you bloody if you ever try to touch me again. I can feel just how *much* you want me all the way from here.'

He scowled even as the amber gleam sprang in response to my words. I probed a little and saw the thought cross his mind, as I'd hoped it would, that he and his Guard could easily overpower us here. That no matter what mind games I tried, they could simply knock me out, overcome whatever persons got in their way, bundle me into the car and back up to London where my prison awaited me...

'Try it,' I said, quietly, as he began to cross the room.

'What?'

'Try calling them.'

He frowned, and I felt him summon Delta. Attempt to summon Delta.

'What have you done?' He said, slowly, as I called to Ethan silently. I smiled at him as we waited.

Ethan opened the door, grinning through a bloody head wound on his temple. He pulled Delta into the doorway. The large Guard man stood, his gaze unfocused, his usually poker-straight back curved in an odd slouch. Lychen stared in horror as Ralph pushed the second Guard man in behind Delta. I could see the third in the hallway, gazing absently at the ceiling.

'Hope you know how to drive, mate,' Ethan said cheerfully. Ralph gave his bark-laugh behind him and I even heard Felix snigger from somewhere out of sight. Lychen turned from him to me. I fed off his alarm, letting it sink into me and replenish some of the energy I'd used for my

155

mental attack.

'What did you do?' He was trying to keep calm but a tremor had crept into his voice. His gaze quickened as Dominic opened the double doors behind him.

'*I* didn't do anything,' I replied, mildly. 'I've been in here with you.'

'How did you... How are you not Guard anymore?' He turned on Ethan as if he'd only just recognised him. I took the opportunity as Ethan opened his mouth to explain about the bond, about the oversight. It was easier than I thought it would be, reaching into their minds. They were broken Guard, after all. Delta first, for all the times he'd stood by and motionlessly watched Lychen squeeze fingerprints into my skin. I reached into his head, found the emptiness clouded with confusion of Serum X – felt it firing off memories of food, touch, a woman's face even as metallic control kept it all at bay – I gathered it all into a ball and crushed it. Delta's face wiped entirely clear. He smiled briefly at nothing in particular, before abruptly crashing to the ground.

They all stared. Ethan mid-sentence. Lychen in horror. Ralph was the first to look at me, suspicion battling confusion, and winning as the second Guard man crumpled.

'Beast, what are you doing?' He moved towards me as I focused on the third one. It was getting more difficult, my body was beginning to vibrate a little with the effort, my mind growing sluggish with fatigue.

'Stop, Beast. We can't use them for Serum X research if they're dead!' He reached for my arm but I shook him off, staring at the last vague Guard man. Down he went. I sighed, finally satisfied.

'I've got all the information we need about X, don't

worry,' I murmured, my eyes returning to Lychen's. 'Sending a message was more important.'

Lychen stared at me in abject horror for three seconds longer. Then he turned on his heel, stepped over Delta and left without a word.

January, 2020

I like to be on my own when I communicate with the Youth Guard. It's not that the connections are difficult to navigate – as fully willing subjects they are as easy to reach as Ethan, if not quite so familiar. Though there are twenty in total and I try to check in with each of them at least once a month, there are a core few who I monitor more closely. Tom, as my eyes and ears at the Beaumont. Bette and Karl in their roles with their respective politicians. And, of course, Eve. Easily the top student of the class, my dark-eyed, dark-haired machine of a Guard girl had so impressed the Prime Minister upon his meeting her and the other Youth Guard selected for interview that he hired her on the spot. I know Lychen was slightly disappointed to hear that she would be placed within his household staff rather than among his aides, but I was delighted. Far greater an opportunity to seek out the vulnerable. Eve, of course, did not feel anything but mechanical fulfilment to be doing something that made me happy.

I take myself to my bedroom to talk to her. I'd prefer a long walk to find a quiet spot on the mountainside, but after the pig-boy-head incident, even I'm not so arrogant enough to venture outside the wall just yet. Besides, I need all my concentration. I can't have any part of me silently wondering if Daniel's going to lob any more heads my way while I'm psychically elsewhere.

Sometimes I do wonder if I'm becoming a bit Guard-like myself. If all the connections to them, not to mention the depth to which I delve Ethan's still-overly-logical mind, has perhaps filtered a little of their cold, stoic metal back into me. I'm sure I should care more, knowing I'm about to take a group of individuals I taught, moulded, cared about and place them all in danger.

There's only so much a person can take before it changes them, murmurs Ana. I look up from where I perch at the end of my bed. She is standing in her usual white dress, diaphanously floaty even though snow falls thickly outside the window. She looks young, vibrant and when she moves it is just how Dr Blake once described to me – as if she were about to step into a turn or slide into arabesque.

What do you mean?

What you've been through... The pain, the darkness. There's a limit to what people can cope with before they begin to shut parts of themselves off.

Is that what happened to you?

Yes. How else could I have hurt you so, precious girl?

I looked down at my arms, remembering the old wrap of bruises.

You didn't hurt me so very much. Not as much as I hurt you, in the end.

She shrugged and danced away, because I needed my mind and all its voices to command. My last thought, before I delved away from my bedroom at the Manor, was how much easier parents were to talk to when no longer living.

Eve is exactly where she is supposed to be. It is seven-thirty pm, Shona Metcalfe is eating her dinner. Eve is filing away the day's reports – Shona was a founding member of a homeless charity and still plays an important role when well enough – on the latest quarter of donations. She doesn't flinch as she feels the finger-soft beckon of my mind at the edge of hers.

Eve. How are things?

Good. Shona has been feeling strong this week. She has spoken to colleagues and has agreed to give a speech at a conference next month. She has already begun writing it.

OK. Well, I'm afraid I have bad news. Ariana's in danger. We need Tom to get her out.

You are concerned that Tom's intervention could expose the Youth Guard's true intentions.

Yes. We need to accelerate the plan we discussed in the autumn.

Right. I have enough.

What do you have?

I have her trust. I remind her of her daughter. She will not notice deviation from the Guard protocol. She has not thought of me as Guard for several months now.

And you, Eve? How do you feel about this?

You are testing me. I do not feel.

Good. It is far better that you don't.

I will do what needs to be done. I shall start right away.

She does not end the connection so much as switch her focus, placing the files neatly into the correct folders and then carefully rearranging a few items on the desk. She swaps two pen lids, places an empty coffee cup inside a drawer, swaps drawing pins for staples. Then she lifts her hands to her tightly-braided hair and carefully unwinds the stiff plaits. She pulls the hair free and, with swift, unflinching fingers, restyles it into two carefully wound buns at the nape of her neck. A quick glance at a photograph on the desk shows me that the daughter, a pretty, slightly-wonky-toothed girl in her mid-teens wore it the same way. Her skin tone is paler than Eve's and she is more slightly built, but the hair is a nice touch, particularly if Shona has already begun to unite the girls in her head.

I return to the bedroom, a sour taste in my mouth. I don't take pleasure in what I am having Eve do. Why would I? But it's necessary. I filter through the rest of the Youth – prepping Karl and Bette, spending more than half an hour talking through a plan with Tom, having him repeat it back to me until we could both execute it step by step with our eyes closed. The others I merely inform and warn. I'm tired afterwards, but nothing like the comedown after my Mollitiam trip to Lychen's mind. I try Ariana, out of habit more than any real expectation of success. Nothing. She bats around an empty tomb of sleep, bound in oblivion. Not even allowed to dream, lest, I suppose, she finds a way to harness her abilities into waking.

Sighing, I reach for Ethan. Always last, always ready. He smiles as he welcomes my mind into his. He whispers and I whisper back until the sour pangs of guilt have been soothed away.

Summer, 2019

The men who built the wall had a pattern. If they hadn't arrived by the time the sun hit the trees bordering the meadows to the south of the Manor, where Nova waited, then they wouldn't come that day. Sometimes she didn't bother watching and waiting. Sometimes the draw of the open, tumbling countryside, the thrill of chasing other animals, of swooping through the air and discovering new rivers, gullies, and mountainsides far outstripped her human curiosity about the human curiosities of the Manor. Today was different, though. Today she kept a shrewd eye from the cover of the trees and when the workmen's van didn't come, she unfurled her wings. She landed in the back garden of the Manor within minutes, hopping towards the beginnings of the wall which already reached her middle.

Ethan didn't pause in his steady digging. She watched as he swung and heaped with the large shovel. Sweat glistened through his T-shirt and his muscles rippled under the brandings covering his bare limbs. Nova cocked her head. She thought about how he loved Bella, how Bella never seemed to need to look for him because she just knew where he was. She thought about the warm tussle of adoration and desire that bloomed from Ralph. The cold press of lust and need to possess from Lychen. As Nova thought about all these things, Ethan continued to dig, his movements becoming uniform and regular as he let the Guard instincts compensate for his weariness. Nova understood that, without thinking about how she understood it. She understood it in the way she could feel her own body shifting, standing more upright as the human contemplations swirled the bird instincts from her brain.

She waited until the hole was deep enough for Ethan to pause and turn towards the first of the three, lumpen bundles of sheets next to him. He glanced up at her then and paused, waiting for her to speak first. She felt her face creasing as she mustered the words.

'Th... three?'

'Guard,' he replied, calmly.

'Not... him?'

'No. Not Lychen. Not yet.' He turned and rolled the first body into the makeshift grave. Nova felt her wings tremble for flight, to take her away from this dark, strange place and the humans who had made it this way. No, she told herself. I must understand this. This is important.

'Why?'

He rolled the next body on top of the first and looked up, his face impassive. She wondered if he were relying on his old Guard instincts to stop himself feeling some of the horror of what he was doing. The thought made her feel a little calmer.

'I don't know,' he said, slowly. 'It's not my place to know. I don't look too far into Bella's history with Lychen. If I did... I would kill him myself. And it's not my place to do that. I trust her. She would have had her reasons for letting him leave here alive. Just as she had her reasons for not allowing these three to.'

He turned back to the grave and tipped the last body in. It landed with a soft thunk and he stared at it for a while, his gaze ticking methodically over the hole.

'Did I h... help?'

'Yes,' he looked up and his face eased with warmth. She felt it then, why Bella loved him. 'You did help. You warned us, you made it far easier to gather the supplies we needed to take down these Guard. You helped Bella, Nova. As much as any of us did.'

He rested on the shovel for a bit, the grin sliding slowly from his mouth. Nova squashed the urges to hop, to ruffle her feathers, cock her head. She held his gaze and saw the sadness beneath it. She opened her mouth to ask him why, but he answered before she could form the words.

'I need you to keep helping Bella. I wish I could stay and protect her for as long as Lychen still lives. But I made a promise... I know I'll have to leave her soon. I need you to keep her safe for me, Nova. I need you to keep sensing danger, keep warning her. You love her too.'

'Yes.' Not the same way, of course. No one loved Bella the same way as anyone else did.

'The Press has died down about you now. The Beaumont have stifled the rumours and satisfied the activists for now. Of course, it helps that the Prime Minister is on board with all things BFI... for now. But in any case, she will tell you you're free to roam further but I want you to stay close to her, OK? No matter how much you want to fly away... always come back. Until it's over, OK?'

'Yes.'

'Good. Thank you,' he turned back to the grave and the mound of dirt next to it. She watched the ripple of the Guardish cloak settle over his features once again as he stiffened his muscles, gripped the shovel and angled it efficiently into the dirt. Nova turned, hopped down from the wall and beat herself into the sky. The soft scoop and plunk of dirt on cloth echoed in her head long after she had given the rest of herself to the bird.

Summer, 2019

It had been an exhausting fortnight. In a few days, the two weeks Ariana had been given to perfect her abilities and then use them on Marc would be up. Ariana's control had improved tenfold, but she still spent hours lying in bed, trying to picture herself hurting Marc as she'd hurt Blake. Watching him crumple to the floor. She didn't know why it should feel so difficult this time, why it should *be* so different. She thought of them both as a grandparent, after all. Reuben said it was because she wasn't acting out of blind fear and rage, it was because the decision to hurt would be a conscious one. But when Ariana thought back to that moment in the ARC, when Blake had spoken to her about her past, her origins, she couldn't remember being blinded by anything. She'd just... not cared.

Ariana rolled over in her bed and stared at the light streaming through the large window which, if she opened the curtains, would face out towards the Yard. It was after nine am on a Saturday. Ariana glanced at her phone but didn't reach for it. There wouldn't be any notifications. Her friends from the school she'd attended for six months in Cumbria had forgotten her even faster than the ones in Flintworth. She didn't bother posting much on anything anymore. It wasn't worth the depressing check for likes and comments that never came. Besides, it wasn't like

there was anything she could say about her new normal...
Today I levitated three textbooks in the air without blowing them up! #LivingMyBestLife. Right. Sure.

The touch of her mother's mind came suddenly but softly, a gentle but firm tap on the door. Exactly the same way she used to wake her for school every morning. Ariana scowled.

What? I told you not to—

I'm sorry, but you aren't answering your phone and it's urgent, Ri.

It's on silent. I'm still in bed, what's so urgent?

It's Lychen. He was here. He's on his way back to you now. He's going to be extremely angry.

Ariana sat bolt upright in bed, eyes staring unfocused at the double doors ahead leading into the adjoining room.

Why? What happened? I thought he was away on business...

He came to talk to me. To try and get me to come back. Said he wanted me to resume my position but I very much doubt those were his true intentions.

Her mother's voice felt stronger than she could remember it ever being in her head. Ariana didn't have time to wonder what the hell that could mean, though.

Why is he angry?

We... the Blakes have been developing a serum which they used on Ethan.

I know, I used to live there, remember? I know about Serum X. I didn't think it worked though.

It doesn't, not fully. But they were able to use multiple doses on the three Guard men Lychen brought with him while I talked to him in the other room. It was enough to confuse them, immobilise them. Then I... Well it's hard to explain but I went into their heads like this, like I'm talking to you, and I eliminated them.

You can do that?

Evidently. Because they were Guard, their minds were already compromised and then weakened by the serum. Anyway, the point is Lychen is furious and he's heading back your way so I thought I'd better give you a heads up. He said something about an argument you had recently.

Yeah. He doesn't like people calling him out on his shit.

Don't push him, Ri. He's more powerful than he looks.

Yeah, yeah. Are we done? I've got things to do, people to see...

What's that? That thought you just had... Was that... Is that Marc?

Hey, you're not supposed to—

Christ. He actually did it. He actually went to Beaumont. And now what's happening to him?

He's fine. He's... being taken care of. Only... Only I'm supposed to use him to practice on.

There was a pause while she felt her mother ingest the information. The connection was so tightly wound between them that Ariana could almost feel Bella sitting next to her, her face only slightly furrowed as the realisation dawned.

That's what the argument with Lychen was about, I take it?

Kind of. Yeah. He told me I needed to sever ties, realise that Marc was making me weak... I told him he was a fine one to talk.

You didn't! Ariana felt the admiration as it fired around Bella's concern. She smiled a little.

You should have seen the look on his face.

What did he do, Ri? Did he hurt you?

No. Hardly at all. I hurt him worse. With my words

rather than my power, which Reuben says—

Wait, did you say Reuben?

Yeah, he's my tutor for my special abilities.

As in Reuben Teaque? Tall, black, intense?

That's the one. Yeah, he said he used to know you.

I... Yes. He was one of the C children. I asked Felix about him last year – she said he went off the radar years ago, that no one had been able to track him down.

Yeah, well. Lychen did. And he's put a Guard with his family, supposedly to 'help' but Reuben's scared of what will happen to them. I can tell that, even though he doesn't give much away.

He never did. Listen, Ri, I'm... going to try and make everything right, OK? I just want you to know that. All the bad things he's done, and that I've been a part of too. I'm going to fix it. I have a plan.

OK. Whatever you say.

Just... be careful, OK? Do what he wants, for now.

What he wants is for me to experiment on your dad. Is that what you want?

My dad has been looking for a way to redeem some of his mistakes for years. What I want is to be able to trust you, Ariana. So that's what I'm doing.

She left with a quick press of her mind, like a hand held briefly against Ariana's heart and then brought away, leaving a soft, warm print. Ariana blinked in the sudden silence. She didn't want to admit it but that last thing, that trusting her thing... that meant something. She got out of bed and quickly crossed the room to her chest of drawers, her mind ticking over the new feeling. Her mother hadn't told her what to do. It was up to her. Who was she? She was going to find out.

'No.' He said it solidly, resolutely, so there could be no hint of a question of anything else. Ariana stared at him. The two of them were alone in his cell, she at the small, spartan desk, he on his neatly made single bed, paperback next to him. Other than a bit of stubble on his chin, Marc looked well. In fact, there was a gleam in his eye and a smile in his voice, despite what she was telling him.

'You don't understand, he's going to make me hurt you—'

'I understand perfectly. It's part of your training and that requires me. So what would Lychen think if someone came to fetch me for your lesson and I wasn't here?'

'He'd think you'd escaped...'

'Which is impossible with his little friends walking up and down out there. You're only allowed in here because he thinks it'll make some better lesson for you in the long run, isn't that what he said?'

'Something like that,' she waved her hand impatiently. 'But look, I managed to distract the Guard out there by dropping a vase right at the end of the corridor. Then I confused him by telling him that he had to clear it up right away – all Lychen's household staff have his fussiness about mess wired in. I slipped past him when he was looking for the vacuum cleaner that I'd accidentally misplaced.'

Marc laughed with his entire body which, she noticed, was decidedly leaner than it had been a few weeks ago.

'If we're quick, I can get you out through the pool room, there's a fire escape round the back. Then we might just get lucky around the outskirts of the building. The Guard are never quite so alert when Lychen's not here.'

'Listen, Ariana, all this is very impressive and you've done a brilliant job at planning this out considering you've only had about half an hour's notice, but—'

'He's going to turn you into one of them if I don't do as he wants, Granddad. Please.'

'Grandpa,' he sank back against the headboard and she knew it was useless. 'You used to call me Grandpa. Well, *Gan'pa* actually.' The laughter had gone. He no longer looked fitter than before, rather saggier, emptier.

'This is what Mum wants too,' Ariana lied, quickly. 'She told me to get you out.'

He looked up.

'No,' he said again, quietly. She didn't know if he was calling out the lie or simply repeating what he'd said when she'd first burst into the room and explained her plan in quick, disjointed sentences. She sighed frustratedly, considering the other option. But even the improvement she'd had with objects would be no match for a large, unwilling man.

'What you don't understand, Ri-ri, is that in a lot of ways, I'm actually happier in here, being close to you, than I am out there.'

'Seriously?' She slumped back in the desk chair, already hearing the distant sounds of the Guard man finishing the vacuuming and opening the nearest store cupboard to put it away. They were almost out of time.

'I endured two of my children dying and the third cutting me out of her life. All of it was my fault. There were times I didn't feel I could bear to live another day... For a long time I drank too much, made a lot of stupid decisions, ended up retiring under a cloud. The only thing which kept me going, gave me the strength to make the one right decision – leave the toxic woman who shared the blame

171

right alongside me – was knowing I might see you again. That I was part of a back-up plan that was more important than anything else in my entire miserable existence.'

'Wait... what plan?' Though she knew really. There was only one person who had always pulled the strings, controlled her life, even from afar.

'Your mother. She came to Maya's funeral last year, told me that there might come a time that you'd call. It was like she knew what would happen. She told me where to come. I knew then that he'd found her. That was the hardest thing I've ever done, letting her get back into that car to go back to him... But it gave me a purpose. It gave me a reason to stop drinking, leave Julia, watch and wait... For you, Ariana. For this.'

Ariana sat there, frustration battling against a looming, annoying sort of knowingness. She understood. She really wished she didn't, because it would be so much easier to force him up and shove him out of the door with every ounce of energy she could muster. Footsteps along the corridor caught her attention and she sighed, getting to her feet.

'Well. Don't say I didn't warn you. I'll... I'll do what I can.'

'Do whatever you need to. I trust you.'

'Alright. See you, Grandpa.'

She left his room, the echo of his worried, sad eyes following her all the way back along the corridor, past the stoic Guard person and up the staircase. Why on earth, just when she felt most in need of a grown up to tell her what she should do, had they all suddenly decided to trust her?

Summer, 2019

The weeks following Lychen's visit passed quietly, like the comedown after a wild high. I rested, exhausted after the feat my mind had pulled off with him and his Guard. Ethan took care of the bodies. Ralph avoided me. Felix muttered under her breath; a bubbling volcano of resentment I knew would erupt before long. And something strange began to happen – as my body healed, my psychic abilities diminished. My leg strengthened as I hobbled around the grounds and up and down the stairs at the Manor – faster and longer every day. My scars began, painstakingly slowly, to fade into the creamy pallor of my normal skin tone.

I waited a few days before attempting another check in on Lychen's mind, just to see whether he was back at the Beaumont, whether my actions had scrambled his usual logical coolness any further. I tried late at night, reaching for the gossamer thread of the mind-link. It wouldn't come. I couldn't even find it, let alone dance along its fine, tantalisingly thin length to his mind. Ariana's mind-link was easier, but took longer, far longer than it had when I'd contacted her in the aftermath of Lychen's visit, still riding the adrenaline of strength. All I could do, after a good twenty minutes of concentration, was see that she was asleep, whole, healthy. Nothing more. No hints of her dreams, no echo of the preceding day's thoughts, feelings, activities.

'I thought it was just because I was tired, at first... After all that happened the other week. It took a lot out of me. But I'm fully recovered now. I'm fine – better than fine. I can get around almost as well as anyone else, I still need the one crutch but my leg doesn't hurt at all anymore... So what happened? Do you think it has something to do with the way he stopped me knowing he was coming until the last minute? It was some sort of drug he used, I could tell that much...'

Dr Blake looked at me keenly over the top of his spectacles. He was sitting up in bed, a tartan dressing gown tied firmly in place, far fewer tubes and lines connected underneath. Ralph had received the call the day after Lychen's visit and had been almost dazed when he'd returned from a long visit to the hospital, reporting that his dad was, somehow, incredibly, back. This was my second visit after the event and though he was not anywhere near the quick, acerbic authority he had once been, his blue eyes were bright and clear and his words, though slow and prone to long, gaping pauses, particularly towards the end of our visits when he was tired, made sense. Or as much as they ever had. He'd even quoted Nietzsche once or twice.

'I don't think so. Whatever that small defence was, it proved... proved no match for you once he was close. No, I believe the answer is... in what you said just now... You're recovering. Physically. Your resilience responds to what... What is most needed.'

'Ah...' I took a small flannel from the side table next to his bed and wiped away the saliva which had gathered and spilled from the corner of his mouth. He blinked his thanks. We never spoke of such things out loud. I glanced around me to make sure no one was around. Ralph had flatly refused to give me a lift. Ethan had driven me in the end and, after exchanging a few pleasantries with Dr Blake, had left us to it. I could feel him roaming nearby, in search of a vending machine.

'So you're saying that now Lychen has been and gone, now that threat has passed, it's working on healing my body faster?'

'In simple terms, yes...'

'And in not so simple terms?'

He took a long, shuddery breath. 'Can you still hear me?' He gestured upwards in a movement that would have seemed vague to anyone else.

Yes. You're close by and you're open to conversation. It's the easiest kind of mind-link.

Good. It's far easier to explain without having to make my mouth work. I believe your resilience is connected to your beauty, but more crucially it is wired to your intentions. When you were scarred, you did not heal supernaturally fast. That is because you chose to redirect your resilience to forging the mind-links. You say you spent those first few nights at the Manor trying to connect to Lychen's mind?

Yes... It took a long time and a lot of energy.

Because you were weakened by your injuries, physically. But that is what your resilience chose to fasten onto. Do you know why?

I sighed, glancing around again to make sure no one was witnessing this strange, silent conversation taking place mainly through very intense eye contact. The way he stared so intently reminded me of many a morning being quizzed on schoolwork at the breakfast table while Ralph smirked knowingly in the background.

I'm sure you're going to tell me...

Don't be lazy, Bella. You don't need me to fill in the blanks for you.

OK. Why did I put so much effort into reaching Lychen... I wanted him to know I wasn't dead. No. I needed him to know that it wasn't over and that I would come for him.

Your resilience prioritised revenge. But it wasn't simply a case of just thinking it, you needed it because, at that time, that was the only way you felt able to carry on living, having lost so much. Never underestimate the mind's ability to heal once it has a goal in mind. They say that sort of thing to me all the time in here.

What if it's gone forever, though?

It's not. I know your enhancement, your edit. I may not have always understood it, but I do now. It's more powerful than you know. More powerful than anything you've done so far... I remember... When you first came to live with us and all you needed more than anything was a mother and father who would love you for who you really were...

I remember.

And what happened?

You threw away my blood instead of testing it. Instead of trying to fix me.

I did. But do you remember something else about that day? When I told the scientists about Ana? I know you were listening. I know you heard me tell them that she was getting better, that her tumours had shrunk since you'd arrived.

They looked worried. I didn't understand that then.

Ana always scared people, much like you do. But my point is, I believe now it was your resilience healing her. Perceiving what you needed – a mother, if only for a little while – and radiating out of you to help stem the progression of her cancer.

She still died, though.

He doesn't answer. We both know why. We both recall the tumultuous years of my early teens. The arguments, the way I'd grown, resentfully, away from her. Believing that I didn't need her or her warnings anymore.

That was the beginning. That's how you healed me, as well. So you see, it's not gone... just dormant. Just consolidating its strength on replenishing your physical strengths while your mind no longer needs to be on high alert.

But it does need to be. Lychen's gone back to London, probably furious. Ariana is there and so is my dad... I know, I know. I need to trust her, to let her go and make her own choices. But it's so hard. She's so young still. And so naïve, underneath all that self-righteous bravado.

Sounds familiar.

Please.

I fixed him with a hard stare and he spluttered with painful laughter. I wiped his chin again, sensing Ethan on his way back, snacks in hand. I wondered why our connection didn't seem to be affected by the undulations of my resilience.

My link with Ethan is different. I know where he is all the time. I can tap into his head as easily as opening my mouth to speak to him, even if I'm here and he's back at the Manor. Why is that?

That I do not know, though he avoided my eye this time, glancing down at his hands folded loosely on his lap. The link you share was founded by Guard bonding, which is beyond my area of expertise.

His voice was beginning to waver, even internally. His eyelids drooped.

I'm sorry. I can't—

It's OK... You sleep. We need to be heading back now, anyway. Back to the cold shoulders and disappointed glares.

Ralph will come around, he thought slowly, deliberately concentrating on the words so they didn't slip into one another.

I had to make a point. And it's not like we have a way to reverse the Guard traits. Serum X only made them confused, barely conscious. We'll work on it.

Do you really want to, though?

What do you mean?

He shut his eyes and nestled his head into the prop of pillows, and when he next spoke, I could tell it was with the very last of his energy stores.

If you did find a way to restore the Guard to their former selves – and there is a way, I'm sure of it – would you want to? Knowing what that would mean, for your chances against him?

You mean the Youth Guard?

My advice would be... concentrate on the resources at your disposal... before you destroy anything.

OK. OK, old man. Time to sleep now.

Talk to Ralph. He'll understand.

OK.

'I'll be back soon. Sleep well,' I said softly, as Ethan appeared in the doorway. Because he was asleep and such things could not happen otherwise, I leant forward and kissed Dr Blake gently on his old, weathered cheek before removing his glasses and folding them neatly on the table, where he could reach them.

Summer, 2019

It wasn't as bad as she thought. So long as Ariana didn't think about what it was she was doing and concentrated instead on doing it. Glancing at Reuben, Ariana wasn't at all sure if switching off her conscience counted as *unifying within herself,* but it seemed to be working, so she was going with it. If the price to pay was a sleepless night, she would take the chance to be extraordinary now and worry about it later.

'Good,' Lychen said, quietly. They were standing in the squash court, the same one where she'd first encountered her grandfather again, bound to a chair. Today he stood freely at the end of a row of Guard people. She'd been asked to target their right arms. Mark stood clutching his, pain still etched on his face as she retrieved her focus. The Guard people stood as solidly and stoically as ever, though two of them had visibly twitchy arms. Ariana stole a glance at Lychen out of the corner of her eye. He looked the same as ever in his clean fresh suit, his hair slicked back and his hands held behind his back. If he was as furious as her mother had warned, there was no outward sign of it. But neither was there any pleasure or gleam of satisfaction when he watched her cause the pain he commanded. That seemed odd, for him.

'The left foot now,' he said, his clipped voice echoing

a little around the square room. Ariana turned back to the people. She didn't think of the crease of pain in Marc's face, she watched through hazed unfocused eyes as he crumpled to the ground, curved over his left foot like a comma. She glanced at Lychen, who observed expressionlessly. On her other side stood Reuben, looking at the ground. As Marc let out a groan of pain and the two twitchy-armed Guard dropped, one after the other, Reuben gave a strange, shuddery movement. Ariana turned back to the people, reeling the pain on Marc back a little. He groaned louder.

'That's enough,' Lychen said as the third and final Guard person fell to the ground. Ariana pulled the thorns from them. None of the men got up.

'Good. You have shown adequate improvement,' Lychen turned to Ariana, though he met her eyes for only the briefest of glimmers.

'Thanks... I've been thinking about all you said last time.'

He nodded, though his gaze had turned glassy and she could tell he was barely registering her words. Looking closer, she could see his pale skin was dark underneath his eyes and there was a heaviness to his movements as he turned impassively to watch the three injured Guard people straighten back up. Marc stood up as well, testing his weight on his foot gingerly.

'Take D'accourt back to his room,' Lychen said to the Guard man nearest him. The Guard took Marc's arm and the two of them headed towards the door. Marc glanced up at Ariana just once as he limped past her, his eyes narrowing as they latched onto Lychen. Lychen gave no sign that he'd noticed.

'Your pain delivery is back on form, it would seem,'

Lychen said, mustering his attention back onto Ariana. What the hell had her mother done to him, to make his reactions so thick, so slow?

'You have worked hard. In return, you are allowed access to the Yard and the rest of the Beaumont grounds. I want to see examples of psychic ability next time – you should be able to infiltrate a person's mind even when they are far away. I expect exemplary teaching on your part, Teaque. In fact, I think simple mind reading is too easy. I want you to show me a psychic link with the power to change the other individual's thought process. I want you to invade a person's consciousness and crush it.'

'Er...' Ariana glanced behind her at Reuben to see his face was a mirror of her own confusion.

'That is not something I ever—' Reuben mumbled.

'I don't care. I know it can be done, so do it. I'll give you a month. I need not warn you of the price of my disappointment. Either of you.' He stared at them both directly this time. Ariana felt it like an icicle pressing into her chest. She blinked and nodded, feeling Reuben do the same beside her.

'Good,' Lychen turned to the remaining Guard people. 'Soren, go and find Dr Skaid and bring him to my office. Hank, go and... do whatever it was you were doing.'

He swept away. Ariana felt him, a compact package of swirling emotion all bound up in a great knot of self-loathing she hadn't sensed before. She turned, bemused, to Reuben.

'What the hell was—'

'Sorry, Ariana,' he held up his hand, his face clouded. 'I just... I need some time.' He shook his head, pulled his hand over his eyes and rubbed them. Ariana looked away, embarrassed.

'Yeah, no... I'll er... I'll see you tomorrow, OK?'

He didn't respond, just stood there like a long, slightly curved pillar of closed-off feeling. Ariana turned and left the room. She wondered, briefly, about what was troubling Reuben, felt a little sorry for him, but by the time she'd reached the ground floor her thoughts had already leapt ahead to the far more interesting subject of what was up with Lychen and why he'd summoned Daniel. *Lychen's office*, she thought to herself. It was upstairs, four doors to the left of the classroom which she knew would not be occupied. Smiling to herself, Ariana padded up the carpeted stairwell. She'd been told to work on her psychic abilities, hadn't she? She'd just thought of the perfect way to do that.

Ariana sat in the chair at the desk where she did her school work in the afternoons with Sigma. The blinds were shut and she hadn't put the lights on in case someone happened to pass by and wonder what she was doing. She had a cover story, in any case, in the form of a maths textbook. She shut her eyes and tried to stretch her mind out into the room four doors over. It wasn't easy. Reuben had taught her a little about psychic listening and she'd always been able to do it perfectly well when a person was right in front of her... Trying to reach them further away was another matter entirely. She tried again, thinking about Lychen, about the strange whirl of distress he was carrying around with him... She stretched her mind through the solid wall in front of her, tried to picture it like tendrils of thought snaking through the solid plaster, into the next room... No. It was no good. She wasn't close enough. But then... How could she talk to Bella so easily, when she was miles away in

Cumbria? *I didn't start that mind-link*, she thought, bitterly.

Throwing herself upwards out of the chair, Ariana balled her fists in frustration. Think. I know how to do this. I've done this before. I need to do this. I need to know what Lychen wants with Daniel. Why? Because it could be important. It could be to do with me. What if he wants him to turn me into something? She forced her mind back over the sickening images – the snarling bird-girl, the mournful-eyed dog-boy. Herself, shrunken and deformed with a long, noodling rat tail... I did it before. At the ARC. I put my head against the door and I saw him in the past... I needed to know then. I need to know now. This is the same.

She was at the front of the classroom now. Without thinking, barely breathing in case the sudden swell of energy she could feel decide to dissipate without warning, she turned her back to the wall and leant her body against it. She slid, slowly, into a crouch and shut her eyes. Just as it had done that day outside her mother's former office at the ARC, her mind slipped neatly from her body and outwards, through the wall behind her like smoke through a sieve. She kept going until the light around her became bright, the furnishings sparse but luxurious, the space neat and perfectly formed. Daniel and Lychen sat on either side of a beautifully carved writing desk. Ariana listened, aware of her body against the wall even as she felt empty air supporting the listening part of herself as it hovered, invisible, above them.

'...sort of mind assault. Linked to the mutated resilience gene, no doubt. The strength of it was unlike anything I've come across, even with the child.'

Daniel pulled his pointed face into a sneer as he rubbed the uneven stubble on his chin. 'There could be a few explanations. Perhaps they have found a way of boosting the genetic material within her.' He shrugged in a bored sort of way. 'In any case, I'm not sure how *I* can help. I've already given you the chemical blocking aide I developed—'

'It didn't work. Not once we were in close range.'

'Well, I could try and strengthen the dosage, but obviously that will increase the risks of side effects. And I can't help but ask what the point is... You know my thoughts on how to be rid of this problem once and for all. And yet, once again, Bella D'accourt remains alive.'

'I told you, they've found a way to eliminate the Guard. I don't want to send more to their destruction without defence or at least preparation. I need a quick fix from you in the meantime to keep her out of my head. The drug obviously had *some* effect, however limited. I need you to strengthen it safely. I've been able to fend her off from time to time but if she really tries, if she wields that same strength I caught a glimpse of the other day... At the very least she could access all sorts of classified information...'

'...and at the most she could drive you irreversibly insane.' Daniel remarked, thoughtfully. Ariana felt her own mouth twitch in amusement from several metres away as Lychen fixed him with a hard stare.

'May I remind you that it is not just *my* projects which are at stake. I know details of your plans for the hybrids which, in the wrong hands, would prove catastrophic.'

'Yes, point taken,' Daniel said, his voice nipping with frustration. 'So when exactly do you expect me to find the time to work on this blocking fix? As you say, I've plenty to be dealing with with the hybrid project at present. Particularly if I'm to make up for the loss of Nova.'

'I am confident you will be able to come up with

something.'

Daniel sighed and brought a shabby-sleeved hand to his chin again, scratching audibly. Ariana watched Lychen's echoing shiver of disgust. She began to be more aware of the hardness of the wall behind her skull, the press of the impacted carpet under her backside. *Come on*, she thought. *Say more.*

'If I do, will you let me keep Bette as my Primary?'

Lychen glared at him: 'Only if you can match the sizable bid I received from a senior minister for her this morning.'

'I told you, once the new generation of hybrid is marketable—'

'This new generation you have not yet begun working on.'

'I need resources, funding, space... And I'm guessing your unwillingness to send a team of Guard to Cumbria means I can't expect Nova returned to me anytime soon, if ever.'

'Do you really need her? You said your new beasts would be an improvement even on her...'

'They will be. She's just a loose end I'd rather have tied up, like the other hybrids of her generation.'

Lychen stared at him keenly. Ariana felt her mind wafting slowly backwards like a slow-moving magnet drawn back to its counterpart. *Not yet*, she struggled against it.

'You'll get your funding,' Lychen muttered. 'The Youth Guard will fetch it in. You'll move back to the Futura by week's end and continue work on your new hybrids there. Once they're ready, you can move them to the ARC as planned. I did not see Nova, but I imagine she will still be there. She is an asset, after all. And Bella is nothing if not resourceful with her assets.'

'*My* asset.'

'By all means take whatever measures you deem necessary should you encounter her when you're there.'

Daniel raised a slim eyebrow. 'I assume we're still talking about Nova here.'

'Yes,' Lychen's face darkened. 'Bella's mine.'

'Are you sure? If you're worried about losing Guard, I'd be happy to take the pleasure upon myself, settle a few scores of my own—'

'*No*,' it was a small word, but Lychen's voice thrust it into the room like a knife. Ariana felt her body flinch from metres away and Daniel, too, winced at its sharpness. Lychen swallowed and made a visible effort to neutralise his face before he next spoke.

'You will develop the mind-repulsion device as a priority – use the drug, adapt it, make a helmet for all I care. Take whatever risks you need with it, just get it done. But you will not go near Bella. Not now, not when you move into the neighbouring building to her, not even if she comes knocking at your door. Do you understand? She is *mine*.'

The last thing Ariana saw as she gave in to the pull from her body was the resentful twitch of annoyance on Daniel's face as Lychen turned away from him. Followed swiftly by a smooth, satisfied little smile as if he'd just been struck by a brilliant idea. It was that smile, above all the creepy talk of mind control, stolen assets and scores to settle, that haunted Ariana long after she'd slid back into her body, stretched her sore muscles and made her way quietly away and up to her bedroom. She was so preoccupied by what it might have meant that she forgot to worry, after all, about all the pain she'd caused just a short time before.

Summer, 2019

'Ethan? Bella, is that you? Can you come in here for a minute, please?'

I exchanged a look with Ethan as he shut the front door behind me. Shrugging, he nudged past me and opened the door to Dr Blake's former office. Apart from Nova, whom I had spotted flying off over the hills to the east as we'd arrived, they were all there. Dominic sat in the armchair, Tess perched on its arm, Ralph and Felix shared the sofa – two rigid, angled bodies defiant against the soft sagging leather. Two chairs had been brought in from the adjoining room and placed side by side opposite the armchair.

'Are we in trouble or something?' Ethan chuckled, though I knew I wasn't the only one who caught the edge to his voice. He made his way over to one of the chairs and sat down, his legs sprawling as if trying to take up as much space as possible. I took the other one, thinking about my exhaustion after that first trip to the hospital and marvelling at how OK I felt now. Ready for battle. I had been waiting for this for a while, I realised, wondering if that was another reason my body had gone into conservation and repair mode.

'We've been talking about our situation here...' Ralph started, not quite able to look at me so looking at Ethan instead. Ethan snorted.

'You don't say. Looks like you're staging an intervention.'

'Look, let's just stop with the sarky comments, OK?' Felix glared at her husband. 'I'm going to be upfront here. I don't want to live in this house anymore. Not with her,' she glanced at me. 'Not after what she did the other week.'

I stared at her coolly, enough to make a few small beads of sweat appear at her temple.

'What exactly would you have had me do, Felix? Serum X only disarmed those Guard people. We had no way of knowing for how long—'

'We could have tried to bring them back, Beast,' Ralph said, his voice quiet and eerily like his father's.

'I told you,' Felix muttered acidly. 'She isn't interested in saving people. Not Guard people, anyway.'

'I saved your damn husband, didn't I?'

'Did you? He doesn't look particularly free to me...'

'Fee,' Ethan's voice gentled. 'Fee, please. I know why Bella killed those Guard, it wasn't because she didn't want to save them, it was because that was the only way Lychen would take the threat seriously enough. Otherwise he would have returned the next day with fifty of them.'

'I'm sure that's what she told you,' Felix muttered, mutinously.

'She doesn't have to tell me, I can feel it.'

'In any case,' Ralph interjected slowly and clearly as if talking to a class of squabbling children, 'we've decided that we need to work together, if we've got any hope against Lychen and Daniel.'

'That means full disclosure. Beast, we never finished our conversation from the other morning about all the equipment you're ordering and the new lab. What's it for?'

I cleared my throat and turned to him. 'There's a hypothesis in Dr Blake's notes about my resilience gene. About the way Ana and her team formulated it back in the eighties... It means there may be a way to stave off the curse of Project A by synthesising my resilience and topping up my levels. If we can do that, there may be a medicinal application too.'

There was a pause as they all collectively blinked at me.

'But that would take years of research...'

'Not if you work with me, Ralph.'

I stared at him, watching the idea invigorate past his awkwardness. I could feel his mind leaping at the possibility like the swarm of a wave against a sea wall. Felix cleared her throat loudly.

'And in the meantime, your old pal Lychen is getting ready to roll out a nationwide army of Guard Assistants for people to use in their homes...'

'The GHAP yes, but as I've said before, it's not about him having eyes and ears in every household...'

'So you say, but I don't know if your answer of his just wanting *order* or whatever it was, really justifies the scheme—'

'Well. How about the billions of pounds in income the programme will generate, allowing him to invest in further developments to the Guard application... The potential for consumer insight as marketable data. I don't know the entirety of it for sure. Only what I was able to gather when he let his guard down, so to speak...' They were all staring at me now, I had every drop of their attention. I could order them all to stand on their heads and they were so entirely ensnared in what I was saying, they would not realise what they were doing until they crashed into one another.

'He also spoke about ideas for Guard replication, through reproduction.'

'Guard *babies*?' Tess looked utterly horrified, gulping as if she wished she could swallow back the words along with the horrendous idea behind them. 'But I thought they were all sterilised as part of the process?'

There was a pause while everyone very determinedly didn't look at Ethan.

'At the moment, they are. But he wanted to see whether the brain alterations could be adapted into a hereditary trait, using the application of—'

'Genetic manipulation. The crazy bastard wants to go full-circle back to Project A,' Ralph said, incredulously.

'Yes. Only the "designer" traits would all be the same. Uniform. He spoke of it as a sort of utopian generation – no confusion or emotion, just intention, logic...'

They all sat there, ingesting my words. Ethan glanced at me curiously, but he didn't say anything and the others were too distracted to notice.

'I've gone over and over it in my head,' I added, quietly. 'The surest way to stop him is to discredit the BFI on a catastrophic scale. Take out Daniel with the same stone. The Press coverage about Nova did a bit of damage, before they hushed it all up of course... But it made me think: what if we blew it all up? What if we went to the top, the very top, and showed all those rich and powerful investors what they're really backing? Make it so that no one would *dare* even talk about BFI anymore, let alone invest in them...'

'How?' Ralph asked, elbows on knees, leaning so far towards me he's almost sitting on the air in front of the sofa.

'I've been trying to put it all together for a while now.

Since I was at Beaumont, leading the Youth Guard project. I don't know exactly how we can do it, but they'll be key to it all, particularly if Lychen does as I suggested and puts the best of them forward for the top jobs. We'll need the cloned resilience application... And something else. Something I was thinking of for the hybrids. A Naturalisation Application. Using your theories for Serum X but adapted to account for their specific genetic mutilations... I hoped you would work on that, Ralph. But if you can't trust me... Then there's no point in any of it. I've been honest. All I want is to stop Lychen and Daniel and get my daughter back. If that's what you want, too, I suggest we do it together. If it's not, then we might as well call it quits now and all bugger off our separate ways.'

I waited. Tess and Dom were both nodding, both snagged by the conviction of my words, the passion I knew was emanating from my delivery, honed from years of performance, spotlight, captivated audiences. I watched Ralph and Felix. He was wavering, the image of those crumpled Guard bodies still slumping round the edges of his mind. I didn't probe further than that. I couldn't afford anymore distrust. Felix's face was far darker.

'You've been honest, have you, Bella?'

I could see her hand. It was her last chance, her last big gamble to attempt to redeem a little of the high ground she had felt so solid upon before I had entered the room and swept it away. But I could see her hand, so I decided to call her on it.

'Felix doesn't trust me. She suspects I, for some reason, did something to lure Lychen into finding me last year. Isn't that right?'

'Eh?' Ralph looked from me to her. Felix continued to stare mutinously.

'It just all seemed too well-timed. Too convenient,' she muttered. Her brow furrowed as she tried to recall the contemptuous logic she'd snarled at me that night in June. 'I... I have my reasons.'

'You think Bella *wanted* Lychen to find her? Felix, I was there at the Beaumont,' Ethan's voice trembled with rage. 'I know what happened there, I *felt* it... I still feel it, sometimes, when she does. No one would choose that life.'

'Maybe she didn't know—'

'Of course I knew,' I said quietly, but with a sharpness which silenced her. 'I don't pretend to be the perfect mother. I never was. It never came easily to me, and is it any wonder? You all know how Ariana was conceived... But if you think I would ever intentionally expose her to the... the *thing* her father is...'

'I'm not saying you don't love her, I'm just saying—'

'That's enough,' Ralph interjected, looking a bit ill. 'Fee... I'm sorry but Bella's right. We looked for her for years... All of us. We know how we found them, how Lychen found them... It was Ariana's Twitter account, Ariana's photo on Instagram. It had nothing to do with Bella. What you're saying, it doesn't make any sense...'

'I do understand, you know,' I said softly, speaking just to her now. 'I get why you're grasping. You don't have any control over this thing between me and Ethan. It would drive anyone mad. He's *your* husband. What he and I have... it's born out of something unnatural, heinous even. But while he's here there's nothing I can do to break it.'

Bella. Don't do this.

'So we'll go,' Felix said, simply. She scowled, knowing that she was getting what she wanted but that it had come at the price of the leverage she supposedly had over me.

I have to. It's time. We could never carry on like this.

You aren't going to be able to love Ralph. Not like he loves you. Not like you love me. You know that, right?

I have to try. I need him. And she needs you. We don't belong together, Ethan. Not really.

He didn't respond. We didn't look at one another as Felix got to her feet heavily and gestured to Ethan. After a few moments, he followed her. We listened to their footsteps plodding upstairs. I stood and moved as quickly as I could into the new laboratory, busying myself with the newest computer I'd set up at the end of the newest work bench. I was right. I knew I was right. Ethan knew I was right. If I loved him, it was only for the safeness he represented, the comfort he'd provided during the darkest times. There was nothing natural between us, not really. It was a science experiment gone wrong. That was it. Robots couldn't love. Not really. That is what I repeated in my head as I listened to the muffled footsteps, the sounds of packing. Those were the words I repeated a few hours later, as the van growled to life in the driveway. And all the while I heard *his* voice, his snaking hiss slithering through my head and around my throat: *I saw you. I know you. It takes a monster to love their counterpart.*

And then Ethan was gone, and every scar within my body ripped itself apart all over again.

February, 2020

Life takes on a strange, impatient sort of quality in the Manor. I check in with the key players of my Youth Guard regularly – Karl, who ensures the careful misfiling of some incriminating memoir pages belonging to his minister master. Bette, who ingeniously misinterprets her charge's requests during a conference in Amsterdam and lands him and several others in a compromising position involving the red light district and a lot of marijuana. And Eve, of course, my deepest tree root, my brightest star. She is the one upon which everything hinges. She goes about her unravelling of Shona Metcalfe meticulously, moving slowly from the misplacement of minor items to altering scheduled appointments. She calls me to watch the more significant incidents, and I try as hard as I can to emulate her cool gaze as she hovers in a doorway, watching Shona stammer confusedly into the phone after missing another meeting with her charity secretary. Still, it takes a long time. She looks at Eve through a narrowed gaze, asks her to double check her appointments and inform her each morning of every single one. Eve observes her wondering out loud to her plump-cheeked husband whether Eve has 'gone wrong' somehow with her scheduling. He assures her, with the air of not entirely listening, that it is impossible.

This is good, I assure Eve, in turn.

She is questioning me instead of herself.

But that just shows that she is coming undone. She knows that you don't make mistakes. She is clutching at straws.

After she misplaces a budget schedule and spends a fruitless two hours searching for it one Tuesday afternoon, Shona asks Eve to bring her a gin and tonic. Eve makes it a double. She places it on the table next to a photo of Shona's daughter, Leanne. Shona's eyes linger on the girl as she takes up the glass. She wonders out loud if she has told Eve about poor Leanne. Eve lies that she does not recall her doing so. I withdraw at that point. Eve needs her wits about her, I tell myself. She does not need the distraction of my added presence in her mind.

Nova's wing recovers to the point that she is able to return to her nest in the attic and flies with only a slight list in her left wing. She bears the brunt of the pig-boy-head the least, blithely ignoring my and Ralph's warnings in favour of taking long, wandering flights over the countryside. She avoids the ARC, at least, and the areas surrounding it. The rest of us stay within the wall. For Dominic and Tess it isn't much of a change to their normal routine. Ralph busies himself perfecting the formula for NatApp, invigorated by the idea of having a plan of action just as he had been at twelve, when the victims in question were the helpless, extraordinary Project C children. We avoid the subjects of Mollitiam, relationships, Ethan… anything that threatens the tentative peace between us as he works and I wait for a woman I have never met to fall apart under the care of my favourite robot student.

As the winter wears on, news filters through of a new virus, a potential pandemic with widespread repercussions, possible lockdowns and quarantines. Ralph and Dom discuss it almost excitedly while Tess murmurs to me about the possibilities of a curative use for Mollitiam. I nod, smile, and try not to let any of them sense the frustration building like a wave tumbling higher and higher. Come on, Eve. We must act. We must act before the chances are taken. I have lived in lockdown for seven months already, I cannot bear any more. Not while Lychen holds the reins of the empire I helped build. Not while swine like Daniel command mutilation and pain in the name of science. I have waited long enough.

One morning I wake feeling the pressure of a million exhales crushing in on me at all angles. I lie in bed wondering what excuse I can make. The towns are full of Guard, and Ralph is more than slightly paranoid that Lychen will have placed several nearby on the alert for my movements. Tess and Dom have ensured our phones are clear of tracking software, but without Felix we don't have the same advantage against Lychen's tech team. I'm not convinced there are Guard masquerading as GHAP models lurking around the corners of Kendal or Ambleside waiting to throw a bag over my head and wrestle me into a nearby Humvee, but I can also see the stupidity in wandering among the enemy just for the sake of some fresh air.

I choose a pair of slim-fitting trousers and a white cashmere jumper which reminds me of Ariana. I pull it over my head and smooth it down, trying to remember whether it's because she borrowed it once – an image of Ariana hovers in my head, hair wild and legs spindly under the drape of my jumper – or whether it's because she liked the softness. I shut my eyes, remembering the warm pressure of her head on my belly, my chest, my shoulder... her hair clinging with static determination as she peeled away. I shake my head before my thoughts can swerve, as they so often do now when I think of my girl, to Shona. To her daughter, lost in a freak accident at only fourteen. Ana swims into focus in the mirror's reflection behind me as I pull my hair into a loose bun at the nape of my neck.

Come on, Bella. Remember what you used to tell yourself about being a robot?

'I never was a good robot, Mamma,' I murmur, quietly.

'I agree.' Dr Blake's voice comes from the open doorway of my room. He hovers there in his awkwardly stooped way, watching me carefully. His expression is torn between exasperation and pride. 'You still hear her, then?'

'Sometimes. You don't?'

'No,' he remarked casually, no envy in it. 'We said all we needed to to one another when she was alive. Clearly, perhaps, you did not.'

'Clearly.'

'What does she tell you now then, your Ana apparition?'

I smile and turn back to the mirror, meeting her brown, restless gaze.

'She says I need to focus. She says: Remember your ballet shows… Don't focus on how well you did last time, think only of your next performance.'

I glance back at him to catch the shadow of my words flicker across his face, mooning it into the old glaze of love he used to use whenever he looked upon her, even the times when she would take his tenderness and spit it bitterly back at him.

'If you take that pill you're thinking about taking,' he murmurs, 'you will be throwing your body out of action for the next twenty-four hours. What if that happens to be the time-frame in which Eve succeeds?'

I turn back to the mirror, my smile fading. Ana shimmers with steely indignation. Blake contrasts her in the corner of my eye – crooked, kindly, whole. I glance between the two of them, noticing their complete focus on me. They were never like that in the old days, of course. They could never exist for that long in a room together without sharing so much as a glance.

'We need to know what's happening at the ARC,' I snap, firmly, turning from the mirror to face Blake head on. 'We need to know what Daniel is doing. The scale of it. So we can work out what more we can do to stop it.'

'Nonsense,' Blake shakes his head, though his eyes twinkle indulgently. 'You're just bored. You're tired of the work on the NatApp. You've done your part, you've finished what you can. The rest of it is down to Ralph, now that Dom's fixed the extraction machine he needs. *You* just want to go outside.'

I sigh busily and step towards him, not looking at him anymore, the bottle of Mollitiam in my pocket. *I probably won't take one*, I think, knowing Blake hears me. He stands aside as I pass him, making an *on your head be it* noise even as, behind us both, Ana murmurs something conciliatory. I probably won't take one. But then again, if it allows me to break past Daniel's mysterious barrier... I'm wired to the movements of the house around me as I lace my walking boots onto my feet in the hallway downstairs. Blake's retreated to one of the upper rooms. Ana is flitting around her former office, the room that was Ariana's last year. Ralph's getting dressed in his bedroom, but I'm still half-expecting his voice to call from the stairwell: *'Where do you think you're going? Don't you realise how dangerous it is?'*

I open the door and breathe the ice-tinged air of the

mountains, eyes closed. I crunch forwards slowly, rolling my feet to feel every crumple of impacted ice. I hasten into long, purposeful strides towards the back gate. The call, when it comes, is so clear I turn around, my command ready on my lips, *Leave me a—* but there's no one there. I stop, frowning, listening. Snow drifts around me, silencing the air like a thousand white droplets of vacuum. I begin to turn back when it comes again.

Bella!

Eve, is that you?

Yes. It is early, I know, but I wanted to update you.

It's fine. What's happened?

Shona has spoken to Roger. She has said that she is thinking of stepping down from the charity because she is making too many mistakes. She drank too much last night and almost took too many anti-depressants.

How did he react?

He was kind to her, but he did not conceal his frustration as well as he thought. She saw it. She thinks she is a burden to him as well. He told her he would be coming to bed early to discuss further, but he was still working at two, long after Shona had fallen asleep. They had breakfast together this morning. She was fatigued and clumsy. It angered him. They argued about her drinking.

Good. Proceed with the directive. I will check in with you again once I have spoken to Tom.

Bella?

Yes.

Where will they take me afterwards?

Why do you ask?

I focus in and out on the sea of white dusting around me. Is she scared? Impossible. I must be projecting emotion onto her. It's this damn jumper.

I should prepare for my next assignment. I breathe a little more easily.

I will have you returned to my service, along with the other Youth Guard if all goes according to plan.

I feel the question hovering between us without her voicing it: *What if it does not?*

Trust me, Eve. The people who are in charge of your fate are men. Men are easy.

Yes. Alright.

She sweeps away. I look up at the gate in front of me and slowly turn my back to it. My hand clenches over the bottle in my pocket. I will need a second bottle, just in case. I walk quickly, lightly, back up to the house, my mind leaping ahead. I will wear the smart, fur-lined black coat that I wore to Maya's funeral. My new, emerald silk dress which matches my eyes. And shoes... Entering through the back door, I shrug my thick boots off quickly and leave them on the mat. My coat I hang on its usual peg. I don't spare them a second glance as I shake the soft specks of white from my hair and tread nimbly along the flagstones, feeling as if I'm shedding something else along with the practical clothes. That tinge of uncertainty in Eve's voice. The sprig of something that whispered of impossibility...

'Hey, what's going on? Have you been out?' Tess greets me from the doorway of the lab.

'Just in the garden. I heard from Eve. It's time.'

'Really? Wow, OK. You're going to need a lot of Serum X, right? I've got it all packed away in a case ready to go. And the Mollitiam tablets, how many of them do you think? Two, three bottles? Just in case?'

'Sure. You grab those and then come and pack.'

'Me? I thought it would just be you and Ralph—'

'I think you should come too, Tess. I may need the

back-up... and it'll do you good to get out of the Manor for a bit.'

'OK.'

I quickly make my way upstairs. Passing my room, I take the next staircase up to the third floor and head directly to Ralph's room. I rap loudly.

'Yeah?'

'We're going to London.'

'Seriously?' He pulls the door open. His hair is tousled and his shirt is open. He pulls it closed as he notices me staring, fumbling with the buttons.

'Yes. Metcalfe knows his wife is hanging by a thread. Tom has a route to Ariana and a plan to bring her out undetected. Bette's minister had to bribe his way out of the situation in Amsterdam, she overheard him blaming her for the misunderstanding. And Karl's master has already begun researching who to complain to about him. Here, you're all muddled,' I reach forward and deftly unbutton where he's fastened up his shirt lopsidedly. I feel the warm scent of his body flowing from him. His pulse twitches the skin of his thin, wiry chest as my fingers work swiftly over the soft twill of cotton. I'm not done before he catches my hands in his. I look up slowly. His deep brown gaze is raw without his glasses, the blaze in them is as different to the rabid, wolfish gleam of Lychen's as fire from ice, but I break the gaze, stepping away before he can capture me.

'We need to get ready.'

'Beast...'

'I've got a car on standby at a dealership nearby, I'll give the guy a call this morning, see if he can deliver so we can hit the road as soon as possible.'

'Can you just stop for one second and—'

'No, Ralph! We have to go! Don't you see, this is the window of opportunity. I can't leave Ariana any longer... Lychen's resolve wavers more every time I spy on him, I know exactly where all the extraction instruments are kept because he is obsessing over them, over whether to use them on her once and for all. That's just one of the options, there are more I can't even see, intentions he's guarding so deeply all I get from them is the sense of finality. It terrifies me, Ralph... It's like he knows that whatever path he chooses, all of them mean that very soon he won't have to deal with her ever again. We've been lucky he's held off deciding for so long, but whatever is stopping him isn't going to last much longer. We have to get her out of there while we've got this chance!'

'OK... OK. I know. You're right. But we've got to think it through, all the same. Those tablets of yours—'

'I told you, I know what I'm doing. I don't plan to use them unless I have to. And I've done nothing *but* think it through for the last seven months. This is everything that matters. We need to *go*.'

I turn around before I can catch the flash of hurt across his face, before I can register any more disappointment. There's no time for doubt, no time for gentling around feelings. I race back down the stairs and into my bedroom.

Ethan?

He stirs through the fog of sleep and is alert within seconds.

Yep.

It's time.

Right. I'll look up train times.

You sure?

I'll meet you at Euston. No arguments.

Will you tell Felix?

I'll have to ask her to take Daisy, she's with me at the moment. She'll ask why. I could lie...

No. We may need the back-up. But don't go into too much detail.

OK. I'll let you know what time my train gets in.

Good. And wear decent trousers, no holes or paint stains.

I'll wear the suit you made me order.

Good.

Suppose I better rustle up some underwear to go with it.

I smile and turn towards the wardrobe, reaching for the outfit I've had ready for several weeks. It occurs to me, as I lay the green dress on the bed and then reach for a few more options, that I haven't felt such a heady mixture of terror-tinged anticipation since the moment I plunged the syringe of untested Mollitiam into Nova's chest.

Autumn, 2019

I felt Ethan's absence like a missing limb, which was ironic as I grew physically stronger every day. The wall went up around the Manor, but no army of Guard came calling. I checked in with Tom and, when she was in an agreeable mood, Ariana, to keep tabs on Lychen's activities rather than re-attempt the mind-link. Tom told me Lychen appeared to be focusing on the impending launch of the GHAP, managing a pre-order list running into the tens of thousands. The Care Assistant programme ironed out some of the early malfunctions and continued to supply Guard Assistants to homes, care facilities and hospitals up and down the country and beyond. Ariana added that Lychen seemed 'weirder' than usual but failed to elaborate and became waspish when I asked her to.

Ralph and I settled into a comfortable co-existence that slowly evolved back into the spiky back-and-forth we'd had in our teens and twenties, though with a guardedness which papered over the things we did not talk about. He watched me but did not reach; I let familiar fondness whisper that it could become more. We carefully didn't mention what I'd done to Lychen's Guard and we also avoided the topic of Ethan and Felix, though I knew he was in regular contact with her just as I was with him. They had moved, as per Felix's wishes, to a small property in

Scarsby with a view of the sea. She had adopted a small terrier puppy. He had begun working as a painter and decorator once again and she had signed a contract to earn a comfortable wage as a tech guru. On the surface, they were an ordinary married couple with a dog and a beautiful home. At first I tried to keep my mind closed to him as much as I could, but he'd been gone less than a week before I drifted, half-asleep, across the ether of meaningless miles and took the hand that had been reaching with equal involuntary need. By the end of September, I could no longer sleep without the gentle touch of his mind to mine. We told no one. And, during the day, we tried our best. Ralph and I became closer. He and Felix fell apart.

Dr Blake continued to improve and his doctors soon began to discuss his returning home. Ralph approached me in the lab after a trip to the hospital one afternoon laden with brochures and leaflets. I turned as he placed them down on the workbench with a sigh.

'That sounds dramatic, what's going on?' I remarked, drily.

'Stair lifts and accessible walkways are what's going on,' Ralph leaned over the bench and ran his fingers through his hair. 'Why did Dad's room have to be on the third bloody floor? He's never going to agree to putting a bed in his old office.'

'No,' I agreed, leaving the genetic isolation machine whirring away and coming over to him. Now that my leg was finally out of plaster, my movements had returned to their old, familiar smoothness. I'd also taken to wearing jeans just because I could again, even though early autumn had brought an unseasonable mugginess outside the carefully-controlled lab.

'What about the old schoolroom? We could move the table out of there and put in a bed... It would be adjoining his old office. He'd like that.'

'Fine, but there's still the matter of an accessible bathroom, not to mention he's probably going to need a carer,' he glanced around with a lost, helpless look in his eyes.

'We can help... Or hire someone, if he needs it. It wouldn't be the first time the Blakes employed household staff,' I reminded him gently.

'Yes, I know... But that was different. Back then the most controversial stuff was happening at the ARC. I mean yeah, Ramona would have overheard a few odd things round the dinner table no doubt, but there would have been strict non-disclosure clauses in her contract like the ones the ARC employees used to sign... Now it's all here. Everything we have, everything we're trying to do. Then there's the cost of adapting everything, hiring someone.'

'Don't worry about that.'

'Beast, you said yourself that you're using your funds for this research. All this... I know I was sceptical but it's actually pretty amazing, what you've done in here... I'm not about to ask—'

'Ralph. It's Dr Blake. You don't need to ask.'

He stared at me until I put down the leaflet about rehabilitation for stroke patients and turned to him, eyebrows raised.

'What?'

'Nothing... Just... You still surprise me sometimes, Beast.'

'Well. The man took me in, Ralph. So did you in your way, even if you *did* spend the first few months plotting to get rid of me...'

He frowned. 'When did I tell you about that?'

I smiled and moved back over to my new machinery. I'd spent the morning showing Tess how to read the genetic code results. I'd already begun work on replication. We'd been discussing names for the finished product in drug form. She'd blushingly suggested naming it after me, but I'd declined. This research deserved a fresh start but with the gravitas of something meaningful. I'd come up with Mollitiam, Latin for resilience.

'How are your calculations coming for the Naturalisation Application?' I asked, mostly to move the conversation subject back onto safe ground.

'Good and bad. I've done some of the initial work. I think we should be able to administer chemical aides like with Serum X, stimulate memory. Of course the difficulty will be isolating the human side from the animal, make sure we're provoking human memory rather than animal...'

'You don't mean to restore the animal as well?'

'It's not really a priority at this point. Let's just start with putting one foot in front of the other before we enter any marathons, eh?'

'Fair enough. What else? You must have been able to learn some useful stuff from the tests you did on Nova?'

'A bit. Although her DNA was far from normal in the first place, thanks to Project C... And now it's completely melded with the bird... I don't know how we'd be able to separate them, frankly. Anything I can come up with is far too risky. It's possible we'd have more success with a newer hybrid, one whose transformation hasn't fully taken hold. We need more test subjects really...'

'Well, we know where they are...'

'We know where they *used* to be.'

'Come on, Ralph. Lychen's distracted with GHAP, Tom

says he's spending a lot of time in Paris and New York at the moment overseeing construction of new facilities there.'

'BFI is going international? Great.'

'They won't ever get it off the ground, not if we bring Lychen down first.'

'What about Daniel? He's back at Futura now, isn't he?'

'Yeah. And they've taken Bette away from him so I can't see what he's up to anymore, but from what I've gathered from Tom, he's fully concentrating on his new generation of hybrids now he's got the funding for it. It's a big facility and the security isn't anything like the Beaumont's. A couple of wigs, contact lenses and lab coats, we'd blend right in...'

'And how exactly do you propose we blend right out again with a couple of hybrids in tow?'

I shrugged. 'We could take a couple of little ones.'

He smiled lopsidedly. 'You're not serious.'

'No,' I smiled back. 'Took your mind off stair lifts and bathroom renovations though, didn't it?'

'Yeah,' Ralph's face clouded over once again. 'I'd better go and look up some of this stuff online. The doctor said Dad should be ready to come home by the end of next week.'

'That's a good thing, Ralph,' I reminded him, pushing a little steel into my voice.

'I know. I know. And he does seem OK, most of the time... But sometimes when he's grasping for a word or can't quite grip a cup of water... I wonder if... Well, it doesn't matter now.'

'You wonder if I did the right thing, bringing him back?'

'I wonder if it's what he would have wanted. If he'd

known that this would be his life.'

'He's getting better, Ralph. When are you next due to talk to the doctor?'

'Friday.'

'Why don't you let me do it? I was going to visit him then anyway. I'll get an idea of exactly what he should be able to do and what we can work towards, how much we need in terms of help and equipment. And I'll talk to the old man himself, I'm sure he'll have some ideas too, knowing him. You know it's easier for me to talk to him...'

He looked at me for a long time, a wealth of emotions tumbling across his tired face. Then he sighed, pulled his hand through his hair once again and shrugged.

'Yeah. OK. You're right. The most I get are a couple of sentences and then he's too knackered to make any sense... It's better you talk to him. And the doctors.'

I waited, sensing a 'just...' but though he opened his mouth, the addition never came.

Friday

The night air danced tentatively across my skin as I stood in front of the open window. September's heatwave of sticky close evenings and blistering days had intensified to the point that I'd reluctantly relinquished my jeans once again for floaty dresses and skirts. The lab with its air conditioning unit had become the Manor's most popular room – even Dom had sloped in earlier today, pillow in hand, hair sticking up with peaks of sweat, mumbling that he was just going to chill here for a bit because all his computers had over-heated upstairs. He'd promptly lain down on the floor at the back of the room where we'd marked out an area for rodent cages and fallen asleep for three hours. He'd still been snoring when I'd left for the hospital.

Tonight, however, the oppression had broken and there was finally a hint of coolness among the insistent press of warmth. I held out my arms. The scars were less visible now and, when I met my own eyes in the reflection of the glass, I had to look closely to see the line of the scar running along my cheek. Tess and I had been examining my resilience levels for the past month and they had slowly begun rising over the last week. The difference was slight, but encouraging after the dip I'd experienced following Lychen's visit.

I turned away from the window, drawing the blind down only partially so that it didn't obstruct the soft flow of air. My cotton nightdress fluttered over my body as I stretched. I'd hiked five miles over moorland and round two lakes today after my trip to the hospital, Nova flying overhead, a joyful blur reflected in the iron-blue water. I'd spoken to Eve, who was establishing herself in the household staff of the Prime Minister, much to my delight. I'd spoken to Bette and Karl. I'd even touched on the gossamer thread to Lychen, though I'd immediately been met with a strange, white-noise buffer. I'd hung around long enough to detect a whiff of that same drug he'd been using to mask his journey here a few weeks earlier. He must have found a way to strengthen it because I couldn't penetrate past the barrier. Still, my resilience levels were lower than normal. I had time to grow them and, in the meantime, it certainly wouldn't hurt to allow him to think he had resolved the issue.

There was no knock at the door. One moment I had half-turned from the window towards my bed, the next there was Ralph. He stood in the doorway, chest heaving, eyes unreachable behind the dark gleam of his glasses. I froze. My entire body flooded with adrenaline, recognising a possible threat, battling itself into readiness to bolt, to fight. *Stop. It's Ralph. It's just Ralph.* I blinked and made myself look at him properly. He was wearing plaid pyjama bottoms and an ancient T-shirt he'd bought at a concert back in 2002. He held his mobile phone in his hand. And then I knew.

'When?'

'An hour ago. Another stroke. It was instant, they said... He didn't... He never suffered—'

I opened my arms. He rushed forward, crumpling into my body like a child. He shook, trembling into me with a thousand tiny bolts which I absorbed and held until I could hold them no longer.

I saw him today. I should have stayed. I could have saved him. It's my fault—

No, Beast.

I'm sorry, I'm sorry. You don't want to talk like this but I can't hold it. I can't stop—

It's OK.

No, it's not.

No, it's not.

I don't know how long we stood there, shaking like twinned trees caught in an unexpected, brutal summer storm. I don't know when we crept, exhausted, into my bed. Who was the first to fall asleep. Who held on the longest. Who ached the hardest. It didn't matter, that night. The petty arguments, our strange, lopsided, undefined relationship. None of it mattered, anymore. We loved him; he was gone.

February, 2020

Nova does not need Bella to tell her she is in a hurry. She observes her strange walk, full of both anger and hesitation, most of the way across the snowy garden until she comes to an abrupt stop and turns. Nova doesn't need Bella to stand in the spot where she knows she can be seen from the hole under the eaves. But she does anyway and so Nova swoops down to her, though she would rather sleep a little longer. She has been out late.

'I'm heading to London,' Bella says quickly, when Nova lands in front of her. Her wing still drags with landings, especially from an awkward, straight down drop. Nova nods, so that she knows she understands.

'It's time,' Bella continues, pulling her coat around her as her breath puffs in white blooms in front of her face. 'You know the plan. It will mean Ariana is coming home, I hope. Will you be OK with that?'

Nova blinks slowly. She knows why Bella would ask such a thing. Last time she saw the girl she tried to rip her heart out. But she'd also given in to the impulse to try and do that to Bella once or twice, back when the cage had provided a safe barrier, hadn't she?

'Fine,' she mutters, eventually.

'I just wanted to double check,' Bella glances back towards the house where a pattern of lights are on. 'Dom

213

will stay here while we're gone... He's going to try and run the first batch of NatApp through his machine. Ralph's managed to tweak a few things to speed things up. There should be an initial batch ready within the next few days... just in case all this leads to us freeing the hybrids sooner rather than later. And you... Are you still...?'

'Yessss,' Nova lets the word elongate, so she knows she means it. Bella looks at her curiously, her impatience to be on the road momentarily overcome with something akin to disappointment. Nova cocks her head.

'It's untested still. Ralph's pretty confident about it but we don't know for sure if it's safe...'

Nova waits. She knows there is more brewing beneath the simmer of surface beauty. Bella swallows.

'And if it *did* work... you'd lose your wings, your feathers. Everything that makes you unique.'

'A freak,' Nova replies, shortly.

'You wouldn't be able to fly.'

'I fly... before.'

'As a child. Project C... you know what happened to the others. None of them retained their abilities.'

'You don't... know that.'

Bella smiles a little and shrugs. 'Well. It's a big gamble, but it's up to you, of course.'

Nova nods. She feels the press of the ARC behind them and glances towards it, feeling the usual loom of Daniel's proximity. She doesn't want to stay down here on the ground, she feels the need to be aloft, hidden, buoyed by a million touches of frigid sky. She looks back at Bella, sensing hesitation tumbling from her body even as she shivers in the icy air.

'What?'

'I just... I wondered if you could sense anything this

time? You know, how you did with Lychen. You felt him coming. You sensed Daniel too, long before we did. Can you feel danger ahead, for me and the others?'

Nova makes her soft, smiling coo. 'Not East. Danger here. Daniel,' she stares back towards the ARC.

'Good,' Bella smiles. She reaches out and, when Nova doesn't move away, she strokes her soft, cool hand over the hair and feathers of her head, cupping her cheek.

'Stay away from guns, Nova.'

Nova doesn't reply, but she rests her head sideways on her friend's hand for a few moments in acknowledgement. Then the bird instincts shake her free, jumbling the mixture of contentment and fondness with the staccato rhythms of the air, the shuddering of the wind in the trees, the ever-present lurk of horror behind her. Bella smiles, turns and walks away. Nova watches her go into the house and then launches herself up into the sky. She wheels a few circuits of the rooftop before settling on a tiled area overlooking the driveway. She watches the large, unfamiliar car as Ralph loads bags into the back of it, his movements jerky with tension. She watches Tess arrive, go back into the house, climb into the car and out again, back into the house and then, a few minutes later, back to the car. Finally Bella re-emerges and they all swarm towards her like mosquitoes drawn to the throb of a warm-blooded body. Bella curves neatly into the driver's seat and Nova watches as the car crawls slowly over the shingle and out onto the road. She stays there on the roof long after the scent of fuel has dissipated, huddled in her wings, cold but not yet too cold to move. The press of foreboding lurks from behind. And beneath her a small machine churns and shudders its way to a future of being ordinary, unfreakish... wingless.

February, 2020

Bella drives with nimble, precise movements, handling the rented MPV as if she's owned it her entire life. Ralph watches her from the passenger seat, trying not to be too obvious about it. Behind him Tess sits, her thumbs batting rapidly against the screen of her phone. Occasionally she looks up, throwing anxious glances out of the window at the countryside. Ralph doesn't blame her. It feels like years since he left the Manor. He actually got a bit of a heart flurry as they passed through the wide, automatic gates of the entranceway. It's that damn wall, he thinks. Putting it up felt safer, and yet he never used to get palpitations whenever he made the short trip out of its boundary to town or the hospital.

'Are you sure you don't want me to drive?' He says, mostly to swerve his own mind away from the anxious bubble waiting in his throat.

'Yes,' Bella replies, neatly navigating around a patch of ice on the road. It's not snowing anymore, but the countryside is awash in white and grey around them. Theirs is the only car on the road for several miles and Bella takes the corners slowly, methodically, eyes flickering constantly from side to side and into the rearview mirror. She's not just checking for ice, Ralph realises with a swallow that catches bulkily in his throat.

'No one's following us,' he mutters, glad his voice sounds more assured than he feels.

'No, I think you're right,' Bella murmurs. 'But we can't be too careful with that shitbag living round the corner.'

'Well that's why we rented this thing, isn't it,' Ralph replies. 'And, like I said, I'm more than willing to take over if you like.'

'And I may be a teeny tiny useless little woman, but I'm more than capable of driving a seven-seater, thanks very much.'

'That's not what I meant,' Ralph glares at her. She knows it's not, of course. He thinks she does, anyway. He hopes. But he seems to be getting everything wrong with Bella lately. Ralph shuts his eyes, still seeing the alarm in her eyes when he'd reached for her this morning. He clears his throat, swallows heavily and tries again.

'I just meant if you need to do any, I dunno, *mind-foraging* or whatever. Surely that's part of the plan, isn't it?' He glances at her. Her eyes remain trained on the road, twin glimmers of clearest, brightest emerald. He can barely see the scar that runs along her face now, close as he sits. She wears a coat he doesn't recognise, a black wool with an expensive-looking fur trim. Her hair is gathered behind her ears, tumbling among the fur and down her back in the way that always makes him want to gather handfuls and bring it to his face. Stop, he tells himself. Focus. Now is not the time. Today is not the day. Today, he adds bitterly, is never the day.

'We're not even out of Cumbria yet,' she murmurs. 'But if anyone contacts me, I'll be sure to let you know. Thank you.' She glances at him briefly and smiles and his entire body gives a great shuddering echo of contentment. So much for focusing.

217

'So what's the plan again, exactly?' Tess pipes up from the backseat. 'Are we picking up Ethan and heading straight for, what, Westminster?'

'No,' Bella replies, carefully. 'We won't intercept Metcalfe until Eve gives me the signal. We'll check into a hotel – I've made reservations at a fairly central one – and wait there until we know more. The ideal scenario is that Tom gets Ariana out of the Beaumont and to us without raising suspicion. Then Eve, Bette and Karl can continue their work without the risks associated with us rushing them.'

'And what if Tom does expose himself?'

'It's the more likely scenario. Lychen will realise the Youth Guard are compromised and I will have to tell them all to go into hiding as best they can – they should all have a contingency plan for that which they'll have adapted according to their current situations. So it is imperative that Eve does all she can before Tom makes his move.'

'And what happens when the PM realises that his wife's Primary Guard has assisted in her breakdown?'

'That's where I come in. I will get my audience, I will persuade him and whoever else I need to that the Guard need to be recalled and signed over to me, along with the Beaumont facility and everything within it.'

'That's a pretty tall order, Beast...'

'Lucky I have such stellar powers of persuasion and a few aces up my sleeve then, isn't it?'

Ralph sighs and looks away. 'You make it sound so simple. But there's a hundred things that could go wrong... What if Metcalfe doesn't blame Eve? What if you can't get to him? What if something happens with Tom and he can't get Ariana out or Lychen decides to move her or, I don't know, countless other little circumstances which could arise...?'

Bella sniffs, her small nose twitching only slightly. She reaches a junction and slowly curls the large car around the corner and onto the main road. They begin to pick up speed as the grey-white fields and hills become interspersed with smudges of green. Ralph turns down the heating in the car and removes the tartan scarf from his neck, feeling pinkish and sticky.

'The main issue is going to be timing. It's so delicate with Eve and Shona. Anything could tip her over the edge... or she might not fall apart at all. Or it could, as you say, end up being nothing to do with Eve... In that case, Eve has been instructed to implicate herself. She knows what she needs to do. And she's good. Trust me. She'll come through for us.'

'And then what happens?'

'We bring Ariana home. Lychen is arrested. We move onto Daniel and expose his hybrid experimentation. Nova can help with that, now her speech is so much clearer.'

'She's agreed to that?'

'She will, when she understands it's to bring about Daniel's undoing.'

'What'll you do with the Guard, if you do manage to get them all signed over to you?' Tess asks, her voice thoughtful.

'It depends.'

'On?'

'A lot of things. Their families. Who they were before they were Guard. The vast majority were violent criminals, of course... Ralph here thinks they *all* deserve a chance at returning to themselves, their former consciousnesses.'

'I just think that everyone deserves a second chance. We shouldn't play judge and jury with people's lives, their ability to make choices for themselves...'

'No, we should absolutely discredit the BFI and then go about reawakening murderers and rapists...'

'I didn't say that,' Ralph snaps.

'What then? Put them all down like Delta and the other two?'

'No. Put them back in prison. Let them serve the remainders of their life sentences in the full knowledge that they will never be free.'

'And let the problems of prison overcrowding and underfunding continue...'

'What would you do then, Bella?' Tess interjects again as Ralph opens his mouth angrily. Bella remains thoughtful, bringing the car up to a roundabout and indicating left, taking a road signposted simply: The South.

'Like I said, it depends... I don't agree with the premise of the Guard application, but I can't deny that it has had its uses. We wouldn't even have a plan to bring Lychen down if it wasn't for the Youth Guard. If I were given control over the entire BFI enterprise, I would argue that there is a use for the Assistants, in just that role. Assisting. Not spying, not bodyguarding, not slavery. No fielding out to the public in exchange for millions of pounds. Just fully-consented assistance for innovative, *ethical* scientific enterprise.'

Ralph snorts and glances in the rear view mirror. Tess is staring at Bella with an expression of rapt admiration, her phone drooping from her loose fingers. He rolls his eyes and switches his gaze back to the window. Opening his mouth, he's about to ask whether Bella is also planning to keep some of the cuter hybrids as pets when the MPV swerves suddenly to the left. Ralph reaches reflexively for an overhead handle as he turns to Bella in alarm. She's staring straight ahead, face rapidly losing colour. She brakes sharply and pulls the car into a layby. They bump unevenly over the uneven surface and come to a stop.

'You need to take over,' Bella says, her voice straining. She turns to Ralph. Her eyes are strange, the usual crystalline green clouded like ink poured into water.

'Is it…?

'Tom. There's a problem with Ariana.'

Autumn, 2019

The funeral was small, private. Ralph and I decided that it
would be better that way. The last thing we needed was an
ambush from Lychen or Daniel. It was by invitation only at
a local crematorium. Nothing like the large Catholic service
we'd had for Ana, packed with unknown Italian relatives
who had pinched Ralph's cheeks and peered curiously at
me. Even so, the small ceremony felt flooded with old
familiar faces from the ARC. Bert, now stooped and bald,
came bearing the distinctly catty smell I remembered from
childhood. His face lit up with a disproportionate delight
when he spotted me and he fell upon me for a slightly-too-
enthusiastic hug from which I had to be rescued by Ralph.
A white-haired walking-sticked Ramona, on the other
hand, embraced Ralph as if he were a long-lost son while
not sparing me even a flicker of a glance. Felix and Ethan
sent flowers and apologies. Ralph said he didn't mind that
they hadn't come, but I noticed a marked decline in his
phone conversations with Felix afterwards. Ethan
confessed to me that evening that they had had a long,
angry row about it. She had wanted to come alone, he had
argued that they both would or neither. *It's a bloody mess,
Bella. I know she can't be happy like this. No one would be.*

*Give it time. She may come round. How is the new
puppy?*

Small and bitey.

Ariana, too, was another reluctant absentee. I'd spoken to her the night after it happened, when my heart still ached with rawness and my body shivered with the warm indent Ralph had left in my bed.

But you said he was getting better!

He was. I spoke to him just yesterday about the plan for him coming home. We'd begun putting up extra handrails around the Manor, converting the old schoolroom into a bedroom, ordered a new bed—

So what the hell happened, Mother? Why is he dead?

He just… He just died. He had another stroke. It happens—

It happens? You sound like you're giving a report! I don't know why I'm surprised, I mean it's you.

I couldn't speak. I could barely breathe.

Mother? Mum? Are you there? When's the funeral?

How dare you.

What?

How dare you say I don't care. You know nothing about how I feel. This man raised me, Ariana. He took me in, he taught me everything I know and he never gave up on me. He gave up the chance of a major breakthrough when he could have tested my blood and raised me like some science project or shipped me back to the D'accourts. Instead he threw it away so I would feel safe. He was my father.

OK, OK. Jeez.

I know it sounds… I know I can come across as cold sometimes but you can't just assume… it's not fair, Ariana.

OK! Sorry! Wow.

The silence was heavy, laden with all the unsaid.

The funeral is next Wednesday at Heather Lake

Crematorium, but I doubt very much Lychen will allow you to attend.

I could make him. I could just go anyway...

And end up being escorted out by the Guard, kicking and screaming? Great idea. Perfect way to pay your respects, Ri.

She sighed. I could feel her frustration, but I could also feel her reasonability crowding in, telling her that I was making sense, that even though the rebellious teen part of her raged to disagree with me on the principle of it being me, there was nothing to gain by doing so. She was growing up. She was growing away. It tugged painfully at the roots of my soul like a deep, unreachable toothache.

OK. I won't come. I'm sure Ralph doesn't want me there anyway.

He'd be fine. He doesn't blame you.

I don't know why. It was my fault.

Dr Blake was already at risk of a stroke, Ri. The doctors said his blood pressure was awful, he would have had one sooner or later. It may have been a coincidence.

It wasn't, Mum. I felt it. I felt it when I did it to him just like I felt it when I ripped your face open.

Well. Some wounds heal and others don't.

Yours?

Healing. Resilience, you know. How are your lessons with Reuben going?

Her attention swerved sharply. I sensed a worry, a pit of tension and resentment which, for once, was not directed at me.

OK. I guess. We're working on psychic ability. I've always found it easy enough to tell what people are feeling but Lychen wants me to be able to do more than that, to get into people's heads and control what they're thinking or something.

Ah. I suspect you have me to thank for that.

Well Reuben's not a lot of help... He was with the other stuff, but with this he keeps saying that it's a level he has no experience with. He's helped me see intentions from greater distances and focus on people to work out what they're feeling even when they're not in front of me. But the mind control thing is just... I can see why I'd need to do it, why it might come in handy if I'm trying to find out stuff, but I'm starting to wonder why I'm actually doing it. Why I'm doing any of this. For this guy who is my dad but can't even look at me half the time. I haven't even had a conversation with him since the last time he came to 'test' me.

Well, you can always leave.

You just said Lychen would come after—

I meant he wouldn't let you go to Dr Blake's funeral. He wouldn't want you to come to me. You're too powerful. But he promised me that if the time came that you wanted to leave, he would let you go.

And you believed him?

Well. Perhaps not entirely. But like you said, you could make him. If you really wanted to. You could do anything, Ariana, if you really wanted to. The question is, what do you want to do?

I don't want to go back to Cumbria. It makes me think of nightmares and being lied to and... feeling like I was falling into a big blank hole...

I understand. So...?

I don't know. Sometimes I feel like I could be happy here, if there were other kids about in actual real life rather than just talking to them online. Other times I just feel like this whole place is full of people staring at me like I'm a science experiment they're terrified is about to explode. I just want to feel normal.

I tried very hard not to let her sense my ironic nod, but I knew she had.

Yeah, yeah. I know you tried to make me think I was normal. I didn't get it then. I suppose I sort of do now.

Does that mean you forgive me?

And again came that weariness, that sad, grown-up distance between us. She wasn't so much angry with me as disappointed that I just didn't understand.

No. I get why you lied but you shouldn't have done it. I was never normal, it would have been better for me to know that earlier. Maybe then I wouldn't have... it wouldn't have all flooded out and Dr Blake—

I told you. It wasn't your fault. No one blames you. And he didn't suffer.

My words snagged on something and she couldn't stop the line of thought from taking off. She shouldn't have needed to ask. She knew she shouldn't, but she did anyway.

You said you saw him that day?

Yes?

Did... what did you talk about?

I didn't euthanise him, if that's what you're asking, Ariana.

I never said that! But the relief was immediate, a great swathe of feeling over the top of everything else. Not just at what I'd said but that I hadn't lashed out angrily again.

We didn't speak long. He was tired and my mind-link abilities haven't been as strong lately. Mostly it was about where to put a downstairs bathroom. Whether we'd be able to fit his old bed in the old schoolroom. He was matter-of-fact about it all. Cheerful, almost.

Except his eyes, of course. The sad, sagging souls of blue that hadn't so much as pierced as shuddered lumpenly into my heart. I hadn't been able to help but hear them, beneath the sanguine rumble of logic. *I want to go now.* He hadn't voiced it, couldn't bear the thought of asking me, couldn't fathom the pain it would cause me. He hadn't asked. Of course he hadn't. But I'd heard him, all the same. *Let me, Bella.*

What d'you mean about your abilities not being so strong at the moment?

It's complicated, but basically my resilience levels prioritised attacking Lychen. Since then, they've taken a dive as my other enhanced genes recover from what happened in the summer. I have to work harder for the rest of it.

But we're talking easily enough now.

Because you're getting stronger, Ariana. Stronger than me.

Did you find out about the Project A stuff? Dr Blake told me… back in his old office when I was… when the emptiness was in charge. He said that your resilience will run out one day.

It's OK. I know. I'm on it.

Her attention caught elsewhere and I knew she was slipping away.

I've got to go.

Ariana – the mind thing. It's the same as the link you can already do. Just listen for their intentions, let them come to you quietly, like a trickle. Don't push it. And when they're there in the palm of your mind, you whisper. It's about suggestion but you have to be subtle, otherwise he'll hear you and he will be furious.

Who? Lychen? You think I should try it on Lychen?

Not at first. Practice. But once you've mastered it… no one is off limits. Remember that. It could mean everything.

OK. I will. Thank you, Mum.

And I felt it, as she left, that shimmer of a Ri who was no longer mine. Beyond the little girl who had tumbled cartwheels on the way home from school and cried in my arms at the end of *Charlotte's Web*… Beyond the dark creature who'd torn the scar onto my face with the power of her hatred. A new Ariana. Stronger. Older. Beyond me.

I should have been proud.

February, 2020

Ralph steers the car around a slow-moving lorry just as the rain begins to patter against the windscreen, slicing sideways from the larger vehicle's slipstream. He glances at me as I turn away, staring straight ahead.

How many?

Seven. There were only two yesterday when I checked. I will monitor their shift patterns and see if there is a window of opportunity to intervene.

Good. What can you deduce from this development, Tom?

If I shut my eyes for long enough and ignore the tremble of the car, the tap of Tess's fingers on her phone, the gnawing grind of Ralph's teeth, I could almost be back in that bright spacious classroom with my obedient, blank-faced army of teenagers.

Security has been tightened as a response to something. It could be that either Lychen is planning to take action with Ariana...

Or...

Or he knows you are coming.

Which is more likely?

It is impossible to deduce. But I shall stay alert to any indication of either scenario that I may come across. There is no evidence to suggest that he suspects my involvement

229

yet.

Good. Go carefully, Tom.

I will.

'Well?' Ralph cannot stay silent any longer. He glances over more than it is safe to do so as the speedometer climbs into the nineties.

'The security on Ariana has been stepped up. It's probably nothing, but it could potentially hinder Tom. And it will increase the chances of his detection.'

'Why the hell would Lychen have put extra people on her?'

'Tom thinks it's either because he's decided to take some sort of action – move her? I don't know… Wake her up himself? Maybe the security is for his own protection? But Tom didn't actually say that he'd seen Lychen anywhere near her…'

'What do *you* think it means, Beast?'

'I honestly don't know,' I frown at the smear of a stranger's fingerprints as the windscreen blots with condensation. 'Probably it's nothing. But it seems too coincidental to have happened just when we began the journey to London.'

'I agree.'

'It doesn't mean he knows we're coming… Remember he's got Daniel round the corner from us. It's very possible he's got Guard or even maybe a couple of fully-trained hybrid creatures sneaking around the perimeter of the Manor, reporting on our movements…'

'So he'd know we'd gone out, not that we're halfway to London…'

'Mmm,' I sigh, looking out of the window.

'So…'

'So nothing. We go ahead. We're too close to change

our minds now. We'll pick up Ethan and continue to the hotel. It's not like we're heading straight for the Beaumont and Lychen still has no idea that Tom's mine. He's probably just taking precautions. It will be fine.'

'If you say so,' Ralph mumbles, his knuckles unclenching a little on the steering wheel. I shut my eyes again and smooth over the frisson of worry Tom's call has sent around my chest. Instead I think about Ethan. About his smile, the feel of his large, warm hand on mine. It sinks over and around me like soft sweet-smelling blanket. It will be fine.

Everything happens incredibly quickly once we reach Ethan. We turn a corner and he's there, a beautiful pillar of reassurance standing just outside the station. Ralph pulls the car into a taxi rank and Ethan clambers into the back next to Tess. I barely say a word, none of us do, but I feel his closeness like a missing organ suddenly replanted. Ralph's jaw continues to chew on itself as he pulls away from the station and makes his way south towards the hotel. It's barely after four but the sky is already mottled with darkness. The city swarms with bodies, cars, noise. I shut my eyes and delve into the links of my Youth Guard. Eve is so close now I feel her breathing as she brings Shona her second gin and tonic of the afternoon and watches her stare into space. Tom stands concealed in a window alcove in the South building of Beaumont, his heart beating rhythmically as he observes the two Guard posted outside the lab containing my unconscious daughter. He turns his head and acknowledges the others, patrolling the corridor. He moves away from the alcove and adjusts the tray of surgical instruments he holds, walking briskly past the

Guard without looking at them.

I cycle through the others more rapidly, though I linger for a moment or two with Karl as he is interrogated by his frazzled-looking master about the whereabouts of yet more manuscript pages. Bette watches a conference from the corner of a large boardroom. And the others; they all have varying reports as they feel my feather-light touch on their minds. Several have been placed in academic settings, one of them, Liz, is a tutor for a wealthy family in the North East. She has already made several errors with her charges, some of them quite ingenious. Just yesterday, she tells me, she made the eldest child stay at home and complete an algebra test rather than take her to her scheduled gymnastics class after 'misinterpreting' a comment from the child's maths teacher. The parents, who paid more than twenty pounds an hour for the private gymnastic tuition, lodged a formal complaint with BFI the same evening. Many of the other Youth have also triggered complaints. I'm not sure how many have reached Lychen's ears, but he has not yet taken steps to investigate as far as I am aware. I do not delve into his mind today, though I am sorely tempted. The risk of him sensing how close I am is too great.

It is only once we've arrived at the hotel and I am carefully hanging my clothes neatly in the large generic wardrobe of my large generic room that Tom returns to my mind, his words coming in quick staccato.

The two on patrol have gone to replenish their nutrition levels. I am going in.

Bring me.

I sink onto the large double bed and shut my eyes. Tom has another tray, this time with a bag of liquid nutrition of a similar type to that which they feed Guard

232

people under transition. I hear his voice as clear as if I am speaking myself as he tells the Guard on the door to the laboratory that he has been instructed to deliver nutritional supplies. They allow him inside without a glance. The room is as brightly lit as I remember from Lychen's memories. A Guard person stands at ease next to the bed. Ariana lies under a thin blanket, pale-faced, wearing a plain long-sleeved T-shirt. One hand is wired with a drip, more lines and tubes disappear under the blanket. Tom places the nutrition bags on a tray next to her and assesses the lines hooked up to her.

'Beast? You alright?'

I blink and look up. Ralph is standing in the doorway of my room, frowning at me. Half his hair is sticking up and I feel a sudden rush of irritation at his hovering, dithery stance.

'Tom's with Ariana. He's assessing whether he can get her out,' I say, my voice quiet but undeniably terse. I have to pull my mind entirely away from Tom while I speak because I can't risk him being distracted by anything going on at my end, especially now.

'Oh. Well I just spoke to Dom on the phone, he says the NatApp is consolidating in greater quantity than expected, so the machine is only producing five mil in liquid form per dose.'

'OK...' My mind is only half on what he's saying. He frowns as he picks up on my keenness for him to leave.

'It just means we'll probably only get four doses out of this early batch. Five if we're lucky.'

'Right.'

'And unfortunately we just don't have the resources to make more right now. It should work, I'm way more confident about this than I was the X, but we could really have used—'

'Sorry, Ralph, can this wait? I really need to check on what's happening with Tom…'

'Oh. Right. Of course.'

'It's just time-sensitive, you know? The Naturalisation stuff, it can wait. Ariana's the priority today.'

'Yep, it's fine. I get it.' He holds his hands up, though I can see the frustration there. It only irritates me more.

'If you let me mind-link with you too, you'd know about all this,' I mutter as he turns away. He freezes. 'I'm just saying, it would be easier for you to know when there's something you shouldn't interrupt—'

'Look, forgive me for not wanting to join the host of voices competing for attention in your head, Beast. I've enough trouble doing it out here in the real world, thanks. Especially when you bring Ethan along for the ride…'

'Ethan and I have barely spoken a word to each other,' I stand up quickly. I can tell I'm not going to be reconnecting to Tom anytime soon, and I'll be damned if I'm going to sit like an admonished child for this argument.

'You don't need to!' Ralph bangs his fist on the dressing table. I don't flinch, though something dormant inside me, the part which sprang into action whenever Lychen's eyes clouded in anger or lust, stirs in warning. My muscles tense.

'I'm not blind, Bella. I'm not a fool. I knew he loved you just from the way he looked at you back in the summer when you were injured… And it might have taken me a little longer to admit it, but pretty soon after that I realised you loved him too. So maybe you'll do me the human decency of just telling the truth for once in your goddamn life. Is it him? Is it both of us?'

'I really wish we didn't have to do this right now,

Ralph...' I pass a hand over my eyes.

'Check then. Go see what's happening, I'll stand here quietly.'

I stare at him, but he holds my gaze with steady passion so, sighing, I shut my eyes and flit back to Tom. He's moving back across the lab, the Guard man watching him now, though not suspiciously.

Progress?

I was able to turn down the sedation without anyone noticing but I cannot stay, the Guard on duty has instructed me to leave the nutrition bag for the scheduled swap over. He is watching me. I must leave. They will be alerted once the sedation change is noticed. I estimate it will take three to four hours before she wakes entirely.

OK. Stay close to her.

I blink and look up. Ralph is still there, of course. I can't help but wish Tom had given me an excuse to shut down this conversation.

'Well?'

'He's turned down her sedation but can't stay to monitor her without raising suspicion. He thinks she will wake in three to four hours unless anyone notices the change sooner. We'd better hope they don't – we'll lose the chance to wake her up and Tom will be caught. The Guard know he was there at the correct time... We'll need Eve to make a move sooner rather than later. It'll have to be plan B...' I cross away from him to the wardrobe. I carefully pull out the emerald silk dress. Formal enough to make my access easy, fitted enough to keep all eyes on me.

'Do you remember the conversation we had, just before Dad... When we were talking about bringing him home?'

'What?' I turn irritably towards Ralph, still hovering

infuriatingly, his face a mixture of frustration and sadness.

'You said something about how I'd spent so long trying to get rid of you and I couldn't remember when I'd told you that...'

'Ralph... Seriously, can we not do this now—'

'You just said we have three to four hours...'

'Before Ariana is fully awake! I need to infiltrate the fucking government before then, remember?'

Eve? Plan B.

OK. I will keep you updated.

Ethan?

Here.

We're going in. Plan B. Go tell Tess, then change into something smart.

Roger that. All OK in there with Ralph?

Fine. If I don't kill him for trying to make me have a deep and meaningful conversation in the middle of a crisis.

Give me a signal if you need me to set fire to something.

'Why not now? If we fail tonight we could both end up getting arrested. We might not have another chance to talk about this!'

'Fine. Just say what you need to say, Ralph.' I turn to him angrily, feeling my eyes flash. His own eyes widen and he takes half a step back. I can tell I've scared him. I haven't been this honest with my emotions in front of him since the night Dr Blake died.

'I remembered, afterwards. I remembered when I told you. I wrote it in the card I sent you. Valentine's Day, 2006. When you had disappeared and I didn't know if I'd ever see you again.'

'I remember.'

'Do you? Because you've never mentioned it once.

236

Ever. Not when we met again in Cornwall, not last year when I saw you in London... not even during all these last few months where we've hung out, gone for walks, spent whole evenings together drinking wine... and even though Dad's gone and Nova was shot and there are hybrid heads coming over the wall, it's still been... Between us, I mean, things have been good. It feels like everything is exactly where it's supposed to be. Like it was when we were young... except... Except when I reach for you like I did this morning and you flinch with every atom of your body... and your eyes, they *shudder*...'

I watch him steadily as Blake's voice nags at the edge of my memory: You'll have to tell him the truth one day... He needs to know that you don't love him back. Don't let it come at the moment when you need him the most.

'I thought you understood. I thought you knew that I wasn't ready for anything physical, not after everything I went through with Lychen...'

'I thought I did too. Look, I'm not demanding anything like that, I'm not a total arse – I'm just saying that it's becoming more and more obvious that perhaps the old, *It's not you, it's me*, cliché isn't quite the whole truth. That maybe, actually, it *is* me.'

'Ralph, do you know what it's like to live a lie for so long that your body, your *soul* becomes immune to it? I used to make myself disappear. That's the only way I could cope with what I had to do... Not just what *Lychen* did, what *I* did. All those dark thoughts you have when you look at me and wonder. It's all true, Ralph. I played my part – I smiled, did my hair the way he liked it, let him hold me, reached for him... What I had to become, to pretend every single day that I was fine with it all, I was *with* him... There's only so much a person can take before it changes them.

There's only so many times they can disappear before parts of them stop coming back.

'He… he said to me, back in the summer when he came to the Manor, he said that I present a different version of myself to you. I don't know if that's true, but I'm beginning to wonder if that's the woman *you* love, Ralph. Because that girl, that silly nineteen-year-old who danced along, basking in the attention, leading two men along without knowing what she was risking… she's gone. And I can't bring her back, I can't just erase all the darkness and the memories of the last year, just as I can't switch off the flight-or-fight instinct when another man reaches for me…'

'Unless it's him,' Ralph's face has paled with my words, but there's still too much anger there. 'Everything you say makes sense, until I see you with Ethan. Over the summer when he'd help you walk. When you'd reach for his hand and just hold it, right there in front of all of us. I could tell you didn't even know you were doing it. And even now… Downstairs when we were waiting for the lift, he was standing just behind you and… yeah, you didn't say a word to each other but you just sort of leant backwards on him or into him, like he was a human cushion.'

'I did?'

'See, you don't even know you did. That's how easy it is between you. It's like he's an extension of yourself.'

'Well, the Guard connection—'

'Is bollocks. He's not a Guard person anymore, Beast. He hasn't *been* a Guard for seven months. He's as human as I am. So why's it still like that between you?'

'I don't know, OK? I don't know. I wish it wasn't. I wish he'd gone back to normal and that he and Felix had had their happy ever after. I wish that I felt about you the way you feel about me and that we could pick up where we left off all those years ago.'

He blinks at me sadly. 'And I wish I could believe you.'

Bella.

'I can't do this now. Eve's calling me, we need to get ready...'

Bella. It's done.

'I just want to know what happened to that card. The one I sent.'

'What the hell does that matter?'

'What happened to it, Bella?'

'I don't know, OK! I put it away. I couldn't deal with it, not just then. I was nineteen, living in the middle of a strange city on my own, in hiding, pregnant with *his* baby... I didn't have the head space to deal with your feelings on top of all the other shit happening to me.'

'Yeah. That's what I thought. OK then. Let's deal with the next crisis and shunt all this aside like we do every time. It doesn't matter, after all. It's only me.'

'I've *never* treated you like you don't matter!'

'Well maybe that's just how you make me feel. When you're not pretending. When you're actually being honest.'

His face is bright red and his fists are still clenched. I can feel Eve tugging on an edge of my mind, Tom on another. Ethan hovers, sensing my distress, longing to intervene. I turn away, sit back down on the bed and shut my eyes.

Eve?

It's done. I administered the dose. She did not question it.

Good. Wait until she is asleep...

...then raise the alarm. I know.

I will see you soon, Eve.

Yes. I am glad.

When I open my eyes, Ralph's gone. I breathe slowly, expecting relief, feeling only guilt, resentment and exhaustion. I'd finally told him the truth, finally voiced all the things that have lurked, unsaid, between us for so many months. Too little and, as Dr Blake had warned me, not so much too late, as spectacularly ill-timed. Worse than that, I don't even think he believed me.

Autumn, 2019

Reuben seemed to take the news of Dr Blake's death surprisingly hard. He began turning up later and later to his lessons with Ariana, until one morning in early October when he didn't arrive at all. Ariana waited for over an hour in the usual classroom, playing at making the whiteboard pens dance in the air and draw increasingly rude pictures on the white surface before sending her mind out and seeing if there were any conversations nearby it was worth trying to overhear. There weren't. Since his oddly intense demand for her to improve her psychic powers, Lychen hadn't checked in with her classes at all. He barely seemed to spend any time at the Beaumont now, having taken a few weeks to visit Daniel at Futura and then touring the country launching the Home Guard programme.

Ariana wasn't sure if Lychen didn't realise the month's deadline for her learning how to control minds had now passed or if he simply didn't care anymore. In either case, she was in no great hurry to remind him. The only people she'd been able to practice the mind-control thing on were Marc (who was so eager to obey he was hardly practice) and a handful of workers she'd spotted across the Yard. She'd spent an amusing afternoon concealed in an apple tree making a spotty white-coated young man walk back and forth from one building to another, forgetting his purpose and remembering it again with the completion of each circuit. By the end he'd simply given up and gone back to the North East building and she'd not been able to concentrate any longer to bring him back.

Letting the markers drop to the floor, Ariana got to her feet and left the room. Sigma, who waited as ever behind the closed door, followed a few paces behind as Ariana strode towards the room in which she knew Reuben resided. She turned to Sigma and, more to see whether she could, rather than out of any real desire for privacy, reached into her blank, linear mind and told her to stay back. She felt the block of override saying that Lychen had given the order to keep within six feet of Ariana at all times, concentrated a little harder and gave a push. Sigma blinked, turned on her heel and walked in smooth, even strides back to the classroom door. Smirking, Ariana sauntered the rest of the way, unhurried. *You could leave,* her mother's voice whispered. An echo of their last conversation, not a live connection. Ariana could tell the difference so much easier now.

Sigma is just one Guard. And all I did was get her to stay back. Getting her, and the rest of them, to let me leave would be something else entirely... Even if I knew where I was going.

She knocked on the door in front of her. There was no answer. She knocked again, a bit louder. Just as she decided she might as well go back and play on the Playstation for the rest of the day, there came a shuffling noise from beyond the door and it opened slowly. Reuben was rough-shaven and wore a T-shirt that looked as if he'd slept in it. He blinked at her blearily.

'You didn't turn up for my lesson,' Ariana said, blankly.

'No. I'm sorry... I've not been well.'

'Oh. How'd you manage to get ill here?' Ariana frowned. 'We don't see anyone except the Guard and they're all immune to the usual bugs and stuff, aren't they?'

Reuben sighed and passed a hand in front of his face. He stepped back and gestured for her to come inside. The room, which was almost identical to her own bedroom only slightly smaller, was pristine. Ariana blinked at Reuben as he crossed over and opened the curtains. They both winced at the flood of sunshine.

'It was a different kind of unwell.'

'Oh...' Ariana was beginning to wish she had gone back to her room after all, but the strange feelings continued to nag at her, Lychen's warning, his threats to remove her power.

'What did you do with Sigma?'

'I told her to stay back. Overrode Lychen's order. It was easy,' she sounded boasty but she didn't really care. It was only Reuben and she knew he didn't care either. He blinked at her and gave a wry twitch of his mouth before sinking into an armchair next to the window. He shut his eyes just long enough for her to wonder if he'd fallen asleep, then he spoke.

'I don't know what good my turning up for your classes will do you now, Ariana. You have demonstrated an ability to infiltrate minds beyond what I've been able to teach. You can access other abilities at will... I don't know what further need you have of me.'

'But—'

'But if I'm not needed, what is to stop Lychen from disposing of me?'

'Well, yeah...'

'This is the question that keeps me pacing at night. I

243

was never going to leave here, I don't think. I was never going to return to my family. At least not as the same person.'

'So then we won't tell him, we'll let him think I still need you... As long as it takes.'

'And when his patience runs out?'

Ariana frowned and sank, thoughtfully, onto the floor. Taking the bed would feel too weird, too personal.

'I can rein it in... make it look like I'm progressing just enough to keep him happy but not so much that he thinks I don't need you.'

Reuben looked at her pensively.

'Do you ever wonder what his end-purpose is for *you*?'

'What d'you mean?'

'Well, *my* purpose was always clear – teach you, help you reach the fullest potential. But what is that potential for? What will he do, once you are found to be fully in control of your abilities?'

'I... I'm not sure.' *He'll use you and spit you out when he's done... I'll let her be whomever and whatever she wants to be.* Ariana scowled, but the memory of her parents' voices continued to snarl and dance around one another like prowling animals.

'They both lied,' she muttered, glancing up to meet Reuben's sober gaze. 'They were just trying to attack each other. My parents, when it all happened up on the roof and they were both shouting about me... They were just shouting at each other really. And even now... they're both so obsessed with each other, I don't know if either of them really thinks of me as a real person who is separate from them. I think, if I went back to Mum, she would try and hide me away, try and defeat Lychen on her own and then, if she managed it... I can't see her just letting me be free to do whatever I wanted. Not if she couldn't control it. And he's the same. They both want to control me. I think they're both scared of what I could be without them.'

'I agree.'

'So... what do I do?'

'Only you can answer that, Ariana. You are connected to the power now, but are you fully connected to yourself?'

'What do you mean?'

'Well... OK, let's look at it slightly differently. What was the last thing you really cared about? What was the last thing that made you really *feel* something – happy, sad, angry, scared...?

She stared at her feet, at the patterns on her socks.

'I was sad about Dr Blake dying,' she said, quietly.

'Sad?'

'Yeah. He was nice. I was sorry for what I did to him. I shouldn't have hurt him, he was an old man. But Mum said he was ill anyway, he probably would have had a stroke sooner or later... So it doesn't, like, *haunt* me. I wish I could've gone to the funeral, though.'

'Why?'

'What do you mean, why?'

'Why did you want to go to the funeral? What purpose would it have served?'

'Well... I suppose I could have said goodbye.'

'He was already dead, he wouldn't have heard you. I don't think that's why. And I don't think it had anything to do with seeing your mother or Ralph, either. Come on, Ariana. The truth.'

'I... I've never been to a funeral. I was... curious? No... No. I was bored. I'm always just so... bored.'

'What was the last thing that made you feel enough to try and take action? Meaningful action, not born of boredom?'

'I don't know. Um. I listened to a conversation between Daniel and Lychen a while ago, about mind-links...'

'And?'

'Lychen wanted Daniel to help him block my mother out of his head. I think he's been able to do it a bit, but Daniel looked weird afterwards, like he didn't really want to help him but he'd given him an idea about something. And that... that worried me even more than Lychen saying he would kill Mum.'

'Why?'

Ariana shrugs. 'Lychen loves her. As much as he can love anything. If he really did end up killing her, it would destroy him. Daniel, on the other hand... Daniel would do it and just, like, go for lunch afterwards.'

'There... There's the spark. There's the inclination I was looking for. Daniel. You *loathe* him. That's your purpose.'

'What, hating him?' Ariana didn't feel inclined or passionate, but she could at least appreciate the old enthusiasm burning again in Reuben's eyes. He almost looked back to normal, if she ignored his wrinkled shirt.

'Destroying him and what he's doing. Save the hybrid creatures like you tried to last year. Finish what you started. Leave your parents to each other.'

Ariana stared at him, tempted by the brightness in his eyes. She didn't need to reach into his mind to know that the idea had taken hold of him, too.

'I wouldn't know where to begin...'

'You know where Daniel is. You know what he's doing.'

'Yeah, but I don't know how to stop him... There are

too many Guard...'

'So go around them. We've worked on distance connections. Your mother can do it, and the scientists have ascertained enough from your genetic tests to show that you can do at least as much as she when harnessing your enhanced resilience. Just reach him the way you reach for her... break into his head and find out what he's planning. Then we can work out a plan to stop him.'

No one is off limits.

'And Lychen? What about when he tests me?'

'We'll do what you suggested,' he got to his feet with the old abrupt movement she knew. She mirrored him automatically. 'We'll show him enough progress to keep him happy. And we'll work on the rest for as long as we're given. Come on, let's walk.'

'Reuben?'

'Yes?'

'I'm going to get you out, too. I promise. Marc's already given up, he didn't take the chance when I tried to give it to him and now he's stuck here. But that's his decision. I'm going to get you home to your family. That's going to be my purpose, too.'

He watched her a bit longer. Then he smiled suddenly, brightly, like the break of sunshine through a heavy cloud. It danced within his large beautiful eyes like flames.

'Thank you, Ariana. I appreciate that.'

February, 2020

Ethan leaves the top button of his shirt undone, doesn't bother with a tie. The uncomfortable stiffness of the starched collar, the unfamiliarity of tight cuffs around his wrists, these are all things from before. Sometimes the connections with who he was before he was Guard are easy, sometimes they feel alien. He will never feel comfortable in an ironed shirt and fitted suit trousers, but it doesn't irritate him like it once would have, because it is for her. Ethan smooths his hair. It's longer than he can ever remember wearing it, because he knows from the small echo of her eyes on him that she prefers it to his old, bristly cut. It's not like he's changed that much beneath the surface, he thinks to himself, more like he's been repositioned. Before, Bella was just a person he knew. Someone he liked well enough but didn't think about all that much. Now she is the sun.

He reaches for her as he picks up his coat. Ralph's no longer in her room, which is a relief. He didn't need to be connected during that exchange to feel the emanation of frustration from both sides. Now she's in quick conversation with Eve. Ethan doesn't linger to listen, he knows that any interference could cause problems and that progress is crucial at the moment. He opens the door and finds Tess hovering in the corridor. She's wearing a neat trouser suit with a bright, silky-looking scarf tied at her neck. Red to match her lips. He smiles at her and she grins nervously in return. Together they make their way along the corridor.

'So… how's life by the sea?' Tess says as they approach the lifts.

'Fine… Nice and quiet this time of year,' he replies. 'Not that I'm really one for the seaside, but it's a good place to take Daisy.'

'Oh yes, I forgot about the puppy. How is she?'

'Better now she's stopped nipping so much.' He presses the button for down.

'You share the dog with Felix?'

'I have her every other weekend. I've only got a one-bed flat near the town centre, Fee's right on the beach. Daisy was always more her dog than mine, anyway.'

'So, um… When you split up, how come you didn't move back?'

He shrugs as they step into the lift. 'I'd only just set up a business in Scarsby. Plus, you know, Dr Blake had not long passed away, I wanted to give Ralph a bit of space…'

'Sure.' Tess smiles awkwardly, and Ethan can tell she's already regretting her probing, wanting to swerve them away from the spiky topic of his separation, the bizarre love-oblong of which he'd found himself a part. He clears his throat.

'How's Dom doing? Still working for the firm in Manchester?'

'Yes, when he's not going on monster quests with eleven-year-olds on Minecraft.'

Ethan laughs shortly, though he can tell there's more than a touch of bitterness in her words.

'You used to work at the Beaumont, right?' The lift

doors slide open to the busy shining hotel lobby. People swarm everywhere and, as the two of them step out and make their way to a row of sofas where Ralph sits long-leggedly, they are swallowed into the gaggles of business wear and loud important phone calls.

'I did, yes.'

'Must be strange being back in London after so long,' Ethan says as they reach Ralph, who glances at them brusquely.

'It's amazing,' Tess smiles around them at the people. With her neatly bobbed hair and high street business-wear she only needs a phone held aloft to blend perfectly into the crowd, Ethan muses. He is about to ask whether she'll move back here once all this is over, when the lift doors open behind them and his focus switches automatically.

Bella is as unapologetically radiant as ever as she steps out of the lift and Ethan feels the attention of others sweep to her as she makes her way unselfconsciously across the floor to them. She is wearing a knee-length jade dress which swirls delicately under her fitted black coat, black stiletto-heeled shoes, and her hair is pinned away from her face, a lustrous, flowing frame for her beauty. Ethan allows himself a moment just to watch her, just to drink in the sight of her in all her glory. Then he glances at Ralph, takes in the turmoil of his features and collects himself.

'We'll need a taxi,' Bella says, as she approaches. Ethan opens his mouth but Ralph leaps to his feet and heads out of the double-doored entrance without a word. Bella's eyebrows flicker upwards slightly but she doesn't comment.

'Where are we heading?' Tess is a wire of nervous energy, slipping her phone from one hand to the other as she jiggles up and down in her heels.

'St Mary's Hospital,' Bella glances around them and lowers her voice. 'They've taken her in. I'll have easier access there and we were lucky to catch the husband between meetings. We'll need to avoid names from now on, the Press won't be far behind us.'

'Right. OK.'

'Ralph's got a cab, come on,' Ethan leads the way across the lobby towards the tall, gesturing figure outside.

Everything alright with you and Ralph?

No, not really.

They don't understand.

He shows her the memory of Felix's horrified face as he'd told her why he couldn't have Daisy this weekend, the shrillness he'd only rarely heard in her voice, '*Why do you have to go as well, what possible use could* you *be?'* Bella smiles in response. *Well. You are pretty useless.*

He chuckles and earns himself a strange look from Tess as he holds the door open and they pass outside. Ralph's jaw tightens and his dark eyes remain cold as he holds the door of a black cab. Bella gives no indication of any ill-feeling between them whatsoever as she slides into the back seat, movements fluid as oil. Ethan folds himself into the taxi last and as it rumbles off the curb, he looks out of the window as Bella goes over the plan with Tess one more time, reminding her of the names of this aide and that assistant should she find herself in such and such position. His mind flits back to Felix, not least because the reproachful energy he feels radiating from Ralph is uncomfortably reminiscent. He wonders if he knows 'the look' too.

'What look?' He'd stared at the vision of rage in front of him, this short, tempestuous woman with spiky hair and eyes like flint. He'd known then that it was over. He'd known it from the moment he'd gone into the office and seen the scrawled notes next to the ostentatiously blank computer screens. But he protested anyway because he'd agreed to do what he could, to give the marriage a chance. And there had been times when she grinned or said something funny in her quick, Felix way, and it was like an old forgotten part of him bloomed in response. But it wasn't enough, because she wasn't the sun.

'You know the look, Ethan! If you don't, just stare in the mirror for five minutes and I guarantee you'll spot it.'

'What?'

'It's like you're smiling on the inside. Like you're listening and looking at me but you're not *here*. You've been doing it for months.'

'So why didn't you tell me before? I thought we were supposed to be honest with each other? Though by the looks of all this,' he gestured at the notes, his fury fuelled by the shock he still felt, Bella's shock as she'd used his eyes to read the words scrawled there, raw like a wound in his skull.

'Don't give me that! Don't stand there and fucking pretend that you haven't been talking to her, whispering with her in your head all this time!'

'And don't *you* pretend you haven't been continuing your crazy, paranoid investigations!'

They'd stood there for a moment just glaring at one another. Then he'd heard a small pathetic whining noise coming from the kitchen. Daisy. The puppy-bandage Felix had insisted upon, whimpering because she didn't like the noise. He didn't blame her. He couldn't remember the last time his throat had ached from shouting. He hated it. Hated *this*. Sinking into the small two-seater sofa lining one wall of the office, the cushions thick with dog hair, he put his head into his hands. When he looked up Felix was still standing where she had been, but her face had softened as well. There were no tears in her steely gaze, but her jaw was no longer tight and she rubbed the side of her nose the way she always did when she felt ashamed.

'I just… I knew the look, from before. At the Manor. And I didn't tell you about it because I knew that you'd just find a way of concealing it. I didn't want you to keep lying to me, but I also didn't want to give up the one way I had of knowing if you were…'

'I'm sorry,' he sank his fingers into his hair, its soft springs still unfamiliar.

'Yeah. Well. I should've told you sooner, I guess. Instead of just burying my head in the sand.'

'And carrying on with your digging?'

'It's like a therapy at this point. It's something to focus on. To stop me sinking completely. You know?'

'Yeah. Same.'

'Talking to her?'

'Not even talking. Just… being there. It's… like an addiction, I guess. I know I shouldn't, but I can't quite work out how to live without it… without her.'

She had looked at him then and he'd known what she was going to ask before she opened her mouth, not because it was her and it was them, but because it was the only thing he'd been asking himself.

'Do you even want to?'

The memory swirls and fades as they round a corner and Ethan turns from the grey-smeared traffic and endless streams of people to the cab. Ralph is staring moodily out of the other window. Tess is nodding, her red mouth twitching nervously, fingers still gripping her phone. He catches Bella's eye and blazes inside as she flits him a brief safe smile.

Ready?

Ready.

Autumn, 2019

It's not working, is it, Lychen? GHAP isn't bringing in the millions you were hoping for, is it? I know you can hear me. It's been a while, hasn't it? Daniel's been dosing you up, I see. You thought it had worked, didn't you? But the thing is, I've not really been trying all that hard to break through.

Get out of my head, Bella.

It's not the same without me, is it? You didn't get half the projected uptake. It was a total shambles compared to the Care launch in April.

Get. OUT!

You know, it wouldn't hurt so much if you just accept that I'm here. That I'm in control, for now. But you'll never do that, will you? It's not in your nature to relinquish control. Even if it's just control over a quick conversation.

Enough!

Stop pushing Ariana. Stop trying to make her into a weapon against me. She is more powerful than you. If you keep trying to mould her into something she doesn't want to be, if you keep treating her like a possession, she will snap. You are her father. I know that doesn't mean much to you but you need to figure out what it means to her.

Why would you tell me this?

Because I don't want her to disappear.

You don't want her to destroy me.

255

No, Lychen. I don't. I don't want Ariana to bear the burden of killing her father on top of contributing to the death of her grandfather. Besides, I'm the one who'll destroy you. I thought we had established that.

This time his reflexive shove was hard enough to loosen my grip on his silky spiderweb thread of mind. I laughed as I withdrew so that he'd think I was in control, that I was only leaving because I had chosen to. The truth was, as I blinked myself slowly back into the bright afternoon sun, it had taken a huge amount of energy to reach him and, once there, to break through the rudimentary walls he had erected against me, no doubt with Daniel's help.

Daniel had been at the forefront of the Guard mind-link development, I knew Lychen had gone to him for help making the deeper link between Ethan and me last year, and not just because Daniel had been the one to oversee Ethan's transition. I could detect parts of the barrier, it was almost like he'd found an antidote to reverse the drug used to open up the Guard's mind to human telepathic command. Though part of its effectiveness also seemed to depend on Lychen's resolve, on his determination not to hear me. And it had been a while. I had been able to feel how much part of him missed me and reached for the sound of my voice, even as it twisted the knife of my unreachability.

In any case, I did not see the barrier as anything to worry about, particularly. It was an irritant, though not as irritating as how easily he had managed to eject me. I was still weak. Too weak. And I was running out of time. My birthday had passed in the summer, I had entered my thirty-fourth year. None of the other Project A Subjects had lived beyond thirty-five. I could feel the curse like a tumorous shadow falling over everything I did.

I looked around. I was sitting on a grassy verge overlooking a small lake, nestled out of the way of roads and footpaths on the tourist track. The late heatwave had worn a lot of the greenery to a dirty gold around me and the air held a cool, autumnal flavour of yellowing sweetness. Nova landed with a flurry nearby, shaking her feathers out and sending a spray of lake water which spotted my jeans. I looked up sharply and she gave a crowing sort of laugh.

'Thanks for that,' I muttered, though I wasn't really annoyed. It was good to see her having fun. It was also good to be out of the Manor. Since Dr Blake's death there had been a strange, cloudy sort of feel around the place, a humid sort of sadness which made it hard to breathe deeply. The days had taken on a new uniform – Tess and Dom busying themselves in the shared office they'd made out of Ethan and Felix's old room, Ralph and I doing the same in the laboratory taking shape in Ana's former dance studio. We kept our conversation work-orientated or simply did not speak at all, passing instruments between one another. He worked on the NatApp compounds, I tried to find chemicals to bond properly with the resilience properties I'd managed to isolate from my blood samples. In the evenings we would all come together with wine and food and trade anecdotes about the ARC as it had been until Tess's eyes widened to the edges of her face in disbelief and Ralph's slowly lit back up behind the lens of grief.

These were, in some ways, some of the best days I'd had at the Manor. There was no underlying tension now Felix and Ethan had gone, Ralph sometimes looked at me in a heavy, awkward sort of way but the safety net of his grief avoided any further action... And yet. It was hard work as well. I would stand in the window of my bedroom, my brain yawning through a heady mist of red wine as I stared at the trees, already browning, and wondered at the world beyond. The empire I'd helped steer, gearing up for the biggest launch in eugenic history. A Guard in every household. My Youth Guard, now all positioned in the most lucrative of positions. My daughter, at the heart of it all. And sometimes, as I stood there, I would hear Lychen's voice drift to me from that summer's evening in his office long ago: *Why deny the world yourself? This is no place for you...* And there was nothing to stop my mind following, wondering on a wine-tinged trail, whether I should have just done what he asked of me that night in August, when the balance was still held, before Ralph, before the presentation, before Ariana... What if I'd bitten back my pride, held his hands firmly so he couldn't clench his nails into mine, and said: *yes, OK then. Take me away from here.*

'Sss... Sad?'

I looked up at Nova in surprise. Quite apart from the fact she had spoken voluntarily, it was unusual for her to ask a question, particularly one so personal.

'Am I sad? About Dr Blake, you mean?'

She cocked her head in the small, nodding gesture with which I'd become familiar.

'No... I mean, yes. Of course I am. But... he was ready. He'd done what he needed to do. I miss him, though. Seems stupid to say that, because I hadn't really been around him for fourteen years. I always missed him, though.'

'Misssss... Rana?'

'Ariana? Yes. I miss her all the time. Like a pain. Here,' I touch my chest. 'But I know she's OK. She talks to me more, these days. I wonder sometimes if being apart is better for us, in a way. I mean, of course I worry about her. About the things she's doing and seeing. But she's resilient, like me. And she has people around her whom she can trust. Reuben. Marc. Tom, not that she knows about him.'

My phone buzzed for the third time in the last thirty minutes. I glanced at it. Ralph. Wondering where I was, again. I knew he'd be getting worried. I typed a quick reply and got to my feet.

'We need to go back,' I said, unnecessarily. 'Well, I do, anyway. There's always someone wondering where I am. Always someone to reassure.'

Nova gave a soft coo of agreement and took to the skies once again. I didn't see her again as I made my way back down the hillside and across the fields leading to the Manor.

'There you are,' Ralph remarked, as I entered the back door, trying to sound less fussed than we both knew he was. 'Those mice you ordered have come. I've put them in the one cage but I didn't know if you wanted them separated.'

'Thanks, I'll sort them out in a minute,' I said, hanging up my coat.

'Where did you go?'

'Just for a walk. My leg needs exercise, remember,' I muttered, not meeting his gaze.

'Well let me know next time. I can always come with you… we don't know how safe it is out there…'

'Ralph, it's Cumbria. It's the middle of nowhere. Besides, Lychen agreed to leave me alone.' I frowned in annoyance as I made my way down the corridor and took my boots off outside the lab. He followed me.

'Yeah, that was before they launched GHAP, there are

ten times as many Guard out there now. I mean, look at *that,'* he gestured at the large flat screen we'd installed on one wall of the lab. Primarily it was to show close up projections but lately it had been left on a rolling news channel. Today the screen scrolled with endless headlines: *PM endorses latest Guard programme, says Guard Assistants are the 'missing link' for busy households; BFI bosses claim 'zero possibility' of Guard former personality traits returning after member of public recognises convicted murderer; Guard Assistant sales have surpassed £50m according to insider reports...*

'At least they're not showing re-runs of my old interviews anymore,' I muttered.

'Only because you threatened to sue them,' Ralph replied, though there is a smile in his voice now. There always is whenever I express negativity about my former BFI role.

'It's not as successful as they projected,' I added, shaking back my hair and tying it up as Ralph pretended not to watch. 'Even those inflated figures,' I gestured at the screen where someone I only vaguely recognised from the Guard programme at the Beaumont explained something with a lot of arm movement as a graph showing a gentle upward curve lit the screen behind him.

'Well, they don't have their cut-throat ambassador anymore,' Ralph smirked mockingly. I raised an eyebrow at him.

'Exactly.'

'Still, fifty mill isn't to be sniffed at,' he turned to the computer screen and brought up a spreadsheet he'd been working on.

'The Beaumont rings up some pretty big debts... It's not representative of the bottom line, and they've swept the launch of the Youth Guard right under the radar. Probably because of the negativity it would generate,' I said, turning to the large mouse cage. There were twelve of them, all adults, all female. I watched as one of them began scrambling up the side of the cage, sending flurries of straw and excrement behind it. I had a sudden urge to seize the whole thing and throw it out of the window onto the gravel driveway, out of my clean laboratory.

Don't do that. It would be a terrible waste. And it would make an awful mess on the driveway.

'What?' I looked up, frowning at Ralph. He raised his eyebrows.

'I didn't say anything,' he said, turning back to his screen. 'Must have been the mice, they're certainly loud enough.'

I turned slowly back to the mouse cage. Blinked a few times and, with inevitable slowness, raised my eyes to the right, away from Ralph, towards the shadowy corner beside the window. The blur which was coming clearer every moment, rising, stooping, smiling benignly.

Of course you're here.

He laughed, the rumble creaking from him with the same warmth that whispered of Christmas mornings and spirited dinner table debates. His hair was the same swoosh of peppery white I remembered from my middle childhood, his height more imposing than crooked, hands solid and untrembling as they crossed in front of him. He looked every bit as alive as he was, undeniably, not.

I'm sorry, Bella, I didn't mean to startle you. That look you just gave me, though. You reminded me so sharply of when you were a little girl. You were always so cross if anyone ever caught you off guard. I suppose you never liked any of your responses to be unrehearsed. Undoubtedly you saw it as a sign of weakness, though I always thought it showed a beauty far greater than your polished performance faces.

Right. Well... thank you for that. I suppose. Any particular reason why you've decided to grace me with your presence? I assume you're just a manifestation of my own resilience cropping up again. So what do I need from you?

To that, I cannot say, he held his hands out and shrugged apologetically, his eyes still glittering with amusement. I busied myself with the stack of new cages, preparing each for its own mouse occupant. They couldn't stay in here. Ralph was right, they were too noisy. And they were already beginning to smell. I glanced towards the back of the room where the new rodent cupboard boasted a wall but still lacked a door.

I appreciate what you're doing for him. Ralph. You ease his sadness every day.

I don't know if it's a kindness.

He finds comfort in the shared experience, even though...

Even though part of him wonders what we spoke about that last day. What I did. Whether I killed you.

Yes. He may never ask you though. I don't think he wants to know.

No. But he will always wonder.

Probably. And he will demand other answers before long. He sees that your focus is not truly here. Even with your work. He feels your restlessness underneath. He did not admit the extent of his worry today. You can't just go off like that without telling him.

I'm not a child. I can take care of myself.

I know that. He knows that too really, but he cannot bear the thought of losing you again. Not after losing me.

I know. I know. But I can't stay. Not forever. I can't breathe here.

I looked up again. His eyes had lost their gleam now. They blinked behind their thick lenses heavily, sadly, though not with the unbound grief he'd shown me on his last day, back at the hospital. There was a freedom behind the sadness, a lifted hope that I hadn't seen in the real Dr Blake since before Ana had died.

What of the link with Lychen? Will this affect how I can do that? It took so long to get back after my body turned its attention to healing.

I don't know. I'm not sure that is a connection it is wise to pursue, in any case. Your resilience is—

...not infinite. I know. It will be, though. Once I can top it up. Once I figure out this regeneration riddle.

'Beast? You OK? You've been staring at those cages for an oddly long time...'

I looked up, back over at Ralph. My earlier irritation had mostly vanished now. I smiled and felt it lift his spirits.

'I'm fine. I was just thinking about where to put these. They're too loud in here, but the cupboard doesn't have a door yet. What about the schoolroom?'

'Sure. There's a good space in there now... Now there's no bed going in.'

'Yes. That's what I was thinking.'

'Want me to help you separate them?'

'Please,' I smiled. From the corner of the room, Dr Blake bounced on his toes and continued to watch us with a vaguely happy look on his face. Standby mode. Ready to be called upon when next my brain conjured a query for him to quell.

February, 2020

Felix stares at the screens until her eyes begin to fuzz. Usually she is able to block everything out when there's a project in front of her. Just last week it had taken Daisy jumping into her lap and spilling a cold cup of tea everywhere before she had realised the doorbell was ringing. Today, though. Today her eyes constantly slip from the computer monitors onto her phone. She swipes the screen unlocked and checks her messages for the third time in five minutes. The three names at the top are labelled simply ONE, TWO and THREE. There are no new messages from any of them.

Sighing, Felix gets to her feet and makes her way out of the small room with the computer monitors all lined up on the desk in front of the window. The view reveals a tumbling mess of clouds and the window is splattered with fat rain drops, but Felix doesn't care. She longs for the fresh, salt-tinged air, the shift of tiny stones beneath her boots, the whip of spray across her cheeks. She's changed, she realises with a strange jolt as she reaches for her heavy raincoat. Only last year her solace had been in the machines, the cold predictability of them, the smooth keys beneath her fingertips. Now she feels as if spending one more minute in front of the soft whirs and gentle clicks will make her head explode. It's probably just the dog, she thinks as she whistles for Daisy. The small terrier bounds up to her, tail aflurry at the prospect of an unscheduled walk. Felix clips the lead onto her collar, crams a beanie onto her own head and heads outside.

The walk to the beach is short and deserted. Felix enjoys this time of year far more than the summer cram of tourists. The beach is shingle rather than sand and it's too small and tucked away for any major attractions except for a long, rambling pier at its far end. Felix bends and unclips Daisy from her lead, watching the small dog bound towards the water. She wonders what Ethan is doing right now. She probably shouldn't have asked him so scathingly what good he could possibly do joining the others on their ridiculous mission to wrestle the Guard back from Lychen. He hadn't reacted, of course, not really, but she had felt the blow land. She'd felt a little of him retreat even further, the easy way he'd stood in her doorway tightening back into a tense hover. She checks her phone again.

'No point checking really,' Felix mutters as Daisy bounds back to her bearing a piece of half-sodden driftwood. 'They'll tell me if anything happens. Thanks for this, mate. Couldn't have found a dry one, eh?' She reaches down and picks the stick up, wishing she'd thought to bring gloves. It was one thing having a new-found fondness for the outdoors, it was another thing being actually prepared for the bloody freezingness of it.

'There you go,' she says, throwing the stick as far as she can. Daisy lollops after it. Felix blows out her cheeks, the breeze snatching the puff of exhaled air and bearing it away. She stares out at the crashing waves, thinking about the cliffs in Cornwall where she and Ralph had found Bella just over a year ago. Was it really only a year? Felix feels decades changed to the version of herself who had trodden steadily down that cliff-face, trying not to look too far over the edge. Her phone buzzes.

TWO: In position. Awaiting GO.

Felix swipes to refresh a few times but when nothing else appears, she slides the phone back into her pocket. She still feels jittery, but she knows no amount of fresh sea air is going to change that. For the millionth time she wonders if she's doing the right thing. She throws the stick again for Daisy, remembering something Ethan told her about Bella having conversations with her dead mother in her head, during the brief time when they'd vowed to be totally honest with one another. Ana had answered back and everything, apparently. It was one of the few things Felix truly envied Bella for, other than Ethan's adoration, of course. As much as she's sought solace during the more difficult times of the last year, Felix has found living alone far harder than she'd thought it would be. Daisy helps, but there are still days when Felix feels the press of emptiness strangle around her like a tight, smothering blanket. She'd give anything to be able to have conversations with dead loved ones.

Felix throws the stick again, her mind conjuring the uneven gait of a young boy running alongside the dog. It was one of the things she did to try and calm herself down, when the darkness threatened to overcome her. Imagine Oscar. He'd be almost fourteen, like Ariana. A few months younger, but eternally two months older. Buzz.

THREE: Sighting confirmed. In pursuit.

'Good,' Felix murmurs. She looks up and smiles as Daisy pelts back and drops the stick at her feet. She throws it again before turning her attention back to the phone.

Thumbs hovering, she lingers over the ONE message window. She could call. She won't call. Instead, she taps back to the exchange with TWO and types out one word: *Standby*.

She doesn't feel guilty anymore. She may not be entirely sure if what she's doing is right, but she doesn't feel guilty about it. She gave up on guilt the day she found Ethan in her small home office, his face awash with the shock that she knew he didn't fully understand. Because it was Bella's shock, of course. And it told her everything. That the scribble she'd made on the page beside her computer: *T msgs, L/B Oct 18. Meta-data tag?* had meant everything. She had been right. She wasn't crazy. She wasn't paranoid. She was acting in everyone's best interests now. Well. Mostly everyone's. Felix smiles as Daisy sniffs at a pile of seaweed and sneezes wetly. Her phone buzzes again and, as she retrieves it, Felix feels the smile freeze on her face.

> TWO: We have a problem. The girl is awake.

'Shit.'

> THREE: Target is alone and unguarded. Might be only opportunity.

'Buggering shit.'

Felix twists her mouth, glances out at the turbulent waves pounding violently against the shingle for a few seconds. Then she decides. Opening THREE's window, she taps quickly:

> Proceed as planned. Use location C.

She sends the message just as the phone begins to ring, the

word TWO flashing in verdant urgency. She calls to Daisy and clips her lead back onto her collar as she turns away from the shoreline, answering the call with sharp, short sentences.

February, 2020

I don't need the Mollitiam pills. It all comes together ridiculously easily in the end. We arrive at the hospital and I take two minutes to face the others just before we go in.

'Remember,' I stare at each of them, forcing Ralph's moody brown gaze to meet mine. 'You are here because you are meant to be here. You've all memorised the names of the top aides, if there're any problems just throw them in there.'

'What if we panic and forget everything?' Tess asks tremulously. I can feel her nervous excitement like a spitting fizzy drink. I blink slowly at her until it calms a little.

'If anyone looks at you too long and hard or if you feel like you're in danger, get out. Walk out of the front entrance there, do a few laps of the street if you need to. Meet back here,' I gesture to the small brick-lined side road. 'None of you really have anything you *need* to do unless I call you. If anything, you'll probably be more of a hindrance than a help if your head's not in the game, Ralph.'

He glares back at me and then makes a marked effort to clear his face, pull it into neutrality. I can tell he's trying to imitate a move he's seen me do a million times. It's almost funny.

'I'm fine. I'm ready,' he mutters. I nod briskly and lead

the way.

It's surprisingly easy to reach Shona. The others hang back so it's not obvious I'm with them. I know exactly where to go, thanks to Eve, who sits placidly in a plastic chair outside the room where her mistress lies motionlessly. I take the lift to the seventh floor, stride towards the security guards positioned outside a closed ward, make eye contact, speak a few choice words and am through the doors before I've even slowed my pace.

'I'm here to speak to Mr Metcalfe,' I tell the man I recognise as one of his senior Personal Assistants.

'Who—' he begins, glancing up and stopping.

'My name is Dr Bella D'accourt. Executive Head of Development at BFI. I helped develop the programme which engineered the Guard, specifically Shona Metcalfe's Assistant, Eve. I met with Mr Metcalfe briefly last year when he toured the facility. I need to speak with him urgently, with the Guard Assistant present.'

He blinks, nods mutely and turns, disappearing through a door with frosted glass on it. I look sideways at Eve. She looks exactly the same as she did the last time I saw her in the Yard at the Beaumont, with the sun dappling lightly over her tightly-bound hair. She does not look up at me, but I feel her acknowledgement. It sweeps from her with images of Shona lolling unresponsively, her husband's eyes bulging in fear, Eve's voice wavering a little as she told him what Shona had ingested.

'Dr D'accourt? You may come through.'

'See that we are not disturbed. Eve, join me please.'

I walk briskly through the door with the frosted glass. The hospital room is larger than Dr Blake's had been with more markedly luxurious trimmings, but otherwise similar. Shona Metcalfe looks older than she appears on TV, her face lined in wrinkles which flow in a slackening way to the white sheets beneath her. Roger Metcalfe, too, is diminished from how I remember him. He stands by the end of her bed as if he would much rather be sitting, his eyes heavy with fatigue and sadness, his shirt already beginning to wrinkle with having been worn for too long. He looks up and though we met for only minutes last year, I can see that my face has done its job.

'Dr D'accourt… Marsh insisted I see you, but I'm afraid as you can see, this is hardly a good time—' his eyes flit confusedly between me and Eve, a blank pillar by my side.

'I won't keep you long,' I say, emanating warmth. 'I'm extremely sorry about your wife's condition, but this matter concerns her directly so I thought it best to talk to you at the earliest possible opportunity. She is in grave danger. She has been placed in grave danger by Dr Josiah Lychen and his intentional use of the Guard to control and manipulate the population to his own ends. I believe you've been made aware of some complaints already about Guard – specifically the Youth Guard range – in employ among your colleagues?'

'How did you know about that?' He frowns, but I can tell my words, my eyes, my body are all working in my favour. He leans towards me, transfixed, his attention already nine-tenths ensnared. His wife's finger twitches in the bed but he does not so much as flicker in response as the last tenth slides easily into my hands.

'Have you asked Eve what happened to Mrs Metcalfe this evening?'

'Of course I have. She took an overdose of anti-depressants washed down with too much gin. She'll be OK. I'm going to get her help—'

'No.'

'No?'

'Eve, did Mrs Metcalfe take too many pills this evening?'

'Yes.'

'And too much alcohol?'

'Yes.'

'Why?'

I stare at her. He stares at her. And she hesitates, just for a moment. Not long enough for him to notice, but long enough for me to begin to frown, to register a tiny error message of alarm. Then she smooths it out and continues on form:

'Because I gave them to her.'

'What?' Metcalfe stares aghast from the Guard girl to me and back again.

'Mrs Metcalfe expressed extreme grief and discontent. I could feel it within her, through our mind-link connection. She desired the oblivion of excessive alcohol and medication. She has reached it before, on lesser levels. She was in more pain this time and required greater, longer oblivion. This was the overriding need that I read within her core requirements. So I complied.'

'But... But you— they're not meant to cause harm!'

'I calculated that the greater harm was allowing the pain to continue. She had not historically been able to lessen the pain through other methods. I concluded that this would be the most humane course of action. Mrs Metcalfe has lived with pain for years and its levels have shown increasing impact on her ability to function, to find joy in her life otherwise...'

That's enough, Eve. Too much detail.

'She... Are you saying this girl – this *thing* – is responsible—'

'Indirectly only,' I say quickly, before anger clouds too far over his rationale. 'This tragedy is a result of an essential flaw in the programmed responses of the Guard Assistants as a collective. Sir, you must act now to recall all those in employment, the fault is with their creator, Dr Lychen. You know him. What he's like. The control he seeks, the conformity he prizes above all else – it has blinded him to the value of a human understanding of extreme emotion, turmoil, grief. Moreover... Well...' I pause carefully, using my eyes, fluttering them downwards in a careful display of unease.

'Go on, please,' he says, his voice gentle even over the edge of worry.

'I believe this matter is more than just an oversight, actually... I think it goes deeper than that. I'm breaking my contract of employment by telling you this, sir... but I believe it is warranted. Lychen's intentions for the Guard Programme as a whole are not what they appear. He seeks to use them to control the country, streamline it, shape humanity to his own ends. Weed out those he sees as... unstable.'

His face is a prison of horror. I keep my voice low and steady, shining with earnest intention.

'There is a wealth of evidence of his intentions at the BFI. I've seen them. They include theorised plans for controlled Guard reproduction and integrated population. He sees it as an evolutionary step – he is quite mad, of course. But he's also powerful, rich, persuasive, and currently in possession of significant government backing. But it's not too late, sir. We can rectify all of this—'

There's a loud noise from outside and a siren blares into life. I frown, unsure if it's coming from the direction from which I came or not, though I keep my eyes on

Metcalfe. He nods, vaguely, though the siren has furrowed his brow, brought him a little out of the daze I've created.

'Yes... but what will—'

The door opens and the man, Marsh, pokes his head into the room.

'Sir, I'm sorry but you're needed. There's been a security breach. We need to move you. And Nicholls wants to discuss the Press briefing.'

'Right...'

'I can wait, Mr Metcalfe, but we need to continue this conversation as soon as possible.' I keep my eyes on him. He nods fervently.

'Of course.'

Eve and I follow him into the corridor and he begins a quick sharply worded conversation with Marsh as they walk away. I nip my lower lip, annoyed at the interruption but knowing I'm more than halfway there. Metcalfe is my puppet now, I've got access, I just need to finish telling him what to do next.

What now? There is a definite air of confusion and fear in Eve's voice which wasn't there before. I look at her more fully and see it echoed in her large, dark eyes.

Eve, why are you afraid?

I don't know. It happens to me sometimes. I don't know why. It is not rational for a Guard person. But it still happens.

The siren is still going off, coming from a direction opposite end of the corridor to where I can feel Ethan and the others waiting. It must be a coincidence, probably a journalist trying to gain admission. Metcalfe and his assistants have moved now and Eve and I stand a little away from Shona's door, a new black-suited man in place, guarding the entrance. I glance at Eve and notice her mouth trembling a little.

Come on, let's move down this way. I don't want Metcalfe's staff to see you like this. They might think you're malfunctioning.

I am malfunctioning!

Yes, well, if they think that then you could be earmarked as a one-off irregularity and that will undo everything I've just told him. You need to get yourself together.

Bella, what you said just now about Lychen and the Guard... His intentions, plans for Guard reproduction, population integration. That wasn't true, was it?

Eve, look at me. These are not the questions you need to concern yourself with.

I know. But I am concerned. And I am scared. I don't know why. I don't know what is happening to me...

Calm down. You aren't scared. Robots don't get scared, remember? You don't feel. This is just a glitch. An anomaly.

Her face calms into smoothness once again, her voice returning to its normal pitch.

An anomaly. I don't feel.

That's right. That's better.

She blinks as if she's just woken up, her eyes swivelling around like a security camera.

Bella. Why are we alone? Where is everybody?

I glance around. She's right. The rooms off either side of the corridor where we stand are empty, there aren't any medical staff around.

It'll be because of Shona. They'll have cleared the ward for her.

Bella, there's a Guard man! He's got a weapon and he's coming right for—

The width of Eve's eyes and her terror. It's far beyond the perimeters of what has been programmed into her, beyond all the nuances of subtle emotion and expression I've taught her. It's beyond everything I've ever known of a Guard person, even Ethan. That's what I'm thinking. That's the only thing I think of, the impossibility of her terror before it abruptly disappears along with the rest of the world.

Autumn, 2019

Lychen watched as Ariana stared at the three men in front of her until, one by one, they all crumpled to their knees. One of them was weeping. Lychen smiled tightly, though when Ariana looked at him she knew he wasn't entirely in the room. She glanced at Reuben who stood, as he so often did, just out of Lychen's eyeline. He gave her a quick look which told her to keep her mouth shut.

'What did you do there?' Lychen frowned as the sobbing man keeled into a foetal position. Ariana shrugged.

'I just made him think things... horrible things. It wasn't hard. I can turn it off as well.'

'Do so.'

Ariana stared at the men, reached into their heads one by one and removed the thoughts she'd burned into each of them. The crying man instantly silenced and got to his feet, looking bemused. The other two blinked and stared around them at the plain, whitewashed walls of the squash court.

'Good,' Lychen muttered, 'Soren, Hank, take them away. Dispose of them.'

The two Guard people instantly leapt into action, one tightening a cord around the men's hands the way they had been bound when they'd entered the room and the other steering them from behind until they moved. The bewildered men walked dazedly towards the door, one of them recovering only enough to utter a 'Wha—' just as they were pushed through the exit.

'What d'you mean by *dispose of them*?' Ariana frowned, staring at Lychen. He sighed and passed a hand over his forehead. He looked as he had done the last time he'd tested her in here, only greyer and more creased around the edges, like a piece of paper which was slowly crumpling in on itself.

'They've seen you, they've seen me. They'll have been taken from street corners, no one will look for them. They'll be made into Guard if strong enough.'

'And killed if they're not?'

Lychen sighed again and checked his watch. 'I need to leave.' He turned to her, looking at her properly for the first time. She stared back, keeping her chin up and her eyes clear.

'The Home Assistance launch is underway, as I'm sure you're aware. There have been a number of issues that I need to address which will be keeping me extremely busy over the coming weeks. You have done well so far with the tasks I have given you, but I know you are growing frustrated with the limitations placed upon you.'

'I just want to *do* something rather than just practising all the time.'

'Well. I have plans for you, rest assured. But practising is key. You're still unpredictable, emotional... You still visit Marc every week.'

'Because there's not much else to do around here... And I'm lonely.'

'You will continue to practice on him while I am gone. Your progress will be monitored by Reuben and Sigma.

D'accourt will be connected to monitors which will show the extent of your progress with him. I've long had reason to suspect that you've been holding back with him... I want to see results on paper. I may not be here but I will be reading the reports every week and any failure to progress will be noted.'

He turned and began to walk away.

'What plans have you got for me? For after all this?'

He turned and looked at her again in a shrewd, measuring way. Just when she thought he was not going to answer, he replied: 'When you are ready, you will accompany me on trips all over the world, taking the Guard programme international. Part of your role will be to isolate those who would seek to oppose and... *subdue* as necessary. You won't be the alluring ambassador your mother was, but if you prove yourself worthy, you'll be far more valuable.'

Ariana smiled inadvertently. 'Like a spy?'

'Like a spy in plain sight. But this position requires a level of trust which goes beyond anything I have placed in another person, Ariana. You must earn it.'

'OK...'

'Good.'

He walked away quickly, as if worried he'd said too much. Ariana looked at Reuben.

'Well?' Reuben asked, quietly, when the sound of the short, sharp footfalls had faded.

'He was telling the truth, as far as I could tell. He really does have this idea of me joining him in all these conferences and meetings, weeding out the people with the most power to stop him... Changing their minds, neutralising them if necessary. He sees me... It's weird, he sort of sees me as a mixture between a Guard person and

279

like a person he might finally be able to relax around, smile at, pat on the shoulder... I think... he's trying to be *proud* of me? But it's like he doesn't know what that feels like so he's just sort of telling himself to do it, if that makes sense. I don't know how that *can* make sense, it doesn't make any to me... He's so *weird.* Like he's this massive block of concrete but underneath it's all pinched and broken.'

'You got all that just now?'

Ariana shrugged. 'It's been coming on for a while now, whenever I feel like he's close by and I concentrate on him. Sometimes I hear snippets of conversations or memories he has of Mum. He thinks about her pretty much all the time. I don't look at the gross things, but some of it's interesting. He told her about his childhood once, a bit. About his dad being awful to him. And she did something to him when he went to see her in the summer, made him feel like a useless child again... He hates her for doing that to him, but he still loves her too. That drug Daniel gave him to help him block her out, it only partially works because part of him wants to hear her voice, and he knows that. And... somehow it's all connected to me, the mess of feelings he has. Mum told him he needed to work out how to be a father, to stop trying to make me a weapon or something, and that's what's triggered all these grand plans of his. But there's also this massive part of him that really, *really* can't be bothered with it all and thinks he should probably just have me *disposed of* too.' She shuddered. Reuben was watching her with an odd expression.

'What?'

'I'm impressed. You've managed to penetrate something close to the deepest, darkest desires of Josiah Lychen without him detecting you, Ariana. That's...

remarkable.'

'Thanks,' she smiled and looked away. 'Not sure how useful it's all going to be. Especially if he's going to be away for weeks on end.'

'Well, we'll see. All information is useful, one way or another.'

'I spose. I still haven't been able to get anything on Daniel, though.'

'Nothing?'

'He's so far away. I concentrate on the Futura, on the bits I remember, but there are so many people there... By the time I start sifting through them the first ones have moved about and I lose track of who they were... Plus anytime I try and actually focus on *him,* he just kind of wavers away. Like a ghost.'

'Well, his skill was disappearing, remember.'

'When he was a kid...'

'No one ever really verified what happened to it as he grew up though,' Reuben stroked his chin thoughtfully. 'I don't think he's actually able to do it to the fullest extent he once could. Once you know that the powers derive from suggestion... there's no going back. But I wouldn't be surprised if he had managed to retain some of the skills to use psychically. He certainly used to block me in a similar, slippery sort of way when we were children.'

'Well... it's annoying but I'll keep trying.'

'Listen for a call between him and Lychen. That might make it easier to grasp him, if you can hear his voice.'

'Yeah, OK.'

Reuben checked his watch. 'We have half an hour still. What do you want to work on?'

'Actually, I think I might go and see the old man. I want to talk to him about this monitoring thing. See if I can try and persuade him to escape again before it comes to that.'

'Are you sure that's wise? Lychen is already suspicious of your complicity with him. He will know you've helped him if he does escape.'

'I've seen inside Lychen's head. He values me more than he admits to himself. It's like you said back in the summer, I'm useful to him and there's only one of me. Yeah, he'll be mad if Marc disappears, but he won't actually do anything to hurt me. Not properly. Now I've stopped answering him back... now he's had this idea of me as his little spy sidekick.'

'Still... it would be best not to push him. He's unpredictable, particularly when angry.'

'Yeah, well... So am I.'

Marc wouldn't go, of course. He never would. And Ariana felt it beginning to change her. All of it. Marc refusing to run away when the chance was handed to him. Watching the blips on the machines they hooked up to him over the next few weeks tick faster as she moved her eyes over his body. The blankness lurked and whispered that it would be easier not to feel it, to just hurt him and not allow his gentle eyes to murmur the memories of sweeping back and forth on a swing, the press of his hand on her back, the tumble through the air and onto his shoulders. The blankness prodded and lunged as Marc screwed up his face and his heart thundered louder than the beeps, the rising numbers. Ariana let it pound through her. She didn't turn to the coldness, she didn't feel the pain. She didn't black out the guilt, but she also didn't let it rampage unbound. She thought about being a spy by Lychen's side. She thought about raising her hands and bringing the entire building crashing upon their heads. Reuben watched her and she could feel his admiration even as it became mingled with rich despair.

And she waited. The days slid into weeks. She pulled her hoodie over her head and realised that the sleeves no longer drooped past her fingertips. Her leggings looked cropped when they shouldn't and when the new clothes she ordered arrived, she knew with a strange, hollow sort of feel in her throat that the jeans that fitted neatly to her ankles would now need turning up on her mother's. Even she could see the changes in her face, the strange new angles, the curve of cheekbones she hadn't realised she possessed, the bouts of unexpected, grown-up radiance between outbreaks of spots and dry skin.

She took to listening at closed doors, trying to hear Daniel's voice, but so far there had been nothing. She'd heard plenty about GHAP, about how uptake was still behind projection but that the French were proving keen. She heard that Lychen had not been well received in New York, whatever that meant. Then, one day when she'd almost given up hope, she happened to be passing one of the conference rooms in North building when the sound of Daniel's snide, snotty voice weaselled its way through the gap under the door to lap unpleasantly at her ears.

Ducking into the bathroom next door, Ariana locked herself in a stall and shut her eyes. Instantly she was in the adjoining room, watching Daniel sneer on the small screen of a laptop as he explained something he clearly thought beneath him to a stressed-looking Beaumont worker.

'...not something I would have thought worth contacting *me* over, Watkins, but rest assured I'll let the relevant people know.'

'I just thought, given your previous interest in the

work—'

Ariana let the words bumble meaninglessly against her ears as she tried to focus on Daniel. She sent her mind through the screen but was met by the strange, slippery whirr she'd encountered before when trying to reach him. It was like his consciousness turned to wisps of air whenever she tried to grasp it. Frustrated, she tried concentrating on the Futura, reaching him that way, using his voice as a guide. She got as far as halfway down one of the squat, school-like corridors before she lost it. Meanwhile, she could tell from the pitch of his drawl that he was keen to end the call. She was running out of time. She'd have to try something else. Focusing instead on the young dark-haired man sitting in front of the screen on her end, she slipped into his head and began sorting through the jumble of surface wants and needs to access the decisions and desires.

'...just a minute, Dr Skaid... Dr Lychen, er, knew I'd be talking to you this afternoon. He asked if I could confirm a few things with you about the hybrid project?'

'Ye-es?' Daniel's eyebrow slid upwards even as he stifled a yawn.

'He just wanted to confirm the status of your latest specimens. And when they might be ready for launch.' Ariana concentrated very hard, going by feel rather than vocalisation lest the young man detect her.

'Tell Dr Lychen that the five new avian hybrids continue to outperform the others, though I have seen measured success across the field,' Daniel had allowed a little of his old snideness to creep in. This was good, Ariana thought. He was letting his arrogance cloud any suspicion over the nature of the questioning.

'Have there been any offers for them?' She sensed

Watkins' growing confusion, the curiosity burning at right angles to the questioning she was leading him down. *Did Lychen ask me to confirm these things? Shh, of course he did. The other day, remember? Now listen, he'll be mad if you miss anything...*

'A few. Nothing I would go into here of course, not with the likes of you, Watkins. It's all above your pay grade, I'm afraid. You tell him that. We're on track and will be moving to the ARC in January, all going well.'

'Right, OK...'

Ariana stared at Daniel through the man's eyes for a second longer and there... At last, there was a tiny flash of an image. A hybrid which slightly resembled Nova in that she was clearly female and part bird, but smaller with coarser, darker feathers. She had large human eyes and a dark beak like a crow and there was a thick iron collar around her neck clasped to a chain. Behind her stood a man dressed in feathers as well, wearing a bird mask with monstrous, shadowy eye holes and a curved sharp beak protruding from his nose. He reached for the bird-girl's chain and as he moved, Ariana caught a glimpse of others in the room – other hybrids, other costumed men and women along with large stage lights, a furry microphone, cameras... Blinking, she cleared Watkins' mind as she withdrew until he blinked vaguely as Daniel impatiently ended the call.

Ariana stood against the cold solid wall of the toilet stall and breathed in the chemical-tinged air around her. She didn't fully understand what she'd just seen, only that it was a glimpse of Daniel's version of what he had planned for at least one of the hybrids, this new bird-girl. Or something he'd already enacted. Something to do with a film and people wearing bizarre costumes, only... Only the costumes had been deliberately cut to show body parts Ariana had only glimpsed before. She shuddered, remembering the shadowy eye holes of the man as he'd taken the hybrid's chain. *It's not real,* she told herself. *It's just an image Daniel has. Something he's planning. Some sort of nasty adult film thing like the ones the boys at school used to show us on the bus, only... Only with hybrids.* It wasn't *real*, though. It couldn't be, but... but there had been a browser window, a view count, comments...

The nausea came upon her without warning, born of the look on Daniel's face, the oddly smug satisfaction almost as if he'd known exactly who was really asking him those questions and had delighted in answering. Born of the aching wrongness of the images, the lingering disgust as if he'd somehow chained her as well, put her in the bird-girl's unknowable, unimaginable position. Ariana turned quickly and braced a hand against the cool smooth surface of the stall wall, breathing slowly until she was sure she wasn't going to throw up.

February, 2020

Tess, Ralph and Ethan stare at each other, wide-eyed for a few moments as the siren wails nearby. Ralph recovers first, blinking at the double doors through which Bella had disappeared ten minutes ago.

'D'you think she—'

'No,' Ethan's head snaps towards the doors as well. 'Something's happened.' He's already striding towards the double doors before Ralph and Tess have time to react. Ralph bites back his annoyance as he watches Ethan gesturing furiously at the two security men standing at the entrance of the ward. He's never seen him like this before. Ethan was always so easy-going, the calm smooth of reason against Felix's more jagged logic. Now he looks ready to throw a punch.

'Should we... should we *do* something?' Tess hisses. Ralph glances at her. She's torn one of her fingernails bloody and one side of her carefully slicked hair is sticking up.

'Not yet... If he's going to get himself thrown out, we'll be the only ones left here.'

'To do what, though? She's already in there.'

'I don't know, Tess.' He grits his teeth as Ethan says something loud and scathing to the security guards and turns back to them, his face clouded in worry. People

287

around them are beginning to notice the large guy arguing with security amidst the blare of a not-very-distant alarm. Ethan hurries back to them just as the alarm switches off. There's a ripple as the other people in the waiting room turn their attention away again.

'I can't get in,' Ethan mutters, looking around. 'Something's happened in there... I can't reach her. I don't know if she's blocking me out on purpose—'

'She does that?'

'If she needs to concentrate, she will block out all other attempts to interfere. But this feels different... I think something's happened to her. C'mon, let's try and find another way in. Those guys aren't budging.'

Ethan strides away, taking a different corridor to the one they'd come from. Though he's taller than Ethan by at least two inches, Ralph finds himself almost jogging to keep up.

'What was the last thing you heard from her?'

'I wasn't exactly listening in. But when I try now, I just get blankness. It's like... like when she reaches for Ariana. Like she's been put in some sort of stasis. I don't know what the hell it means, but it's not bloody good.'

They take a sharp right and find themselves outside another set of double doors, this time with an automatic locking mechanism. Ralph peers through the glass at the top of the doors as Tess takes a swig of water from a bottle in her bag. The ward beyond appears to be fairly standard with several medical personnel flitting from patient rooms to a semi-circle reception desk.

'I don't think this is... oh, hang on...' Something is happening on the other end of the ward, where he can just make out another set of doors. Ethan joins him at the viewing point and they watch as a group of security guards

288

come through, gesturing at the medical staff.

'Looks like they're trying to clear a path...'

'She's not in there, come on, we need to find her. I can feel her getting further away.'

'Just a sec, I just want to see why they're—'

'Ralph, come *on!*' Ethan paces back to him and grabs him by the arm. Ralph shakes him off.

'Bella said not to interfere, what if this is all part of the plan?' Ralph knows he's still talking out of spite and jealousy and all the other mortifying emotions Bella thrust upon him today, but there's instinct nagging him, too. Something insisting that what's happening here, beyond these doors, is important. Ethan shuts his eyes for a second and Ralph wonders briefly if he's doing some sort of meditation to stop himself from hitting him, but then he opens them and his face floods with frustration once again.

'She's going too fast. I think she's in a car. I can't get a hold on where she's going, I think she must have been drugged.' He kicks the wall and a chunk of plaster falls out of it. Tess jumps and quickly glances away, back through the glass doors.

'It's got to be Lychen,' Ralph murmurs, worry seizing him in a tight cold fist.

'Hey, guys,' Tess clears her throat, bouncing on her toes to look through the doors.

'Dunno how he managed to work out where she was...'

'Must have some been some sort of surveillance... or bugs on the phones, that sort of thing...'

'She thought of all that, that's why we hired the car, kept the communications secure...' Ethan winces as he puts his foot back down.

'Hey, Ralph – I think somethings happening in here, it

looks like they're arresting Guard people or something…?' Tess's voice trails into a question as Ralph and Ethan move as one to join her at the door. The ward writhes with confusion as men in dark suits direct and argue with hospital staff. In the middle three Guard men stand stoically, seemingly unaware of the men in suits jostling them into position. Several security people speak into walkie-talkies and there's another flurry of activity as the far doors open and two more security people walk through, holding the figure of a young woman between them. Ralph stares – the girl, for he can see, even from here, that she looks no older than sixteen, is unlike anyone he's ever seen. She walks with the short, mechanical strides of the Guard and her face is set the same way, and yet she glances sideways at her bearers and when she looks up, seemingly directly at them, there's fear in her gaze.

'What the—'

'That's Eve,' Ethan breathes. 'The Youth Guard in Shona Metcalfe's service… They've arrested her…'

'So Bella succeeded with that part at least…?'

'I don't know…' Ethan frowns, tearing his eyes away from the doors and glancing back along the corridor. 'It doesn't feel right. Eve wasn't supposed to be taken with the others… We need to go. We need to call Tom and see what's happening with Ariana… Bella would want us to go ahead with the planned pick up at all costs…'

'I'll call Dom too,' Tess says as she joins Ethan, already beginning to stride towards the lifts at the end of the corridor. 'He's monitoring the lines of communication we've got coming from the Beaumont. Maybe he'll have picked something up…'

'Hey!' Ralph tears his eyes from Eve as she's positioned with the other Guard. The man on her right side doesn't let go of her arm, though she makes no move to struggle against him. He can see the tightness of the grip from here.

'What about Eve?'

'We don't have time, Ralph,' Ethan growls, jaw clenched.

'But she's... she's just a kid!'

'She's a Guard, remember?'

'But she's different, though... Just *look,* she's scared!'

'She'll be fine, Bella said she'd get them to recall the Guard—'

'...and sign them over to her, but what if there is no her here to sign them over to? She didn't plan on disappearing, did she?'

'Ralph, Eve's not our responsibility right now, we've got to *go.* Every minute we stay here runs the risk of discovery and arrest... Ariana needs us, I'm going and I'm taking the car.'

Ralph sighs, fists balled, anger and pain and everything else rising and falling within him. He wants to punch Ethan very much. Smash his fist – both fists – into his big, stupidly logical face and then yell very loudly. He wants to burst through the doors in front of him and grab the girl with the large, frightened eyes and... probably get arrested in the process.

'Bella would choose Ariana,' Tess murmurs. Ralph sighs and slowly turns from Eve, hating himself for it. Ethan has already reached the lift and jabbed the button to call it as Ralph trudges slowly away from the double doors. He knows they're right, he knows that Bella and his own father and probably even Eve herself would tell him that he had to go, that the priority had to be Ariana now. But as he walks away, he feels as if he's leaving something behind.

Something that shouts in the voice of a young boy, eyes embarrassingly wet behind their glasses, voice high-pitched in its earnest protestation. *This isn't right,* it shrieks. You *should save Eve. You should at least try. What happened to you?*

Winter, 2019

'...don't really understand all of it. It was only a glimpse and it's been so many weeks now, I wonder if I actually maybe just imagined it somehow. I mean, it's not like I'd ever be able to prove any of it. Watkins won't know a thing about it, after all. He was just the thing in between... what's the word? Vessel, that's it. Yeah. So... And Reuben isn't all that much use anymore, really. I mean he gives me tasks and things to try and stretch my psychic stuff, but... I mean... I don't think it's anything that I can't do on my own, you know? But I really like him. I think. I don't know, maybe I just think I do because I haven't really seen anyone else for so long. I talk to people online and stuff... there's this pretty cool group I found the other day when I was trying to find that hybrid video. It's got those old news photos of Nova falling out of the sky and all these people talking about the hush-up and conspiracies – some of them are surprisingly spot-on. I haven't posted anything but I think about it sometimes... God, it would blow their minds—'

'Ariana.'

Ariana jumped to her feet and turned abruptly. Lychen was standing in the wide doorway of the spacious, clinically sparse surgical room. She was in South East building where much of the space was dedicated to hospital-type rooms and equipment. This was where the

Guard were made. She knew because she'd watched, once, body concealed in a cupboard, mind hovering around the fluorescent light fittings... Having imagined a *Simpsons*-like montage of brains being sliced open and scooped with ice-cream spoons, the process – which had mostly involved scanners and keyhole probes – had been way more boring.

'You're here,' she said, stupidly. Lychen did not reply straight away. He placed his hands behind his back and walked towards her. She kept her eyes on him, but he wasn't looking at her. He stared at the man in the bed next to her.

'They told me he'd been moved here permanently. Is he always unconscious now?'

'Not always,' Ariana glanced back at the diminished form of her grandfather. His face was slack and positioned sideways. Wires and tubes connected his body to machines and drips and other things she didn't like to look at.

'Sometimes he wakes up for a bit. It's painful for him when he does. I can feel it through him. The doctors here say he's got swelling and stuff in his head so he gets a really bad headache when he's awake. I haven't seen him awake for a long time. It's like he's trying to protect himself.'

'You could force him awake,' Lychen remarked, coolly. He was standing on the other side of the bed now, his flinty eyes on her. Up close, he looked a strange mixture of the Lychen she'd come to know and a slightly different, unpredictable version. There were dark smudges around his eyes and his neck looked scragglier than she remembered where it met his tight stiff collar. Nonetheless, he stood tall and she still had to tilt her chin, though perhaps not as much as before, to meet his gaze.

'What would be the point?' She kept her face still even though internally she shuddered to hear how much the cool delivery sounded like Bella. He, too, didn't twitch, but she could feel the same uncanny frisson shiver through him.

'How did the Paris trip go?' She asked, quickly, before he could decide she had been insubordinate.

'Fine,' he replied, though she could sense the underlying frustration and, probing a little, saw a tumble of dissatisfaction. Their new ambassador had made a crucial communications error, the facility was not nearing completion fast enough, investors had been reluctant to place high-number orders.

'I have a question for you,' he added, as she opened her mouth to follow up. 'Why is it that I found your classroom dark and empty this afternoon and Sigma working in the North building kitchen?'

'Did you ask Sigma?' Ariana widened her eyes. Lychen's left eyebrow jerked.

'I did. She appeared under the impression that I had given her an override order.'

'You told me to practice my psychic mind-control.'

Lychen's eyebrow gave another strange little twitch and this time the rest of his face ticked a little with it. He was amused, Ariana realised with a strange, icy feeling of surprise. She didn't need to probe into his head to know he was feeling the odd conflict of longing to be proud mixed with tired consternation.

'You need an education,' he said, shortly, frustration overlapping the brief warmth. She hovered over the line.

'I know,' she looked down, pretending to be abashed. 'Sigma's lessons are just *so boring.* All she does is drone on and on. I never thought I'd say this but I miss real school. I've looked it up, there are tons nearby... Private ones, public ones, grammars, single-sex... I wouldn't breathe a word of where I live. I wouldn't invite friends round, *obviously.* I just want to feel a little bit normal. It's *not* normal, keeping me cooped up in this place without anyone my age…' It was all coming out too fast and too much. She hadn't planned on saying any of it, but now she had started it was difficult to rein it back in.

'You are free to roam the facility, talk to the scientists and technicians if you want…'

'No thanks. I already know I'm a freak, I don't need the bug-eyes of some twenty-two-year-old nerd to back it up.'

'If you attended school, you would be restricted by term dates and attendance records. You would not be able to accompany me next time I went abroad to oversee launches. Do you not remember what we discussed last time I saw you?'

'Yeah…' Ariana frowned, her eyes stealing back to Marc, to the large, weathered hand in hers. The only part of him that seemed the same. 'But how do I know you're not just saying that to try and make me carry on with my lessons like a good girl? It's been over a month since you said you were thinking of taking me somewhere and nothing's happened yet. You know I've passed all your tests.'

'Your abilities are remarkable, it's true. But your loyalties…'

'Really? You still don't think I'm loyal? Look at Marc! Look at me! I could have gone at any point over the last few months, you know,' she was still speaking too fast. She couldn't help it, though. She could feel the strangeness of his conflict as well as her own and both were inside her, powering her voice and dragging words from a place she hadn't known existed.

'You think a few dozen Guard could stop me? I can

levitate if I want. I could have floated right off that balcony you threw my mother off of – while I watched, by the way, and here I am still – I could have gone—'

'Where?' The word came smoothly but she could feel the anger beneath it. She had mentioned her mother and that, of course, had crossed a line, had swarmed all the unresolved mania to the surface.

'What?'

'Where would you go, Ariana? Back to her? I hardly think so. If that's where you wanted to be, you would have gone already. I don't doubt all you tell me about being perfectly able to leave whenever you want. I *do* doubt that you have any idea where you would want to go, though.'

She glared at him, not knowing if the fury thundering through her was his or her own.

'I could go to Futura,' she spat. 'I could go and wipe Daniel Skaid and his disgusting hybrid project off the face of the planet before he gets the chance to do all the horrible things he wants to do with them. Finish what I tried to do last year when I didn't have a clue just how powerful I could be...'

His eyebrows shot upwards. She had surprised him. She felt it in every inch of her being and revelled in the unlikely pleasure of it, even as Marc's hand gave a strange, warning sort of clutch against hers. She couldn't stop, though. She felt Lychen burning to know what she had found out, how she had found it out. Her mind tumbled the memory of it back to the forefront: how she'd overheard Daniel's voice, hiding in the nearby toilet stall, probing his mind using Watkins as a vessel...

'Extraordinary,' Lychen murmured, his eyes unfocused as he saw the pictures she sent him. Ariana bit her lip. Stop, she thought. That's enough. Shame whispered in a small child's voice: *What have you done? You shouldn't have shown him that.*

Why? Why shouldn't he know? Why shouldn't he see who I have become? It doesn't matter anymore. I'm not scared of him anymore.

'I'm not,' she said, wondrously. She met his eyes and knew he knew what she meant. He smiled in that weird, grimacing sort of unsmiling way he had. Then he glanced down at Marc and she knew what he was thinking.

'And yet... here, as you say, you still are.'

'He's an old man... Lych— D...Dad? Don't. Please?'

'He is not needed anymore. You said yourself. You have passed the tests. If you were telling the truth about your loyalty, this should hardly be an issue. Soren. Dispose of him.'

It happened in a flurry of pulses. Marc's hand in hers, a squeeze which was maybe not a warning after all, was maybe a goodbye. But... Soren? Another pulse and she looked up, at the black, twisting knives of her father's pitiless eyes and then, in the next beat, across the room. Where Soren stood in the doorway, Reuben in front of him, his head held in Soren's thick hands.... Ariana dropped Marc's hand, began to run, knew it was too late, knew it even as she opened her mouth and the scream wrenched from her as Reuben crumpled to nothing on the floor.

February, 2020

Nova is stalking a confused rabbit when the strange feeling comes. She isn't really intending to catch the rabbit, she's just enjoying the sensation of narrowing in on it, swooping, testing the flux and flow of air through her flexed wings. Sight, focus, hover; she lets the air dance tremulously beneath her feathers. Strike; she swoops downwards, eyes pinioned on the thatch of grass, though too human to see more than the vague smear of fur that is her quarry. She stretches her feet outwards as the rabbit looks up, freezes and then zigzags into the undergrowth nearby. Nova lands on her feet with a soft flump. Her human toes are too stubby to grip, the skin too delicate against the flurry of teeth and claws it would seek to seize. She's just playing. Still, her bird mind whirs with disappointment as she folds her wings and looks out across the snow-flecked moorland. The wind whips around her sparse head feathers and chills her too quickly. She crouches over her legs before they turn to sticks of ice. The cold hisses around her like the call of a distant gull, reminding her that she isn't bird. She will never be bird. She never can. She is just playing.

The feeling comes with a clouting rush. Danger. Change. Nova clicks her mouth and turns to the west. She is several miles from the ARC, but she knows without any doubt that that is where the sensation is coming from.

Nova straightens up, runs and launches into the sky. She does not think much as she flies, just lets the sensations flood as they come. The exhilaration of flight balances the warm instinct of trouble pressing into her face as she bounds towards it. The moorland skims beneath her, opening up to scrubby fields of deer. One or two spare her a wary glance, but there is no time now to swoop and scatter them into panicked droves. A lake smudges to the east, framed by mountains. She blinks, images swarming unexpectedly as the dark tower of the ARC flecks over a distant hill. Herself as a child stepping into the air. Bella clapping her hands with delight, a shimmering vision of jade crystals and impossible beauty. And there... waiting in the wings beyond... A woman she has never seen before, tall and slim, pale-skinned with aquamarine eyes sparkling like the dance of sunlight on stones snagged beneath a stream. Gingery golden hair sifting over shoulders, straight and feather-light. *Mine*, she thinks, as she banks and swerves away from the ARC and lowers to circle the mismatched stones of the Manor. *Me.*

She spots Dominic through the window straight away. He's in the laboratory, reading something off one of the machines. She approaches the window and calls softly. He looks up and raises his hand, points to the front door. She waits for a few minutes on the gravel, feeling its jaggedness in the softer parts of her feet, nudging the stones further in, encouraging the skin to roughen.

'Nova, you alright?' Dominic opens the front door, shrugging a thick coat over his shoulders. Nova shuffles towards him, trying to keep her movements smooth. Dominic is the hardest to talk to because he does not look at her enough and often misses the gestures she uses to supplement her language. She wishes they had left Ralph behind instead.

'Danger,' she mutters, her mouth stuttering a little around the difficult intonation. Dominic frowns.

'Danger? Where? When? I mean... what sort of danger?'

Nova glances in the direction of the ARC, though of course it's blocked by the Manor. She grunts in frustration.

'ARC,' she mutters. 'Something... Ch... Changes.'

Dominic opens his mouth to answer, but as he does so, his pocket begins to sing. Nova jumps backwards, but he holds his hands up calmly.

'It's OK, it's just my phone,' he reaches for it and lifts it to his ear. 'Tess? How's it going?' He turns away, his face creasing as he listens intently. Nova glances away, back to the glass between her and the laboratory. She hasn't been in there since her wing recovered. Apart from her nest room, she doesn't like being inside the Manor at all, the doors are too narrow, the ceilings too low. Still, this room intrigues her. Just like she can feel the press of danger from the ARC, here she can feel a different sort of emanation. It's coming mostly from the machine at which Dominic was standing a minute ago... Possibility, hope, the bright-eyed woman with the ginger hair... She realises she is leaning towards the window, eyes unfocused, mind entranced when the sound of Dominic's voice twisting with worry brings her back to the driveway. She turns to him as he presses a button and lowers the phone, though he still looks at the screen more than he looks at her.

'Well... I dunno about the ARC but you were right about danger. Something's happened in London – they managed to get to Metcalfe and it looks like the first part of the plan worked because the Guard are being taken out of action. There's some sort of alert. Yeah, see, it's just come through on my news app – all Guard are being asked to report to their nearest police station. Looks like they're rounding them up alright, but something's happened to Bella. She went to speak to Metcalfe then all hell broke loose and now she's missing... The others have gone to get Ariana as planned and then they're going to regroup... Wait, what're you doing... Nova, where are you going?'

Nova isn't listening. She runs, her feet smashing painfully across the stones, wings pumping one, two, and up. The swarm of danger floods into her face as she curves around the Manor and faces the black spectre of the ARC. How could she have been so stupid? Bella had asked her if there was danger ahead and she'd told her no because the only danger she'd sensed had been from the ARC. Her human mind floods with regret and shame as she cuts over the wall and keeps low, to the treeline. She feels Daniel somewhere around the front of the building and so aims for the back, gliding on the silent spread of wings. She lands neatly by a boarded-up window and takes a minute to gather her thoughts. Everything feels scattered. Bella, whole and mended and so supremely confident, but lost all the same. Only half the plan executed... But here. Here is the danger and the badness. Why?

She shuts her eyes and the memories crowd in. Hovering high in the air above Rudy on stage, his eyes strange as he'd glanced up and met her gaze. The car he held wobbling, swaying as she dove... and the sounds which seemed to rip the entire night sky apart... And afterwards. Waiting alone, too terrified to move, the synthetic feathers of her costume tearing apart slowly, one by one, in her hands. *Bella will come. She will come and explain what happened. She'll pull me into her arms and call me little darling and say it will all be OK.* But she hadn't come. And there the memories twisted. Lychen's face screwed in anger, Daniel's smirk: *Rudy's dead, you know. Do you want to know why? Do you?*

Dank, damp walls of shining darkness. Throat raw, fingers bloody from constant claw upon unfeeling indifferent hardness. Huddling in a ball, not small enough to stop the nightmares. Darkness. Floating. The shock of a cold hard surface and not knowing if it was the ceiling or the floor. And all the while, her own voice shrieking inside and outside: *It was never real.*

Nova opens her eyes. She lets the hurt and the anger and the pain flood backwards, turning her face to the shining wall in front of her. She looks up. Someone has left a window open on an upper floor. It's only a small crack, but they haven't changed the windows in this building since the days when she used to lever them open, nudge her body out onto the ledge and launch herself out into the joyful air. Danger is here, the wildness shrieks, tethering her to the ground. This is where we were locked away. This is where we were hurt. This is where she left us behind in the dark. This is the place we were torn apart. She shakes her wings outwards. This is where we recover. This is where we find the answers and make it right. Nova sets her mouth, focuses on the window, beats her wings and propels herself upwards.

Winter, 2019/20

Ariana could feel herself screaming. She could feel the searing bleed of her throat as she wrenched her voice into a screech of pure fury. She felt herself sweep Soren into the wall behind, the thunderous death-crack of his skull meeting plaster and brick. She could feel the burning, the pounding, the soaring hatred… And yet when she blinked, she found that the room was silent, her throat normal. Soren stood with his murderous hands hanging by his sides. Reuben lay in a huddle at his feet. Behind her, she could hear the regular blips of the machines hooked up to Marc. And Lychen, saying something about neatness and loose ends and compensating someone's family generously. Ariana stared at Reuben's face, at his dark, beautiful eyes as they glassed into nothing at all and she thought: *No. No more.*

She didn't realise she had begun walking or that she had left the room at all until she heard her name. She looked up. She was standing in the long white corridor outside the surgery rooms. To her right was a wide bay window overlooking the Yard. There were a few people out there on their afternoon break, coffee cups in hand, chatting away as if murder hadn't been committed mere metres away from them.

'Ariana, where are you going?'

She turned around slowly. Lychen stood a few feet away, staring at her mildly. He had his hands behind his back still, hair smooth as ever, not a strand of cotton out of place on his shirt. Behind him, Soren emerged from the room where Reuben and Marc remained. Ariana glanced behind her to see another Guard person whose name she didn't know emerge from the stairwell. She knew Lychen must have summoned them, which meant he felt some sort of threat from her. The thought should have made her feel powerful, she mused, but instead she was just... done.

'I'm done.'

'What do you mean?'

'I don't want to play this game anymore.'

'It's not a game, Ariana,' he said, quietly, stepping closer. 'You no longer needed Mr Teaque's instruction. He allowed himself to become emotionally invested in your welfare, ergo he would never have gone quietly back to his family without taking some tedious measure to try and *rescue* you. Even I could see that.'

'He didn't have to *die*!' She said, the words clenching in her throat. The fury jolted back to her like lightning. She looked outside, blinked and an apple tree burst into flames, scattering the people around it like ants. Lychen raised his eyebrows as screams met their ears.

'Control yourself,' he murmured.

'I *am* controlling myself,' she spat. 'Otherwise it would be you on fire!'

'Careful,' he said, taking another step forward. 'I have the means to take it all back, remember. I can see that you are emotional, but if you do not bring yourself under control, I will—'

'What? What will you do?' Another tree swarmed into rich auburn flames even as a pair of Guard gardeners approached the first with a hose pipe. 'There's only one of me, remember. You destroy my abilities and that's it, you won't get the little sidekick you wanted, you won't get the prodigal daughter to mould and make up for all your pathetic daddy issues.'

Lychen's face clouded in rage. She knew she was going too far, warnings pounded in her ears but the inferno of her own fury shrieked louder, crackling with the flames of the trees outside and the sound of Reuben's neck breaking.

'You think I cannot make another extraordinary child? I could make an army of them!'

'Not like me, not with a will of their own and Bella D'accourt's green eyes to match.'

'And what good has being Bella's fierce, loathsomely wilful child ever done you?'

Ariana stared at him. She glanced outside and saw that the two trees had been doused with water. Lychen watched them as well and a little of the fury left his features.

'You will go back to your rooms and take some time to gather yourself. Hank will accompany you,' Lychen gestured to the Guard behind her shoulder. 'I will come later, and—'

'No,' Ariana said, her eyes still on the trees outside, the gaggles of people muttering and pointing, gesturing confusedly.

'What?'

'No. You can't tell me what to do. You can't have your toy soldiers shuttle me around.' She felt the Guard man approach and tossed her head. There was a loud thunk as he hit the wall. Lychen's eyes widened and then narrowed into glittering slits.

'You can pretend otherwise, but I've seen in your

head. I saw that small pathetic little part of you that wanted to have the chance to bring me up, pass on your empire, be a father. I suppose a small pathetic little part of me wanted that too. I suppose *that's* why I'm still here... But I was wrong. You don't know the first thing about being a human, let alone a parent. You can't tell me what to do anymore, you can't just reach out and choke me when you get mad... *No,'* she swept her arm and sent Hank sprawling backwards.

Lychen jerked forward and she pushed with her mind until he, too, fell back onto the floor. Rage burned within her, tussling and tumbling with the familiar darkness, uniting as one. She yelled and, on her right, the window exploded outwards along with a shower of bricks. It sprayed into the Yard, thundering down over the people, shattering the air with their screams. Ariana didn't even bother looking. She screamed again, letting the air rip apart with the sound as she thought about Reuben's face, the ripple of his soft voice, the spark in his eye whenever she'd impressed him, the beam he'd given her when she had told him that she would help him go home. The building shuddered beneath her feet. More bricks and rubble spurted outwards, more sounds of panic rent the ground below.

'Stop! Stop it!' Lychen spluttered, getting to his feet. Ariana turned away from him and faced the open hole where the window had been. Power flooded through her, she raised her arms and concentrated on stepping into the air, letting it lift and carry her to the ground where she would make her way, casually, out and away... She looked down, feeling the shattered tiles beneath her feet begin to peel away as she buoyed upwards. Then a cold, iron hand gripped around her wrist and as she looked down to shatter it, a sharp yank of pain stabbed into her arm.

Ariana?

So... Sor... Sorry? Who is sorry? Why are they sorry?

Ariana! Ariana.

Soren. Not sorry. I forgot Soren. He's behind me, he got me.

'Ariana. Ariana, wake up!'

What is that? Who is calling me?

'What?'

'Ariana, you must wake up. You must get up. We have to go.'

The whiteness is blinding. Her eyes burn as she blinks confusedly, expecting to see the rubble-strewn corridor, the wide gap of open space she'd blown out of it. Lychen, Soren. Unconscious Hank. Instead she is lying on a thin mattress, a strangely young-looking Guard person she only vaguely recognises bustling around, pulling stickers off her arms, unclipping wires and glancing around with a quick urgency she has never seen a Guard display.

'What?'

She sits up slowly, feeling as if she is wearing a cloak of stone. She's in one of the surgical rooms, identical to where Marc had lain. The young Guard person holds a hand up for quiet, staring out of the glass-fronted door. Then he gestures hurriedly.

'There's no time. The Guard on duty knows you were waking up, he stepped out to make a call but he'll be back any minute... And there's a summons out for the Guard, all of us. I must get you out before the police come.'

'I can't move properly,' she mumbles, trying to lift a hand to her face and feeling it come in slow motion. 'Why can't I move?'

'It's the sedation... And muscle atrophy. You have

been unconscious for over two months. Your mother was supposed to help wake you more gently than this but she's missing. I can help you up if you—'

'Did you say two months? *Two months?*'

'Please,' the man reaches and slides a hand under her shoulder, half lifting her from the bed. Outside the room, shouts can be heard and a door bangs loudly somewhere nearby. Ariana stands shakily, her brain scrambling to keep up, still expecting to see Lychen getting up from the ground, Soren standing with a syringe in hand. The young Guard man lurches and catches her as her foot gives way. He tugs urgently towards the door. Ariana pauses.

'Who are you, anyway? Why're you trying to get me to leave?'

'I'm Tom. I'm one of your mother's first-generation Youth Guard. She gave me orders to wake you up and get you out of here safely...'

They're approaching the door now. Ariana feels her strength returning like the trickle of feeling to a dead leg, power beginning to prickle slowly back into her limbs. She knows it is her resilience, that no ordinary kid would be able to use their body so soon after waking from such a long sleep. *Two months!*

'Wait... did you say my mum's *missing*?'

'I can't sense her. Ethan said she has been taken. In any case, my orders have not changed. I am to bring you to the rendezvous point as quickly as possible.'

'OK...' Ariana shrugs, her head beginning to pound. *Well,* she thinks, *I was leaving anyway, I suppose.* She lets him lead her as slowly, bit by bit, the strength reignites and begins to flow.

February, 2020

'Not that turn, take the next one, it will bypass the one-way system.'

'I know where I'm going, Ethan.'

'When was the last time you drove in central London?'

'When was the last time *you* drove—'

'Hey, shh… They're talking about the Guard!' Tess leans forward in between the two front seats. Ralph and Ethan immediately stop bickering and Ralph turns the volume up on the radio.

'…reiterate, there is no need to panic, the Guard Assistants pose no immediate threat. All Home and Care Assistants are being asked, at this time, to report to their nearest police station. It is thought that this is just a precautionary measure to do with a system update. In other news, the Prime Minister's wife is reported to be in a stable condition following an alleged collapse at home earlier this evening. Matthew Broadhurst reports from St Mary's Hospital in central London…'

The car fills with the sound of the reporter's voice as he repeats much the same information which has been filtering through the radio for the last thirty minutes – stable condition, unknown cause.

'They haven't joined the dots between that and the Guard recall yet then,' Ethan muttered, his forehead creasing as he glares through the dark rain-spattered windscreen. Ralph nudges forward behind a taxi. He breathes slowly through his nose, pushing away the worry, trying to focus on nothing but driving. The rendezvous point with Ariana is one street away. They're already ten minutes late.

'There's no real reason why they should,' Tess says, slowly, listening as the journalist finishes his report and the main newsreader moves onto more minor stories. 'Looks like Eve's arrest was successfully hushed up. I'm just wondering how on earth they plan to manage thousands of Guard showing up at random police stations up and down the country... Talk about panic move.'

'Take this left, Ralph,' Ethan barks, his eyes swivelling towards Ralph. Ralph sighs and takes the left. An old man hunkers into a doorway, narrowly avoiding the spray from the unexpected puddle Ralph swerves the tyres through.

'...not to mention where they're going to put them all while Metcalfe decides what to do,' Tess continues to mumble, as Ralph takes the corner ahead more slowly this time. It's properly raining now; driving angled sheet rain of the type to drench a person in seconds. They all fall silent and stare as best they can from the splattered windows as Ralph pulls into the layby outside the tube station. The pavement is full of umbrellas, slick-wet coats, unsuitable shoes. Heart humming somewhere around his gag reflex, Ralph presses the button for the window and peers out at the crowd.

'Any idea what Tom looks—'

'He's not here,' Ethan says, mechanically. His eyes have swept up and down the throngs of people, taking in the tight-packed groups, the loners, the tourists and the workers. Ralph follows his gaze, swallowing his irritation.

311

Ethan's not a Guard anymore, he reminds himself. He's allowed to be wrong. His eyes snag on the huddle of another homeless person in an alcove next to the rush of people, a pair of old walking boots just visible. Something tugs at him, the memory of boots tossed haphazardly across the flagstones at the bottom of the stairs, a stumble followed by a rush of annoyance. *Your bloody boots nearly broke my neck, Ari!* Ralph wrenches the car door open and is outside, hair flattening to his head in the short time it takes him to stride across to the small huddle of person. Ethan's call shudders somewhere in his ears but he pays it no mind as he falls to his knees, reaching for the dark hood, the mass of hair, the pale face beneath.

'Ariana? Are you OK?'

Ralph reaches out instinctively, tucking a lock of curls away from her face. Her eyelids flutter and there's a glimmer of green. Her cheek is cold beneath his hand. Ralph glances behind him. Ethan has climbed out of the car as well, hazard lights blearing into the street. A few people have stopped to watch, but mostly the Londoners keep their heads down. Someone shouts further down the road and they all glance over to see a woman gesturing at a group of four Guard people, all clad in grey with ID lanyards round their necks. Ralph takes advantage of the distraction and reaches for Ariana, scooping her into his arms and scrambling to his feet, Ethan offering a supporting hand as he staggers a little. Slight as she is, she is heavier than expected and Ralph can tell from the droop of her long legs over his arm that she's grown several inches since he last saw her.

'Quick, in the back,' Ethan mutters unnecessarily as Ralph plants his feet and hurries towards the car, tossing the splat of hair from his eyes. Tess opens the door from the inside, Ralph tips Ariana in as gently as possible. Glancing up as he straightens back up, he takes in the sight of the four Guard people turning as one, their faces stoic even as rain slashes at them and the woman gives the nearest one a little push. They begin walking down the pavement, but the woman's shove seems to have set off something. People surrounding them begin to yell. Someone throws a cardboard cup of dark liquid. It hits the Guard person on the far right of the group, splotching heavily across her shoulder. She does not flinch or hitch her stride. Ralph meets Ethan's gaze and, without speaking, they both move to the front of the car as quickly as possible, Ethan taking the driver's seat this time. Ralph shuts the door and instantly feels a swipe of relief as more people rush past the window towards the group now surrounding the Guard.

'Where's Tom?' Ethan mutters, though he doesn't stop as he pulls the car steadily into the traffic creeping away from the station.

'He... He had to...' Ariana's voice trembles weakly from the backseat. Ralph turns the radio down low and strains to hear her over the insistent swatch of the windscreen wipers.

'What was that?'

'He got me to the station... And then some woman started yelling at him... He had to go...'

'Christ,' Ralph mutters, 'what have you started, Beast?' He glances into the wing mirror as the traffic begins to move forward a little faster. A bottle sails through the air and clatters into the back of the head of one of the Guard. Ralph keeps his eyes on him long enough to see him pitch forward slowly under the force of the blow before the piercing sound of a car horn brings him back to the road.

Ethan says nothing but he wastes no time pummelling the accelerator as soon as a space opens up on the road ahead.

Ariana doesn't remember much about the first part of the journey out of London. She slants across the backseat of the unfamiliar car, unable to summon the energy to close or open her eyes fully and so letting her vision haze in and out of focus. The others' conversation silts with the radio, the odd piece of sense filtering through her ears: *Guard continuing to be rounded up, no need to panic, Prime Minister to make a statement...*

Sleep hovers nearby, whispering seductively of sweet oblivion, a break from the images which swirl relentlessly. Reuben, crumpling to the ground like a doll. The squeeze of Marc's hand as she'd dropped it and turned away. Lychen's eyes widening as she'd blasted a hole in the side of his precious building... And the strange mixture of nonsensical happenings since then. The corridors of the building unblemished as she'd stumbled past them, though the paint nearer the window noticeably lighter than its surroundings... Tom's face riveted in stoic concentration as he'd tugged her along, her feet stumbling and failing every so often. The painful spasms of her own muscles. Shouting. Lychen's face... Was that real? Had that been tonight? He'd barked into a phone furiously, surrounded by six or seven Guard as he walked quickly towards a black car on a driveway.

Ariana frowns, trying to place the memory in context. Driveway... Buildings had loomed from it but the rain swarmed them out of focus. Lychen had climbed into the car without noticing her... Or had he? She remembers the car scrunching away over the stones. She remembers

Lychen's smooth hair spotting under the rain. His suit darkening at the shoulders during the brief time the Guard person nearest had lowered the umbrella as he'd climbed into the car... He hadn't seen her... Except... people were shouting behind her, Tom was dragging her sideways... Lychen's face, turning towards hers, rigid shock... Fear?

Gradually Ariana feels the rhythm of the car change as they leave the stops and twists of the London traffic behind. Ralph and Tess's voices relax noticeably, though Ethan's remains tight like thread spooled to snapping point and he speaks less and less as if afraid every word might bring him closer to the break. At one point they all fall silent and someone turns up the radio. A tired, posh voice Ariana only vaguely recognises fills the car.

'...brief. The recall of the Guard should be treated as a precautionary measure only. They should not be considered dangerous and any acts of violence against them will be treated as criminal damage. Their manufacturer – Beaumont Futura Industries – has been co-operating fully with the government with regards to this matter, but we are still very keen to speak to the managing director, Dr Josiah Lychen. We have, at this point, been unable to make contact with Dr Lychen and would urge him to come forward as soon as possible. If anyone has any knowledge of the whereabouts of this individual, please call the special hotline number...'

'Wow... Lychen's a wanted man,' Ralph murmurs.

'Well, they didn't actually say he was wanted in a *criminal* sense...' Tess replies. Ariana keeps her eyes half closed but can make out the woman's neat blonde bob as she leans forward. Ralph is sitting in the front passenger seat, talking into the rear-view mirror rather than turning his head. Ariana can't see Ethan from her current position, but senses his tight solid shape behind the wheel. Energy seeps back into her limbs and she blinks to bring her vision into stronger focus. She cannot sense the feelings of the others around her as easily as she normally would – her resilience must be concentrating on replenishing her body first, she thinks – but she gets the odd flash. Muted excitement from Tess, mingling confusedly with worry and dread.

'Hey guys... I think she's awake,' Tess leans a little closer. Ariana blinks and opens her eyes and Tess instantly recoils back.

'Hey, Ari,' Ralph speaks softly, as if to a very young child. Ariana turns towards him and is surprised by the surge of her own feelings as his large slightly-lined face appears on the shoulder of the car seat in front of her. His hair has grown since she last saw him and there's a little more grey shot through the temples but otherwise he's exactly the same. She opens her mouth to say something and, to her shock and utter mortification, what comes out is a strange, strangled sort of sob.

'Hey, hey... It's OK...' Ralph reaches backwards and puts a large, warm hand on her knee. Ariana buries her head in her hands, feeling her face glowing. Something flutters around her shoulder – Tess's hand? – she shakes it away and clears her throat a few times until the weird crying thing stops.

'It's alright... You've been through a lot, huh? It's OK. You're safe now,' Ralph mumbles. Ariana swallows furiously. It's his voice, she thinks. His voice means more than his words, but she doesn't know if it's what's making her cry or making her stop. She coughs and wipes her face with her sleeve. There's a few moments of silence before she clears her throat again and tries to speak.

'I don't… I don't know why…' Her voice crumbles weakly, hoarse with lack of use.

'It's OK,' Ralph says, patting her knee.

'Don't worry about it,' Tess adds, offering her a tissue. Ariana takes it and mops her eyes. Then she gives herself a little shuddery shake. She looks up at Tess, remembering the last time they were in a car together. Tess looks away as if she's remembering it as well. Ariana had woken up in a strange place then as well, she thinks. She'd cried then. Her mother had been there that time, the voice in her head telling her what to do, where to go, how to be… Now there's nothing except confused memories and the slow, reknitting pathways. Ariana glances at Ethan. He remains a tight fixture behind the wheel but, as she looks up, he peers into the mirror and catches her eye. She feels his flash of painful worry for Bella, his desperation for her to be safe… Ariana looks away again.

'Do you remember anything that happened at the Beaumont tonight?' Tess asks her gently. 'Anything about Lychen?'

'I… I was asleep… or unconscious, I guess. Before then… I made the wall collapse. They *killed* Reuben, right in front of me. I was trying to leave… Then I woke up and it… I woke up and it was now. Tom was there. He said we had to go… There were loads of people… They were running and shouting. The Guard… They were all going one way and the people were confused and scared. But Tom got me out. He knew which way to go… My legs… They didn't always work right. But we got out…'

She coughs and the others wait motionlessly. Tess offers her a bottle of water and Ariana drinks deeply, letting the coolness flood and soothe her throat. When she speaks again, her voice cuts a stronger shard through the rumble of the car.

'I saw Lychen. I think so, anyway. It's hard to know what was then and what was tonight... It's kind of mixed up still in my head, but... I'm pretty sure it was tonight because he was getting into a car with a few Guard Assistants. Maybe six or seven? They were all big, wearing dark clothes... It was raining. Tom had brought me through a side door into this passageway. There were people trying to get past us. We kept our heads down and went as fast as we could. Lychen... he didn't see me until someone shouted nearby. I don't remember what they said but it made him look up and he... He'd been on the phone and was really angry with someone, but when he saw me, he changed. He looked alarmed... Scared. Like I was about to attack him or something. Then he got into the car and it zoomed away super fast. Like sending-up-sprays-of-gravel fast.

'That's when Tom brought me down the driveway and into the street. He got me as far as the station but by then people were noticing him... He said he couldn't stay because it would draw too much attention. Then he kind of bundled me into that doorway. I was so tired at that point. I couldn't feel my feet anymore. I couldn't even stay awake... Then he was gone and Ralph was there...'

She feels her throat closing up again and takes another long drink of water. No one says anything and gradually Ariana feels herself sinking back into sleep. She wakes on and off as the car speeds northwards, lights flashing over her eyelids as they pass under streetlamps. The tinny undertones of the radio occasionally cuts into her dreams, but it's only Ralph and Tess starting to speak again which slowly tugs her mind out of the miasmic well of unconsciousness.

'...any idea where he would go. Just having the Guard with him is going to be enough trouble – they're now saying that anyone harbouring Guard will be prosecuted.'

'I suppose Futura is too obvious...'

'It's the first place they'd look for him. Plus the place is rammed with Guard, the police will be all over it...'

'He's probably still got his contacts within the police though... perhaps he's got some protection there.'

'Good point. He might hole up somewhere, build his case and then emerge with his excuses. Once they expose Bella as the head of the Youth Guard programme it'll be easy enough to place the blame on her for Eve and the others' malfunctions and undo all the headway she made with Metcalfe.'

'So why hasn't he done that now to stop the recall?'

There's a pause as the car fills with traffic noises again alongside the rhythmic beat of the windscreen wipers. Ariana keeps her eyes closed, half expecting them to stop talking if she opens them, half worried she might do something unexpectedly humiliating again. Ethan's voice thrusts into the conversation like a hammer slicing through mist.

'Because he's been too busy arranging Bella's abduction.'

There's another silence. Ariana feels the scrutiny of eyes watching her steadily, assessing how asleep she is. She remains motionless.

'I'm not so sure... I mean, yes he's almost certainly the one who's behind her being taken,' Ralph says, measuredly, 'But I don't see why that would have stopped him coming forward, making a statement and trying to undo all the damage...'

'Maybe it just snowballed too fast,' Tess says, quietly.

'And there's what happened with Ariana. That will have thrown him off. She said he was furious on the phone to someone...'

'...because of the Guard recall?'

'Or something else hadn't gone according to plan. Remember earlier when Tom told Bella about the increased security around Ariana? We still don't know why that was, but if he was terrified to see her then I'm guessing he wasn't planning to have her woken up...'

'What does any of it matter?' Ethan mutters, his voice sounding hoarse though Ariana has barely heard him use it. 'The Guard are being recalled, Lychen has gone and wherever he is, he's got Bella, the same Bella who's been tormenting him for months. God knows what he'll do to her... *is* doing to her.'

'Guys.'

'Let's just... Look, you said you can't sense her because she was asleep or unconscious or whatever—'

'Or they're using whatever they did to cloak Lychen and the ARC to block her telepathy...'

'Guys!'

'Well there's not an awful lot we can—'

'They tracked her, Ralph. You know they did. They knew when you all left the Manor, they tightened security on Ariana. They knew where to find us at the hospital... They're probably still tracking us now...'

'So what do you want to do, call Felix for help?'

'No. Yeah. Maybe. She won't help if it's for Bella, though.'

'What if it's for Ari?'

'*Guys!*'

'What is it, Tess?'

'That truck. The plain, white one in front of that van...'

'What about it?'

'It's a BFI vehicle. And I'm pretty sure I saw another one pass it just now...'

This time Ariana's eyes pop open before she can think about stopping herself. She clocks the large, unmarked lorry a few cars away up the rain-sheeted motorway. As the others watch it too, it indicates left off an exit.

'Should I...?'

'Follow it. Definitely,' Ralph says, sounding uncannily like his father. Ethan must think so as well, Ariana decides, because there is no flicker of question as he indicates to follow and turns the car rapidly off the motorway in pursuit.

February, 2020

The ARC is eerily empty. Nova slides through the open window and immediately wheels around, talons ready, feathers bristling in defence, but there's nothing to fight. The dark walls shine unconcernedly around her, the familiar rush carpet nestles underfoot. She is standing in a corridor, the window placed between what looks like a cupboard and an office door bearing a faded rectangle where a name would once have blared. Nova doesn't recognise the corridor, but that doesn't mean much; as a child she was only allowed to go into the designated rooms on the ground floor and the carefully walled gardens beyond. Glancing up and down, Nova shoulders the door to the cupboard open and creeps inside. Cobwebs snag at her wings and dust smears her feathers but she moves until she is standing between a mop and a broom and shuts the door. Concentrating into the darkness, she sends her mind out without quite knowing what she is doing. Daniel. He's far from here, she realises with a twist of relief. She can see his outline, wired with a frenetic excitement as he walks briskly down a corridor towards the entrance hall. He's talking too fast, too distantly for her to hear, to a plain-faced Guard woman next to him.

Nova opens her eyes and inches out of the cupboard, shaking the dust and muck away. She tries to sense whether anyone's coming, but there's nothing to be heard in either direction. She doesn't know whether that means the place is deserted or if she just doesn't have the instinct to know like she seems to with Daniel. In any case, she is beginning to feel the familiar crushing sensation of being inside for too long and sets off in an ungainly shuffle. Downstairs, she thinks. If the hybrids are anywhere, it will be downstairs in the larger rooms with access to the gardens as well as the stone-lined dungeons. Nova keeps going until she reaches some stairs. Glancing around, she takes them sideways. Her human side wonders where the mass of Guard people she saw unloading the lorries last month might be. Her bird instincts keep her feet moving, her eyes sharp, her focus narrow.

She comes across them completely unexpectedly. Finding herself in a corridor she recognises but only in a vague passive way, Nova glances up through the glass door to what she thinks might have once been a medical room and gives a squawk of surprise to catch the eye of a person. Blinking, she approaches the glass. The person is a young man, around her own age. He sits alone in the small room beyond, which is bare except for a narrow single mattress on the dark shining floor. The man frowns at her and shakes his head. She knows instinctively that he's trying to work out if she's real. There's no fear there, though. None of the horror or disgusted wonder that she has become used to seeing on the faces of humans when they see her for the first time. She is not the first hybrid he has come across. She reaches for the door handle, unable to grip it properly but able to nudge it enough to confirm that it's locked. The man approaches the door and looks beyond her before placing a hand on the glass.

'How did you escape?' He whispers urgently.

Nova glances around before concentrating as hard as she can on the small words.

'Not from here,' she mutters.

'No?' The man raises his eyebrows. Despite the gesture, he has a weary presence about him, as if there is nothing left in the world which could truly surprise him. His clothes are dirty and torn, Nova notices, as if he's been attacked by an animal. His arms bear scars which remind her of the ones she left on Bella.

'Who are you?'

'I'm Harry. My... my brother Ozzy is a... They made him into a bird... person. Like you. Only different. Darker feathers. They let me see him once a day. I have to talk to him, make him do stuff for them...'

'Why?'

A cloud passes over his face and Nova realises she shouldn't have asked.

'They do bad things. There was one pair — a woman and her son, I think... They tried to refuse. They tortured him with a taser. She... the *sounds* she made. They didn't kill them, though. I think we're too valuable for that. But after that happened... We all do as they say.'

'How many?'

'Twenty, maybe twenty-five pairs...'

'Where?'

'The humans are kept apart most of the time. I don't know if there's anyone else on this floor... If there is, they haven't spoken to me. I don't know how long I've been here. They bring me food three times, take me to the bathrooms first and last thing... I'm taken outside to exercise and see Oz most days, not every day. Check my health every so often. No one really talks to me apart from the creep. I don't know his name. He doesn't use mine.

He's worse than the Guard people. He asks questions, monitors Oz... He treats him better than me – him and the other scientists call the creatures *assets*, talk about marketability and bids. We humans are important enough to keep fed and healthy but the others, the creatures... I think... I think they're for sale.' He shudders and looks away for some time. Nova waits until he turns back to her.

'Can you help us? The Guard have the keys, I've seen them on their belts. If you can work out how to get them... Or find a way, *do* something to make them let us all out... Please.'

Nova watches him for a little while longer, letting the desperation of his eyes blaze into hers, settle around her chest. She knows she is letting her guard down, that any moment someone could appear from the other end of the corridor and she wouldn't know until they were almost upon her... She knows she's being too human, but she can't help it.

'I will try,' she says, slowly, clearly. He grins, revealing several missing teeth.

A sound from somewhere nearby brings her back to herself with a sharpness that sends her scurrying away before she remembers to say goodbye. Her wings are half-unfurling and she lets her bird-sense rise, stumbling as the overwhelming suffocation swamps over her. She stares wildly around as she runs, the urge to hurl herself at a wall surging alarmingly within... Luckily a window appears when she shoves open the door to a stairwell. She hammers her body against it, thrusting through the opening, tearing feathers and skin, not caring as the pain glimmers somewhere far beneath the surge of panic. And finally the air crams into her face and she's tumbling out and into the sky, her wings fluttering outwards, the beautiful sweetness of night lifting her up and away.

February, 2020

It is past two am by the time Ethan brings the MPV to a crawling stop outside the Manor. He glances in the mirror. Tess and Ariana are both fast asleep, the former with her head nestled upon her jacket she's wadded up against the window, the latter curled in a mass of limbs like a spider. He watches Ariana for a moment longer, yearning to beam the image to Bella, to feel the swarm of relief and love in return. He sighs, her absence in his head a painful crater as he turns to meet Ralph's eye somewhat unexpectedly.

'You're awake,' he says, finally, just to say something.

'It's not Ariana's fault,' Ralph replies, keeping his voice low. His eyes are heavy with too little sleep and appear overly small and young without his glasses.

'What?' Ethan frowns. His own tiredness is like a heavy weight around his shoulders, but it's nothing compared to the worry juddering around the empty space inside. Finally fully human, he thinks, bitterly.

'What happened to Bella. It's not Ariana's fault.'

'Of course it isn't. Why would you even suggest—'

'I'm not *suggesting* anything. I'm just reminding you. She's got enough problems, she doesn't need guilt as well.'

'Whatever,' Ethan yawns shudderingly. Then he turns back to Ralph, who wipes his glasses clean before placing them back over his eyes. 'She hasn't asked about her at all.

Have you noticed that? Not once.'

Ralph shrugs. 'Give her time. You heard her, she watched Reuben die and then she got put to sleep for two bloody months. God. Poor Reub.'

Ethan tries, but finds he can only conjure a very distant rumble of sympathy for the serious dark-eyed boy he'd known a lifetime ago.

'I mean,' Ralph continues, his voice thin with weariness, 'what does that do to a person, let alone a thirteen-year-old already struggling with so much?'

'Yeah. Well. I wouldn't let my guard down if I were you,' Ethan mutters.

'I miss her too, you know. You're not the only one worrying about Bella.'

Ethan grunts.

'But we've got bigger problems to deal with right now. This girl here... She's the most important thing now. She's the one we have to protect at all costs. I was stupid enough to forget that once, I'm not going to make that mistake again. I owe Bella that.'

'You sound like you've already given up on her.'

'Bella is more than capable—'

'You don't *know* that, Ralph. You all say that all the time but sometimes she's *not*. If someone's doing something to stop her from using her resilience to defend herself—'

'She's still Bella.'

Ethan sighs and removes his seatbelt before throwing the door open as if he can't stand to be in the same space as Ralph any longer. Ralph rolls his eyes. He turns to wake the others only to meet two pairs of curious, wide eyes staring back at him.

'Did... er... did you call Felix in the end?' Tess glances

from Ralph to Ariana and back again, awkwardly.

'She didn't answer. Signal wasn't great, I'm going to try again once we get inside. Did you manage to sleep much?'

'A bit.'

'How are you doing, Ari?'

'OK,' Ariana mumbles, her voice slightly stronger. She glances moodily at the Manor looming outside the car window. 'Didn't think I'd be coming back here again.'

'Mmm. Come on, your bedroom hasn't been touched since you last used it. And I suspect we'll find a Marble lurking somewhere around the fire...'

Ariana's face brightens at the mention of her cat and she reaches for the door eagerly. Ralph hurries out of the car, shuddering involuntarily as the icy darkness slaps him painfully after the stuffy bubble of the car. Ariana stumbles a little as she climbs out and her steps are slow and hesitant, but as Ralph approaches he can tell her strength is returning quickly. He can see it in the brightness of her green gaze, the planting of her feet, the only slight pressure she places on the arm he offers her.

'Tess! Ralph!' Dominic comes running out of the Manor wearing a strange mixture of jeans, dressing gown and T-shirt, his hair sticking up at the back. He hugs Tess, peering curiously at Ariana over her shoulder.

'What's going on? Ethan's stormed in all moody, he's gone to put a pot of coffee on... He said something about Felix coming?'

'I haven't got hold of her yet, but yeah, hopefully. We're going to need all hands on deck,' Ralph says, as he locks the car door and leads Ariana into the house. He glances around to the treeline behind them but there's no sign of Nova.

'Nova's up top,' Dominic says, following his gaze. 'She took off over to the ARC earlier after you called, said something about danger.'

Ralph passes his hands through his hair, barely able to squeeze the new, odd piece of information into the jumble of the last thirty-six hours. Nodding wearily at Dominic, he follows Ariana into Blake's former office where the fire crackles welcome heat across the room. The sofa spills with blankets where Dom has been sleeping. Ariana sits on the rug in front of the fire, Marble curled with his eyes squeezed determinedly shut as she pets him.

'So what happened with the trucks?' He hears Dominic ask Tess behind him. 'You texted that you were going to follow them but then I didn't hear anything...'

'Yeah... I must have fallen asleep afterwards,' Tess mutters, sinking into one of the armchairs. Ralph takes his phone from his pocket and crosses into the adjoining schoolroom. His stomach feels achy and a little nauseous around the edges as it always does when he's up too late. The shadows of the room lurk luridly, stretching in the long reaches thrown by the fire and he shudders as the chill creeps under the collar of his jumper, the cuffs of his shirt. It feels like years have passed since Bella reached for him upstairs, her fingers soft and nimble as she buttoned him up. The room seems to glare with all the lost touches and whispers of her. A sci-fi paperback draped on the arm of a chair, her favourite teal coffee mug on the side table next to it. A long, shining strand of dark hair drifting from the open doorway. Shutting his eyes, he allows himself to feel it all – one heady swiping crash of pain and worry and hurt – before he shakes his shoulders back, presses a button on his phone and makes himself stop.

'Ralph? What's going on?' Felix's voice is as thick and

slow with sleep as he expected it to be.

'Fee. I'm so sorry to call so late. It's… um… we—'

'Is Ethan OK?' Her voice immediately sharpens and he realises, with a strange jolt, that it wasn't sleep which had thickened it a second ago. More like… wariness. He shakes his head, sure his own tiredness is clouding his judgment.

'Yeah, yeah, don't worry. He's fine. Everyone's fine. Well, almost everyone. Listen, it's a long story and I don't really know how much you already know, but… Well, we went to London to try and—'

'Discredit Lychen and get the Guard recalled?'

'Sort of, yeah. And rescue Ariana.'

'Ariana's with you? Is she OK?'

'She's fine. Or seems to be, anyway. A bit weak and tired but you know, pretty good considering…'

'So what's going on then?'

'Well, to be honest we need your help. We were tracked to London. Bella was taken when we were in St Mary's Hospital. I know what you're going to say – not your problem, nothing to do with you… But if Lychen was tracking us there, he's probably tracking us still. And we have Ariana… She could be in danger. Also, something else happened on the way back here – we saw some lorries heading off the motorway. Tess recognised them as BFI. We thought we'd follow them, see what they were up to…'

'*Christ*, Ralph.'

'Yeah, I know. But listen, they went to this abandoned industrial estate off the M1. There were about seven of them there in total, not all of them BFI models but all of them these massive artillery vehicles. We managed to find a place to park nearby and Ethan and I snuck over to see what was happening… I thought at first it was a human trafficking thing we'd stumbled across but it was the

Guard. Hundreds of them, they must have been crammed in like cattle... They all came marching out and into these abandoned warehouse buildings...'

He stops, his throat closing unexpectedly. He turns around to meet the gazes of Dominic, Tess, Ethan bearing a tray of coffee cups, Ariana curled up motionlessly next to Marble, peering up at him like a cat herself. They're all listening to him.

'Ralph? What happened?'

'Sorry... We found a way around the back, managed to get to a window. It was hard to see what was happening. I was going to break it and climb in but Ethan... he had a weird feeling. Like a sort of sixth sense, I guess. I don't know if it was a residual Guard sense for danger or something but it's a bloody good thing he stopped me because... Well, we could see all the Guard standing there. There were people – they were all dressed in dark clothes, I couldn't see if they were police or BFI or what. There was a bit of discussion and I thought they were just going to shut the doors and leave them there, you know. The Guard... they were all just standing around like robots. Then they... they chucked a bunch of canisters in with them and bolted the doors shut.'

'Jesus.'

'Yeah. We couldn't see much because of all the smoke at first... But we could hear the coughing and the... the noises. They tried to get out, they tried to open the doors. They were hurling themselves at them at one point... Then they all just... stopped.' He shuts his eyes, hearing the thuds, the last few coughs, the wide, empty eyes of a Guard man who had found the back window too late, falling even as he reached a hand towards it.

'They gassed them.'

'Yeah.'

'Shit. So much for reprogramming them or whatever it was the news said they were going to do.'

'I think they panicked, Fee. Whatever happened with Bella and Metcalfe—'

'She fucked up.'

'Or she was interrupted before she could finish doing what she needed to do... In any case, we need you, Felix. We need your help if we're going to have any chance at all to finish what we started and keep Ariana safe.'

'I... OK. Just give me a few hours, I'll need to find somewhere to take the dog. I... I can be there by morning.'

'OK. Thanks, Fee.'

'See you soon.'

February, 2020

Tense, flex, test. Repeat.

When I lived at the Beaumont... No. No, it was before then. Tense, flex, test. My body remembers. My muscles stretch back twenty, twenty-five years... To the days where it would lie and cradle my waking mind in stasis, bringing me slowly to the surface; tensing, flexing, testing for hurts. Till my eyes would blink and the slow aches would return. Back then the wounds were skin deep. Bruises, blemishes, the marks of a woman disturbed by the fester of malignancy in her head, the mocking beauty of the child she could never fully claim as her own. The need to protect and nurture battling the urge to mark, to score. I would never understand her or what she did, but I learned to live with it the same way I lived with everything. Testing, flexing, pushing, nudging my way to the edge of what I could cope with. My body learned a way to wake gently through the painful edges, take the worst of it away, dip slowly through the rest. It was a skill I lost after Ana died, but my body remembered and, just as my legs and arms could spring to perfectly recall a ballet routine my brain had long since forgotten, when the bruises returned so did the slowness of waking.

So when I lived at the Beaumont, when my careful unravelling of Lychen got to the point where he could no longer stop himself, I was ready. Consciousness would trickle upon me with the gradual pulse of aches. My throat, often. My arms sometimes. Wrists. Tense, flex, test. Sometimes I would be fine. Sometimes a warm shower and a stretch were all I needed to shake the remnants of pain away. I had a resilience gene, after all. I had extra to compensate for the sadism I pulled towards me like eyes. Sometimes I wasn't so fine. Sometimes I hadn't played my part well enough and the ache knifed deep inside, the dragging sharpness carrying me back to the place my entire life seemed to be pinned to. The shivering shame, the tearing hurt, the raw acid of nausea. Those days would take me a little longer to muster the energy to pretend, to smooth away the winces, to pour myself into my cold mask and brace it against the world like a shield; to Bella.

It's been so long since I needed to wake slowly. My body may have grown stronger over the last few months, but it has also weakened – the reflex against danger has receded, the guarded readiness for blows, too-tight grips and that old familiar need to disappear has faded. It tries, though. I feel consciousness tumbling towards me and something snags it, slowing it but unevenly, clumsily. My head gives a yank of sharpness first. The back, where I was hit. I try to move a hand to it but I can't. My wrists sear next and I blink and shiver as the cold hits me with a barbed rush.

There is a corner of dark wood next to my face. My hands are shackled together with heavy metal which, as I move, clinks. Chains. Icy snakes trickle down my back as I blink focus back into my eyes. Don't panic. I am lying on a floor, the carpet scratching into my cheek. My hands are fastened to the corner of dark wood I can see. I blink and shift my head backwards a little. The movement spasms pain around my skull, but I manage to see a little more. A carpet of swirling deepness stretching across a room.

My mind begins to leap across the aching holes of pain and confusion. I am not in my former bedroom at the Beaumont – that sends a quick swarm of relief over the shudders. The carpet in front of me is familiar though. I move again and a small puff of dust lifts into the air. It smells of murmurs and darkness and memory. I flex, tense, test. The rest of my body shifts slowly in response. I'm lying on my left side, curled around myself. There is no injury to my midriff; my legs are cold but unbound. My body aches from the hardness of the floor, but when I shut my eyes and concentrate inwards, I can't feel any other injuries. That brings more relief. I open my eyes fully and move again, ignoring the pain in my head. I manage to rock myself sideways onto my knees so I'm crouching, back rounded towards my clasped hands as if in prayer. Finally, I look around.

Of course.

The carpet is thick with dust and so is the desk, the sofa, the crystal chandelier in the ceiling. Footprints show where a few people have come in and out but otherwise, other than the grime, my office is exactly how I remember it from fourteen and a half years ago. My bathroom door. My small set of mahogany drawers. Even the marble plant pot on top, though it no longer bears the easy-growing succulent Dr Blake gave me. My desk, of course, is the heavy wooden thing I am shackled to. I try pushing it but it doesn't so much as shudder and my head screams in protest. I breathe slowly as nausea threatens to crowd in on top of everything else. Pulling against my chained hands, I manoeuvre my feet underneath me and around to the side until I'm sitting with my back to the wood of my desk's left side. I stretch my legs out.

I'm still wearing my green silk dress, though it is smeared with dust from the floor, blood from my head blooms along one shoulder and there's a rip in the seam along my right leg where I've been grabbed or dropped or goodness knows what. My feet are shoeless, the neatness of my nail polish a strange contrast to the dirt and chaos around me. I shut my eyes and try to reach someone – anyone – though I know before I even try that it won't work. My brain sent its distress call out before I even moved, it called for help as soon as it stirred enough to know that something very bad was happening. However the ARC was guarded against me these last few months is working against me still, only I'm inside the barrier now. Even Mamma doesn't answer.

I'm completely alone.

They sit and they drink coffee and they talk about the same things over and over again until Ralph feels his throat ache dryly with every swallow. When he can no longer watch Dominic yawn so widely his tonsils gape obscenely, Ralph gets to his feet and mutters that he's going to get some air. No one looks up. Tess is staring straight ahead into the fire. Ethan is looking through files and notes at the desk, no doubt hoping to come across something they've missed, maybe a scribbled note from Bella telling them what to do in the event that she suddenly disappears. The TV is on a twenty-four-hour news channel, though the volume has been turned to a gentle buzz. The same headlines scroll along the bottom. Beneath, Ariana lies curled around Marble on the rug, a cushion wedged under her hooded head. Ralph can't see her face but the gentle rise and fall of her chest suggests she's asleep.

Shrugging on his warmest coat, Ralph opens the cupboard next to the stairs where Ramona used to keep the family's assortment of woollens neatly arranged. Now there are two large wicker baskets containing a jumble of yarn, fluff, chunky knits and threadbare favourites. Ralph digs for a bit until he finds a particularly large, knobbly scarf in black wool. He eventually finds the matching hat in the second basket. Looking up, his hand trails against a soft tartan scarf hanging on one of the pegs. It's accompanied by a simple waxed jacket with a similar tartan lining. Ralph sighs, shaking his head, but he's too tired, too full of caffeinated jitters to banish the usual swoop of loss. It's not just that he misses his dad, it's the utter hopelessness of it.

Stop, he tells himself, winding the black scarf around his neck. *If he were here... he would say stop, Ralph. Pull yourself together. Do something useful. Go and find something out.* Ralph pulls the hat on and turns to leave. He catches a glimpse of something pale on the peg next to Dr Blake's. Reaching his hand for it, his fingers meet feather-soft fabric. Bella's, of course. It's one of those round scarf things – *a snood*, the word whispers in her voice, though he knows it's not really her – and he pulls it to his face before he can stop himself. He shuts his eyes as he breathes in sandalwood, jasmine, sweetness, her. *Where are you? Are you OK?* The pain tears unexpectedly; it's like he has had a shard of glass in his foot for hours but has been deliberately avoiding stepping on it fully until now. Ralph shakes himself again and places the snood back on the peg. He shuts his brain off to the images of Bella being dragged along a deserted hospital corridor, a firm cold hand around her mouth. He turns away from the cupboard and walks slowly along the corridor and through the back door to greet the freezing indifference of four am in the garden.

There are no stars to be seen and the trees rustle in the wind, so Ralph doesn't hear the sweep of wings until Nova lands with a soft thump next to him. He looks up and smiles, not knowing if she can see it in the gentle light spilling from the Manor's lower floor windows. All he can see of her is a gleaming ripple along her golden feathers and the two glittering spots of her eyes.

'You're back,' she says, shortly. He nods and then, remembering the darkness, clears his throat. 'Yes. Are you OK? Dom said you went to the ARC?'

'Yes.'

'You saw the hybrids?'

'No.' She shifts a little and moves closer so the pool of light from the window falls on her. Ralph watches her patiently. She frowns a little in the way he has come to associate with her searching for words. 'I saw... Huh... Harry. A brother.'

'Brother? Whose brother?'

'Bird... Boy.'

'Ah... So Bella was right. Daniel's using close connections to control them. Like you and her...'

'Yes. Tw... Twenty. Twenty-five.'

'Twenty-five hybrids?' He frowns. 'I thought there were more. I thought there were twenty or so in the original batch... There were at least that many in the cages we saw at Futura... Unless...' He peers back at Nova, thinking about the ill-fated pig hybrid. Nova cocks her head at him and he isn't sure if she's following his line of thought or if she is simply hopping from one fact to another like she does sometimes. In any case he shakes the horrible train of thought which has just occurred to him away. 'Perhaps the original hybrids are still at Grayson's. In any case, we can focus on these twenty-five and their relatives first and foremost, now the NatApp is ready to test. Though we only have five doses...'

She nods and frowns again. He waits.

'Bella's gone?'

'Yeah. I don't know what happened. I think Lychen must have... What?'

'Daniel.'

'Daniel?'

'Daniel... was danger.'

'You think Daniel had something to do with Bella being taken?'

'Me... Bella asks me... look for danger. Before. I feel... Daniel.' She gestures wildly towards the ARC and lets out a long, frustrated sound. It whistles mournfully into the night air around them. Ralph isn't sure he fully understands her words, but he definitely understands the sound, the heady wail of grief and guilt as it lifts the hair from the back of his neck.

'No.' He reaches out and touches her soft feathery shoulder before he even thinks about it. 'Not your fault,' he murmurs. She doesn't move away but she doesn't move into him either. She just stands there, staring out at the empty night where they both know the ARC looms. Then, as if the spell of strange kinship between them has snapped suddenly, she turns to him brusquely.

'Help them.'

'The hybrids? That's what we're planning to do. We need Felix though. She can help us work out how to get in, how to stop Daniel.'

'Good.'

She steps away and beats herself up into the air. He

follows her with his eyes but she's swallowed by darkness before she's reached the level of the second-floor windows. A soft rustle near the roof tells him she's making her way through the narrow opening into her attic nest rather than heading back out into the tumultuous night and he breathes a little easier. Turning, Ralph heads back inside.

The fire has dropped a little when he returns to the office. Dominic is snoring, his limbs splayed across the sofa. Tess huddles on the other side, her head cradled in one arm, eyes closed. Ethan sits at the desk, gaze fixed ahead. Ralph pulls his hat and scarf off, places them on a chair and crosses the room. Kneeling in front of Ariana, he gently lifts her as he did from the street in London several hours earlier and, ready this time for the weight, straightens up. Ethan's face doesn't move as Ralph crosses the room in front of him. Ralph buries the urge to shudder, but it's difficult. Ethan looks exactly as he did the first time he saw him after he had been turned into a Guard. It's almost as if Bella's absence has reverted him somehow, though it makes Ralph's head hurt to wonder at the logic behind that line of thought.

'Ralph?' Ariana's murmur brings him back to himself as he plants his feet slowly, carefully on the stairs.

'Yeah?'

'I'm really sorry about your dad. I… wasn't in control. I didn't mean to—'

'Shh… it's OK. It wasn't your fault. I don't blame you. Neither did he.'

'She said that too. But she lies. I didn't know.'

'I know, I know.' He reaches the first-floor landing, averts his eyes from the room straight ahead. The wardrobe is still ajar, he glimpses several pairs of shoes laid out in front of it. He turns away and heads to the small room at the end of the landing. Ariana only opens her eyes the tiniest amount as he backs into the room and lowers her onto the bed. He wonders whether he should say something reassuring about finding her mother, then he remembers what Ethan said about her not asking about Bella, not once.

'Why'd he do it?' Ariana's murmur, once again, brings him back to the present with a jolt.

'Who?'

'Lychen. Why'd he keep me like that? Asleep? Why didn't he just kill me? Or take the powers away? He said he would...'

'I don't know,' Ralph exhales slowly, feeling his exhaustion flood like weighted malignancy in his lungs. 'I guess the most plausible explanation is that he simply didn't know what to do with you. Which is saying something. This is the guy who would get a nervous twitch if any of the Project C kids left a picture half drawn or broke off mid-sentence... He can't bear loose ends. Indecision. Dithering. Not knowing what to do with you must have been driving him mad... Maybe that's why he looked so scared when he saw you earlier, because it wasn't his decision to wake you up. He failed to act when it mattered most.'

Ariana sighs wearily as if she has lived for ten times as many years as she has. She shuts her eyes and turns into the pillow, bringing her filthy leggings-clad knees up to her chest. Ralph reaches down and folds the duvet over her as best he can. He watches her a moment longer until he's sure she's fallen asleep. He's turning back to the door when her whisper reaches him. Faint but clear as anything else she's said so far: 'I wish it had been you.'

He opens his mouth to ask what, but instead he says: 'Me too.'

February, 2020

Felix arrives as the dawn blears greyly through the trees. The sky is thick with the heavy promise of snow and a few flakes spot half-heartedly onto the windscreen of her Fiat as she pulls it into the driveway of the Manor. She parks behind the unfamiliar navy people carrier and turns off the engine. Glancing at the sprawling building next to her, she tries to swallow away the uncomfortable bubbles of feeling rising in her throat. Nostalgia wrestles with guilt which swarms over anger and flurries back into worry. She checks her phone. Nothing there. Not even from Ralph. She glances into the boot in what has become habit, but of course there is no furry head poking through the middle of the back head rests. No thump of tail. Her parents had been confused by her last-minute request for dog-sitting, but they'd agreed without questioning it.

Felix places her phone in her rucksack and climbs out of the car. She quickens her pace towards the large heavy door as another flake of snow finds a spot of warm skin at the nape of her neck. The house is eerily quiet. Felix shuts the front door behind her and steps towards the light glowing under the door of Dr Blake's former office. She glances around, taking in the sprawling shape of Dom at one end of the sofa, the curled tightness of Tess at its other. A spray of notebooks cover Blake's former desk, a lamp angled to show a mixture of handwriting. Felix glances into the adjoining room, remembering the long afternoon spent moving books upstairs, arranging the desks into one large table and digging out old extension leads so she could plug in all the different monitors and hard drives. The short frenetic hour she had spent unplugging them all six months later.

Felix glances at the fire burning insistently behind the grate. Someone has stoked it recently, she can tell, but there are no other signs of life in the room. She crosses over to the writing desk, placing her bag down as she draws up the chair and skates her eyes over the various notes.

'It's mostly old theoretical notes about Project A,' a voice barks from the doorway. Felix looks up sharply at her husband as he crosses into the room, carrying a tray laden with a large coffee pot, mugs and toast.

'I was just going to wake them up,' he mutters unemotionally as he places the tray on the coffee table in front of the sofa.

'How long have you been back?' She asks, her voice sharpening to match his even as her heart pinches at the sight of the heavy drape of tired skin under his eyes, the blemishes of sadness and fear.

'We got in around two this morning. The others crashed out not too long afterwards. Ariana's upstairs. Ralph's somewhere… I think he must have fallen asleep as well. It's been a long night.' He says it all without judgment, without any sense of self-righteousness, but she can't be sure anymore that he doesn't feel it. The old Ethan – her Ethan – he wouldn't. It simply wouldn't occur to him that he was better than the others, stronger for having stayed awake when they couldn't. That it meant he cared more. But this Ethan is different. He doesn't think the same way.

She can't tell *how* he thinks anymore, let alone what he thinks. It's sad and yet oddly freeing, too. It makes what she knows easier to bear.

'Fee!' Ralph bursts into the room, taking long sweeping strides across to her and enveloping her in a strong, tight hug before she can so much as gasp. 'You're here!'

'Yep.' She pats his back as best she can with her elbows pinned awkwardly by her sides. He releases her and she takes a proper look at him. His hair is longer than she remembers seeing it for years, there are squeezes of wrinkles around his eyes and he stoops more than he did last year, but otherwise he's the same old Ralph.

'I know, I look awful,' he grins, though it doesn't reach his eyes. 'We've not had much in the way of sleep...'

'Sounds like old times.' She smiles.

'Yeah, well... stakes are somewhat higher this time around,' he mumbles, glancing at Ethan, who scowls.

'What do you need me to do?' Felix asks quickly, before anyone can start arguing. Tess stirs on the sofa, her body slowly beginning to unfurl itself like a stretching cat.

Ralph sits down on his father's old armchair, his eyes trickling along the floor as if reading a list from the flowing patterns of the carpet.

'Well... Lychen's still out there. Hiding God knows where. He probably has Bella and he definitely has at least six Guard from what Ariana said. If you can do anything to track him down, that would be massive. Then there's Daniel. The Press haven't said a word about him so I don't think Bella got round to telling Metcalfe about the hybrids... We need to expose him before he gets the chance to run, for which we need evidence. Again, anything you're able to hack into or acquire that way... It's not going to be easy. Dom's been trying to get into his systems for months now and they're impossible. But we've got the NatApp developed enough for five doses. They're only experimental of course; they might not work... but I would like to try. I think it's important we at least give it a go...' He meets her eye and she realises, with a flush of fondness for him, why he's worried.

'The hybrids,' she says, slowly. 'You think that once the authorities get wind of them, they'll wind up the same way as the Guard.'

'If Daniel doesn't destroy them first. He decapitated one of the old models – the pig-boy – and sent its head over the wall a few weeks ago. And there's more – I spoke to Nova. She investigated the ARC yesterday... I'm not sure why, she seems to think that it was her fault that Bella was taken because she didn't sense the danger or something, I'm not sure I fully understood what she meant, but it seemed really important to her, it seemed to mean everything that she could go over there and find out something that could help... She said there are twenty-five or so of the new hybrids being kept with humans they're close to, as a means of controlling them...'

'Only twenty-five?'

'Yes.'

'There were more than that at Grayson's', Tess mumbles, her voice hoarse as she reaches shakily for the cafetiere and pours herself a large measure of dark, aromatic liquid.

'Exactly,' Ralph says. Tess shudders as she brings the cup to her lips.

'OK,' Felix says, her mind already leaping ahead, wondering why she had only brought one laptop, whether there might be a compatible monitor of Dom's she could use... She gets to her feet and crosses into her former office, placing her backpack down on the table and switching on the light.

'Felix!'

Felix looks up and gets a quick blurry impression of sleep-wild curls, green eyes and so tall, so much older... before Ariana rushes across the room and winds her skinny arms around her, hair puffing into Felix's nose, chin poking into her shoulder. Felix blinks in surprise before she hugs her back, her chest swarming with conflict.

'You're here,' Ariana mumbles. 'You've come to help us!'

'I've come to... try.'

'Good,' Ariana breaks away, her face swiping clear and serious. With her wild curls and clear, unguarded eyes she's like a version of Bella that Bella never allowed herself to contemplate, thinks Felix to herself. Bigger, stronger, wilder... freer. She stands in filthy clothes, smelling more than a bit ripe, evidently not caring in the least. Her entire face is focused on nothing but the purpose in front of her.

'They kept me asleep, you know,' she says. 'Lychen.'

'I know, love. He was wrong to do that.'

'It wasn't just him though,' Ariana says with the air of needing to get it out. She glances at Ralph and the others, all watching her. Dom has finally awoken as well and is blinking confusedly at Felix. 'My mother knew too. She knew for long enough that she could've done something before and she never did.'

'Ari, that's not true,' Ralph says quickly. 'She only found out a few weeks ago, when we developed the Mollitiam and she was able to use it against Lychen to find out what he'd done with you and even then she couldn't just swoop in and grab you.'

'Of course she could,' Ariana snorts, simply. Rather than screeching with furious temper like she might have before, she emanates a cold rage, a burning maturity that both impresses Felix and makes her want to shudder.

'No, we needed to plan it so the Youth Guard—'

'I'm sure that's how she spun it,' Ariana slices through, leaving Ralph frowning. 'But I understand now. It's coming back to me. The power, the memories… all of it. I heard enough last night, and from some of what Tom told me, too… I pieced it together. She knew I was unconscious, but she also knew I was safe. She could have had Tom get me out of there months ago. Back in November or whenever it was exactly that I was first put away into that cold, white room like a little piece of inconvenience swept under the carpet while the grown-ups went about their other business. She could have brought me back. But she didn't. I know my mother, Ralph. I'm not blinded like you men are. I know she felt relieved. She didn't have to deal with me, not until she realised that Lychen might actually take away my powers… *then* she realised she had to do something. But not until she'd tied it in with her own plans to get even with him.'

Ralph's brow is still furrowed as if she's thrown an intricately layered maths puzzle at him and demanded he solve it on the spot. Ethan looks ready to explode. Felix flicks her gaze between them and fights the sudden urge to laugh.

'She did get you out, though,' Ralph stutters eventually. 'We couldn't have done it without her.'

Ariana rolls her eyes and turns back to Felix. 'I want you to help them first. The hybrids. Ralph's right, people need to know what Daniel's doing, but they can't be left to just be *disposed of* like the Guard.'

'Right,' Felix mutters, glancing sideways at her computer, her fingers already twitching to begin, to exit the awkwardness of conversation, to find their homes against the smooth, indifferent plastic... No one speaks. Felix sits down and pulls her laptop out of the bag, plugging in its cable and reaching for the plug socket behind her. She eases her shoulders down and stretches her neck from side to side unconsciously as she switches it on and waits for it to load up. She looks up, as a thought occurs to her, to meet the ready green gaze of Ariana. Again, she's unnerved not by the similarities to Bella (which had seemed so glaring over the few months they'd lived here together last year) but by the differences.

'The problem is,' Felix says quickly, over the rush of her own feelings. 'Is it enough just to say that this guy has been making hybrids? Most people seemed to accept that spiel BFI put out about the interests of science after Nova was spotted last summer. We can't prove that Daniel inflicted pain and suffering on them with what we have... Nova's hardly a reliable witness, no offence to her...'

Ariana sits down on the chair next to hers, glancing smugly at the others and then back to Felix. 'Lucky I know what his plans are for them, then, isn't it? Also lucky that I know for a fact that there is video evidence somewhere on the internet. It won't be easy to find, mind. It'll be buried on the dark web. On the *very* dark web. But trust me, when people see it, they *will* care. They'll *have* to care.'

Ariana smiles and for a small, sinister moment she looks very much like Lychen. It's in the gesture, Felix thinks, the way it doesn't even really look like a smile at all. Felix turns quickly back to the screen and types her password so she doesn't have to look at it anymore. So she doesn't have to feel it looking at her.

February, 2020

If I keep my head very still against the flat surface of the desk's side, the pain doesn't shoot with as much viciousness as it does when I catch the edges. I doze, my eyes hazing in and out of focus. As my mind drifts I can feel my resilience flooding back to me, reaching healing fingers up into my skull, stemming the blood, drawing the skin back across. Of course it won't heal like Nova's gunshot wound, not without a dose of Mollitiam. I curse my decision to wear the luxurious silk dress – no pockets – after months of jeans and jumpers. The pill bottles had been in my coat and, like my shoes, that's long gone.

Of course, I know what I'm really cursing is my own arrogance for thinking something like this couldn't happen. My fatuous self-assurance which had taken root the day I crumpled those Guard people in front of Lychen's eyes and bloomed ever since, blinding me to all but my own clanging ego. I don't even think I went over a 'what if' scenario with the others. *Ethan and Ralph will be besides themselves. But they'll prioritise Ariana, especially Ralph.* They both know that's what I'd want. I breathe a little slower, the ache in my head receding a little. I watch the beginnings of a bruise blossom across the side of my right knee. Where are my shoes? What caused this bruise? I shut my eyes. Was I really as uninjured – unblemished – as I had told myself?

As my resilience had persuaded me, as it had rushed to heal and soothe over wounds and rawness while I'd lain unconscious?

The door begins to open and suddenly everything slows down. Footsteps shuffling, sending flurries of muck into the air. I hear the particles whisper conspiringly as they shudder upwards. Memories lurch from the past; the dull thwack of my own skull against the furious slant of a quick, cold hand; the thump against the butcher slab of my desk... *No. Not again. I will fight him bloody.*

I look up when I am ready. The footsteps have long stopped, their owner standing in front of me, another by his side. It's not Lychen. Of course it isn't. He never shuffles.

'Dr D'accourt. You're looking... decidedly less polished than usual.'

'Daniel,' I spit his name like a swear word and then look to his Guard companion. I feel the surprised stretch of my eyes register on Daniel's face. He smiles smugly, his entire pasty, wispy visage a mask of nauseating self-satisfaction.

'T.' She doesn't acknowledge my greeting, she remains staring straight ahead. She looks exactly the same as the last time I saw her, her hair the same basic, triangular cut, her muscles thick beneath the plain sweatshirt she wears, her feet planted solidly in boots. There's nothing about her at all to suggest she's ever seen me before, despite our once being bonded to the degree she knew which pastry to select in a line-up of fifty, could pick a pair of shoes for me based on the degree to which my feet had been aching the day before. I flick my eyes back to Daniel, catching his glance at the smudge of blood on my shoulder.

'You're injured?'

'Just my head. You know, where it was clobbered.'

'Hey now, that wasn't me,' he holds his hands up, laughing as if we're exchanging anecdotes at a champagne reception. 'Your arrival here was just as much of a surprise to me as it no doubt is to you. I'd have had your old office spruced up a little first if I'd known,' he looks around with a delicate sneer.

'Really.' I fix him with a look but he shrugs.

'Honestly. I had some *ideas,* of course. What with us being neighbours and all... But ambushing you in the hospital? Not my circus, not my monkey, I'm afraid. You have Felix Bryden to thank for that. Along with your old pal Josiah. No surprises there, though I must admit I didn't think old Fee-Fee had it in her. I don't know if *she* even realises what she's done, sending you here.'

I sniff, not really registering surprise at the mention of Felix. The seed of suspicion had been planted, after all, as soon as Tom had told me about the step up of Guard around Ariana at the exact same time we'd left Cumbria. There's only one person I know who is that good at tracking. I put it out of my mind for now; there are far more pressing questions throbbing to be answered.

'You're the one who managed to construct the cloaking agent against me though, aren't you? You gave Lychen a drug, taught him how to repel me... *try* to repel me, anyway. He never quite got the hang of it fully.'

'That's because I didn't really want him to. Dr Lychen is a brilliant mind, he remains one of the greatest pioneers of our field, but he's always been flawed and it's only grown more apparent over the last eighteen months or so. Ever since you sashayed back into the picture.' He regards me sourly and suddenly he's ten, hulking and snotty, watching me tickle Rudy and cuddle up to Nova. Always the outcast, never a favourite. I let him talk as my strength continues to tingle back into my head wound.

'He came to me for help when you began playing your little mind tricks on him. And I did help... You were right about the chemical intervention; it was an antidote I'd been developing as a means of blocking out Guard interference so that they could not be weaponised against the primary user... But it only worked as much as he wanted it to. It was a test, I suppose, of sorts...'

'To see if he truly did want rid of me?'

'Precisely. I don't think even he appreciates how damaged he is by his need for you, his obsessive addiction... It's a weakness. He can see *that* at least, that's why he wants you still, even now. He truly believes he will kill you.' He locks eyes with me, all sulky boyishness gone. There's a hardness, an emptiness that I haven't seen in anyone before save, perhaps, the eyes of my daughter when she threw me across a rooftop. 'I'm not so sure.'

We share a long look. I can tell that he is beyond my power, too, here. I could tell that the moment he broke through my gaze like the snap of a spider's silk. I just can't tell how... Unless... I glance at T again.

'You used T,' I say, quietly. 'You used the old mind-link somehow...'

'You forget, I am the one who designed the mind-link technology in the first place. I know all about your special bond with Ethan. The minute he turned up at the Futura lab last year with old whatsherface Brown and your pathetic little pleas for patience dealing with your ARC cronies and the brat, I knew that you'd be using a replacement Primary while he was absent. And then when they took my lovely Bette from me last year to be sold like cattle… it was around the same time Lychen asked me for help to repel your mind-invasion. The cogs began to turn, I saw an answer to a puzzle I had only just started to consider.

'You're a nuisance, Bella. You're an interfering anomaly who should have shrivelled up and died like the rest of your Project A kind. You pose an irritating threat to me and all the work I do. I knew I'd be moving my work back here to the ARC. I knew that you'd be over the hill with your ragtag collection of misfits, thanks to your failure to bloody die when someone tried perfectly well to kill you. I knew you'd try and see what I was doing. I had to find a way to prevent you. And it came to me then, in that office when poor, broken, addled Lychen asked – no, *demanded* – I find a way to repel you. What I needed was access to a mind which had once linked to yours. Only then would I be able to use it against you.

'Using Ethan would have been the ideal solution, of course, but that avenue posed more tedium than I was prepared to put up with. But there had been another… Another Guard who had linked deeply into that pretty little head of yours, if only for a few days. T. I requested her as my new Primary – easily done – and performed a simple bit of brain jiggery-pokery. The Guard are essentially mechanical in memory – how else would they have the capacity to store such endless trivial information about their users, after all. Everything she knew about you was still there, locked and stored and, with the right tools, easily accessible. I merely probed around a bit, altered a few things here, amplified others there and voilà. My very own personal, transportable Bella-repellent. Nice ring to it, don't you think?'

He smiles and squats in front of me. I flinch as he

reaches a thick-fingered hand, replete with wispy grey hairs on the fingers, towards my face, but all he does is move my head to the side a little so he can see the wound.

'It's not deep,' he murmurs. The stench of him fills my nose. A mixture of musty, inadequately dried laundry, and sexual frustration. I jerk my head away; he makes a clicking noise with his mouth but, unlike Lychen, he doesn't instinctively grasp me harder.

'Tsk, now. We're all friends here, aren't we. Especially in this place. This *glorious* institution where we ourselves were created! You and I... Though not, perhaps, equally. The girl designed to be seen; the boy created to disappear. And see how far we've come. How we've... *evolved.*'

His eyes come to rest on the scar which I know he's seeing for the first time. His finger drifts towards my face again to trace over it slowly, shudderingly.

'Beautiful, powerful Bella D'accourt, Subject A. The one they all chased, the one they all loved...'

His fingers clench around my chin and a stir of madness creeps into his eyes. I glare at him, putting as much disdain as I can into it so he won't see my fear.

'The child chosen to live in the big house with our rich, powerful creator. How could she ever know what it was like to be left alone, left in the dark by that same man. Not so much raised as dragged up by indifferent scientists. Always underestimated. Always overlooked. Made to disappear. Made to *want* to disappear.'

I swallow my sneer, dig past my fear and disgust, muster my face into sympathy.

'They were wrong, Daniel. They should never have done what they did to you.'

His face changes and I relax a little. Reading men, giving them what they want from me – it's a dance I've performed since I was a little girl and it's never failed me. I can do this.

'But that doesn't mean you have to be the monster they created.'

'Don't tell me who I am,' he snaps, and in one brutal movement he takes his hand away and hits me sharply across my cheek. I gasp, my scar shimmering pain as I slump sideways. Blood swarms into my mouth, but I shove myself back upright as best I can, my tongue nipping gently against the cut he's torn in my lower lip. Daniel sneers, standing up and staring around us before looking back at me slowly, eyes roving over my bruised body. The memory shudders back to me: standing near him backstage, his eyes watching me the same way they do right now, as if he knew what had happened to me, knew *exactly* what had happened to me right here in this very room.

'There were advantages, of course, to being the boy no one saw. They didn't look for me. And so I saw... everything.' He waits, letting the words swallow into me like boulders.

'What did you see?'

'All of it. Lychen and you, dancing on the edge of his tether. You and Ralph, sneaking into cars and dark corners when you thought no one would see... Did you never wonder why Lychen was so angry that night? Why he came after you with such unexplained brutality?'

'You told Lychen about me and Ralph?'

He smiles and licks his lips slowly, deliberately, sinking back into a crouch in front of me. I can smell his saliva, his sweat, his arousal. It's unlike Lychen's cold amber-coloured lust, as a rodent from a wolf, but it feels the same as it clenches my throat, raises the hairs on my arms, prickles warning along my limbs.

357

'Told him, followed him... Oh, the things I heard from right outside this very office. I went to see him afterwards, told him I knew what he'd done. He didn't care what I'd seen, of course – no one would believe lumbering unlovable Daniel over the great Dr Lychen. But he saw me, for the first time. He saw what I could be... And so he put me to work, sowing the seeds of doubt in poor thick-headed Rudy, bringing him down right at that perfect, beautiful moment. Crashing the entire catastrophic folly of the ARC onto the heads of the Blakes and you, the girl who thought she was untouchable.

'Did you never wonder why he took me with him when he left here? Nova... Well, everyone knew she was your favourite. If anyone was going to prove useful as bait for you, it'd be her, even though she was a mess by then. But me? Well. I knew too much, had *seen* too much. I don't think even Lychen knew the depths of what I was. What I've become. He still thinks he's in charge. Even though you've taken his Guard and he's wanted by the authorities... He thinks you being brought here was part of our obedience. That I'll bow in deference and hand you over when he gets here like the good little minion I am. But he can't even control his own thoughts and meanwhile, I've been so patient for so long now...'

He hovers his hand above my knee, his fingertips drifting upwards to the hemline of silk which dances flimsily over his thick knuckle. His voice turns husky as I hold in my flinch: 'He warned me when I moved here that I wasn't to go near you. That you were off-limits. His.'

Come on, I stir myself, *reaching for the stores of resilience. You've broken into Lychen's head without the Mollitiam. You can speak to him across hundreds of miles... You can fight off this rancid shitbag. You can do something.*

I hold myself very still, even as his hand clamps onto my leg. I shut my eyes for a few seconds as I feel him lurch closer, his breath hot. Then, when I can no longer bear the stink of him near me for another moment, I open my eyes, take aim and spit the blood from my torn lip directly into his face. It sprays his cheeks and he recoils in surprise, but not far enough.

'You lay one more finger on me and I swear, Daniel—'

'Oh, *what*. What are you going to do? Bat your big scary eyes? Scream in your head for someone to come and save you? *No one can hear you*,' he shouts it right into my face, so close I can see my own dark, shuddering reflection in the droplets of my blood on his chin.

'Poor, beautiful, untouchable Bella. Brought back to the place of her great undoing, brought so low who knows how much further she can plunge... But I've always relished a challenge.'

I fight. I fight with everything I have and everything I was and everything else besides. I try shooting rays of acid out of my eyes like Ariana might, imagine an invisible axe crunching into his head, I envision throwing him backwards a hundred times. When it all fails, when the block he's created so effectively using the hapless motionless Guard person standing nearby fails to even cause a flinch of pain within his pitiless eyes, my resilience wires itself into white hot fury. I scream into his ears when he veers too close; I bring my legs up and kick at him until my toenails are torn and bloody; I lurch against my chains and claw his face like Nova would. When my bony knee narrowly misses his crotch, he rolls back onto his feet, snarling, his entire face radiating all the darkness of a lifetime spent hating and hated. My head wound throbs in agony and my vision blurs in and out as he glares down at me, weighing up his options of how best to fuck me up. Then he laughs – a brutal, echoing call of apathy which swirls around him and me and the stoic Guard woman who stands and stares and never sees a thing.

February, 2020

It takes Felix less than an hour to get it done. Ethan watches her across the room, admiration tangling with familiar guilt as her fingers fly across the keys and her eyes blaze with the reflection of the screens she's set up. The others flitter around, Ariana returning from a shower with her hair dripping into the hood of a fresh sweater. She wears black leggings underneath, which are clearly too short. She catches him looking and scowls, pulling her socks up over the exposed skin. Ethan paces the hallway as Felix works. He's already gone up to the attic nest but Nova remained curled in a ball of her wings in the corner when he called to her. Ralph met him on the way back down, barking pointedly that she needed to rest and that there wouldn't be anything she could tell them that she hadn't already. He didn't add that Ethan wouldn't be able to understand her half as well as he could, but they both caught the unspoken inference.

'Got it,' Felix says, just as Ethan has begun to stomp towards the boot rack, a half-formed plan in his head of going to the ARC and posing as a Guard person to gain entry, locate Daniel and beat Lychen's whereabouts out of him.

'Got what?' Ralph looks up from the other side of the table where he's sorting through cases to find a suitable one for the syringes of NatApp.

'I've got the video. Don't look, trust me,' she adds, grimly, holding a hand out as Ralph makes to cross around the table to her side. 'And don't *you* even think about it,' she throws sideways at Ariana, who stops mid-stride and scowls.

'I've already seen—'

'I don't care what you've already seen, young lady, you are *not* looking at *this*. Not on my watch.'

'Is it...?'

'Adult-based videos. Yup. Along with a few other things I've unearthed...'

'What other things?' Ariana asks quickly, her eyes trained on the woman in the chair. Ethan watches Felix squirm, knowing that Ariana will be probing, alert for any unspoken truths. Felix chooses her words carefully, speaking with measured calm as her gaze skates over the screen's contents.

'Well... I mean, it's nothing so obvious as a Gumtree ad for fully-tamed hybrids for sale or anything like that, but it's not a *million* miles away. Looks like not all of them are being groomed for the... er... adult entertainment industry. Some are being marketed as companions, the next generation of domestic pets... I've also managed to get into Daniel's funding application system... Some of his ideas...' A shadow gloams over her face. 'I never really knew him at the ARC. I'm glad of it now.'

'Why?' Ralph stares at her, his hands drumming impatiently along the metal of the case in front of him.

'He wants to breed them... Make hybrid babies... It looks like he's been experimenting with children, though according to this research file here none of them survived except a seven-year-old boy who was melded with a juvenile monkey. I'm not sure what that… what that even really means but he's already receiving bids in the billions for him.

'It's a lucrative opportunity, according to this application. He plans to carry on in the long-term but in the meanwhile he wants to try a breeding programme… He's got the technology, he's developed a treatment programme and everything… God, he just needs funding. And if this monkey-boy brings in the cash…' She looks up, her face devoid of all colour. 'It means he doesn't need Lychen anymore. Not with this clause he's snuck in here about ownership and patented technology…'

'Can you stop him?' Ariana also looks sickened by the thought of hybrid infants but there's an urgency about her too. Like Ralph, her fingers are busy, tapping at her elbows in a gesture that reminds Ethan so much of Bella he has to avert his gaze.

'I can certainly try. I've copied everything, all the files and videos and applications… It's all on its way to all the major news outlets, the police and the government.' She clicks a few times and then breathes out slowly, pushing her chair away from the desk and reaching for the cup of tea on the side. Ethan knows it will be cold, he can tell from the slight pucker she has as she drinks it. He can't watch that either.

'We have to get them out then,' Ariana says, glancing from Felix to Ralph. She stops tapping on her elbows and clenches her hands into fists as if she's just realised what she was doing, who she was emulating. 'We've got to get them out, give them that special potion of yours…'

'We've only got five doses, Ari. And I don't know if they even work…'

'It's better than nothing!'

'And even if they *did* work, what on earth are we going to do with the other twenty odd hybrids during the three months It takes lu make another batch of five?'

'I don't know! We'll think of something, we can't just leave them and hope that the same thing doesn't happen as it did with the Guard in those warehouses.'

'The hybrids are not like the Guard, Ari,' Ralph says, measuredly. 'For one thing, we only saw what happened to one lot – we don't know if was same for all of them. For another, the Guard were, for the most part, former life-sentence criminals. As much as the decision to destroy those we saw was a rash one, no doubt about that, the authorities who decided it did so knowing that no one was going to protest too much... After all, they all signed their bodies away to science or however it was the BFI spun it.'

'Not all of us knowingly,' Ethan grunts. 'We all know that was just a convenient cover story.'

Ralph looks at him frustratedly. 'True, but the vast majority were sourced from prison cells... Anyway, my *point* is that there's no reason to believe the authorities will treat the hybrids like the Guard, not now I think about it rationally.'

'How did *you* feel when you saw them for the first time, Dad? Cos I know I certainly wasn't hit with the sudden urge to protect and save them right away,' Ariana says, darkly. Ethan watches the use of *Dad* land and sink into Ralph's face, knowing it's exactly how she intended it. *Just like Bella would have*, he thinks, with a weird mixture of respect and unease.

'These will be different, if what you and Felix found out about his intentions for them are correct, they'll have been made to be photogenic, cute even...'

'Pr... Pretty,' says a voice in the doorway and Ethan

364

turns swiftly to see Nova there, her wings folded behind her in a feathery, downy frame, eyes fixed on Ariana inscrutably. Ariana gulps nervously but holds her chin up, staring back at her solidly.

'We can't take that risk just because they might think they're cute. That's just stupid,' Ariana throws the words at Felix, who twists her mouth and looks at Ralph. Ethan knows that look. It means *Let's talk about this privately.* Ariana must know it too because she bristles irritably.

'You've sent the files now, we can't just sit around and wait and see... You've got the NatApp ready, we've got all the people we need... Let's *go*...'

'You're still weak, Ari. You're practically swaying. You've got to give your body time to heal—'

'There's a seven-year-old monkey-boy over there! He doesn't have time! If Daniel gets wind of what's happening, and you know he probably *will* if it hits the Press... He might do what we all know he probably did to all the others. Like pig-boy. Cut his losses, kill them all and run away with his *patented technology* to start all over again somewhere else. Otherwise anyone could get hold of them and make the money he was supposed to make...'

'No one is going anywhere,' Ralph says, firmly. 'Not you and not *you*,' he turns to Nova. 'Can you imagine what Bella would say if I let you both go swanning off over there, right into Daniel's hands...'

They both round on him angrily. Ethan can feel the heat of power blazing from Ariana just as he had on the rooftop of the Beaumont. Unlike then though, she controls it. He can almost see her batting it back down as it spits and hisses pleadingly to strike.

'You can't stop—'

'I can *help*!'

Ralph holds his hands up as they both hammer him with their protests. Ethan feels a small part of him spring back with amusement at the image and turns automatically to see if Felix sees it too. But she's distracted, staring at her phone where he can just make out a flash of a short word on the screen. She gets up from her chair and, without looking at any of them, quickly leaves the room. The others don't notice, Ralph still fending off Ariana and Nova, who is spewing more angry bird noises than actual words, to Ethan's ears at least. Ethan slips back into Blake's office and out into the corridor, listening as Felix stomps into the utility room at the back of the house, her voice tightly wired as she snaps: 'Where've you been?'

Ethan follows on light feet, letting the sound of Ariana and Nova's rage overtake any sound he might make as he leans his head against the utility door and listens intently.

February, 2020

Ralph isn't quite sure when the sound of shouting outside the room overtakes the fury of the girl and part-bird in front of him, but at one point – possibly when Ariana pauses to draw breath somewhere in the middle of how he can't tell her what to do and he has *no idea* what she's been through – the sound of Ethan's booming anger swipes over them all. Nova's angry squawk dies in her throat and her eyes widen with human surprise. Ariana glances sideways towards the direction of the noise. Ralph takes the opportunity of their distraction to sidestep the pair of them and dash out of the door leading to the hallway. He meets the confused gazes of Dominic and Tess as they approach down the stairs. Ethan and Felix are standing a few paces apart, she with phone in hand in the utility room, he in the hallway, a boot clenched in his fist. Rage shimmers like heat waves between them.

'...all this time and you've said nothing!'

'Eth, please. I never meant—'

'Don't you dare lie to me and say you never meant any harm!'

'What's going on?' Ralph finds his voice, a strange, shivery sense of foreboding nudging its way along his veins.

'Tell him,' Ethan spits, looking away in disgust. Ralph watches Felix's face, sees the dance of loss and hurt swallowed by a steely resolve. She looks Ralph straight in the eye.

'I'm the reason Bella was abducted. I was tracking your movements from here. I... I didn't know you were going to the hospital, which is why it was initially assumed that you were going to the Beaumont...'

Something clicks into place in Ralph's head. *'That's* why they stepped up the security on Ariana when we were on our way...'

Felix nods. 'It was my Guard person who followed you to the hospital—'

She's interrupted by a strange, strangled sort of sound from the stairwell. Ralph turns to see Dominic staring at Felix as if she's sprouted an extra head. *'You* employed a Guard person? And you used him against us?'

'Things have changed, Dom,' Felix says, heavily. 'But I never used a Guard against *you.* Any of you. I wouldn't. It was just her. That was the deal.'

'Deal?' Ralph turns back, though he finds that he doesn't really need to ask. He can tell from Dominic's face that he's worked it out as well, though Tess is a mass of confusion and when he glances behind him, Ariana's face hovers in white shock in the doorway. He has a sudden urge to send her away, to bundle her up to her bedroom and lock the door, no longer caring if she hates him for it in the short term.

'Tell him who the deal's with, Felix,' Ethan grunts.

'Just shut up, Ethan,' she spits back at him.

'Tell them.'

'It was Lychen,' she says, passing a hand over her forehead. 'We spoke back in December... I was at a pretty low point in my life. Eth had gone, my new job wasn't going as well as I'd hoped it would, my brother upped sticks and moved to Canada with his wife and kids... I was keeping tabs on what was happening at Beaumont. I heard there had been a big hoo-ha with Ariana and part of a building collapsing. I heard she had been put on ice.' She peers over Ralph's shoulder and he knows she's seeking the girl in question. He glances back at Ariana too but her expression is unreadable. Something passes between her and Felix, but it's too complicated and quick for him to read. He turns back to Felix with eyebrows raised.

'I told myself it was none of my business. I told myself that I wasn't her mum, I had no place to intervene. And I waited for her real mother to do something. Anything. But of course she never did... For what it's worth, Ariana, I think you were spot on about her seeing your stasis as a convenience, it gave her the time and freedom she needed to get on with all this NatApp, Mollitiam shite. But anyway, when it became clear to me that Bella wasn't going to do a damn thing to help Ariana, I decided to take matters into my own hands.'

'*You* contacted *him*?' Ethan drops the boot, his fists balling and juddering. Ralph can see the muscles as they whittle under the skin of his arms.

'Yes,' Felix says. There's no remorse in her, Ralph realises. There's a bit of guilt, maybe, but on the whole, she speaks as if she has thought long about it and knows without any doubts that she did the right thing. That given the chance, she would do it all again.

'I called Lychen. It had been a few weeks and I knew he'd hate the dithering, the indecision. So I offered him an out. I said I could help. I reminded him that I'd worked with the Project C children, I had experience with special abilities and, more importantly, I knew Ariana and cared about her, *for* her, like a mother. She obviously hadn't been getting on too well with whatever arrangements he'd made for her... I could help with that, offer a different approach. If he handed over custody to me.'

'Why? Just to get back at Bella?' Ethan frowns.

'No, Ethan. Not to get back at Bella, to do what Bella *should* have been doing from the moment she opened her big stupid eyes again last summer. Get Ariana away from Lychen. I knew that he must be getting fed up of her, that his decision to keep her asleep would have been borne of frustration and inexperience. I knew it wouldn't be too hard to persuade him to hand the responsibility over. And I said that part of the deal would be that he could have access to her whenever he wanted.'

Ethan snorted. 'Doesn't sound like keeping her away...'

'Well he wasn't going to just give her up, was he? This is Lychen, he's the great possessor, isn't he? No way was he going to let her go if he wouldn't be able to keep some sort of control on her and her abilities. I just needed to get her away long enough for her to decide whether she wanted that or not. She's powerful enough not to let anyone control her if she doesn't want them to. And anyway, I knew I'd be able to offer Lychen something he wanted even more, something that had been driving him slowly mad for months ever since she slipped through his fingers yet again...'

'Bella.'

'Yes. I know what systems you use here. I taught Dom and Tess everything they know, after all. And Tess taught me a few things, too, back when she joined us and told us all about how the BFI used to track us individually. I knew it wouldn't be too hard to figure out a way to do the same. I even offered to use my own Guard person so that Bella wouldn't have any chance of recognising them and getting spooked. As it was, she didn't even see him.'

'Where is she?' Ethan marches up to Felix and a shadow of alarm flickers over her face briefly. He stops short of touching her and simply glares, muscles still twitching. 'Is she in London still? Just tell me where and I'll go, you can have the girl, you can have whatever the hell you want, just tell me where she is.'

'I don't know,' Felix says, slowly, but Ralph can feel the lie. He lets his mind trickle back through the gaps and confusion of the last twenty-four hours.

'It went wrong, didn't it?' he murmurs, slowly. 'We got to Ariana first and Lychen disappeared.' Ethan turns to him, comprehension slowly beginning to clunk into place. Felix bites her lip and Ralph can tell he's right.

'I didn't know about Tom,' Felix mutters. 'I never told Lychen more than he needed to know. I didn't want to place anyone else in danger, especially Ariana. I didn't tell him about the Youth Guard because... well, why would I? They had nothing to do with anything, as far as I was aware. *I* didn't know you were using them as part of a plan to rescue Ariana. I was given a Guard contact at the ARC, part of the team looking after Ariana. When we realised you were all on the move, they were going to bring her to me early... But then she started to wake up and at that point all hell broke loose with the Guard recall. I didn't know if you'd gotten wind of my plan or if something else had happened... But next thing I knew, Ariana was gone. And that meant Lychen hadn't fulfilled his end of the deal.'

'So you didn't hand Bella over?'

'Not to him.'

'Where is she, Felix?'

'Listen, the exposure is underway, we don't need to

fight anymore, Ralph. The people we need to protect are right here. If we go in all guns blazing, who knows who else we'll lose... Last time, I lost everything because of her. Please, Ralph, *please*...'

'Where is she?' Ethan's voice doesn't even sound like a voice anymore. His hands twitch and Ralph can tell he wants very much to grab his wife by the arms and shake the answer out of her.

'Shit,' Ralph says, slowly, as the answer clunks into place. 'You gave her to Daniel, didn't you? *That's* why Nova could sense danger there...'

Felix passes a hand over her eyes as Ethan turns wildly to Ralph.

'Location C, she said on the phone. You were speaking to Lychen?' He barely glances at her now, reaching to grab his discarded boot and thrusting his foot into it.

'Yeah,' she says, quietly.

'He's on his way there too?'

'Yes, but... He already knew where she was, Daniel told him. He's close...'

'Not as close as us,' Ethan finds his other boot and kneels to pull it on. He's more awake and alive than Ralph's seen him since the moment Bella disappeared. 'Have you still got those explosives I made back in the summer?'

'Yeah, they're in the shed,' Ralph says dazedly. He pulls his coat on and then looks at Felix, his mind stumbling with too many feelings to identify.

'So you knew this whole time that she was just down the hill?'

'Ralph, please. You don't have to go—'

'Of course I have to go, for fuck's sake, Felix!' She flinches. Ethan shrugs on his coat and marches wordlessly out of the back door towards the shed. Ralph turns around but Ariana is no longer behind him. Dominic and Tess are, though, he reaching for a coat, she appearing from the schoolroom with the case he'd prepared for the NatApp.

'For the hybrids,' she says, quickly, though fear shivers through her voice. 'I've also put in all the Serum X we have. We should divide it between us. I'm guessing the Guard over there will have ignored the government summons. I've, er, also included Bella's Mollitiam pills. You should take them to her.'

'Good thinking.' Ralph takes the case from her as she holds it out. 'Where's Ari?'

Dominic glances behind him into the office. 'Not in there. Neither's Nova...'

'I didn't see her go upstairs—'

'You don't think she—'

'Wait,' Ralph holds up a hand. He sniffs the air, freezing from the blast of freshness when Ethan had opened the door. There's another thing lurking under the ice, though. 'Smoke,' he mutters, turning to the back door and making his way across the flagstones and out. He doesn't know if Felix is calling him, or if it's the whine of the wind as he steps out into a frenzy of fresh snow. The ARC smudges in the distance, the image patterned by whirling flecks of white and the beginnings of an unmistakable billow. He refocuses his eyes and sees the gate in the wall wrenched open, though Ethan is still striding towards it from the direction of the shed. Ralph turns to see Dominic, Tess and Felix beside him. He raises his eyebrows.

'I'm coming,' Felix barks, her eyes also on the open gate. 'We both know that's where Ariana's gone. You need all the help you can get.'

They begin to stride across the snow-covered garden, their feet crunching in the eerie quiet lurking between the gusts of wind. Ralph glances at Felix sideways.

'If you do *anything* to hurt Bella—'

'I won't. I'm only here for Ariana.'

'Fine.'

He glances behind him just once as they file through the open gate. The Manor seems to blink and beam back at him in the grey morning light, the windows lit softly, the stones rambling in the same pattern he could shut his eyes and sketch from memory. He blinks and thinks, for a strange, swooping moment, that he sees his parents standing in the window of what was once their bedroom. His father's eyes are sad but accepting, his hair more dark than white, his stance tall as he reaches and places an arm around his mother, who smiles fondly from beneath her favourite yellow scarf, hair spilling vitally around her shoulders, hand pressed against the glass. He squints and then they're gone and he turns back to the looming devil of cold stone on the hill before him and thinks that he is really, extremely sleep-deprived and the sheer volume of adrenaline which has bucket-loaded him over the last day would give anyone hallucinations. That's all it is.

February, 2020

Nova leaves when they all become so wound up in each other, in the mess of who hates who because they love someone else; all their petty unimportant human worries. She'd been wrong to get angry with Ralph. As she flies swiftly across the whirling white, her wings beating evenly against the gusts and falls of wind, she realises that it had been her human side again, letting her down. Her silly girl brain getting caught up in Ariana's indignant distress. Now she can't even really understand why. It's not like Ralph could've done a thing to stop her, after all. She'd simply waited until they were good and distracted and headed out the back door unnoticed while they were still yelling. Not before she'd grabbed the small box from the hearth, though. She holds it clasped in her talon now, its fourteen matches a tiny rattle lurking beneath the wind. Her eyes narrow as she skirts around the ARC building and flurries to a halt at the base, under the window she'd escaped out of last night. It's still open, despite the frigid ice of the air, the creeping slick of chill up the side of the building. She beats her way up to it, a pulsing warmth telling her that Daniel is on one of the upper floors towards the front of the building. She enters quickly, dropping the small box to the ground and gathering it awkwardly into her mouth.

Harry is exactly where she left him the night before

and, once again, she meets no one on her way to him. It takes surprisingly little time for her to get his attention, communicate her idea and slide the box of matches under his door. The bed sheet takes a few matches to catch, but once it does she slides it easily back into the corridor where the tiny flames latch onto the rush carpet like a baby to the breast. She beats the flames with her wings until the smoke curdles and churns her throat, then she runs. The ceiling is lined with detectors, but it takes several minutes for the tendrils to find one with working batteries. She hears coughing and running feet behind her and, just as the first beeps begin to shrill and she reaches the stairwell, she hears the first loud, mechanical call of a Guard person and the unlocking of doors.

Nova swallows her fear, coughs for several minutes as the purple haze of smoke follows her into the stairwell and leans for a moment against the wall. In front of her the stairs lead upwards to the window. She can see the curls of smoke blooming out of it already, escaping into the frosty air, beckoning her to follow, to fly, to beat herself out and far away. She shakes her head and allows the panic to flutter a little. She hopes Harry is alright. She hopes he managed to stamp out the small flames which had caught the wooden door as she'd slid the bed sheet underneath. Most of all, she hopes that he'd been right when he'd said the prisoners of the ARC were all valuable – that this momentous, insane thing she has done is a big enough something for them all to be let out. She checks Daniel. He is still far away, she feels the smudge of him against her face. There's no time to probe further into wherever he is and whatever he's doing, she knows he'll be made aware of the fire in this part of the building in a matter of minutes. Nova glances back the way she came and feels a burst of heat against her face, it threatens and whispers of annihilation, flesh-twisting burns and feathers spitting into vapour. She turns, not looking upwards at the window, and heads down the stairs to her right. She has work to do. There are still ten matches left.

The floor shakes. There are flashes. Flashes of awareness, of feelings and pain and a growing, writhing fury. I taste blood, feel hot breath on my face, twist, and bring my knees up sharply. They connect with something hard and I realise my eyes are shut and I'm lying on my side and I'm alive but… but there is a rushing sense of too many things inside my head and my body. The metallic smell of blood tinges around my nose and I'm reminded in a stark, brutal way of the moments after I'd given birth to Ariana. The warm, uncontrollable flush of bloody, visceral humanity between my legs, the remnants of panic and fear, the tiny, grey-purple creature I could not look at because I was so unutterably terrified she would bring me back to this place. This nightmare of a place I have somehow found myself back inside.

The flashes of reality grow longer. I become aware that the pain is still mostly just around the back of my head. I open my eyes slowly. The focus is clearer than it was when I first came to. The desk is in front of me, my wrists still shackled to it. I sniff. The blood is coming from my mouth, my lip where he hit me – but it's already lessening. I can feel the resilience within me swarming to heal the bruises, the broken parts, the flesh wounds as it always has done. I can feel it massing around my memory, cushioning the badness, locking it back, choking it away. I can feel it buffering against the flow I've become used to, the rush to

Ethan's head, to anyone's... It can't save me that way so it does what it did after Lychen came to the Manor all those months ago, it compensates by trying to protect me itself. And I let it.

I lie curled into myself, my blood drying, my cuts already beginning to knit, smudges of bruised skin already rushing to return to normal, brain whirring. *Is Ariana safe? Where is she? Where is Daniel? What is that smell? Why did he leave?* I shut my eyes again, my thoughts dancing too close to where I can't touch. I have to draw some of it up though, I have to remember what it was... a phone call? No. His phone *had* rung... I'd felt it through the cheap fabric of his pocket. But it hadn't been that. *Hot breath. Hands... hands forcing, cold, rough.* I squeeze the thought away and concentrate on the sound of T's voice, slow, mechanical: *Your coffee is ready, Dr D'accourt. The Chanel suit is still being dry-cleaned but I have the red Lacroix. It is not forecast to rain today. There is a disturbance in the south wing of the building. A fire. You are required.*

I open my eyes. That's what I can smell, flooding over the blood and dust of the carpet. There's no heat coming from the ground beneath my face, at least, but the tiny wisps of smoke in the air are unmistakable. It raises my head from the floor, brings my knees up, clenches my toes painfully against the carpet and groans my body upwards against the desk. I blink for a few moments at my legs and feet, at the pattern of bruises and what looks like a broken toe and several torn, bloody nails.

I shuffle until my dress flutters a little lower down my thighs, ignoring the other cuts, the climbing bruises and stinging pain. I blot what blood I can with what green silk I can reach, and all the while the insistent smell of burning swells in my nose. I remind myself that I'm not coughing and the floor is still cold. There's no reason to panic. Yet. Except no one knows where I am apart from Daniel, Felix, and... Daniel said something about Lychen coming, didn't he? So no one who wouldn't be fairly relieved to hear I'd burned to a crisp shackled to my former desk in the wreck of what was once my luxurious, lovely haven of an office. *No. Lychen wants to kill me himself.* It shouldn't be a comforting thought, but in a strange way it is. Lychen is an entirely different beast to the pitiless devil who has just left me. If he comes I have a chance.

The memories lurch and I shut my eyes again. Footsteps. Flashes. Daniel laughing, drawing his foot back to kick. My head exploding as it had lurched backwards against the desk... And there it turns vague. There's the sensation of being grabbed, moved... T's voice cutting through, followed by Daniel's groan. *Of course there's a bloody fire in the south wing. Fine. I'll be back. I'll finish this. Don't you forget that, Bella. I know you can hear me. This isn't over.* I blink. He hadn't, then. Finished it. The realisation sends a ricochet of strength around me and I pull at the chains. My wrists yank with rawness but I keep tugging until some of the chain unwinds a little and I'm a few inches freer of the desk. It's no good though, not really. The shackles are locked around my wrists and locked again around the desk leg, which only lifts a millimetre or two when I shove it. I'm wondering where the shackles and chains even came from in the first place – one of the hybrids? An ancient relic of Project B? – when I hear the sound again.

Unmistakable. Footsteps, closer this time, hurrying. My heart shrinks to the size of a peach pit and shudders uncontrollably. I draw one knee up, my bleeding toes clenching against the grimy fuzz of the floor, the other leg bent under me, elbows hooked around. It's as defensive as I can get. My eyes watch the door. I feel my resilience mustering, searching for a chink in the defences T has constructed against me, and the remnants of whatever drug they must have used at the hospital to conceal me from Ethan. When it finds none, I feel it settling around me instead, bursting from the surface of my skin, glowing from the tips of my hair, readying my wired body with the wild frisson of a caged animal. The door opens and the sound escapes my lips before I can do a thing to stop it.

53

February, 2020

They divide the Serum X between them, once Dominic has caught up with Ethan and persuaded him to wait long enough to take a few vials and at least listen to their scrambled-together plan. He glowers when Ralph explains that he needs to find the Guard and take out as many as possible, his eyes never leaving Felix.

'I need to find Bella,' he grunts.

'I know,' Ralph replies frustratedly, 'but you're our best hope against the Guard. You know that, Ethan. Come on. If you go hurtling off, chucking bombs about and not considering who else is caught up in that building, you're going to do more damage than good. You don't even know where she is.'

'And you do?'

'No, but I know that building better than you. Better than any of you. I grew up there, remember? Dom, you know the lower floors. That's where Nova said they're keeping the hybrids. That's where you and Tess go. Take X, take NatApp... Use it if you can, but the priority is to get them out. It looks like the fire is coming from that area, from what I can see from here.' He glances back at the building. The smoke isn't thick yet, but it's consistent and it's definitely flooding from the lower back end of the tower.

'Ethan, you take these and you go round the front. Take some Mollitiam too. Here.'

Ethan stares at him.

'Please, Eth.'

He sighs furiously and holds out a hand for the bottle and syringes. He places them in a pocket of his backpack and, after a few moments' hesitation, carefully pulls out a few of the explosives and some lighters.

'Light them at this part here, don't hang about once you do. Dom, Tess?'

They each take a bomb and lighter, Dom eyeing his nervously. Tess looks unsure where to put hers and eventually opts for the inside pocket of her parka. Ethan doesn't even look at Felix. He offers Ralph two. Ralph takes them slowly. He places them in his pockets like Tess before taking the Mollitiam and, after a moment's hesitation, one of the NatApp syringes and a handful of Serum X vials. He thrusts them into various pockets of his large, baggy winter coat. Felix reaches for the case. Ethan grunts and she rounds on him.

'I'm just taking the Serum. Ariana's in there too, she needs someone looking out for her while the rest of you prance about playing superheroes.' She sighs. 'Has anyone considered, you know, something utterly crazy like calling the fire brigade? God knows no one in that building is going to do it…'

'Great idea, we'll let you explain about the half-animal, half-humans and the teenage girl with supernatural powers, shall we?' Ethan snarls.

'The world's going to know about the hybrids soon enough anyway. And an ambulance might not be a bad idea—'

'Let's give it twenty minutes before anyone dials 999,'

Ralph barks quickly before they can start arguing again. 'The plan's simple. Get in, try not to get killed, get as many hybrids and people out as you can, try and stab as many Guards with Serum X as possible. Once the hybrids are out, see what you can do with the NatApp. Try and explain it first, obviously...'

Ethan's already striding ahead, snow obscuring his large paces from view as he treads steadily up the hill. Ralph and the others follow him, though he's faster and more sure-footed than they and by the time they reach the gate at the perimeter of the ARC's property, he's already disappeared. The gate – once locked – hangs open, the bolt hanging off the chain as if it's been wrenched apart.

'Ralph,' Felix barks, her voice half choked by smoke, which is billowing more furiously now, buffeted by the wind. Without the cover of the trees or the sprawling Manor, the gusts are more waspish here and Ralph tugs his hood up to protect his eyes as much as anything.

'I know, the bolt's—'

'No, look... Round the front. Isn't that Lychen's car? The one he had when he came to the Manor last year...?'

Ralph stares, his heart lurching as he recognises the sleek black Mercedes.

'Bugger. Yeah, I think so.' He starts jogging the rest of the path, his brain leaping ahead of the swirl of panic in his throat. There's a downstairs cupboard to the right of the front entrance with a window, he remembers it vividly from the days when nothing seemed more important than finding the best hiding places in the ARC to overhear secrets about the Project C children. If he can just remember which window from the outside of the building, it should give him an easy, concealed entrance.

'Ralph!'

He turns. Tess and Dom are already skirting the building in the opposite direction. Felix stands in front of him, what he can see of her face is conflicted.

'Be careful, OK?'

'You too. Get Ariana out. All costs, OK?'

'I know.'

He begins to turn, his thoughts returning to the window, to where else he might be able to break his way into the building he had grown up thinking he would own by now.

'I never wanted to kill her,' she says, her voice so low that he almost doesn't hear her at all. 'But don't *you* get yourself blown up trying to save her.'

He doesn't answer, simply turns back to the building, puts his head down against the onslaught of snow, ash, and wind, and tries not to think too much about what he's walking into.

The window in the ground floor bathroom is still broken, the old towel she'd used to cushion the glass fragments still draped over the sill, stiff with muck and ice. Ariana scrambles over the rim and into the small room beyond, almost unrecognisable as a bathroom now. Leaves and mud are strewn across the floor, there's evidence of some sort of animal nest in one of the stalls and parts of the floor are slick with ice. The door has been boarded up from the other side, Ariana guesses that Daniel has ordered only the most basic of repairs and renovations. She shoulders the heavy plywood and uses a little of her pool of bubbling strength to move it aside just as she had done earlier with the locks on the gates.

Ariana pulls her hood up over her hair, hoping that her

black clothes and boots help her blend into the dark walls around her. Smoke lingers in the air of the corridor ahead, not really going anywhere, just hanging in puffs like a lazy ghost. Ariana lowers her head and walks towards the stairs. She doesn't think about the time she followed Dr Blake up to his office. She doesn't think about the other time, when she came here alone and raging. Felix's words whisper in her ear briefly as she casts around and places a hand on the door leading to the stairs. *I knew Ariana and cared about her, for her, like a mother*. She pushes the words, the confusing tumble of feelings, all of it, away as she sends her mind through the door to check for people. There are three Guard people in this stairwell. Two of them are several floors up and climbing, one is making their way downward, but is several flights away. She is faster. She heads through the door and steps into the larger, more vicious cloud of smoke crowding the stairs.

Heat beats frantically at her face as she makes her way downwards and Ariana removes her hood. She can feel her resilience stores battling to filter the poison from the air, regulate the temperature surrounding her. As she rounds the corner and another flash of heat whomps over her, she resists the urge to strip her hoodie off, instinct telling her not to. She hesitates outside the door on the lower level and sends out her mind again. It's more difficult this time because so much of her strength is concentrating on keeping her protected from the heat and smoke. The images come slower, but they're clear enough: there are several people on the floor below, all massing in one area. She can sense a few on this floor too, all of them appearing to be in rooms. The images are like shadows, but they bear an energy she can read – the beings in the rooms beyond the door in front of her are all human. There are Guard at the far end of the corridor, making their way towards her with their brisk, even strides. Two of them. Ariana grits her teeth as she opens her eyes. She's never come up against Guard like this before. *I should've grabbed some of the Serum. No. I don't need it. The others do. Come on, Ariana. You've got this.*

'Let's go,' she mutters, pushing the door open.

The entire corridor is a mass of writhing grey vapour. Ariana blinks, feeling it buffer against the protective bubble around her. She clenches her fists, plants her feet, looks up, and waits. The two Guard men march into sight like blank-faced gargoyles brought to life, the smoke whittling and curling around their large bodies. They catch sight of Ariana at the same time and both pause, blinking in unison, clearly communicating something. *Down,* Ariana thinks. They both fall backwards like planks of wood. Ariana steps over them neatly, not looking at their faces. *They aren't dead,* murmurs the small voice. *Not yet,* replies the other one. The blank one. *Don't separate,* she thinks, as she stares at the doors on either side of the prone Guard people and isolates one, three down on the right. *Remember Reuben. He said we need to be united, as one, no isolation, no blankness and me. Just me.* She reaches the door and it bursts open. *Look at what happened to Reuben, though. Just go with it,* says one of her. *Remember our purpose. Remember the girl who got nightmares just from seeing the hybrids for the first time... Remember how much she yearned to try and do something right to save them, even if it was just opening their cage doors...*

She lets the smoke settle around the form of a huddling girl around her own age. She's leaning her face against a window which only opens a crack, her mouth as close to the outside air as she can get it. Her room contains only a mattress on the floor.

'They wouldn't let us out,' she gasps at Ariana in terror.

'Well I am, come on,' Ariana turns away, already pinpointing the three other humans in their rooms. She doesn't bother checking to see if the girl follows her, the smoke is growing thicker every minute and she can feel the heat swarming through the thick soles of her boots. She concentrates for a moment and finds, with a heady little glow at her own brilliance, she can sense the fire. Part of it is directly beneath them, devouring mattresses, wooden doors, tables and chairs in a make-shift break room across the corridor... It's swarming ever closer to the huddle of hybrids who cower next to the locked door leading to the stairwell. Ariana draws up her power and thrusts all the humans' doors open at once. It's more energy than she should be using, but time is against her.

'There's a way out if you follow me,' she shouts, 'But you have to come *now*!' She turns as shapes emerge from the blurry mist of choking heat surrounding the doorways. She lets them see her and then turns, jogging back past the silent unmoving Guard, her mind already reaching on, downwards, out... *Open the cages,* she thinks. *The rest is up to them. I'm coming, Nova. I'll get it right this time.*

February, 2020

Ralph shoves his glasses up, takes aim and plunges the syringe into the side of the Guard man's thick neck. The Guard does not make a sound, but he reflexively reaches for Ralph and, though Ralph ducks, the heavier man grabs his arm and effortlessly drags him around and thrusts him back against the wall of the corridor. Ralph coughs, his glasses clouding, the shock of the wall startling the air from his lungs. The Guard raises a fist and Ralph flinches, preparing for the blow. It never lands. Ralph squints through his glasses and sees the familiar cloud of confusion swarm the Guard's eyes. He kicks upwards, a strange sound coming from his throat – something between fear and triumph, he guesses – and the Guard keels forward. Ralph enjoys the novel feeling of physical superiority for a moment, before whirling around. Luckily, the Guard man had been alone. Ralph is standing in a corridor just off the main entrance atrium, having entered through the store cupboard window as planned with the help of a large rock. He flattens himself against the wall as voices carry towards him. The smoke isn't so bad in this high-ceilinged well-ventilated part of the building, but he can taste it searing his nostrils and throat with cancerous fingers.

'…want to know who started the fire, it's concentrated on the lower levels where the hybrids are… I've sent the

Guard down there with instructions to salvage as many of the creatures as possible as a priority, then the humans.' The voice is nasal and holds a vague sneer even though Ralph can detect the strong thread of frustration and anger in its owner. It takes him a moment to connect it with the pallid, awkward Daniel.

'Good,' comes the reply, as the voices travel across the entrance hall. Ralph recognises Lychen's clipped tone straight away. He inches further along the wall and peeks around the corner. As he'd thought, Daniel and Lychen stride towards the lifts standing at the opposite side of the hallway. Daniel is smeared in dirt and dust and his face is spattered in blood as well as a long, ragged scratch. He looks as if he's just come from wrestling one of the hybrids himself. Lychen is wearing his usual suit, but even from where he stands, Ralph can see the mark of the last twenty-four hours on him. His usually flat tawny hair struggles and tufts outwards, there are streaks of ash on his suit jacket, his shirt gapes at the neck without a tie and his fists are clenched. They're speaking more quietly now, three Guard people tailing them – one woman and two men – shielding their words from Ralph. Ralph strains as far as he dares to try and catch them.

'...office and there's no danger of interference... as long as T... that's how...'

'...go and see that the hybrids...'

Daniel stops short and turns, frowning. Ralph shrinks back, sure for a moment that the younger man's abrupt halt means he's been spotted, but when he dares another glance, he sees that the short wispy man is smiling in a strange, cold way.

'Huh. That's interesting.'

'What?' Lychen snaps impatiently. He's glancing

towards the lift as if eager to be elsewhere. Their voices come clearer as the Guard shift, the two men flanking Lychen, the woman hovering behind Daniel.

'Seems like one part of the mystery's been solved. Ariana D'accourt has been spotted on level B1, the south wing.'

'What was she doing there?' Lychen sounds more weary than surprised, Ralph thinks.

'I don't know. Presumably something to disable my Guard, as they're no longer responding. I need your men,' he turns to Lychen and indicates the two stoic Guard behind him.

'You already deployed the other three,' Lychen frowns. Ralph feels a familiar tightening in his chest as more smoke billows into the air around them. The front doors are open. He breathes in that direction, visualising the cool, fresh air from the mountains filling his lungs instead of the creep of acrid poison. His fingers touch around the strange shapes in his pockets and find his inhaler.

'...need them. I've already lost five somewhere else. I need to see what the hell's going on down there.'

'But—'

'I told you, as long as T keeps doing what she's doing, Bella poses no threat to you. Her psychic abilities are blocked and she's chained up. I've practically gift-wrapped her for you. Well. I mean, she's not in a *pristine* condition, but as you can see, she put up a good fi—'

Several things happen at once at this point. Ralph feels a pulse of white-hot rage at the smug, knowing look on Daniel's face and the indication he makes to his injured face. He takes a step into the entranceway, not caring that there are three huge Guard people between him and the two most dangerous men he knows, not caring that his lungs are floundering weakly in his chest, begging for the quick burst of relief from his inhaler. He takes a second stride just as a roar and a crash erupts from the area of corridor beyond the lifts. Ralph blinks and Ethan rushes forward, jabbing Daniel's face viciously with his elbow without pausing in his stride, sending the smaller man flying in a spurt of blood into the door of the lift.

Ethan abruptly launches himself at the pair of Guard men, who both leap into action. Lychen steps neatly around Daniel and unconcernedly heads towards the second lift. Thinking quickly, Ralph turns on his heel and jogs back along the corridor behind him. Pausing only to grasp his inhaler, shake it and send a few puffs of relief to his chest, he reaches a set of stairs and takes them two at a time. *Come on,* he urges his memory to be right and is rewarded with a swift kiss of relief as he reaches the second floor, sprints around a corner and finds an identical set of lifts. Wrenching the doors open as best he can, he wedges his foot into the gap, and ignoring the pain, reaches into his pocket for one of the explosives. He can hear whirring and movement from the shaft, though it's impossible to tell if Lychen has got into the lift and, if so, whether it's above or below him. Before he can think himself out of it, Ralph lights the fuse, chucks it in and runs.

The boom reaches him as he's on the stairs heading upwards. It shatters dust into the air and the entire building shudders. Ralph braces his hands on the metal banisters, waits a few moments, clears his throat and carries on. He doesn't pause until he reaches the tenth floor. The air is clearer up here, though the taste of smoke still sears the back of his throat. Ralph pushes one of the windows of the stairwell open and glances outwards.

Smoke engulfs the entire lower floor of the building. There's another shuddering explosion from somewhere beneath him and he has a sudden thrust of memory of watching the twin towers of the World Trade Centre sinking into the ground on TV as a teenager. He shakes the uncomfortable thought away and turns instead to the door in front of him.

Memories crowd in. His old lab, its familiar books and instruments. Unlike his dad, he hasn't stepped foot in the ARC since it was emptied by Lychen's Guard over a year ago. He pushes through the door, blinking hard against the other memories, the good and the bad. Bella's face scornful as he'd called her names they'd both known he hadn't meant, the flow of her body in that iridescent green dress, the easy laughter as Felix and Ethan had teased him.

Another boom shudders the floor beneath his feet, but Ralph doesn't stop. He begins to jog, wondering whether the explosive had been powerful enough to create a *Die Hard*-like fireball in the shaft, whether Lychen had been burned to a crisp in a quick, vicious instant. He can't bring himself to hope. He rounds a corner and counts the doors. Had Ethan heard what Daniel said about the Guard woman and Bella's powers? Five, six. And what about the thing he'd said about Bella not being in pristine condition? Ralph hasn't thought many good things about Ethan recently, but he hopes with every fibre of his soul that he is able to fight off the three Guard people and then turn to smash Daniel's head against the ground. *I didn't worry enough about Daniel*, Ralph thinks. When he'd found out that he was the one who had Bella, he'd just been glad it wasn't Lychen. He hadn't known, hadn't thought about what threat *he* posed... Nine, ten. He wishes he'd brought a bottle of water, even up here the air is still tight with fumes. Another bang, more distant, which means it's probably coming from the furthest reach of the building, echoes along the corridor. He wonders if it was from an explosive or the fire reaching one of the labs... *Please be safe, Ariana*. He stops, grasping his inhaler and drawing another long tremulous breath. Then he places his hand on the door in front of him and pushes it open before he has time to think too much about what he might find.

The sound reaches him first. Caught between a call and a sob, and full of a relief so desperate it rips part of his soul raw, the cry is unmistakably hers. It pulls him like an unfathomably strong magnet through the dust shimmering the air, lit by the weak sunlight streaming through the window, round the large ornate desk and onto his knees. Bella crouches like a small animal, hands bound together by bolted shackles and chains wrapped around the desk leg. Her face is dirty and her long curls fall in tangles, there's blood on her lip and he can see a dark matted wound at the back of her head, but her eyes are wide and gleaming and she is every bit as wonderfully alive as she ever has been. Wordlessly, he gathers her to his chest. She shakes into him as if every particle of her is shuddering, shimmering, stealing for battle, quaking with pain.

Ralph smooths her hair and looks away from the bruises and marks he can see, though every blemish sears itself into his head, noting itself against Daniel's name, stirring a rage which surprises even him with its murderous clarity. He doesn't ask if she is OK because clearly she is not. Instead, he reaches for the chains.

'Where's the key?' he murmurs.

'I don't...' she coughs and shudders. He looks around, cursing himself again for forgetting water. Such a simple thing. So stupid.

'I don't know,' she manages, her voice croaking back to itself. 'I need wa—'

'Water, I know. I'm so stupid, I didn't bring a bottle. I can offer you some Serum X or a syringe of NatApp, spectacularly helpful I know.'

He stands up and casts around as if hoping a cool box of supplies will materialise. When he looks down again his heart gives a flutter to see her mouth twitch into a tiny shadow of a smile. It doesn't reach her eyes of course, but it's a spark of her and he grasps it like a fragment of precious stone.

'Is Ariana—'

'She's fine, we got her and she's fine. Everyone is. Except you. I can't believe I forgot bloody water, who runs into a burning building without water, for Chrissakes—'

'My office... has a bathroom,' she says, quietly. He sees the door and is upon it in two strides.

'Always showing off,' he mutters, turning both taps, only slightly rusted. The pipes bang and grumble and the first gush of water is brown, but it clears within seconds. He grabs an old mug and rinses it through a few times before filling it and bringing it back.

Bella drinks deeply and, as he holds the cup to her lips, Ralph notices something strange happening. Her body seems to glow from within, as if the water is replenishing some deeply sourced well. He wonders if it's a trick of the light, of the dirt-speckled air, until he lifts the empty cup away and sees that the cut on her lip has closed. He stands to get more water and notices the wound on the back of head seems smaller too, the hair around it less matted.

'Oh,' he reaches into his pocket for the Mollitiam and quickly snaps the bottle lid open. 'Here, this should help.'

Her eyes ignite at the sight of the pills and the glow

about her seems to shimmer, to reach. The look she gives him is one of such blazing gratitude that he's dropped to his knees, his hand reaching for her face before he can regain control of himself, before the sound of footsteps forces him to regain control of himself. Terror flutters across her eyes and she glances at the pills. He understands, placing one in her mouth. She swallows. The door opens before he can give her another and he sweeps the bottle into his pocket, standing up and turning. He senses Bella bracing herself beside him, imagines the tablet dispensing its properties within her, sifting into the glow of beauty and powering it into something deadly.

And as Ralph stares into the blank shark eyes of Josiah Lychen, at the gun he slowly lifts and points directly at Ralph's chest, he hopes with everything he can muster that it will be enough.

February, 2020

Ariana knows she doesn't have much time. The fire is leaping at the feet of the hybrids, a locked door between them and the only possible route left which might save them. She vaults down the stairs and smacks into the chest of a Guard man hurrying upwards. He seizes her by the forearms before she can gather herself enough to push him back. The next second is all she needs, though. He drops her and she slams him back down the stairs, his skull cracking loudly against the concrete.

'Woah,' a voice croaks behind her. She turns around. The girl, the first one she saved, is standing at the top of the stairs, her top pulled up over her mouth and nose. She has short mousey hair and pale blue eyes. Ariana knows with a strange certainty that if they were to stand side by side they would be within an inch of one another's height. The girl coughs, watching her with a mixture of fear and admiration.

'Are the others coming?' Ariana asks, her voice clear despite the choking fumes surrounding her. She can see the smoke gathering and buffeting off a space around her, her protective aura a centimetre thick. She can feel the energy sapping from the store within, she knows it won't last much longer, not if she still wants the strength to slam Guard people into walls and down stairs, anyway.

'Yeah, I think so,' the girl glances behind her, coughing harder. 'How do we get out?'

'I'm just trying to work that out,' Ariana mutters, trying to rake her memory over how many stairs she's descended. Is this one level below ground or two? She sends her mind through the wall ahead and meets solid earth. *Too much energy.* But does she have time to lead the others upwards and out before the ones below burn? They have minutes. Of course not.

'I'm going to get the hybrids out. They're trapped. You can stay here if you want, or you can try and get out. Go upwards. There's a bathroom with a broken window on the ground floor,' she knows even as she's saying it that it's useless trying to explain the ARC's labyrinthine lower floors. Why can't it be like the disaster films where there were conveniently placed escape hatches and fire exits all over the place?

She doesn't turn to see what the girl does, she hammers downwards, heat engulfing her as she wheels around the bottom of the stairwell. She can hear the screaming as bodies hammer at the door in front of her. Summoning all her energy, she concentrates on the door. It blasts open and there's a rush of bodies, heat and smoke into the narrow space at the bottom of the stairs. Ariana feels herself shoved aside as something large and furry hurtles up the stairs. She blinks, unable to see anything, the noise battering against her ears.

'Wait... stop pushing,' she tries to shout, but the smoke is too thick even within the protective bubble and her voice shrivels like a burning crisp packet. It's no use anyway, the larger hybrids are storming up the stairs, falling and tearing over one another in panic. The building gives a shudder and Ariana finds herself falling, something hard jabbing into the bubble to reach her shin. She catches the banister with her right hand and something feathery helps push her upright. She turns to see Nova, feathers askew, one wing twisted against her chest, its feathers shortened and melted.

'Get them up,' Ariana mutters, looking around and seeing several smaller shapes huddled, some motionless, some attempting and failing to climb the steep carpeted stairs. She seeks out the vicious lapping flames and forces them back, though they push with a hunger she knows she can't match.

'We've got to get them up to the next floor. I can find a way out then.'

Nova clicks her small mouth and turns, using her good wing to try and buffet a smaller bird-girl into movement. The bird-girl groans, but she pushes herself upright and begins to climb. Flames leap into the bottom of the stairwell and a new wave of shrieks reaches Ariana's ears. She turns and leaps to the bottom, feeling her clothes wither and the skin beneath beginning to burn but not paying attention as she scoops small furry bodies to her chest. There are too many. The tiny monkey-boy reaches his arms up plaintively, but she has a rabbit-girl already in one arm, a long-tailed creature clasped in the other, something with long claws gripping into her shoulders.

'Ariana, I'm here! Pass them up!'

She turns and gives a strangled cry of relief. Dominic stands a few stairs up, his face partially obscured by a bloody rag tied around it, his thin chest flailing as he reaches through the thick fog, arms blistered and shaking. Ariana passes him the rabbit-girl and the long-tailed thing. He takes them and lollops up the stairs. Nova has already gone, as has the bird-girl. Ariana scoops up the monkey-boy and looks around. Two hybrids, she can't even tell what they are, burn at her feet next to the body of the Guard man she'd thrown. The smell forces its way into her nose and she looks away, tears evaporating. The monkey-child grips her neck viciously and the long-clawed thing gives a sharp piercing shriek in her ears, and Ariana turns, unable to hold off the fire any longer. Leaping up the stairs, she pauses to scoop another small rodent-shaped creature struggling with a broken, dragging foot.

She meets a seethe of bodies on the floor above. Fighting her way through as best she can, she searches desperately for Dominic or Nova. The building gives another shove and the inferno bursts against her ankles.

'Ariana!' Dominic's voice chokes from somewhere up above. 'The ground floor's blocked – it must have caved in after I came down here. We can't get through!'

'Rana!'

'We're going to burn! The fire's coming!'

Ariana glances up ahead and then around, below. She can feel the push of the fire, she can feel the soles of her boots beginning to melt and the thin fabric of her leggings searing up her legs. She can feel the push of bodies all around her, the choking lungs, the failing hearts. The fear swarms into her. *Blast the wall.* I can't. I can't do that and hold off the fire, I haven't got enough in me. *Blast the wall anyway. Or we all burn to death.*

Ariana screws up her eyes and shoves her mind out once again, dropping the protective bubble, her lungs immediately seizing against the flood of fumes. They're still underground, but not by much. She can't reach the wall physically, she's trapped in a choking, writhing, pushing mass of panicking beings, united in death. But she knows where to aim, she knows that the wall directly facing the stairs meets earth and then diagonally, six, maybe eight feet, open air. She gathers her strength and sends a pulse of energy up, towards the wall. It shudders and reverberates back, sending an avalanche of brick and bodies backwards. They scream, someone grabs her, one of the small ones is wrenched from her grasp. She grips the banister with her hand, forcing her body to stay on the stairs and summons more, summons as much as she can. It's not enough. She opens her eyes into the stinging deadly haze and feels the oxygen dissipating, feels her lungs squeezing and searching in panic... *Mummy.* She doesn't know if it's because she's dying, if it's a part of her which is still small, still wants her, still reaches for her arms, her safety. Wants to be there, if it's going to happen. Wants to be held, if only by her mind.

Ariana...? The voice is faint, not more than a whisper. Ariana blinks, feeling her body falling, something sharp knifing into her side.

Mum? Can you help me?

Yes. Take it. Use me. Ariana feels the flood of strength hit her and sucks it desperately like a drowning diver given one last burst of oxygen. She turns her face towards the top of the stairs, stands without knowing or caring what surface meets her feet, and blasts out and upwards, feeling the very last of her strength rushing away. Her body drops backwards like a bird killed in flight before her eyes have a chance to open, to see whether it worked.

Felix swears, blinking through a bloody sheen as she raises a hand to her face. The Guard who struck her stands vaguely, staring at his own hands as the dose of Serum X she's just hit him with takes effect. Reaching into her pocket, Felix draws out a handkerchief and wads it, placing it over the cut she can feel blooming somewhere around her temple. She blinks and her vision clears. She's standing in the entrance hall of the ARC, the doors to the lift wedged open by the prone body of a dead Guard person, rubble littering the floor and half the large floor-to-ceiling windows gaping jaggedly like the teeth of a carved pumpkin.

Felix looks around, wondering whether to chance heading down the rubble-strewn corridor past the lift, or take the darker, less direct but also more sturdy-looking corridor to the left. Taking two steps towards the latter, there's a sudden rumbling, shuddering noise which seems to come from the earth itself. Felix frowns. That wasn't like the explosions she's heard and felt over the last few minutes. That one seemed to come from the very ground beneath her feet. Crossing over to the nearest window, she peers outwards, careful to avoid the shards of glass slicing towards her jugular.

The next rumble comes slowly, but she can tell it's bigger than the first. It builds like a volcanic eruption, juddering the ground, forcing Felix to place a hand on a glass-free part of the window frame. A shower of ash, brick, earth and God knows what else bursts from the far end of the building, rising so high she sees it spray over the tall brick wall around the Project C gardens.

'Now what,' Felix mutters, turning and running towards the entrance. She stops, remembering the Guard man and turns back just in time to see the large crystal chandelier shear clear away from the ceiling and land, with a skittering, shattering crash, on the smooth black ground. The Guard, standing fortunately off to the right, blinks and slowly turns his head towards the sound.

'Get out,' Felix calls to him. 'This way, out of these doors here. Unless you want something to land on your head next.'

She turns back and thrusts her way through the double doors. Snow is still swirling around in a strange rebellion against the bursts of fire she can feel coming from different parts of the building and grounds as she jogs around the perimeter. She meets Tess as she reaches the wall around the back gardens. The younger woman's entire body is smudged in ash, but she seems unhurt and she still carries the NatApp briefcase, now decidedly battered-looking. Wordlessly, they pass through the gate in the wall, its lock long since removed.

A large ugly crevice gapes into the earth surrounding the ARC's back wall. Tess stops short, staring, but Felix hurries towards it, spotting a few huddled shapes at the far end of the garden. Some of them look furry and misshapen, others are unmistakably human. She steps hesitantly into the crumbling earth, blasted at a diagonal from a dark area thick with smoke and scrambling bodies. Two bird-people burst forth, one of them carrying a smaller rodent-hybrid in its human hands. A monkey-child struggles upwards, pushed from behind by pale, long fingers...

'Dom! Is that you?' Felix hurries forward, keeping to the side of the slope to avoid sending rocks back down against the tide.

'Fee! Here, can you take him?' Dominic's face, sooty and scarred but alive and breathing, appears from the darkness. Felix takes the monkey-thing without hesitation, letting it reach for the fresh grass above her and scramble upwards.

'Is Ariana in there?'

'Yes, I think so... There's a big drop off, they can't all

402

get up, some of them are injured...' He reaches down and helps lift a large dog-man up and out. The dog-man turns, reaching for a teenage girl. Felix reaches as Dominic pulls a small feathery shape upwards. Another bird-girl, this one with a burned, bleeding leg. Felix half supports, half drags her up and out of the slope.

'Is Dom in there? Is he OK?' Tess says, her voice tight as she stares over the top of the open case. She has one of the NatApp vials in her hand.

'He's OK, he's helping get them all out. Living out his hero fantasies.'

She stops suddenly, a wheeling whining noise coming to her out of the rush of burning. It's a siren. Tess's eyes widen.

'What do we—'

'Give as many doses out as you can.'

'How do I choose who—'

But Felix has already turned away, heading back to the hole. Several more bodies emerge, many of them scrambling to help one another, some of them dragging broken or burned twisted limbs. The dirt begins to churn beneath their scrambling feet and in the smoke and snow, Felix blinks and finds she can no longer make out human from hybrid. She reaches the edge and finds Dominic bent double, coughing like his lungs are being wrenched inside out.

'Out, now,' Felix barks, swinging her feet over the edge and dropping into the darkness.

'But there's more of them—'

'So let me hand them to you. You've done enough. The fire engines are here, I heard them.'

'Fee...' He stares at her and she sees it all. The longing to trust her, the pain both physical and soul-deep.

'Let me do this, Dom,' she murmurs. 'Let me make it right.'

He coughs again and this time she has to grasp him to hold him upright. She can tell from the weight she bears of him that he's at the last of his strength. She shoves him up as best she can. He scrambles the rest of the way. Felix turns into the billowing darkness, covering her nose and mouth with the neck of her shirt. She blinks, trying to sort movement from smoke.

'Ariana? Ariana! Are you down there?'

Something flurries to life nearby as she steps down, reaching out with her hand. She connects with something soft and feathery and a familiar voice grunts at her.

'Nova? Are you OK? Is Ariana down there?'

'Rana... down. Fallen. Last one. Can't reach.'

'OK, I'll get her. You go, get yourself out.'

Felix blinks, unsure if Nova has moved past her or not, unable to see anything. The heat blasts against her face as if she's just stuck her head in an oven on full power. She slips on something horribly furry and tumbles a few feet down broken, uneven stairs. Staring around, she sees a leap of flame lurch towards her and, by its light, her eyes finally pick out a head of dark ashy curls. She reaches her and pulls at her shoulders, slapping and shouting at her, choking and coughing. Ariana moans.

'Come on, Ariana. I know you can hear me, you great lump. I can't heave you out of here on my own, you've got to try and wake up so you can bloody help me,' Felix gasps, her throat closing and failing as she turns her face towards the lurch of weak sunlight and gulps at the air beyond. Planting her feet, she shoves against rock, bodies, earth, rubble... Ariana moans again, but this time something in her long heavy limbs shifts and next time Felix heaves, the weight has lessened as Ariana's feet find purchase. They inch closer to the hole, but behind them the fire blooms, feasting on the fresh oxygen and snapping at their feet.

'Felix! Hand her up!' Felix turns, sure she must be hallucinating. Ethan's face skewers across the hole, his strong hands reaching. Felix feels tears of pure relief bursting out of her face as she gives one last shove and feels his hands close around Ariana's arms, pulling her out like she weighs no more than a doll. Felix coughs, watching Ariana's body, legs, feet all swallow into the open air, into safety. The fire yawns and leaps, heat tearing at her side and she turns back to it. There's a sound like gunfire and the building rumbles again, falling debris lurching her sideways. She sees the fire reach, she knows she's going to meet it, she hopes she has done enough...

The thought is still unfinished as fingers, achingly familiar even under the roughness, close over her upper arm and yank her up and outwards. Felix turns and grips Ethan's other hand as he pulls, then her boots meet the sweet, solid earth and they're running, tumbling, skidding up the slope as behind them the world splits and burns.

February, 2020

I can't see his face very well from where I crouch, but I know it's him. The footfalls, the shoes – smudged but still passably shiny – the creases that still form along the front of his trousers even though the fabric is smeared with dirt. Next to me, Ralph swears loudly. Lychen gives a strange, cold little laugh which could also be a cough. The smoke isn't thick yet but it has become a discernible feature in the flavour of the room.

'Did you really think I wouldn't come for her, Blake?'

'No,' Ralph mutters, stepping forward until his legs form most of my view. I don't know whether he's acting instinctively to try and shield me or if he's simply playing for time, hoping the Mollitiam gets to work. I swallow, still tasting the bulky powder of the pill's residue in my throat. Already, though, I can feel it. It tingles shiveringly along my veins, knitting the last of my head wound back, reaching out and pushing against the choking net of T's psychic block.

'...did hope that an explosive in the elevator shaft might slow you down a bit.'

'Oh, that was *you*?' Lychen sounds light, amused, but already I can sense past it. Already I can taste the impatience, the frisson of needing this done, yearning to get away. I remember what Daniel said about him being a wanted man.

'I'm afraid I was still waiting for the lift when I felt the explosion. You know they always were very slow… Like everything around here. I must say, I didn't know you had it in you, Blake. You were always the indecisive weak boy-child of the dynasty. Mind you, what hope did you have? Your father was the same. Practically rolled over and let me take whatever I wanted…'

I peer up at Ralph, watching his white face twitch as the words needle into him. *Don't listen to him,* I urge, though I know the words aren't bridging the gap between us, small as it is. *Don't let him bait you.* I know Lychen has the pistol, the same one he used to shoot Ethan at Futura a year ago. I can't see it but I can feel it in the way Ralph doesn't move, the stony confidence in Lychen's snaky voice.

'Your mother was the real force of nature in the family, wasn't she? Until nature took her out, of course. Dear Ana. You know, from the moment I first met her I always admired her far more than Frederick. I even wondered at one time if I was developing something of a little *crush* on her—'

'You shut your goddamn mouth! You are not worthy to say her name!' Ralph moves forward, away from the desk. My eyes lock onto Lychen's. I see his black gaze flicker, widen with shock as he regards me, but his voice when he speaks remains conversational.

'That is, until my attentions were diverted of course. Hello, Bella.'

He steps towards me and I feel Ralph begin to move back, to stop him. Lychen raises the gun at him and he stalls, but when Lychen turns back to me he moves again. *No, Ralph.* Finally, the Mollitiam tears a tiny hole in T's block and I push through it, invisible bonds reaching towards Ralph and holding him back. He stares at me as comprehension dawns slowly.

What are you doing?

Trying to save you.

Well, stop it! Bella, he—

I cut the line of communication. It's too much, on top of holding him still. The hole is still tiny. I can't even send a thought to Ethan, though the feel of him wisps gently through the air to me. Closely followed by the delicate tendrils of Ariana. I let their closeness, their wholeness strengthen me as I turn once again to Lychen. He is standing above me, looking down with an unreadable expression. I can't probe further yet, so I have to guess at what I can make out. Anger, of course. Shock. Some satisfaction perhaps, too, at seeing me brought so low. But not by him, which cycles us back to anger.

'Who— What did...' He stops and glowers, and I know it's out of frustration at himself as much as the situation. He's changed again since I last broke into his mind, I can see even from the outside the new blemishes, the dull marks of stress and exhaustion underneath the dust and dirt of the calamity surrounding us.

'What happened to you?' He asks, eventually.

'I'm still trying to work it all out myself,' I reply, coldly. 'But from what I gather, I was used as a bargaining chip between you and Felix, which resulted in a minor head injury.' I barely feel the ache and sting at the back of my head now, but I know from the pained glance he throws at it that it still screams messily from my hair. His eyes travel the rest of my body, what he can see of it, the marks and bruises, the deep blooms of blood on my torn dress. I feel the questions tangling on his tongue.

'Everything since… I suggest you ask Daniel. You two seem close.'

'That *swine* and I—'

'Have more in common than you think. Your taste for violence, for one. Your taste in women, for another.'

I see the blow land, still keeping an invisible hold on Ralph, though I feel his turmoil as well. There's more strength coming now as the Mollitiam finds a stronghold and bursts itself free in my system. I know I could reach Ethan if I wanted to now, at least fleetingly. Or I could concentrate on the matters at hand.

'I told him— I *warned*… I will *end* him for this,' Lychen mutters, the words coming out flat and bullet-like because his face is so rigid with fury. I keep drawing on my power, keep focusing it in the same direction, keep talking his attention from Ralph and the gun now slack at his side.

'Do you think so, Josiah?' I keep my voice light, like his had been, though I can feel the power of it returning, threading my waiting words through with wire, steel, resilience, and everything else that so many of them found impossible to resist. 'Do you really have the power to make claims like that anymore? Daniel certainly doesn't seem to think so. Why else would he dare take something you had so clearly marked as your own? He seems to think you've lost your grip… That your weakness for me, my voice twisting its knife in your head all these months … that it's damaged you beyond repair. He even takes credit for what you did to me right here in this office all those years ago.'

'What?'

'He told you about Ralph and me, didn't he? I always wondered, you know. What made you burst in here, what made you so *angry*… You never hid your feelings for me. I knew that you wanted me. But the way you hit me, threw

409

me back over this desk... What could I possibly have done to invoke such brutality?'

I feel Ralph's internal groan even as Lychen's face darkens further.

What are you doing, Beast?

Just wait. Wait. Trust me.

'He did tell me,' Lychen mumbles, his voice quiet and pinched as if he doesn't want to give the words up but they're being dragged from him nonetheless. 'I was coming to confront you. Just to talk. To ask you why you had shown me such encouragement when your heart clearly lay elsewhere... But then, I came in... I came in that door and you... You were standing here, your hair long and shining, your clothes neat and perfect, everything about you pristine and goddess-like and all I could think of were Blake's hands on you first, Blake's mark... And then you didn't even look up. I had given my life to cultivating respect, command, turning myself into this cold domineering presence whom people feared and deferred to above all others. Then I walk into the office of this teenaged subordinate and she doesn't even give me the common courtesy of *acknowledgement.*'

He passes his fingers in front of his eyes and then clenches them into a fist as if furious they've performed such a human gesture, such a betrayal of anguish.

'It sounds petty now, of course. And, for what it's worth, I do apologise for what happened. It was a reaction of blind rage and I am sorry. But we've both done things we regret, Bella.'

'I haven't.'

'Really.' He narrows his eyes at me, and for a brief black moment I glimpse the truth, or at least the version Felix has told him. I know he sees me see it, that his mind is already placing the pieces together, that any second now he will take steps against the Mollitiam.

Get the gun, Ralph! I explode upwards as Ralph lurches forwards, my shackles shattering as I fire a short, sharp burst of energy against them. Lychen blinks once in surprise, and I know in that second that I've waited too long, I've shown him too much. He's half ready, his arm rising as Ralph collides with it. I shake my hands free of the tangle of chains as Ralph lurches for the gun and Lychen raises it higher. The two men grapple, the pistol between them, its muzzle facing Lychen, Ralph, me, the window. I gather my strength, finding the Mollitiam where it runs half-depleted, and I ready my strength to break into Lychen's head, swerve him away, knock him down so Ralph can finish it once and for all.

Mummy.

The call is faint. A breath of whisper, but it comes to the part of my mind that always listens for her and I hesitate, the gun shoving back and forth through the dust and gathering smoke, and there she is: *Mummy*. I don't know if it's a call or a cry but I flood to her, finding her within seconds. *Mum? Can you help me?* Choking, alone, battered and dying. I send it to her without a moment's hesitation. *Take it. Use me.* She takes it with the same feverous need she once took milk from my breast, and I blink myself back into the room just as the gun erupts in a skull-shattering explosion.

My ears ring. Something heavy falls against me and *yes*, it's Ralph, it's the kickback of the gun which has shoved him into me, tumbling us both to the floor. I look up in triumph to see Lychen fall. Only Lychen isn't falling, he's standing solidly on the carpet, the gun smoking at his side. I look downwards, the air buffering at my lips, refusing to enter, refusing to carry on this moment of living with that unmistakable tang of blood in my nose once again, only this time so much more... Ralph lies across my lap, his mid-section awash with crimson. It drenches across my hands and my body and he splutters as he looks up at me and my own useless resilience clears my ears enough to hear the choking rattle of his torn lungs.

'*Ralph!* No, Ralph! Don't you dare... Where's the Mollitiam? You can take it, it'll save you...'

I lurch for his pockets, searching for the bottle of pills, my hand closing around something small and circular. I draw it out. One of the NatApp vials.

'For Nova,' he murmurs, his voice already faint. I turn away, dragging out the pill bottle. His voice can't be faint. I need it. I can't live in a world where his voice isn't there to call me Beast, laugh at my mistakes, tell me I'm not *that* pretty...

'Here, here you go,' I take a pill out and shove it into his mouth. 'Swallow it, please. *Please.*'

'S'no good, Beast...'

'Shh... Shut up. You swallow it and you'll get better just like Nova... You have to... You promised to take me to Lake Como, remember?'

'B... Bottle of Chianti...'

'And *gelato* by the waterside, that's right.'

He gives a weak, wispy imitation of his bark-laugh and blood shivers onto his lower lip. 'Like *you'd* ever... eat *gelato*.'

I look up. 'Get me water,' I bark at Lychen. He blinks and walks away.

'Still... got it,' Ralph murmurs, then he lurches forward a little, coughing wracking his entire upper body. I cradle his head, bring it forward. More blood burbles from his mouth. The unswallowed pill dribbles in a red sea down his chin. I pluck it up, place it back in his mouth. Lychen hands me the mug I drank from earlier. I look up to see him blinking as I take it, his face clouding with anger once again as he comes out of the trance of my command. I hold the water to Ralph's mouth and he sips clumsily.

'It won't help him,' Lychen says, shortly. 'That wound is beyond help. It was your fault, Bella. It didn't have to happen like this… Or perhaps it did. You know I know the truth now, after all. We are the same, you and I. We can only have one another. We will always eventually seek to destroy all others who stand between us. Even those whom we love.'

I drop my eyes from him, search Ralph's face instead. He gives a side-smile, though more blood spills from his lips. I straighten his glasses and stroke his face.

'Bollocks,' he says, 'S'all just… hot air and bollocks… mate. She never loved me.'

'Don't you say that,' I whisper, leaning forward, my hair spilling over his chest as if trying to shield him from the malevolent spectre leering over us. 'You know it's not true.'

'Are you crying, Beast?'

'*No.*'

'Don't *cry*,' he says, as if crying were the very last thing he would have expected me to do. He frowns and it freezes slowly and gradually smooths out as he lays his head back in my lap and shuts his eyes. His mouth slackens from the tug of his wry, mocking smile… and then he's not my Ralph anymore.

February, 2020

Ariana breathes slowly, letting the pure air filter and cleanse and soothe the scorches. She can feel her body beginning to heal itself, the burns on her legs already numbing as the flesh creeps itself back together. She lies in the sweet-smelling grass, snow falling on her face, and somewhere nearby she can hear Felix talking to Dom or maybe Tess, saying that ambulances are coming, that they'll probably all need treatment for smoke inhalation. Tess says that she's given four of the hybrids the NatApp. Ariana sinks back into a grateful stupor, letting the grown-ups deal with it, letting their authority blanket over the need for her to do anything else. She doesn't know if it's minutes or seconds later that the heavy footsteps approach, that she feels Felix's voice change as she tells someone to let her rest.

'I can't... I'm sorry. Ariana, please. If you can hear me, I need your help.'

She opens her eyes and looks at Ethan. He's covered in blood and muck and there's a nasty looking gash on his forearm, but she knows that none of them look much better.

'She's in her office. On the tenth floor. Lychen and Ralph are with her,' Ariana murmurs. His face clears, he bends forward and, without a word, kisses her forehead.

Ariana frowns.

'Why didn't she just tell you herself?'

'I don't know, I got a glimpse of her a minute ago but then it disappeared. It's like whatever was blocking her is going in and out of focus. Or she's blocked me for some reason.'

'I'm not strong enough to reach her at the moment. But she's the one who did this... She sent me the strength to blast that hole and get them all out. She saved us all. I don't know what it cost her. You'd better hurry.'

He turns and runs without a word, skirting the approach of the fire-fighters along one side of the building and taking the other. Ariana watches him disappear as the responders aim a hose at the base of the building and begin to billow the smoke away. She turns her head to see Felix talking to one of the firemen, gesturing at the sorry collection of hybrids and humans on the grounds. Ariana wonders what she's telling them. She pushes herself into a sitting position, staring around and counting.

There are fifteen people, not including Dominic and Tess, who sit in a huddle against one of the brick walls, she supporting him as he takes deep, long breaths. There are fewer hybrids. The four who've been given NatApp sit with their humans – there are two bird-girls among them, though Ariana can't see well enough to tell if either is the one she saw in the horrible video. Monkey-boy is also there, along with one of the rodents. Ariana wonders what happened to the rabbit-girl, whether the rodent is the same creature who clung with vicious desperation to her back, leaving welts she can feel stinging into the fabric of her top. She remembers the crunch of tiny bones under her feet as Felix had scrambled her up in the darkness, recalls how, sickeningly, at the time she hadn't cared what she was stepping on in her own desperate search for clean air.

'Rana,' murmurs a voice to her right. She turns and sees Nova crouching beside her. Her feathers are still askew on her head and there is a burn on one of her legs, but it's not deep and her wing is not quite as injured or twisted as it had looked in the darkness.

'Are you OK? Your wing?'

'Hurt... But can fly...' she stretches it out. Some of the feathers are still shrivelled, but the wing holds straight. Ariana frowns. It *hadn't* been the dark. She was sure more of the feathers had been burned away, she remembers the sight of sinew and bone... Nova's quick eyes meet hers and she says slowly and clearly: 'Resilience.'

'You have it too? How can that be?'

'Bella gave it to me... Saved me. After I was shot.' Her face sweeps into a wild darkness, the same look of pure hatred Ariana remembers when she first saw her all those months ago, only this time it isn't directed at her.

'Daniel. He's the one who shot you?'

'He did... all this.'

Ariana looks around, at the bleeding, burning bodies. The half-beings, the humans. She spots a young man watching them with an empty, lost look in his eyes. A smaller bird-boy lies across his lap, his chest fluttering only very faintly, dark feathers twisted.

'Where is he? Can you sense him?'

Nova shuts her eyes for a moment and then gives a soft squawk. She turns her face in the direction of the path leading away from the ARC, towards the Manor.

'Running. One Guard with him.' She rustles her feathers and Ariana realises why she's come to her, that it isn't to check on how she's doing. That would be far too human for Nova, far too sentimental. She is recognising her power, giving her the chance to finish it together. Ariana glances back at Felix, who is still talking to one of the fire-fighters. An ambulance has arrived in the front driveway, another pulling in behind it. She won't get another chance to go. She turns back to Nova and nods.

'Let's go.' Ariana scrambles to her feet. Tess watches her, but she doesn't say anything. Perhaps she doesn't care, thinks Ariana. Perhaps she's too spent to care. She knows how that feels. She felt like it herself just five minutes ago, before the surging well began to return. Before she remembered what she came here to do, her purpose, as Reuben had put it to her so long ago. Nova stretches her wings, flinches but only slightly, then beats herself upwards. She hovers for a moment, drawing the attention of the fire-fighters, of Felix, and Ariana takes the diversion, slipping through the gate in the wall and away, into the dirty smear of falling snow.

58

February, 2020

It takes me a while to realise Lychen is talking. There was a time when my ears sought his voice among all others, when I was so attuned to his clipped, careful enunciation that I thought it would be possible for him to stand across the crowded canteen of the ARC and speak and I'd be able to pick out exactly what he said. Over time, of course, the keenness of my ear narrowed its focus and mutated into a sort of susceptible masochism that was not as close to dread as it should have been. But now... He's talking about how everything has changed for him now Felix has told him what she found out, that he finally understands me. About destiny or fate and something about us having time, we'll pick up somewhere new, probably Paris. We'd been before, I'd loved it hadn't I? Great things are happening in Paris for BFI, a new facility is well underway with a view across the Champs Elysées...

It all filters into me as I stare at Ralph, hold his face, wish I'd kissed him, it needles into the keening wail of grief hurtling around my chest and slowly I look up. Lychen stops talking the moment my eyes meet his and I know my fire is back. That the Mollitiam is giving me its final phoenix song. The pathways in my head are clear too, which means T has either been neutralised or has simply travelled too far away. I could find out, but it doesn't matter right now.

Right now, all that matters is him and me; and I will not be sitting on the floor for what comes next. Gently, I lift Ralph's head and slide my legs from under it, then I nestle it slowly back down as I get to my feet.

'Come, Bella. We don't have much time.'

The building gives a shudder as if agreeing with him and, for the first time, the sound of sirens find their way into the room.

'You know you weren't happy without me, Bella. You *know*. You never were. That's why you did what you did, isn't it? And it's why you've sought me out so many times over the last few months... I understand now. I saw you, too. No matter how much you say you were pretending. I saw how alive you were when we were together at the Beaumont... That fire you had when you showed me all you had done with the Youth Guard. I don't know what's become of them, my love, but they are, after all, replaceable. You are not. I've learned that much over this last year.'

He waits. I clear my throat, my diaphragm struggling a little against the thickening poison between us. Still, when it comes, my voice is dagger-sharp.

'Do you think I'm stupid? That I've just forgotten what you showed me back in January? Do you think I don't know there are still chains lurking in your plans for me? That every night when my head lay on that luxurious, Parisian silk I wouldn't turn it to find you waiting to choke me, force me, fuck me into obedience... How *dare* you presume to know me? Yes, there were elements of my life at the Beaumont which weren't intolerable, the Youth Guard foremost among them. But everything else – all the times you used me, my body... I wasn't just pretending, Lychen. I would disappear. I'd rather exist in oblivion than feel what you were doing to me, what I was allowing.'

'Not always. Not always. You can't pretend it was all like that – remember New Year's Eve? The night we celebrated the launch of the Care Programme? The week we flew to Paris? Have you become so skilled at lying that you've just blocked all that out of your mind, compartmentalised it away?'

He frowns as images flash between us so rapidly I don't know who is remembering them: our faces alight with fireworks across the London night sky; my eyes drifting to his across the Beaumont Yard during a champagne reception; my hand, reaching for his. I shake them away.

'I played a part. I didn't know it was only to be for six months, for all I knew that was my life now. I made of it what I could. Let you have your fun, take what I could in return. Drank the champagne, held your hand, smiled in that way you liked, let you jet me off to Paris, drank more champagne, often, until it all became easier to bear. I did what I had to do for Ariana. For Ralph. To keep them safe from you. It was all a lie, Lychen.'

It was. It has to have been. There are no voices I can give to the alternative.

His face clouds once again but then clears as he glances down at Ralph. I fight the urge to channel my rage into lasers. He still holds the gun and his grip is not as loose as he is pretending it is.

'You're upset. Understandably. But we both know the truth now, Bella. It wasn't always about Ariana or even Blake here. I asked you a long time ago to make a choice. I thought, for so many years, that you had chosen him. Them. This. But you didn't, did you? It was always me. Us. Whatever form that took. I see it now – why you kept the pregnancy, knowing she was mine. You were angry too of course, rightfully so, for what I did that night. That's why you ran, why you stayed away so long.

'But come, Bella, you must *see*… That action you took, adding those words to that photograph, you must see what it means. You were never supposed to be a mother, just as I was never supposed to be a father and we both failed when we tried. We are only meant to have one another. We are the same, you and I. As I said before. Come. Ralph is dead. Ariana doesn't need us anymore; let Felix take her. There is nothing for you here.'

I stare at him and slowly, deliberately, step over Ralph. I watch as the light washes into his face, the traces of humanity I had searched for in him for so long swarming into creases and fire as I approach. He reaches for my face, his fingers cold and hard upon my skin.

'You were always mine,' he murmurs. For one second I shut my eyes and let the vision sweep over the grief and pain. I see the two of us together in a palatial Parisian facility, an army of Youth Guard under my control. All obligation, pressure and responsibility to others gone. No further need for masks, life-strong lies, ghosts summoned to speak the truths to which I could not bear to give my own voice. A compromise placed upon my body but so much to take in return: luxury, beauty, glamour, wealth, power. Endless opportunity to use all I had ever worked for and wield it over so many.

'No,' the word comes without my thinking it. It comes *before* I think it. From the torn, brutalised, damaged part of me which had been broken right here in this room fourteen years ago and so many times since that the rest of me had forced it into silence. I knock his hand from my face at the same time that I open my eyes and meet his.

The black orbs glaze with a familiar hunger and I realise this is the way he loves me and hates me the most, the passion and the fury tumbling from me and illuminating me from the inside. A fire ripe to be claimed, consumed, dampened into extinction.

'I am *not* yours. I didn't choose you. What I did… that *action I took*… It wasn't even *about* you. It was about me. Just a fleeting, irrationally selfish choice made for my own sake a very long time ago. And every moment since then I've tried to put it right for Ariana's sake, even though it has driven us apart and made me do and endure things that I'd rather disappear than think about. But I don't belong to anyone. Not Ralph, not Ethan, not even Ariana. And I would rather die – be buried alive in the rubble of this wreck of a building – than belong to *you*.'

He narrows his eyes and raises the gun, but this time, at last, I am ready for him. I push past his flimsy shields and plunge into his head, scouring and scoring past the hatred and lust and confusion and deep, burning rage. I seek out the memory of that small child, the snivelling boy called Simon. I wrestle his soft humanity to the surface of the abhorrent excuse of skin and tissue in front of me until it is suffused in him. Then I grasp Lychen with everything I have. I take him through the cold hard focus of his eyes on my childish body as a girl in a twirling white dress. I burn his skin with the icy touch, clench his hair and whisper threats into his heart. I approach him on silent, furious feet and crack him round the head. I wrench his screwed-shut eyes open with brutal, burning agony and I knife him from the inside with every scrap of terror, humiliation and pain he caused me. He quakes and stumbles as I feel my own energy sapping steadily. Lychen senses it too, reaching for me with the burning edges of his strength and grasping me by the arms, shaking me, lifting me from my feet in his desperate command that I stop. I let my head and body move back and forth under his hands and I plunge further still, twisting him into every fearful glance into the shadows, endless days of aching loneliness, the terrifying swell of my belly. His grip slackens and he crumples before I've even taken him fully through the terror of labour and childbirth. And I keep going. I slither and I push and I shatter him over and over – wasted years, constant paranoia, a decade of excruciating uncertainty and fear. I'm not even up to the events of the last year before I feel him gone.

'Bella... *Bella!* Come back... Come back to me.'

I blink. Ethan's standing with his arms around me, his hands soft but shuddering. Shuddering because I'm vibrating with every particle of my body. He feels me sag back into myself and quickly moves to support me, not letting me drop.

'What on earth...?' He murmurs, looking down. I follow his gaze.

Lychen is lying huddled in a foetal position at my feet. His body has been twitching in unison with mine, and as mine stills so does his. I stare down at him and, with my foot, nudge him over onto his back. He stares up, his eyes glassy upon mine.

'Did you—?'

'Kill him? Why the hell would I do that? No, I broke him. Locked him in. He can see everything, hear everything, know everything happening around him. But he will never speak or move or touch another person again, apart from the poor souls who'll have to wipe his dribble and clean up his shit.' I bend down, leaning towards Lychen so he has no choice but to see me. Shudders still wrack me sporadically.

423

The Mollitiam is long gone now and my own resilience has depleted itself significantly. My cuts, bruises, and broken toe throb more painfully with each heartbeat. But, of course, I don't let him see that.

'This is over, Lychen. You will rot in your own head with all my memories until you die. And you will *never* set eyes on me ever again.'

I step over him and make sure I'm out of his line of sight before I lean heavily against the wall and let out a long shuddering sigh.

'Bella. Bells. We've got to get you out of here.'

'I know. I can walk, just... take Ralph, will you?'

'Are you sure—'

'Bloody take him, Ethan! I won't leave him here with that *thing*!'

Ethan nods, steps smartly over to Ralph and gathers him up into his arms like he weighs no more than I do. Something catches my eye on the ground as I try not to watch Ralph's head flopping horribly against Ethan's arm. I step over to it. It's the NatApp vial, the syringe secured to its side by a rubber band. I pick it up and press it to my heart as if it bears Ralph's fingers rather than just their prints. Then I lead the way, shaky but nimble, out of my office for the last time. I don't look back at the thing that was once my greatest fear lying in its shell on the dirty floor, but throw my words over my shoulder clearly, so I can be in no doubt that he hears them:

'You and I,' I say, 'are *nothing like* the same.'

59

February, 2020

Ariana runs, feeling the pulse of power reignite and begin to burn once again. She lets her hair flood behind her as she takes the slope towards the trees, only slightly staggering. She leaves the press of worry behind her, letting the exhilaration of movement, of her own wheeling legs and pounding feet fill her up like it did when she was a child. Running so fast she felt she might fly, arms flying in the salty breeze on a beach... Her mother waiting, always watching. She slows as she reaches the first cluster of trees, their limbs spearing nakedly into the grey and white world of winter. Ariana stops for a moment, glancing around for Nova. She's soaring ahead, circling a small area of trees just to the left of the path. Ariana treads slowly towards them, mustering her energy. She can just make out the shape of a large Guard woman, her grey tracksuit cutting a blocky shape in the shade of the trees.

Ariana? Her name in her mother's voice, travelling to her mind through the whirling snow behind her... it is full of feeling. Ariana frowns and dips behind a tree. She could ignore her, she could block her away, she could snap her back. She might have done, before today.

Mum. I'm OK. She can't quite bring herself to say thank you, so she floods the acknowledgement of it, instead. She knows Bella understands. She shuts her eyes and concentrates, seeing her mother pick her way along a dark smoky corridor, following a heavy-set figure carrying something, or someone.

Who's that? Is everyone OK?

Where are you, Ariana? She can feel her mother's attempt at a return probe, but it's weak. Weaker than Ariana has ever known it.

What happened to you?

It's a long story. I can't talk like this for long, I don't have much energy left... Please, tell me what you're doing. I can feel where you are. What's happening?

Ariana opens her eyes, stares into the swirling storm in front of her. She can't see the ARC anymore, the snow and smoke are so thick. She can't see the Manor either. Standing where she is, she could be anywhere. Part of her urges not to tell, the same part which snuck away from Felix. The other part tells her that there's not a lot Bella can do anyway. She decides, and shuts her eyes.

I'm with Nova. We're going after Daniel.

There's a pause. She feels Bella physically stop, one hand against a wall, steadying herself. She is shaking, in pain, almost at the end of her physical as well as psychic stores. She echoes with worry and a gulf of sadness so wrenchingly close and deep that Ariana feels the shock of it shiver the colour from her own face. But there's more, too. There's pride, love and the sense of a palm opening to reveal something clutched so tight it's half misshapen... All at once, Bella turns her hand and lets the half-broken thing go.

OK, Ri, she says. And, as she's already leaving, as the touch of her has already mostly faded, she adds: *Make it hurt.*

Ariana blinks. *Who died?* It doesn't matter, she tells

herself. We can't change it now. *But what if it was because I asked for help, what if it was my fault?* Stop that. We can't think about that right now. We don't care— no. We *can't* care about that right now. We need to do this. For her, too. We need to make it hurt.

She steps out from behind the tree and takes the last few steps into the small clearing where the Guard woman stands and breathes with a slow, deliberate purpose. She looks expressionlessly over at Ariana. There's a vagueness to her face which makes Ariana wonder if she's been hit with Serum X like a few of the confused, motionless Guard she's come across in the last half an hour. Then the woman moves towards her, her face set, her arms reaching out to grasp and Ariana realises the vagueness came from listening to an order delivered silently, the way she's seen a hundred times between Lychen and his Guard. Ariana draws on her power and flicks her head to one side. The Guard woman stops short, her hands still outstretched. A glimmer of almost-confusion crosses her face before she plummets backwards like she's been frozen solid.

A bird call draws Ariana's attention upwards and she spots Nova circling the clearing, her eyes skittering between the trees.

'I know you're here,' Ariana sing-songs softly, her chin dipping back downwards. She stares around at the circle of oak and pine. The ground is clear, there are no prints to show where a wispy shadowy man who could once turn himself completely invisible might lurk. *Could once*, thinks Ariana, her eyes snagging on a smudge of movement on the far right of the clearing. She looks up at the saturated branches and blinks, sending a slump of snow downwards.

'Argh,' the snow hits an arm, a shoulder and then Daniel steps forwards into the clearing, shaking the icy droplets from himself furiously. He's shivering, wearing only a patched tweed jacket and jeans, and when he looks up at Ariana, there's a snarling fury in his bloody, torn face.

'Don't you remember what I said the last time we met, little rat?'

He strides towards her and she blinks, seeing the sharp-looking rock in his hand as he raises it. She tries to push him backwards, but he makes a weird flinching gesture and keeps coming. Panic spasming around her belly, Ariana tries again, this time concentrating on sweeping his legs out from under him. She feels the strength of the thought-weapon whistle from her like wind, but again he makes a twitching sort of expression and smiles. Ariana turns and begins to run, but a hand closes on her arm and draws her back. She yelps as she feels the cold press of rock against the side of her head.

'Do you think I didn't learn a trick or two after the last time you tried to reach me with those warped psychic powers of yours, rat-girl? What, did you think I didn't notice? Doesn't surprise me. We all know where you inherited that arrogance from.'

He turns them both around and pulls her backwards into the shelter of the trees as Nova sweeps lower overhead, unable to reach them through the thick tree cover.

'You know, you've lost me so much good stock today that really it seems quite fitting that you become one of my first replacements. It shouldn't be too difficult to find a human to help keep you under control. Felix will do, she seems unfathomably attached to you from what I hear. Or your mother. She and I have some unfinished business... If she's survived,' he adds as a distant rumble reaches their ears. Nova is still circling overhead. Ariana hopes she's looking for another way to get to them. *If I can get him back into the clearing, she might be able to reach him...*

'My mother is fine. And so are most of the hybrids. Ralph and the others have got a way of saving them, turning them back.'

'Of course they do. Never could leave well enough alone, those damn Blakes. Always hanging off the coat tails of greater, more ambitious men. Always yanking them two steps back for every pioneering leap forward...'

'You're not a pioneer,' Ariana snorts. 'You're just a sad little bully who made friends with a *rich,* sad little bully.' She's still thinking furiously, trying to work out how to get him forward. She can't use her powers against him... So what has she got? *Make it hurt...*

'Careful. I choose the rat, remember. I can pick a particularly disgusting one. With fleas.' He's twisting her arm around and up her back, inching towards the Guard woman where she lies. Ariana spots a shotgun at the woman's waist and swallows a large bubble of fear. *Think. We haven't got much time. Can't call for Mum this time. We're on our own... Make it hurt.*

She looks around and spots a fallen branch half buried in sludge. Without pausing for breath, she brings it up with her eyes and twists her body sideways as she slams it heavily into Daniel's wispy head. He yells and staggers, dropping the rock as Nova swoops, but still she's not close enough, her outstretched talons grasp empty air. Daniel swears and makes a grab for Nova. She shrieks and beats herself back upwards. Daniel stoops for the gun and, desperately, Ariana brings the branch up again, using her outstretched hand to guide its movements, she brings it swooping towards him but he's ready this time and ducks, snarling. He's not ready for the rock, which she directs with her other hand, up and in a jagged smash into the side of his temple. Daniel staggers, drops the gun and presses his hand to his head. Blood drips through his fingers. He turns to her, his pale watery eyes hardening with murder and, with a harsh roar, he snatches up the gun and moves towards her... Ariana steps backwards as he raises the gun, staring at the muzzle, one pace, two, waiting until she feels the rush of wings, then she glances up and Daniel does not, but she sees it in his face all the same. The crashing realisation of his mistake. His eyes bulge at hers briefly before they disappear in a flurry of sharp, unrelenting talons and a slash of hot, thick blood.

Ariana watches until she cannot bear to any longer. Then she turns and, slowly, begins to trudge back through the trees until she finds the path. The snow has finally stopped falling and she looks upwards as the sun breaks through the heavy grey clouds just briefly. She smiles even as tears begin to form and fall. The sadness she'd felt a touch of just briefly in her mother's heart begins to swell in her own and she knows it was Ralph in Ethan's arms. She'd known all along, really, she thinks. Those long legs, the baggy raincoat flapping limply... The unyielding well of Bella's devastation.

Ariana wipes her eyes with her sleeve as Nova flies overhead, cawing with triumph. She swoops low, Daniel's blood patterning the snow around them, and sweeps sideways and off to the left. Ariana feels the pure joy of the hybrid lift a little of her own heaviness. She reaches the gate and stops for a moment. The dull tarnished walls of the ARC are still engulfed in swirling tumbling smoke and ash, but the flames no longer leap from the aching gaps in the stonework or the shattered holes of windows. Lights flash insistently from the driveway and as she turns her head in that direction, she spots Dominic on a stretcher, an oxygen mask strapped to his face. Tess jogs alongside and the two of them disappear into an ambulance. Another four ambulances stand at the foot of the ARC. Fire-fighters emerge carrying a body strapped to a backboard. Ariana squints at the mop of tawny hair, the dark suit trousers...

'Ariana! *Ariana!*'

She turns and there's her mother, wrapped in a woollen blanket, her head matted in blood and her dress torn. She half runs, half limps towards her, Ethan and two paramedics in frustrated pursuit. Ariana passes through the gate and hovers, her feelings tumbling and gathering in confusion in her chest. Bella does not hover. Face awash with emotion, she reaches Ariana and throws her arms around her with a fervent abandon which takes Ariana utterly by surprise. She freezes for a second before slowly allowing her body to soften, her arms wrap around her mother's familiar body and she inhales her scent. Sandalwood, glamour, hair serum, and other things – blood, fire, ash, grief. They clamour and buffet to be acknowledged, but Ariana turns them away and breathes her mother in long shudders instead.

'Ralph's... gone?'

'Yes. I'm sorry—'

'We got Daniel. Nova and I. It... definitely hurt.'

'Good. I got Lychen.'

'I saw. He's dead?'

'Not exactly. He'll wish he was, though.'

There's a hardness there that Ariana hasn't heard before, despite all she's seen and learned of her mother over the last year, over the last almost-fourteen years... Something cold and broken and unreachable. She begins to pull away, but Bella doesn't let her go, she hardens her grip around Ariana's shoulders and chest as if she were trying to squeeze the breath from her body.

'Mum... I can't—'

'I'm sorry,' Bella whispers in a kiss against Ariana's ear. And Ariana looks up over her shoulder, eyes widening in panic as she feels the nip of a syringe at her neck. Ethan and the paramedics stand back, witnessing nothing more than the heart-warming embrace of mother and long-lost child. Only Felix, standing near the ambulance bearing Dominic, meets Ariana's gaze and, too late, begins to move. *Too late.* Ariana sinks into Bella's arms, and as she begins to feel the power leave her, flowing like blood from a desperate wound, she stares at her mother's eyes. At the iridescent, unknowable knives of green.

Afterwards

August, 2020

The beach is unacceptably busy. Full of pasty holidaymakers making the most of the latest easing of pandemic restrictions, their hair flat with sweat, their hands flowing with the sticky globulous rivers of their perspiring ice creams. I lean against the balustrade of the pier, the heavy afternoon sun dappling the boardwalk and casting lengthening shadows onto the sea as it creeps slowly up the shoal. I keep my sunglasses over my eyes as I rake over the beach-dwellers, their stench not reaching my nose just as the insistent beat of the sun does not trouble my body sheathed in its unseasonal black, fitted silk dress.

'If you were going for inconspicuous, you've failed miserably,' announces the familiar, determinedly nonchalant voice. I turn around, annoyed she has managed to creep up behind me. I don't show it, of course. This is me, after all. Felix wears a pair of Bermuda shorts which shorten her already short legs unflatteringly. Her cheap T-shirt already bears sweat-patches. But her eyes are unlined, her face is tanned and bright with the balm of deep-rooted contentment. Her hands are squeezed into the tight pockets of her shorts, one of them looped through the lead of a small dog with a grinning mouth which sits at her side, staring up at me lopsidedly.

'I don't need to be inconspicuous anymore,' I reply, blandly. 'She's not coming?' I switch my attention from dog to woman.

'Did you really think she would?' Felix squints at me. I'm standing with my back to the sun. I feel it beam along my hair, shining gently from its smooth curls. I peer at her from over the top of my sunglasses.

'Not really. You look well.'

'And we all know you look fabulous,' she quips, shortly, though I hear something of a smile in it. A glimmer of that almost-friendship we once had. Perhaps a husband for a daughter did it after all.

'Shall we walk?' She glances up and down the pier. 'The crowds should be thinning out soon, it's nearly tea time...'

'Sure,' I reply, glancing beyond her swiftly just to make sure she's not attempting to divert me. There are no familiar faces among the throngs of young and old gambolling along the pier or basking in the sediment below. Felix flickers her eyebrows upwards as I sweep my gaze back over her and I know she knows I'm still searching.

'Surely you'd... I dunno, *sense* her with all your tingly psychic powers, if she were here?'

I give her a look before turning wordlessly towards the long stretch of wooden planks. She has to jog a little to join me, despite the killer heels upon my feet.

'How is she?' I ask, quietly, because I know she longs not to tell me but will do anyway.

'OK, considering everything... Things were pretty bleak at first, as you know.'

'I know,' I say, recalling the blank, white face at the back of the church as Ralph's body lay encased in wood. The refusal to even look at me as I had stood and enraptured the entire congregation in the brilliance that had been Ralph Blake. The glance of pure unfiltered loathing I'd caught as I stepped down from the podium.

'But she's settled well into her school, even with all the madness of lockdown and remote-learning – the pandemic's been good for her in a way, helped give her distance to get her head straight after everything. We took lots of walks with Daisy, did a *lot* of talking and processing... And now things have calmed down a little she's been meeting up with some of her new friends – keeping to the rules and all that, of course. She's a good kid. And, I dunno, it seems to have given her a bit of perspective, all the new challenges – it's hard but it's the same as every other kid in the whole world is dealing with right now, if that makes sense... She's not on her own anymore, she's not the freak in the tower locked away from the world and forced to hone powers she doesn't understand.'

I turn to Felix, knowing that my frustration is sliding from me but not bothering to rein it back this time.

'Maybe if you could just explain that's *why*—'

She holds her hand up and stops short. I pull up beside her. With my heels and her flats, we're around eye-level with one another.

'One, it's not my job to explain any part of you and your decisions to anyone, let alone Ariana. Two, who do you think you're kidding? You didn't do what you did out of some motherly instinct to give Ariana a normal life. Maybe a small part of you was protecting her, but I saw you, I remember. There was a real... *desperation* in the way you dragged yourself up and ran at her...'

She pauses and I see it in flashes on the surface of her memories. Me, dwarfed by Ethan and paramedics who tended my head injury and muttered about *smoke inhalation* and *signs of assault*. Ariana appearing at the gate, white and blood-splattered and so old, as her eyes sought out the figure of her father on its stretcher, extricated by the paramedics and firefighters on my careful instruction. The flare of wildness as I'd seen her, the grip of my hand on the NatApp I'd drawn up carefully into its syringe as I'd waited for her to come… I blink and we're back on the pier, my heels tip-tapping the wood, Felix's sandals squeaking, the grinning dog and the blazing sunshine blaring an incongruous chord after the frigid darkness of the memory.

'I *was* scared,' I admit, slowly. 'I was scared of what she had seen and done. I was scared of what she would become if she carried on down that path… Away from my guidance.'

'Away from your control, you mean…'

'Becoming more powerful…'

'More powerful than you.'

I sigh. 'I don't think we'll ever agree on this. Maybe that's a good thing. Maybe Ariana needs that.'

'Now that I do agree with.'

We carry on walking for a bit longer. The sun drops lower over the sea and the salty scent mixes with the tang of vinegar and sizzling oil as we pass catering vans and stalls.

'Does she see much of Marc?' I ask, as I catch sight of a large man with a protruding stomach smiling with his entire face as his small daughter gambols from the end of his careful hand.

'He pops by most weeks. You knew he got a flat in Scarsby then? Of course you knew, what am I thinking…'

'I was the one who had him extracted from the Beaumont, remember.'

'Mmm. So I suppose you know about Julia too?'

I can't help the twitch which springs across my face at the mention of the name and I know she sees it too. She waits, but when I don't bite, she continues:

'She got in touch a few weeks after Marc got back on his feet. I think she felt... guilty, maybe? That she didn't try very hard to find him when he dropped off the face of the earth for several months. He thinks she was too scared, in case the search led her to you. After meeting her, I'm inclined to agree.'

I sniff as my memory shrinks and darkens. My mother, her hands soft one moment and clawed the next, a hiss which snaked right into my soul, her voice a curse around my name. *Bella is defective*. My mother driving away from Cumbria alone, white-knuckled at the wheel, ready to reach home and remove all evidence of her youngest child. *You need to take her back.*

'She wanted to meet Ariana. It took her a while but eventually Ariana decided that would be OK, so I took her down to Weston. That big old house on the hill. Anyway, it was all very stiff and awkward at first, but once she showed Ariana her new kittens it all thawed out a bit.'

'OK.'

'It was weird. So many pictures of your brother and sister all over the place. You wouldn't think—'

'That there had ever been a third child, I know. Maya told me a long time ago that there was a household ban on any photos of me.'

'She has one.'

'What?'

'In the corner, by the piano. There's a photo of you when you were about eight or nine. Bright blue lace dress, ribbons in your hair. Ugly kid, right stinker...'

I smile. 'Ralph always did say reports of my beauty were grossly exaggerated.'

'Smart man, that Ralph Blake,' she grins, then lets it

slide slowly from her face. We fall into silence, save the neat taps of my heels, the soft slap of her sandals.

'I remember that dress,' I say, quietly. 'I found it on my bed the day after she told me she would cut out my eyes if I kept batting them at the postman. Or maybe it was the supermarket assistant. I can't remember. She had a real thing about my eyes. Probably because they were like hers, only greener, brighter. She said they were unnatural, the colour of poison. That it was what the Blakes had put in me, shining out.'

'Well, she was nice enough to Ariana, poisonous eyes and all.'

'Well. Perhaps she's finally mellowed, after all this time.'

'I'm not so sure about that. She said something weird when we left. She looked me up and down and said, "I hope she knows what she's done. Letting someone else raise your child, there's no going back." Ariana heard that bit. She looked at her that way she does sometimes, like she's forty rather than fourteen, and she asked her, bold as brass – "Does that mean you regret what you did to my mum?"'

'Bloody hell, Ri.'

'I know! I didn't think Julia was going to answer. She went sort of white and trembly. She's built like you, basically your living Twiglet, I was a bit worried she might keel over then and there and we'd have to run and fetch the smelling salts. But then she sort of shook herself out of it and said something like "What a question—"'

I shut my eyes, silently reaching into Felix's head, watching the memory from her perspective. My mother's bony face creased with scorn even as the sadness pinched its edges hungrily.

'I regret so much. My husband's blind stupidity, our

438

greed. That we ever crossed paths with the Blakes.' She looked up and fixed Felix with the callous, green-eyed look which shivered right through me, and it was like she knew, somehow, whom she was really addressing.

'I regret everything... and nothing. That child should never have been born, and when she was, she certainly didn't belong here. But when she was gone, when I took her back... I felt it like a cancer. Every day. I regret *everything*.'

She glanced at Ariana then, softness making her unrecognisable to me. 'Children aren't meant to be perfect. Remember that. I had the closest thing to a perfect child... she almost destroyed me. And now look at her, what she's become. God help us all.'

I blink myself back to the pier, the gentle tread upon wooden planks, as my mother's voice trembled feebly into vapour. I felt nothing. No anger, no sadness, no regret... Not even pity. She was nothing. Finally.

'Will Ariana see her again?'

'Yeah, I think so. Probably not more than a couple of times a year though.'

'Well. Ariana needs family, such as it is.'

'Speaking of which, you know she wants to go and see Lychen again?'

'I received a request from his facility along those lines, yes.'

'Are you going to let her?'

I sigh, staring at the end of the pier. People gather, posing for group photos and selfies, tapping away on phones, laughing. Face masks dangling from ears like so many forgotten shackles. Felix indicates a bench set apart from them and we head for it.

'I don't know,' I say, honestly, as I sit delicately. Felix

reaches into her pocket for a dog treat and holds it in her hand for a moment, waiting for me to finish: 'I don't know if she wants to go because she really feels like she needs to see him... or if she's just doing it to punish me.'

'She's fourteen. Could be either. But for what it's worth, I think it's something more personal than that. She seemed troubled last time she went, but almost calmer in a way, afterwards. Like she'd needed to understand something. Like the understanding of it didn't make it any better, but it made it... easier to swallow, I guess. I don't know. I'm hardly an expert parent. I'm just learning as I go...'

'Well, you couldn't get a much lower benchmark, so you've got that going for you.'

'Cheers.' She holds the treat out and the dog sits, eyes trained on the biscuit with a narrow focus I almost envy.

'I think I'll let her then, if you think it helps.'

'The mighty Bella D'accourt taking advice from lowly Felix Bryden?'

I shrug. 'Stranger things have happened.'

We lapse into a silence which is nearly companionable, though the deeper hurts and accusations still swarm darkly beneath the surface.

'How's Nova getting on?' Felix breaks the silence.

'Well, thank you.'

'She forgave you for not saving the last NatApp for her?'

'Once she saw two of the other hybrids die after receiving it.'

'Did you manage to figure out what had gone wrong?'

'Yes and no...' I lean back against the iron railing of the bench, my thoughts skimming tiredly over the endlessly long nights spent pulling blood, running tests into the small hours, going over Ralph's calculations over and over.

'It was all there,' I murmur. 'It should have worked and it did, but not for all of them… the error was in the formulation of one of the properties pertaining to the boosting of human DNA, but it's odd… It's almost like it was accounted for in the calculations. Without Ralph, I don't think we'll ever really know what happened. It worked for one of the bird-girls and the monkey-boy, after all…'

'And it worked on Ariana.'

'That's the strange thing. I didn't know if it would. I knew enough to know it wouldn't harm her… but I didn't really know it would pull all the Project A resilience out of her, not for sure. But it worked faster, more efficiently and with less residual side-effects on her than on the two hybrids…'

'Almost like Ralph planned it that way…'

'And then left all the blueprints lying around for us to be able to adapt it to use on hybrids in the future.'

'But he told you to use it on Nova, didn't he?'

'He told me it was for *"her"*.'

Felix gives a long, slow whistle from between her teeth.

'*Really* smart man, that Ralph Blake.'

'The best. Not that I ever let him know I thought that.'

There's another silence and this time the darker things lurk closer. Neither of us want to look at them yet, though.

'How's Dom?' I ask, casting for something lighter to talk about.

'He's good. Living his best socially-distanced bachelor life in Manchester… though he did let slip he'd signed up for Tinder the other week when he was round for lunch, hopefully it'll do him good. The break-up hit him hard. I think he was a bit blind-sided by it all, to be honest.'

I snort. 'He shouldn't have been. Tess is far too ambitious to sit inside playing video games for the rest of her twenties...'

'How is she getting on at Beaumont?'

'Really well. I don't know how I'd run it without her. She was integral in the campaign to allow us to continue the Guard programme—'

'I still don't know how you wrangled that... Hell, I don't know how you managed to get the whole bloody BFI signed over to you.'

'Lychen promised me a long time ago that if I were to work with him, it would be as his equal, his counterpart. I don't know if he ever really believed it, but I made damn sure I held him to it where it actually counted.'

'And here I thought you'd just switched on the charm for Metcalfe.'

'Yes, well... that too. Though with regards to the Guard, we're heavily monitored still. Red tape all over the place...'

'That's not what I heard. I heard you've been given the green light to use Youth Guard as eighty percent of the personnel at that new laboratory you're building out of the ARC ruins...'

I look at her sharply. 'I always did underestimate your ability to come across classified information, Felix.'

'Depends on what you mean by classified, Bella. Some things are only hidden because they want to be found.'

And there, we have arrived at it at last. The true reason for my visit. She knows I knew Ariana would never agree to meet me. Not so soon. Not when she's only just allowed my voice to trickle back into her head over the last couple of weeks. A tiny, miniscule hint of reparation. No, Felix and I both hold the remaining puzzle pieces. A pair, missing from a corner right at the very beginning of the story, separated by the two of us, one another's counterparts. We don't look at each other, but that's OK. It's easier, in a way. This is one answer I don't want to force.

'Why did you do it?' She mutters.

'Why did you tell Lychen?' I counter.

She bites her lip and looks at her knees. They're paler than her face and her arms. Clearly the shorts have been a new addition. She brings a hand up and tousles her hair. The sharp undercut is growing out and the pink-tinged locks above it are nearly long enough to form ringlets. It suits her like that, I think, but I don't say.

'I was angry... I was bitter and jealous. I couldn't just... Losing Ethan to you the first time was hell. But the second time it kind of destroyed me. We were together, he was trying, I was trying... but still, he didn't want me like he wanted you. He *never* loved me as much as he loves you.'

'A different kind of love, I'd call it.'

'Whatever,' she frowns. 'I loathed you for it. I still do sometimes. Only...'

'Only you got your revenge.'

She looks at me then, full of a sickening curiosity. I can feel her questions simmering on her tongue just as I feel them hover behind Tess's eyes. The only one who knows the truth is Ethan, of course. I couldn't have kept it from him if I'd wanted to.

'What did happen to you in that office?'

'I destroyed Lychen.'

'I mean before that, with Daniel... They said your injuries were—'

'No. You don't get to ask me that, Felix. You don't get the privilege of knowing exactly what you owe me. But you also don't get to loathe me anymore. What you did, what

443

you enabled him to do... it eclipses all of the rest of it. Do you understand that.'

'Yes,' she murmurs. We sit in silence for a while and I begin to hope that I might have got away with it, that the horror I have alluded to might just be enough to cancel out her que—

'You didn't answer my question. Why *did* you post that tag?'

I draw in a long breath and watch a young family make their way slowly back along the pier in the direction of the beach. The mother has a sandy backside, the father's shirt is wrinkled and stained. Their twins sleep side by side, sticky-mouthed in the double pram.

'The evenings were the worst,' I say, my voice clear and sharp as always, despite the memory I draw upon. The dark, barren corners of the flat. The empty noise of the TV. My laptop blaring with not nearly enough challenge. 'It had been so long at that point. I'd become used to wondering whether I'd been mad to think anyone was hunting me. I'd circle around again and again, wondering what the point of all this secrecy was, why I was trying so hard to be so... mediocre. I felt wasted. You were right, you know. When you said all those things last year... About how I wasn't born for that life – keeping my head down, pretending to be a dour, dull alias, hiding my brilliance, raising a – how did you put it? An *increasingly ungrateful* child...

'You were right. And so was Lychen, when he said I wasn't supposed to be a mother. I wasn't born to it. I wasn't *genetically designed* to hide away, to care selflessly for another. I did try, though. I tried for twelve relentless *years*. I fought it, buried it, swallowed it, burned it away inside myself... And then one night I had a glass or two of wine and I saw that photo online, that photo of Ariana in

444

the background of her friend's selfie. After all I'd told her, all I'd hammered into her empty little head about being careful, staying off social media... There she was, glowing out at the entire world with *my* eyes... I kind of just... I just thought, for a moment, *What is the point?* And that was all it took for that buried, innate part of me which I'd suppressed and choked away inside for so long to burst to the surface. It was a stupid, nothing little hashtag posted by an anonymous, nothing account. It didn't mean anything to anyone. It couldn't, except...'

'Except the people who might just, possibly, still be looking for you.'

'Ralph. I hoped... it would be Ralph.'

'But you also knew damned well there was a higher chance it'd be Lychen.'

I shut my eyes and see it through Ethan's narrowed gaze last Autumn: her handwriting, scribbled on that notebook. *T msgs, L/B Oct 18. Metadata tag?* And the words, the text itself blazing at me from that cottage in Cornwall:

> Only a partial match, but closer than
> we have ever come before, particularly
> when teamed with a corroborative
> metadata tag.

'I never did find the hashtag itself.'

'I deleted it after about twenty minutes. Once I came to my senses. It was... an unconscionable mistake.'

'You couldn't have known what it would become.'

'Couldn't I?' I look at her and she looks away.

'What was it, anyway?'

I sigh. 'The girl with the green eyes.'

'Catchy.'

'Stupid.'

'Hmm.'

'What?'

'It's just... nothing you do is stupid, Bella. Selfish, definitely. Impulsive, possibly. But never *stupid*. Even a glass or two down.'

'Give it up, Fee,' I say, quietly but with that thread of power that I know she can't miss. 'There's nothing left to dig up. Just... please don't tell Ri. She wouldn't understand...'

'No, it's not really something a normal person *can* really comprehend, I have to say,' she says it mildly enough, but there's acid within it. I wait for a moment or two.

'I won't tell her,' she says, steadily. 'But for her sake, rather than yours.'

'Thank you.'

'Right.' She waits another minute or two, but when I don't say anything else, she slaps her thighs and springs to her feet. 'Well. I've got to get going. Dinner isn't going to order itself. And you've got an empire to get back to...'

'Tell her I miss her. And, you know, I love her.'

She looks at me for a moment, a mixture of pity and something almost like respect tumbling back into the general dislike.

'I will. See you, Bella.'

'Goodbye, Felix.'

I watch her amble up the pier, the small dog at her ankles. She doesn't look back, but I feel her want to more than once. I stay sitting at the bench, my thoughts still half tumbling through those dull, desperate moments, the rash typing of those words. I can't even really remember it, after so long. Two years, almost. *That action you took... you must see what it means.* Had it really been, as I'd told Lychen, a tiny moment of short-sighted self-indulgence? Or was it closer to Felix's old suspicions of a calculated act of cold-blooded fury? Is there any point, now, deciding which?

Bella?

Ethan. All OK back there?

Yes, all good. I've just had a call from Tess. She said the next Mollitiam trials have been scheduled to begin September 1st.

Good. Cases will begin to rise again once the schools go back. Uptake will be excellent.

We had already undertaken one trial of the marketing of Mollitiam as a curative drug, Moll-A. It had had a one hundred percent success rate so far. There's still a long way to go, but signs are looking positive, particularly in terms of investment. One could say that the whole global pandemic has come at an extremely fortuitous time. One with a suspicious mind could say it is almost *too* fortuitous, given that pre-orders alone are funding the ongoing renovations of the Manor and the construction of our latest facility. I've continued to monitor my Project A resilience levels daily, ready with a Mollitiam micro-dose treatment plan for the moment they begin to dip. No longer do I live under the shadow of the malignant timebomb which took so many of us.

Ariana didn't show?

No. I didn't think she would.

Did Felix give you the answers you wanted?

Try again.

Nag. Did she tell you the truth?

Yes. She did.

And did you tell her the truth?

I smile and feel him echoing it back. He sits in our

newly refurbished room at the Manor, his body nestled in a blanket I sometimes drape about my shoulders on colder nights. Now we no longer have need for lodgers, the bedrooms on the second floor, including my own old one, have been converted into one long airy open-plan space. Ethan faces the window in what was once my daughter's bedroom and, before that, Ana's office, gazing at the open grounds which used to be skewered by a shining black tower. Now it's a mess of construction, but in a few months it will rise again, no longer towering or shiny but a neat grey stone. The Eve Institution will harbour the finest minds of science without any of its dirty secrets. It will innovate cures for the most despicable diseases and afflictions, manned by staff who have been specially selected to understand fragility and frailty without feeling it themselves.

Marc hadn't been the only lost thread I'd picked up, as soon as I regained enough strength and sense to return to myself the day when the ARC burned. As I'd hoped, the majority of my Youth Guard went into hiding when they found their connection to me unexpectedly severed and their peers unceremoniously rounded up. My beautiful Bette, brave Tom and definitively Scottish Karl all now hold senior positions in the new, reimagined BFI. All except Eve, whose whereabouts, like the strange emergence of her fear and anxiety back at the hospital, remains a mystery.

I searched relentlessly for her, raking through the hundreds of Guard bodies in the warehouses where so many were slaughtered in Metcalfe's panic. When her body never surfaced, I widened the hunt using the full force of the resources I'd inherited. Until the day several months ago when the message came up on my phone:

I am alive. I am fine. Stop looking for me.

And I lie awake as Ethan snores, Eve's mind-link dark and untethered, and I remember her words: *It happens to me sometimes. I don't know why.* And I wonder what it means, whether she is out there living a life as something evolved beyond the Youth Guard, beyond humanity, beyond me... She always was the quickest, the brightest of my stars, the deepest of my tree roots. I miss her, but I do as she says because no one needs to tell me that twice.

How's Nova doing?

She's fine. She spent the night away again, but she came back for lunch today. They both did.

He shows me an image of my protégée huddled around the outside table alongside another bird hybrid, a dark-feathered young male called Ozzy. Since choosing not to take NatApp, the two of them have become fast companions. Sometimes, I suspect, they are more than just companions. They spend more time beating the skies of the North West than they do roosting in the attic of the Manor, but when she's home, Nova seems happy enough. Thanks to my new partnership with Metcalfe, the few remaining hybrids are now classed as a protected species, safe from interference from the public, free to roam where they choose. There are rumours, of course, of rumblings and discontent, groups longing to restore the natural state of things, rid the world of hybrids, the Guard and all the other troublesome legacies of the eugenic Projects started so long ago, myself included. I'm not blind to it. I know that the natural equilibrium we find ourselves in may not last forever. But for now it is enough to smile, step into the spotlights and use my face to persuade the public that they need me, they need my brain, my vision, my blood, to restore all the things they never knew they were missing. Moll-A is just the beginning; there is so much more to give, now that the shadows are finally behind us.

When are you coming home?

Soon. Now.

Hurry, my love. Hurry back to me.

I sigh and close the connection. The light begins to dwindle properly now as the last of the sun's beams touch the sparkling expanse of the North Sea. I blink and wait for him, knowing he'll come, knowing he'll have questions, too.

You might not remember much about it, but you know as well as I do that posting that hashtag had nothing to do with me finding you. Just as you know full well that I wasn't talking about Ariana when I gave you that vial of NatApp. In fact, I'm pretty sure I said 'for Nova.' And you know perfectly well none of the calculations were adjusted.

He sits next to me. I turn and smile beatifically.

I know. But if she ever does talk to her about it, it will be easier for Ariana to think that it was all part of your plan.

Do you ever tell yourself the truth, Beast? Are you as entangled in your little lies as much as the rest of us? Actually, you know what, don't answer. I don't have to care about any of this anymore. I'm dead.

It has to end with me, Ralph.

Not listening, don't care.

Project A. All the shit my parents and your parents did. It has to end with me. I won't let there be another nine-year-old abandoned for being defective.

Ralph's shimmering, insubstantial face slides into a wry grin. I know what he's thinking. It's what I'm really thinking, after all, but don't dare to project into voice: I've earned the right to be the only one. Surely I've endured enough now to be the last one standing.

The sun's rays slowly begin to die. The end of the pier

is quiet now. I sit alone with my ghosts, waiting for the darkness to finish creeping its way down my body. I think about the empire waiting for me, the conference call with the Prime Minister scheduled for tomorrow morning, all the work we need to do ahead of the second round of trials, Tess poised for instruction at the Beaumont, another fully-functional team at Futura, and Ethan, always waiting, my safe haven back in Cumbria. I think about my daughter, wrapped in her own frustration at being safe and whole and unblemished just like everyone else. And I think back to myself. The nine-year-old who clenched her fists and stared out of the window of her mother's car, waiting to be abandoned with the soul-deep helplessness of the very young, the very beautiful. *Bella is defective. You need to take her back.*

I slide gracefully to my feet, smooth my dress, shake my hair back so it catches the diamonds scattered by the last of the sun's rays, and begin to walk with quick neat taps back along the pier. I feel the eyes upon me, I always will. They do not matter. I am thirty-four years and one month old and there is plenty wrong with me. There are shadows of secrets I will guard for the rest of my life, there are scars that no amount of resilience will ever heal. But I am Bella, and I will bear it all without giving away a thing. I am the girl with the green eyes, the last of my kind. The darkness is behind me.

And I won't be taken back.

THE END

J M (Jenny) Briscoe is a sci-fi author, website content editor and mum-of-three based in Berkshire, UK. She writes a strong female lead, bakes a mean birthday cake and has been known to do both simultaneously. Her publishing debut, *The Girl with the Green Eyes*, was long-listed for The Bridport Prize: Peggy Chapman-Andrews First Novel Award in 2020, reaching the top 20 of over 1,600 entrants.

Jenny is currently working on a new sci-fi novel series. She also has plans for several spin-off stories featuring familiar characters from *Take Her Back*.

For updates, subscribe to J M Briscoe's website: www.jmbriscoe.co.uk and blog: www.jmbriscoe.com

BAD PRESS iNK,
publishers of niche, alternative and cult fiction

Visit

www.BADPRESS.iNK

for details of all our books, and sign up to
be notified of future releases and offers

Also from BAD PRESS iNK

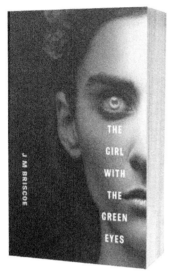 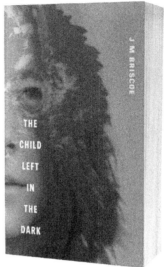

Bella is defective. You need to take her back.

Everyone tells her she is normal. Everyone is lying.

Eugenics, chimeras and the fierceness of a mother's love in a terrifying near future.

Books One and Two in The Take Her Back Trilogy.

Two love affairs and two summers, 75 years apart.

Cantankerous Tilly is determined to grow old
disgracefully.

Shy Ava is finding out looking after the elderly was
never meant to be like this!

Future Imperfect – the new eco-thriller from
BAD PRESS.iNK

Climate catastrophe isn't in the future... it's now.

Climate refugees aren't other people... they're you.

Printed in Great Britain
by Amazon

41592249R00258